Capri
In a perfect world...

Jahquel J.

Copyright © 2024

Published by Jahquel J.
www.Jahquel.com
ALL RIGHTS RESERVED
Any unauthorized reprint or use of the material is prohibited. No part of this book may be reproduced or transmitted in any form or by any means, electronic, or mechanical, including photocopying, recording, or by any information storage without express permission by the publisher. This is an original work of fiction. Names, characters, places, and incidents are either products of the author's imagination or are used fictitiously and any resemblance to actual persons, living or dead is entirely coincidental.
Contains explicit languages and adult themes.
suitable for ages 16+

Jahquel J's Catalog

Synopsis:

She's a homie hopper. She's confused. She doesn't take accountability for anything. She's f*cking her way through all her brothers' friends.
I've heard more than a few of those when people talk about me, and I have even felt the same way my damn self. I didn't know what I wanted. I mean, I knew what I wanted.
I wanted marriage, love, and the commitment that I made to my husband – ex-husband. I've found myself confused after my divorce to Naheim. It would have been easier to stay and forgive him for something that broke me. It would have been easier for him to stay and forgive me for sleeping with one of his friends.
Nothing worth ever having is easy.
My personal life aside – Let's also remember:
I'm THAT girl.
The girl who let that shit go with one hand, popping my shoulder out of place. I'm that same girl that protected both of my sister-in-law's. I'm also that girl that rides with the Inferno Gods and can hold my own on a bike.
nose swipe and spit included

Hey There

This is Capri's story, and we all know sis' has gone through the ringer in both her brothers' books. Like I said about Cappadonna's book after wrapping up Capone's book: **this is Capri's book... don't compare her book to her brothers.**

Like both her brothers are different, her story will be, too. There's ground that needs to be covered, so consider this a slow burn – kinda.

We're introducing new characters and Capri again, as her healed self. Remember how we set the scene for Capone before we tore shit up?

Like my teen says.... Lemme cook. ***wink***

To every woman who has ever lost herself and had to fight to find her again.

Translations:

Translations:
Cabeça nas nuvens – Head in the clouds
o tempo todo hoje em dia – all the time these days
é sobre aquela mulher? seu amor? – is it about that woman? Your love?
Não entre aqui meu amor.. estou fumando - don't come in here my love... I'm smoking.
Eu não vou - I won't
Aceite isso como uma boa menina, meu amor – take it like a good girl, my love
meu tudo – my everything

Prologue

I STARED AT MY SISTERS AND WANTED TO CRY, BUT THE both of them had already beat me to the punch. Alaia was wiping her eyes on Cappy's shirt, while Erin held her stomach and stared at me. She was due any day now and should have been sitting her butt down and resting. Instead, she insisted on bringing me to the airport with my brothers.

"I'm going to cry so hard on the plane... because you two have beat me to it." I pulled my bag up on my arm.

Capp looked at Capone, and they both looked at me. I knew they both were keeping it together because both of their wives were acting a whole fool. "Then don't go... why the fuck you wanna travel anyway?"

"I never had time for myself, Capone. During law school, I settled into being a wife, and then life happened. I never got the chance to be alone... I have to learn how to be alone."

"Keep that fucking necklace around your neck, Capri," Cappadonna looked down at me, and I stepped into his arms.

"Gonna miss you the most, Cappy."

I was close with both my brothers, but me and Cappadonna's bond was that much tighter. He was the oldest and had always protected us, even from the inside of prison walls. He squeezed me so tight as he kissed the top of my head a few times.

"Just fuck me then," Capone pulled me into his arms and kissed my forehead before wrapping his arms around me. "Be safe out there."

"I will... I promise."

My parents were in Barbados, so I planned to stop there for a week before truly continuing my travel journey. Cappadonna held my chin and looked me in the eyes. "We're proud of you, Capri. You doing what you need to do for you... nobody can take that from you."

"Thank you." I gulped down the knot in my throat that was threatening the tears that were going to come.

I looked at the security line and then smiled at them. "Love you, Capri... call me soon as you land, okay?" Erin sniffled while Capone rubbed her stomach and kissed her.

Alaia settled by her husband's side, hugging him around the stomach while crying. He held her tightly while he stared me in the eyes. "Love you the most, Baby Doll."

"A year isn't that bad, right?" I shrugged, knowing that a year would feel like a decade away from my family.

"Will breeze right on by," Capp lied through his teeth to make Alaia feel better. "Big Pri over and out," he saluted and smiled at me as I rolled my carry on beside me.

Capone and Capp had already helped me check in all of my bags. I breezed through security and found my gate, propping my feet up on the suitcase and scrolling my phone. A year would breeze right on through, and I would be able to mark this off my bucket list. I had finally done something for me, and not a man.

I looked at everyone getting up and ready to board. It never mattered when I traveled, I was always going to get here right before boarding because of my lack of time management on travel days.

Capri

Even though I had first class tickets, I never rushed to board first. It's not like I had to work through the aisles like everyone else. My seat was right in the front, and I never had to worry about shoving by people.

"Damn, Suga, all I got was a text message." I turned my head and Quameer sat in the empty seat beside me.

"Quamee...Quameer, what are you doing here?" I stammered.

He smirked. "I bought a cheap little flight so I can see you walk through the gate. One year without my homie is gonna suck."

"You're the one who told me to travel."

"Didn't think you would do it... or that it would hurt to see you go." He shrugged and looked at me.

I stood up. "Did you come for a hug, Meer?"

He stood up, towering over me. I watched as he patted his jeans and then pulled out a lighter. "Take this with you."

"A lighter?" I held it in my hand, confused.

"My favorite lighter, Suga... hold it when you miss home. Do a little flick when you're thinking about me."

The tears I had successfully been holding at bay came crawling down my face. He held his arms open, and I stepped into them, hugging him. "Thank you, Meer."

"Take this time and fall in love with Capri. Get to know you, and when you come back, be ready for whatever is to happen."

I looked up into his eyes and he smiled, as I ran my hand across the burns on his face. "I will. Can I facetime you if the lighter trick doesn't work?"

"Anytime you want to... you got the number."

"Meer?"

"Yeah."

I looked up at him. "You still have to be celibate... you not slick," I giggled, while wiping my tears.

He laughed. "Ain't shit out there I wanna slide into... you the one that need to keep that shit on lock."

They made the call for last boarding, and I slowly rolled my suitcase over toward the door and looked back at him for once. He held his index and middle finger together and instead of sliding it under his nose, he kissed them and winked at me.

"I'll be here when you get back... *bestie*," he teased.

I smiled, wiping my tears. "I never learned that one."

"It's only for you." He winked.

I swiped my tears, returning the gesture. "Later, Meer."

"Until you return, Suga."

Chapter 1
Capri

FLYING HAD ALWAYS INTRIGUED ME. I LOVED HOW A PLANE could go full force down a runway and up into the sky holding thousands of pounds of people, luggage, and equipment. Alaia hated when I pointed out the obvious because she was a bad flyer, but I always found comfort in being up in the clouds.

As I started reading Forever My Lady by C. Wilson, I peeped the man looking at me. The only reason I noticed is because I looked up after I had finished reading Finding My Way Out Of Darkness by Briyanna Michelle. He was trying to be discreet, and he had been failing horribly. He had to have had some money because he was sitting up in business class with me on an Emirates flight.

I was so excited to be back home. After traveling for a few months, I decided the backpacker life wasn't for me and settled in Singapore for the remainder of my time abroad. After my tearful goodbye at the airport, I refused to return home after only a few months, so I settled there and enjoyed being somewhere without my family. I wasn't Capri Delgato in Singapore, nobody gave a hell about who I was. I didn't have to watch my back, carry a gun, or worry about someone walking up on me.

I needed to stand on my own as a woman, a single woman.

Jahquel J.

One who needed to find herself. I was so used to being Capone and Cappadonna's little sister, Naheim's wife, and Kincaid's shorty that I forgot what it was like to just be Capri.

The woman who loved law, even though I broke it often. I was also a woman who loved being in love. For a while, I pretended like I didn't need love, and the truth was that everyone needed love. We all needed that person that ignited us. You saw them, and then your entire world lit up. This year taught me how to be comfortable with being alone. Being alone used to hurt so bad because I was afraid of it. When you had no choice but to be alone, you learned to become comfortable in it. I remember when I first moved into my place in Singapore, the first night I sat there crying because I missed home.

I missed having someone.

I remember calling Cappadonna and crying to him, and he had bought a flight to bring me home. I called him the next morning and told him to stay home. He couldn't come and save me, even though I knew he would.

When Alaia texted to ask what she should pack him for the weather there, I knew I needed to stand on my own. Cappadonna had his own family and shouldn't have been rushing across the world because I called him crying.

I would sit on my balcony, crying because I didn't know how I ended up in this head space. I wasn't supposed to return back until next month, right before my birthday, and I was coming home early without telling anyone.

I turned my location off on my phone and prayed that nobody was tracking my necklace. The pilot made the announcement that we were about to land in New York, and I was excited. Too excited to be back home, and right in time for the good weather.

As I struggled to grab my carry on, I felt a strong hand reach above me. "Let me help you with that."

I backed away because he was too damn close. "Um,

thanks." I smiled, realizing that I was grilling the hell out of him.

He was tall, dark, and handsome with a short fade. I noticed the suit he was wearing, and the typical businessman suitcase. It was like every man that was in business bought the same suitcase. I noticed the vintage Rolex watch sitting on his wrist, so I could tell that he had some taste.

"You're welcome. I hate to see a woman struggling."

I folded my arms offended. "I was not struggling."

He smirked, revealing a set of perfectly white teeth. "You right. My apologies."

I looked him up and down and clocked his designer suit and shoes. When he reached to grab my bag, I could see the tattoo on the inside of his wrist, too. He wasn't totally a square, I guess.

"Enjoy, New York," I tossed over my shoulder and rushed off the plane.

Whenever it was an international flight, everyone damn near rushed to customs because the line was always long. I was lucky that I had global entry, so I didn't have to worry about a long line. I hadn't even left the airport, and I was already excited to be back home. I missed my family and knew they would be excited to see me home early.

My driver was already waiting when I finished with customs. He held a sign up and I paused when I saw my brother walk in behind him. Cappadonna looked around, and then smiled when he spotted me.

I was so excited to see him that I didn't bother to ask him how or why he was here. Rushing into his arms, he picked me up and spun me around. "Hey Baby Doll. You didn't think you could sneak back in the country without me knowing?"

"Cappy, I was trying to surprise you!" He put me down on the floor and held my face, kissing me a bunch of times on the forehead before squeezing me again.

Jahquel J.

"Felt like hell not being able to do that for the past year." He paused and looked at the driver. "My man, put those suitcases in my whip, she ain't riding with yo' weird looking ass."

I shook my head and looked at the driver who rushed to grab my suitcases and do exactly what my brother said. Cappadonna didn't lie, he did look weird, and I was glad that he had come. I held onto my brother's arm as we walked out the airport and he held the door open for me.

"I love the smell of pollution, ahhh," I took a big whiff of the air, and closed my eyes while leaning back in the seat.

"Missed you, Baby Doll," he said as soon as he got in the car, pulling right off while putting his seatbelt on.

"Missed you, too. Does anybody know that I am back home?"

"Nah, I told Alaia that I was going to handle something."

I smiled. "Good. I want to surprise everyone at Jaiden's tournament this weekend." Jaiden was home from college, and he was playing in a tournament at Rucker Park in Harlem. It was all over social media since there was a lot of talk about Jaiden being drafted. He was a first-round pick, or whatever that meant. He was going to the pros, and because everyone wanted to be close to Jaiden Cooper, he was playing in this tournament that was benefiting underserved youth in New York City.

The entire family had been chatting about it in the group chat and everyone was going. I decided after the six hundredth message that I was going to come home and surprise everyone.

"I got you. I can keep a secret."

I side-eyed you. "Cappadonna, you better keep it a secret because Alaia will get it out of you. Neither of you stand on business when it comes to each other," I called him out.

He looked over at me. "How the fuck I'm supposed to stand on business when my wife looks like that, Baby Doll."

I laughed because they both made me sick. "You would

Capri

think going into year two of marriage you both would be sick of each other."

"When you marry your soul mate you could never be sick of them... me and my baby locked the fuck in."

I shook my head because both he and Capone were so lovesick. Erin and Alaia had both my brothers whipped. All they had to say is jump and both of them would be jumping up and down. The same applied to Alaia and Erin, too. Those bitches didn't know how to stand on business even if the business was standing on them. I wanted that for myself one day, and it was something I spent the last year praying for.

"How are the babies? Is the surrogate doing alright."

I could never grow tired of seeing my brother smile whenever his family was mentioned. It was the only thing I dreamed about when he was locked up. I knew Capp pretended on visits for us, so we never felt down about him being there. With him being home and seeing how happy he was with his family; it was something I had always imagined.

"My boys are straight... we on countdown now. three month until we holding them in our arms... if she don't have them early."

Alaia and Cappadonna were having twin boys, and we were so excited for them. Adding more babies to the family was always a blessing. I loved being an auntie, even to my overly grown nephew who hated for me to call him Sugar Plum.

"Capp, you know you're so blessed right?"

He looked over at me. "More than you know. Count my blessings every day."

"I know you do."

With me being gone for a year, I missed so much but somehow felt I hadn't missed anything. My family kept me so in touch with everything that I didn't feel like I missed out on anything.

"What you doing with your land, Baby Doll? Mom and

Pop's house is completed, Capella is on track to be done next, and me and Capo's house is damn near done... just waiting on a few things. Yours is the only one sitting there with dirt, and honestly, it's fucking up my property value."

I punched him. "Oh, shut up. I don't know what I want to do right now. Let me just ease back into life and then I will decide. No big decisions right now, Cappy."

He pinched my cheek. "I got you."

"Do you sit and watch that damn app with all of our chains?"

He smirked. "Yeah, it's like my own little Sims... I can't sleep unless I know everybody good."

"Creep."

"Call me what you want... I got here before you had to get in that damn car with fucking Beetlejuice."

I snorted while laughing so hard. "I've missed you so much."

"Big Pri back home!" He did a celebratory beep of his horn and scared an elderly woman trying to merge into the next lane. "Her ass shouldn't have been driving any fucking way." He grilled her while she stuck her middle finger at him.

I SPENT THE NEXT FEW DAYS HOME DECOMPRESSING AND praying that my brother didn't have a big mouth and tell Alaia. I half expected for her to pull up after he went home. Capp stayed over for a few hours, and we talked about everything going on.

As nice as it was to travel and then settle in Singapore, nothing felt better than being back in my home. Even after being gone for a year, I could still smell my signature floral scent that my house and car smelled like.

Capri

> **Meer Cat:** Shouldn't you be sleep? This open legs hours, Suga!
>
> **Me:** I'm reading and enjoying the view.

He had no idea that I was back home and was going to see him in a few. Today was Jaiden's tournament, so everyone in the family group chat was promising to send me pictures and videos of today.

> **Meer Cat:** I'll send you videos and shit today.
>
> **Me:** Thank you.

Me and Meer spoke almost every day since I had been gone. We faithfully played our game and checked in on each other. I don't think I would have lasted if it wasn't for him being in my ear. Every time I told him I was going to come home; it was his words that reminded me that I had this. I was stronger than what I thought, and this was for me, no one else.

We weren't together and never had any conversation about it. He had literally become my best friend, and I couldn't picture my life without him. Did I have feelings for him?

Yes.

I've always had a little crush on Quameer, but never acted on it because he was in a relationship. Call me a homie hopper all you want; I did have some decorum back in college. I don't know what happened after that, but back then I knew not to cross those lines. Plus, Quameer was very much caught up in Brandi.

As much as we spoke, he never gave too much. How did he and Brandi end up broken up and her married to another man? I thought I would never see the day those two would be over and living separate lives. Even when they broke up in college, they eventually ended up back together.

It showed that two people who were in love could co-exist.

Jahquel J.

I never thought it was possible, especially when it came to me and Naheim. I went an entire year without a man I thought I couldn't live without.

Even after his mother passed, I thought I would be rushing to fly back to be by his side, and all I did was talk to him and send my condolences. Nellie was his girlfriend, and that was her place to be there, not mine.

Naheim did send me pictures of NJ from time to time, and my heart always ached seeing him grow up. I had been there ever since he was born and now, I was reduced to pictures while Nellie helped Naheim raise him. As much as it hurt, I made the decision to step back because I needed to. Raising my ex-husband's side chick's baby was some crazy tail mess, and because I was so caught up in life, I never realized it until I stepped away.

With enough time away, I figured out that I was nuts for even accepting the shit. Anger always consumed me when I thought about my marriage to Naheim. We were so good together; our marriage was everything. Until I realized that I was only seeing things from one side and ignoring most of the red flags.

The cheating, jealousy, and arguments over the pettiest shit. I used to tell myself that it was because he was adjusting to being home, giving myself any excuse to keep going in this marriage. I didn't want to prove my brothers right, especially Capone. When Capp gave his blessing, Capone wasn't so convinced. For Nellie's sake, I prayed Naheim really changed and was being everything he couldn't be for me to her.

Nellie was a good woman, and I could see them being together for the long haul. As excited as I was to see my family, I was the most nervous about seeing Naheim. When I decided to leave, I never sat down and had a conversation with him. He found out from my brothers that I was leaving for a year. We never said bye, and I knew he probably still felt a way about it.

Capri

If seeing Naheim made me nervous, knowing I would see Kincaid added another wave of nervousness.

I looked myself over in the mirror and pulled my red Yankee snapback over my curls. I had freshly washed, and finger coiled my curls, so they were soft and bouncy. It was a basketball game, so I didn't have to do too much. I wore a pair of ripped jean shorts, oversized men's tank top and a sports bra underneath since the arms were big and would expose side boob. Finishing the outfit off with a pair of red dunks and my purse, I was ready to head out.

Cappadonna bought me a black Bronco like his for Christmas since I wasn't there. He parked it in my garage next to my challenger and motorcycle. I fixed the mirror, checked myself over once more and pulled out the garage to head to Harlem, excited to see everyone that I loved.

Chapter 2
Quameer

"Like I told you, I want my money when he win this game... look at all of them struggling and my guy breezing," I told some little nigga that came to watch the game.

His ass just knew his big-headed brother was going to win from the other team. His brother was having trouble trying to balance that big ass head of his and he thought he was about to win.

"You wild, Meer... he like seventeen." Goon laughed, as we walked toward the entrance to smoke.

Between Capone and Cappadonna, they were probably gonna kick all our asses out anyway. I ain't never seen two men more competitive in my life. Alaia had balled her husband's lips up a few times because his ass was hollering at everybody from the other team.

Everybody was out here deep, including the Gods. We all wanted to see Jaiden bust some heads. This game was big because he could be going into the league soon. They had media out here hard covering this game.

> Water head: Are you picking Ryder up tomorrow?

Capri

I looked at the text message from my baby mama and wanted to slam my phone onto the pavement.

I hated when her water head ass asked stupid ass questions. She knew I always picked Ryder up on Sunday and brought her back by Wednesday. It had been our schedule since Ryder was four, and she acted brand new every damn week. As if I didn't pull into her driveway and wait until she sent Ryder running out to my truck.

"Who the fuck is that?" Goon asked, as we watched a blacked-out Bronco double park and hit their hazards. I could feel the base from the music within my chest as I leaned on the gate and watched. The person remained in the car, as we watched, ready for whatever. Nobody was stupid enough to try some shit with all the media coverage out here today.

Then again, I've met stupid people so anything could go. We saw the door open, but still couldn't see who was getting out because the truck was so damn high. The spliff I was about to light dropped to the floor when *my* Suga walked around the truck.

Cappadonna came out the court and met her and hugged her tightly. It wasn't a hug like he didn't know she was going to be there though, so he had to have known she was going to show up. Her curly hair was tamed under her hat, and those shorts. I watched her thigh jiggle as she released her brother from his hug and then laughed at something he said.

The shorts she wore had me ready to run over there and tossed this damn vest over her legs. "Shit, she fine as shit... think I might shoot my shot."

"I'll fucking shoot this shot if you even look in her direction, lil' nigga," I snarled as I showed him the gun that rested behind my vest.

I didn't even know who the fuck this nigga was, but he had me fucked up if he thought he was about to talk to *my* Suga. Every nigga had eyes for her as she continued to talk to her brother as if she wasn't standing there looking good as shit.

As if she knew I was watching her, our eyes connected, and she smiled widely as she skipped over toward me. I waited a year, held onto her voice over the phone and our text messages for this moment.

"Meer!" she squealed and leaped into my arms, and I held her tightly, kissing her on the cheek. I continued to hold her, not wanting to let her ass go. "Um, Meer, you gotta let me go." Capri giggled in my ear.

"Yeah, let her ass go, *Meer*," Capp looked at me and I smirked.

"Damn, you always somewhere... let me hug my best friend... ain't seen her in a damn year." I chuckled and took a quick look over her.

She pulled on my loose loc, and then smiled up at me. "Let me go see my sisters and then I'll come back out here."

"Bet."

Capp gave me that big brother look, knowing what I told him in Miami. When she was ready, I was going to sit down and have that conversation with both he and Capone. I was a man of my word, and I would never step to Capri without having their blessing. I've always been intrigued with Capri since I saw her shuffling across campus with glasses on and some football nigga following behind her.

It was clear he had done some fuck shit to cause her to act that way toward him. When she saw me, even though we had only seen each other a handful of times at that point, she instantly tossed her arms around me and pretended like we were going to study so he would leave her alone. I played along, knowing I was waiting for Brandi to come on so we could go to some banquet dinner that her parents forced her to attend.

I didn't know how it was possible for both Erin and Alaia to scream louder than the damn game. Even from out here I could

Capri

hear them screaming and probably jumping all over her. Goon looked over at me as he handed me my spliff that I had dropped.

"Nigga, wipe the drool from your lips... the look on your face when she came around the truck... damn. You ready to go toe to toe with both Capo and Capp's ass?" Goon laughed, nudging me with his shoulder as he continued to people watch.

I tucked my spliff back behind my ear and headed back into the court, no longer interested in smoking. Like I expected, Alaia and Erin were all over Capri hugging and kissing her. I watched as Capone grabbed Capri, tossing her around and kissing her on the head a few times.

As much as Capp was strong and shit, I knew a piece of him was missing with her being gone. I think everyone expected her to return home and not stay away the full year and she did. Only I knew the struggle she went through during the holidays, and how lonely she was. There was a few times that I wanted to jump on the plane and come to her. I also knew that I had to let her be and give her that space. Capri needed to stand on her own and learn who she was without a man.

After Capone put her back on the floor and she found her balance, Chubs came over. She hugged him, and then was picked up when Jaiden flew off the court mid-game and grabbed her up.

He hugged her, spun her around, and then caught the ball, dunking it. I looked over at lil' homie and his ass was sweating bullets because he owed me money. "I want cash, too... none of that bitcoin shit, either." I raised an eyebrow and looked at him.

"I...I got you," he stammered, knowing his brother wasn't winning today and he was going to leave broke.

I took a seat in the bleachers and watched my Suga do her rounds, hugging and loving on her family. Her smile was infectious, had me over here smiling all creepy and shit just because she was smiling.

Facetime wasn't enough for me. I missed seeing her face in person and watching that little dimple on her left side deepen whenever she smiled. Capone had the same damn dimple on his left cheek, and so did their mother, so I could only assume they got it from her.

> Water head: Hello?
>
> Me: yeah.

My fingers lingered over the screen wanting to say some next shit and decided not to when I smelled that familiar scent. The only scent that tickled my nose, and only one person I cared about wore it.

Capri plopped down next to me and gently nudged my shoulder with hers. "Sooo, you surprised?"

"Reading and taking in the view my ass... why you didn't tell me?" I smirked.

Capri looked me in the eyes and smiled. "I couldn't ruin the surprise. Probably the best surprise you've ever had, huh?"

I could tell she was being sarcastic and had no clue that this was the best surprise to me. "What happened to our plan?"

She looked confused. "What plan?"

"Me picking you up and then having you run right into my arms as we scream, you're back from the war."

Capri broke out into laughter and then watched my face. "Boy, we were both drunk on facetime... you didn't actually believe we would do that, did you?"

"Hell yeah... was going to get a sign made and everything." I snickered.

Capone and Cappadonna was back to pretending to be coach while everyone was cheering Jaiden on. Capri remained next to me as we watched the game, and she reached over and squeezed my knee when that hater fouled Jaiden.

I was looking around for Naheim's ass and didn't see him. We were familiar because he ran with Capone and Cappadonna, but we weren't on no friendly shit. I knew the nigga didn't like me because me and Capri were close. Every time I was around his ass, it was like he was trying to figure out what I knew about his ex-wife.

Half the time, I wanted to let him know that his ex-wife was about to become my new wife, and I would be damned if I allowed her to slip away because I didn't have self-control. When the game was over, Erin went over with Jaiden to talk to reporters.

I peeped how Capone and Cappadonna remained out of the camera view. Capp even threatened to shove the camera up one of the cameramen's ass if he got him or Capone on camera. When I turned to look at Capri, she was already staring at me.

"What are you doing after this?" she asked.

"I got a few things to handle and then gonna head home... I got Peach tomorrow."

"Awe, Daddy and Peach time... tell her I said hey."

I didn't bring any women around my daughter. When it was my time with her, I took that shit personally. Ryder wouldn't be able to say I put anybody before her. I didn't even tolerate bitches texting me when I was with Ryder. So many situationships ended because they accused me of being with another woman, when all I was doing was spending time with my daughter. My time with her was special and I cherished that.

After witnessing my brother have to bury his own daughter, my niece, I spent all the time I got with her. I never took that shit for granted because my entire family hurt when he lost Harley. I watched a piece of him die when his baby mother passed, but I saw the rest of him die when he had to put Harley in that grave next to her mother.

When I had Ryder, I was locked all the way into daddy mode. Nothing was more important than spending time with my daughter. So, when it came to women, I never gave a fuck if they came and went because Ryder was the number one woman in my life.

Suga was different though. She facetimed me once when I was with Ryder, and the rest was history. Any time I was on the phone with my Suga, my Peaches always would pop her head in and say hi to her.

They had a cute little rapport, nothing too serious. I didn't take meeting my daughter lightly, so even though I knew I wanted Capri, I needed to know she felt the same way before I even brought her around my daughter romantically.

She was cool to meet Ryder as my friend, but when it came to calling her anything other than that, I wasn't there with her.

"I got you," I nudged her back with my shoulder.

"So, can we kick it on Thursday? I know you have Peach 'til Wednesday and I'm gonna be catching up with my family."

"I got you." She stood up, and then climbed down onto the court before turning to look at me. "Suga, you got thick."

She blushed and then twirled. "All that rice I been eating. It's time to tone it though, so Capp gonna train me."

I laughed. "That nigga be trying to get anybody to run with his ass. He turned Capella into a workout junkie."

"We gonna have to stop calling him Baby Capp soon." She smiled, exposing her perfect ass smile.

My eyes took in every part of her because I missed seeing her in person. Having to be reduced to over a screen for the past year was fucking painful. I wanted to be with her, holding, and loving her, but I also knew she needed this past year. She needed to get away and she needed to find herself before we could ever be.

Capri

If we would ever be.

"Word."

"Where's Quasim?"

"He was here earlier and had to dip to handle something."

She folded her arms. "We need to talk to him about Blair, because why is he acting like the woman doesn't exist? You know she's dating someone, right?"

My brother acted like Blair had the fucking cooties with the way he avoided her. I knew he was feeling her because whenever we happened to be in the same space as her, his ass couldn't keep his eyes away from her. His eyes always scanned the spot until they landed on her, and then the nigga acted like he didn't fucking know her.

"I'm not getting involved in another grown man's business... especially when I'm trying to get my own love life together." I pulled the spliff from behind my ear and prepared myself to spark it the moment I walked out the court.

"Tell me about it... I just got back, and my friend Jesse already wants to hook me up with one of the groomsmen in her wedding." The problem with being friends with Capri was that she vented to me about things.

Things being other men that were interested in her. I already knew Suga was pressure, and so did other niggas, which in return had me tapping into that side that I had worked this year to control. I was a rational unhinged nigga, like I could rationalize with myself, but that other side took over and it was all bets off.

"Oh yeah."

"Don't even be like that," she climbed back up and mushed me in the head, while laughing. "I'm sure you have plenty of dates lined up yourself."

"Just one."

"Oh yeah? You haven't told me about no potentials... who is this girl?"

"The future Mrs. Inferno." I pulled her shorts down and she swatted my hands. "You out here showing too much, Suga... I'm surprised Capp ain't lose his shit."

"He tried to put his shirt around me," she rolled her eyes and laughed at the same time. "Anyway, who is the future Mrs. Inferno?"

I looked up into her eyes with my spliff tucked between my lips. "You, Suga."

Capri's breath was caught in her chest as she looked down at me. "Capri!"

We both turned to Aimee running over toward us and Capri jumping down the bleachers and embracing her. "Aimee!"

"Hey Quameer!" Aimee greeted me before turning her attention back to Capri. "Why didn't you tell us that you were coming home early? We have to go out tonight...we have so much to catch up on." Aimee was speaking a mile a minute while Capri tried to catch up with everything she was saying.

Capri looked over at me before Aimee pulled her toward Alaia and Erin. "Later, Meer."

I winked as I remained seated while watching her walk away. Watching Capri had me lost for a second before I remembered that I rode with Goon, and his ass wouldn't hesitate to leave a nigga if he couldn't find me. When I left the court, I found him shooting the breeze with Capone and Cappadonna.

"I was just about to breeze on yo' ass." Goon laughed as I finally sparked my spliff and leaned on his car. "Where the fuck you slid off to?"

"His ass was too busy grinning in Capri's face," Capone called me out.

"Fuck up," I snorted.

It was no secret how I felt about their sister. Both Capone

Capri

and Cappadonna knew it was only a matter of time before I approached them and asked for their blessing. Right now, I was playing it cool and seeing where Capri was.

As much as we spent the last year growing closer in our friendship, she may not even feel the same way as I did. "I don't fucking know about this lounge idea they told me about," Capp's overprotective ass said.

"They gonna be good... the lounge is in IG territory, and I'll be around," Goon replied, tossing his empty water bottle into the trash can.

"Yeah, last time I thought my wife was good some dusty bitch snatched her ass," he snarled. The thought of someone taking his wife still had his ass fired up and a whole year and some months had already passed. I don't think that emotion would ever leave him whenever the subject was brought up.

Goon checked his phone and held his hand out. "You got my word, I got them."

"I'll swing by if I finish whatever I'm doing. Got Ryder tomorrow so gotta food shop and shit."

"Daddy shit, I respect it." Capp held his index and middle finger together and I did the same, as we tapped them twice on the front and once on the back.

"Capo, I'mma holla." I saluted and headed to Goon's whip.

Everyone assumed because Capp was now an Inferno God that his brother would join, too. Capone wasn't into all of that, but if we needed him to ride, that nigga was going to ride, just like we would do the same for him.

As I slowly pulled into the suburban neighborhood in Staten Island, I always took note of the manicured lawns, tree lined streets and children playing signs that were positioned in the streets to avoid speeding. Every driveway had either a big ass suburban or a Mercedes in it. I could feel the hives forming on my skin while I pulled into the driveway that belonged to the brick colonial house with black shutters and black double doors. It was one of the biggest houses in the neighborhood.

The hydrangeas were fully bloomed, and a bike was sprawled across the front lawn. Peach never put her shit up, even when she was at my house, so I knew it was hers. Plus, she was the only child, so who else bike could it have been?

> Me: Outside.

I sent Brandi's ass a text message and waited for her extra ass to reply. She always had to reply instead of just sending Ryder out to me.

> Water head: One sec.

I leaned my head back and mentally prepared myself to go into daddy mode. It was hard living two different lives, but I was grateful for it. My daughter was my world, and I would do anything for her. Being honest, Peach was my broke judgmental ass best friend.

Everybody needed one of those.

She drove her mother crazy because she acted just like me. I expected my daughter to be this prissy stuck up child because of the way her mother acted, and she was the complete opposite of her. It was like she wanted to be the complete opposite of her mother, and the shit made me proud.

It was no secret that I couldn't stand my baby mother. At one point, I loved the fuck out of her and wanted to marry her. Brandi Devaughn used to be my everything, and that was rare for me. Nobody had ever been my everything and here I was

Capri

admitting that this woman used to be that. Even knowing that we came from two different worlds, I thought we could have forever together.

Shit was stupid for me to even think. Brandi's father was the police commissioner, and nobody was good enough for his pumpkin. Especially not the boy whose father was the head of the motorcycle gang that he despised.

The odds were stacked against me before I even met her father. Then when I met him, I knew he would never approve of us being together. Shit, I never needed him to approve of us being together, he just needed to respect it. When me and Brandi got together, we were grown and smart enough to understand what we were getting into with each other.

I was a grown man and not living at home, so why the fuck did I need his approval? Even though I didn't give a fuck about his approval, Brandi did. She was all about pleasing her father. Since she was the youngest, he watched her ass like a hawk, especially when she brought me home. I could tell Reggie didn't like shit about me and thought his daughter was too good for me.

He wasn't wrong.

Brandi grew up with a silver spoon in her mouth, never experienced struggle and couldn't identify a ramen noodle box to save her fucking life. We came from different worlds, and even though I knew we could never relate on certain shit, I fell in love with her anyway. Our relationship was always so up and down because she fucking cared about what her father thought.

Even with me being in college and doing my own thing, his ass never liked me. The feeling was mutual because I couldn't stand a Black man who forgot where he came from. Reggie's ass grew up with my father. He came from the same hood as he did, and you would have thought he grew up with the same silver spoon that was shoved in his daughter's mouth.

Jahquel J.

Brandi always made the shit hard, forcing me to get close with her dad or change who I was so he could like me. I attended more stuffy ass events than I cared to be a part of. She tried to change me into what she wanted me to be.

During our relationship I noticed nothing I did was ever good enough for Brandi. It never mattered how much I loved that woman, she always had something to complain about. I started to change into someone that I barely recognized because I wanted the relationship to work so bad. I stopped hanging with my brother and the Gods and was tied into her and whatever she wanted. Attending events and being fucking boring was all I did with Brandi.

Even with me being everything to her, the shit was never enough for her. Whenever I did hang out with my brother or the Gods, she always had an attitude or something to say. Shit was always tense between us because she wanted me to be the kind of man that her father would approve of. Since his ass didn't approve of the relationship, I felt like she never gave us a fair chance. She kept me close enough to feed me lies, but she never saw a future with me, and that was hurt that I had to carry.

She tried to change me into someone else and I allowed that shit because I loved her. Brandi didn't understand the hold that she had over me, and how much I loved her ass. I would do anything for her because that was how I was when I was in love. While I was serious and thought we were working toward our future, she had no plans on actually having a future with me.

I learned our relationship was a game when I asked her to marry me, and she accepted the ring. Months went by and while I was telling anybody that had fucking ears, excited for what was to come, she was mute. Imagine my surprise when I ran into her father and mentioned our engagement and the nigga didn't know what I was talking about. Her ass never told her family and had been lying to me about her mother and sisters being excited about planning the wedding.

Shit broke me when she handed me back my ring and told me she couldn't marry me. I was willing to give up everything and everyone for her, and she couldn't stand up to her parents for me. I wasn't worth enough for her to go to bat against her family for our love.

It wouldn't be the last time that she broke my fucking heart and then stomped on it.

A few months later, I found out that she was pregnant. Brandi played games all throughout her pregnancy. She denied me the chance to experience my child growing in her womb. Some shit you could never forgive someone for, and that was one of the things that made me hate her. I was cordial because of our daughter, but other than that, I wanted nothing to do with the bitch.

She played me and had me looking like a goofy and that was some shit that I could never forgive her for. The shit still kept me up at night when I thought about how soft I was for her, how vulnerable I was when it came to her. Brandi fucked it up for other women that had come into my life.

The door opened and Ryder came skipping out the house, and I hopped out my truck. She came crashing into my arms, with a bright smile on her face. Her soft curls were pulled up into a high pony, and her hazel eyes stared up at me.

"Hey Daddy!" she smiled, squeezing me as hard as she could.

I picked her up and kissed her on the cheek. "What up, Peach?"

Ryder gave me a tight squeeze around the neck and whispered into my ear. "Mom and Martin are arguing again." She referred to her mother and stepfather, Martin.

"Oh shit…. again?" I snickered as I put my daughter down and watched my baby mother saunter out the house like everything was all good. Her big-headed ass had always been good with pretending. Her entire world could be in flames, and she would pop out like her life was marvelous.

When Brandi married her politician husband, I knew the shit wouldn't work out. She may have been born with a silver spoon in her mouth, but her ass liked that hood dick that yanked her hair and had her ass sucking dick shot gun in the whip.

Brandi like the allure of being with men involved in the streets. The only reason she tried to change me was because of her father. Had her father not had a stick up his ass, her ass wouldn't have changed a thing about me. Now she was married to some overweight politician that probably only fucked her missionary.

I knew her freaky ass was sexually frustrated as fuck. Brandi folded her arms and looked over at me with a smile on her face, per usual. The bitch was always so giddy to see me like I ever gave her more than five words when I picked our daughter up.

Her sienna skin glistened under the sun as she ran her hand through her jet-black hair, and then crossed her arms again. I remember when I used to kiss the beauty mark that was above her thick pink lip. Now all I wanted to do was smear shit on her face and watch her fucking gag over the smell.

"Hey Quameer... her teacher complained about her homework not getting done when she's with you."

"Her teacher just wants to fuck," I replied honestly.

Brandi looked to see where Ryder was before she rolled her eyes. "I'm being serious, Quameer. She sent an email saying that the homework isn't being completed, and she wants to schedule a meeting to talk."

Ms. Adams wanted me to come sit in her classroom to talk about imaginary work because Ryder did all her work. I knew my daughter and I was always on top of her schoolwork

Capri

because education was important to me. Both her parents had degrees, so her ass was going to get one, too. Between me and Brandi, I had a more relaxed parenting style, which made it easy for Ryder. I wasn't on her back about her homework, so she always took it upon herself to get it done. She was seven years old and more responsible than half the niggas I knew.

Ever since I picked Ryder up from school at the beginning of the year, her teacher had been making any excuse to have a conversation with me alone. She never had a problem when Ryder was with her mother. It was always some problem when she was with me since she learned our schedule.

"School damn near about to be over and she wanna have a conference now. You going to be there?"

"I asked her if I needed to attend, and she told me that I didn't need to come. Plus, Martin has this conference in DC this week, so I'm going to drive up and surprise him."

She snapped her fingers like she forgot something. I watched her jog back to the house to grab Ryder's school bag. She rummaged through it before closing it and handing it over to me. "Can you keep her until Friday? Martin's mom has been in and out the hospital, so I was thinking we could drive to visit her while in DC."

While Ryder was climbing up in my pickup truck, I opened the backdoor and placed her bookbag in the backseat. "If you need more time for you and big draws, I got you."

If this was the first time she did this shit, then I wouldn't have had an attitude about it. Brandi did this shit all the time, acting like it was a problem for me to keep my daughter longer than my assigned days. If it was up to me, I would have had Ryder live with me full time. The days I had her weren't enough and I always hated having to bring her back to Brandi's ass. Unlike other parents, I enjoyed being around my kid all the time. I was raising a dope fucking kid, and I enjoyed her company as much as she enjoyed mine.

"Daddy, Capri is calling you!" Ryder yelled out the window. "Can I answer the phone, please," she begged.

Brandi didn't get the chance to address the new nickname for her square ass husband. Whatever thought she had left the minute she heard Ryder yell Capri's name out the window.

"Tell her I'm gonna call her back," I told Ryder, and she put the window back up, as she answered the phone excited.

"Capri Delgato?" Brandi stood there with her arms folded, waiting for me to confirm what she probably already knew.

I chuckled as I walked backward to my truck. "This is where those boundaries we discussed kick in... mind your business, Brandi."

"You run for her brothers, so it doesn't surprise me."

I paused. "I don't run for nobody... the only fucking running is your mouth, and then you don't even know what the fuck you talking about. Brandi, mind your fucking business," I checked her stupid ass.

She stood there looking stupid and not knowing what to say because she was loud and wrong. I should have asked why she knew the Capri that Ryder was referring to was even Capri Delgato. The name Capri was fucking common, so she could have been talking about anybody.

Even though they ran in the same circles and had mutual friends, Capri and Brandi were never friends. Brandi actually couldn't stand Capri, and I always had to hear her ass complain. When Capri pulled onto campus with a brand new whip, I listened to her ass talk during our whole date about how Capri thought she was better than her because her brothers bought her a brand new BMW. The shit that always confused me was how down to earth Capri was. She never acted like she was better than anybody.

If anything, it was Brandi's ass that acted like she was better than every person she met. Only a select few knew she came from money, and even then, she didn't always come from

Capri

money. Capone and Cappadonna didn't always have the bread they had now. She didn't toss her money in people's face. Unlike Brandi's ass, she couldn't wait to toss out who her father was and what neighborhood she lived in.

That was the difference between Capri and Brandi, and I guess it was easier to hate on someone that you really wanted to be. No matter how much she tried, she could never compete with Capri. Funny shit was that Capri never had to do too much and she was still shutting Brandi down. That was how I knew I was a fool over Brandi. All the shit I realized now, I should have back then, and I would have saved myself a whole lot of heartache.

Completely ignoring me, she stood with her hand on her hips. "Why is she even calling you?"

I checked inside my truck and watched Ryder running her mouth on the phone. "You sucking this dick, Brandi?"

"Quame—"

I cut her stammering ass off. "You don't get to ask me why the fuck anybody is calling my phone. I'll see you on Friday, Brandi. You need to be worried about that nigga, not me." I snorted, and then climbed back into my truck, leaving her ass speechless.

Brandi must have been snorting fucking paint if she thought she had any right to question me about my shit. The only reason this co-parenting relationship worked was because I didn't give a fuck about what she had going on. As long as my daughter was safe and happy under her roof, that was all I cared about.

Martin might have been a fat bitch, but he loved my daughter like his own and treated her like gold. For that, I had no choice but to be a real man and be cordial whenever his ass was around, which wasn't often.

Brandi was always concerned with how I felt about her moving on. The shit hurt when she was floating around with that ring on her finger like she didn't hand mine back. When she showed up the night before her wedding, I should have turned her ass away. All that apologizing and shit didn't mean shit for the way she had fucked me over.

"Maybe your father will finally allow us to meet over the summer, and you can come visit my lake house," I overheard Suga as I backed out the driveway, while Brandi was still trying to find her words.

"Yes, please... I love swimming and I never swam in a lake before, just an ocean," Ryder told her.

"What up, Suga?" I finally made my presence known.

"Hey Meer... I was calling to see what you were doing... I forgot that quick you told me it's you and Peach's time... sorry."

"You good... you needed me?"

She giggled. "I would have texted you INY... I just wanted to see what you were doing. Us girls decided to come to the lake houses."

INY was an inside joke between us that meant *I need you*. Whenever the lighter I had gave her didn't work, Capri would shoot me that text and I would facetime her right away. It didn't matter where or what I was doing, I was going to pause whatever just to facetime Suga. Even if it was for a few seconds, I always responded when she sent those letters.

"What's INY?" Ryder's nosey ass asked.

"What I tell you about grown folks' business, Peach?"

"To stay in a child's place... sorry, Daddy and Pri," she sulked, looking out the window with a pouty face on.

Brandi spoke so freely around her and allowed her to stay in rooms she shouldn't have. When I was growing up, soon as the adults got to running their mouth, you were supposed to scatter. They didn't give a fuck where you went, as long as you weren't in their face listening to the conversation.

As relaxed as I was when it came to my daughter, there was certain things that I didn't rock with, and Ryder already knew.

"It's alright, Ryder. Spend your time with Ryder and I'll see you on Thursday, right?"

"Nah... I'm going to have Ryder longer."

"Oh okay... call me later?"

"I got you."

When we pulled into Quasim's driveway, Ryder's attitude and silent treatment had melted away. She was ripping the seatbelt off just to get out the car. I grabbed my phone and followed behind her as she rang his doorbell. I knew his hermit ass was home because he hardly ever went anywhere. Unless he had to handle some business, Quasim's ass was usually home.

He pulled the door opened and stood there in his pajamas. It was the middle of the day, and this nigga wasn't even dressed for the day. "Ry, you came to see your favorite uncle?" His face always lit up whenever he saw his niece.

Aside from Harley, she was his favorite person in the world. I think she reminded him a lot of his own daughter, which is why I brought Ryder over here as much as I could. It would never bring back Harley, but I enjoyed witnessing Ryder's relationship with her uncle.

Ryder kissed her uncle's cheek when he picked her up. "You are my only uncle, silly."

"And the favorite, right?"

Ryder hugged her uncle around the neck, and he put her down. "Do you have ice cream, Uncle Sim?"

"Yeah... I always keep ice cream in the house for you."

Ryder didn't wait before she rushed inside the house in search for the ice cream. Quasim held the door open for me and I strolled in, looking at how he had all the damn curtains drawn. "You a fucking vampire or something? Why the fuck is everything dark in here?"

The only thing that was on was the TV, then he had the nerve to be watching some boring ass civil war documentary on the history channel. Quasim had always been into history and shit like that. I always figured he would be the one to attend and graduate from college because he was so damn smart.

"It's Sunday, what the fuck you expect me to be doing?" Quasim sat on the couch, kicking his feet up on the expensive coffee table.

I plopped down on his couch and looked at the documentary before deciding that giving myself a headache wasn't worth it. "Which is every reason why you need a girlfriend or something." I looked toward the kitchen to see where Ryder was. "At least somebody to fuck on... when the last time you got some pussy, Qua?"

"You think being in a relationship or fucking some random gonna prevent me from being at peace in my house on a Sunday?" he chuckled and turned his TV up.

When Cherie was murdered, I saw a piece of my brother die. Cherie wasn't some random baby mama; she was the love of his life, and he had planned on making her his wife. He bought this house for her when she got pregnant with Harley. Quasim had planned a full proposal, and never got the chance to because she was murdered by a Chrome Viper.

Quasim had become a fucking savage, and I never saw that from him before. He was laying bodies out like the shit was legal, and it was his daytime job. Despite having a daughter, he didn't give a fuck what happened to him. Cherie was everything to him and they had a whole future together, and her life was taken away because of a stupid ass beef.

After ending the nigga that was responsible, the founders of both Inferno Gods and Chrome Vipers had to step in and squash things. The death toll was high and gaining unwanted attention from the authorities. The imaginary treaty was put into place to avoid any more violence in either city. I don't think Quasim really forgave my father for stepping in and

Capri

squashing it, because in his heart nothing would ever be squashed when it came to Chrome Vipers and Inferno Gods.

It was beef forever when it came to those niggas, and I always had my gun cocked ready to follow up behind Quasim. Soon as life settled and he was trying to live life without Cherie while raising their daughter, Harley was diagnosed with cancer.

I remember the day I came over and found my brother sitting on the bathroom floor with a gun to his head. Quasim had always been the strength when we were growing up. Whenever I was scared, I would always look to my brother and his strength and bravery always told me that shit was going to be alright.

Even now, when we were riding side by side, all I had to receive was that nod from him and it was go time. The day I walked into his bathroom and found him on the floor with that gun to his head scared the shit out of me. Harley was down the hall taking a nap and he was in his bathroom ready to end it all.

In that moment I didn't understand that he was on the verge of losing another member of his family. It hadn't been even two years since he lost Cherie, and now he was faced with having less than eighteen months with his daughter.

The kind of cancer that Harley had been diagnosed with was the worst type of brain cancer and there wasn't any happy outcomes for children diagnosed with it. Qua fought tooth and nail for his daughter. Traveling out of state for clinical trials and doing any and everything to make sure that Harley had a chance of survival.

Even in the fogginess of his own grief, he was still superman for his daughter and did any and everything to save her life. Harley was five years old when she lost her battle with cancer. When we dropped that dirt on her casket, I believed we buried the rest of my brother with Harley and Cherie.

He hadn't been the same and had become a recluse. Since

Cappadonna had been home, this was the most I had seen him out the house. Quasim stopped living and the shit broke my heart because life was passing him by. Cherie wouldn't want him in the house living in their past memories.

Not much in this house had changed since Harley and Cherie passed away. Harley's room was still the same, and when you walked into his bedroom, you would have thought Cherie was still alive.

The house was a reminder of his past and the future that he would never have with them. Shit broke my heart every time I came over here. As much as I wanted to stop his pain, I knew nothing I could do or say would ever make the pain stop. When Suga asked me how Quasim felt about Ryder since he lost his own daughter, I couldn't answer that because I didn't know the answer to it.

Quasim had never been the type that was open with his emotions. I could count on one hand how often we had heart to heart conversations about Harley or Cherie. He just moved forward and although he never acted like he was fine, he pushed forward like he was.

"You heard from Pops?"

Quasim's eyes remained on the TV while he shook his head no. "Should I have?"

I struggled with finding something to talk about because it was clear he didn't want to have a conversation right now. Ryder came running out the kitchen with a bowl of ice cream for herself, and plopped down next to her uncle, handing him the second spoon.

Quasim didn't need to tell me how he felt about Ryder because his smile whenever he saw her told me everything. Despite losing his daughter, Ryder healed something inside of him. He took the spoon from her and scooped some ice cream on the spoon.

"You excited to be done with school soon?"

Capri

Ryder smiled as she shoved more ice cream down her throat. "Yes. Daddy said I can stay with him the entire summer instead of going away to summer camp."

"Oh yeah?" Quasim chuckled as he spooned more ice cream into his mouth. "How is Brandi going to feel about that?"

Brandi usually sent her away to some expensive ass summer camp where she spent six weeks away from both of us. I hated it because by the time she came home, summer was damn near over and we both were trying to scramble to figure out who got time with her first. As much as Ryder enjoyed summer camp, she would enjoy spending time with me for the summer.

"I'm her father... what else could she say?"

Ryder quickly realized we were talking about her mother and grabbed the bowl, and quickly went back to the kitchen. "Brandi could say a lot and you know she won't hesitate to make things difficult."

He wasn't wrong.

Brandi had always gotten her way with me because she liked to make shit harder for me when it came to being a father to my daughter. She knew the only way to control me was with Ryder, so whenever shit didn't go her way, she knew how to use her to get me to bend, and nine times out of ten the shit always worked.

"The only reason she sends her to that camp is so she can travel with her husband. No sooner than Ryder is on that bus, she's out the country living her best life. How many parent days have I attended alone because she was in a different country."

"You prepared to take Ryder on for the entire summer? Who is going to watch her when you have shit to handle?"

"Gammy."

"As if she doesn't have enough shit going on," he referred to all the shit our grandmother had going on.

Jahquel J.

I leaned forward, becoming pissed because he was making it seem like I couldn't take care of my damn child. If push came to shove, I would always make sure Ryder was safe and taken care of. "I know how to handle my seed."

"Never saying you don't know how to. I'm here, too... if you need me."

"Appreciate that."

Ryder stuck her around the corner. "Daddy, can I come back and eat ice cream with Uncle Sim?"

"Yeah, come on."

She rushed back over to the couch with even more ice cream in the bowl than she had left with. "Capri told me that I can swim in her lake." Ryder looked over at her uncle, excited to share the news of Capri's invite.

Quasim chuckled. "Oh really? Do you even know how to swim in a lake?"

"I can swim in an ocean, so a lake isn't that much harder... I need more sprinkles," she hopped back down and went back into the kitchen.

"You introducing her to Capri?"

"I ain't say all of that."

Quasim laughed, now more interested in my shit than the boring ass documentary that was on. "What are you saying exactly?"

I shrugged and leaned back on the couch. "I don't fucking know... you know how I am with bringing anybody around Peach."

"What the fuck are you both doing 'cause I'm confused."

"We friends."

Quasim laughed before becoming serious. "You already know what you need to do if you decide to cross that line, Blaze," he warned using the nickname that only he and my father called me.

A lot came with making Capri Delgato mine. I couldn't and

Capri

would never approach her like a regular chick because Capri was far from that. She had been through a lot of shit and had her heart broken more than a few times. Despite dedicating the last year to her and only her, she still had trouble trusting her heart.

Shit. I had trouble trusting my own.

Chapter 3
Capri

THE SMELL OF BACON CAUSED ME TO RISE UP OUT THE guest bedroom and float down the steps to the kitchen where Alaia was cooking breakfast with Promise and Rory sitting on the counter. She laughed as she pinched their cheeks and carefully took the cooked bacon out of the pan.

"Aht... don't touch hot... blow," she coached them as they tried to snatch the bacon off the plate, she had just placed it on.

"Quack-Quack, hot," Rory said in his low raspy voice. His raspy voice was one of the cutest things about him.

Alaia smiled, pinching, and kissing his cheeks. "You are so smart, Rory."

Promise looked at Rory, then her mother like she had betrayed her before she broke out screaming. Alaia looked at her daughter before kissing her on the cheeks like she had done Rory seconds before.

"Joy, why my daughter screaming?" Cappadonna came through the garage door, kicking his running sneakers off, and washing his hands before grabbing a screaming Promise off the counter.

No sooner than she was in her father's arms she had

Capri

stopped crying and looked down at her mother. "Cause she's dramatic like her father."

Capp dropped a few kisses on his wife's lips, and then kissed his grandson on the head. Rory had already stolen a piece of the hot bacon and was satisfied with the attention not being on him. It was funny how he mirrored similar qualities of his father and grandfather, and he was only over a year old.

"The smell of bacon woke me up out of bed," I made my presence known, taking a seat at the counter, nuzzling Rory's curly hair.

He was so into his bacon that he paid me no mind. Since I had been gone for a full year, they only knew me as the woman in the screen. Promise kept looking at me like she knew I was familiar but was wondering why I wasn't on the screen of her mom or dad's phone that she constantly held hostage from them.

I don't know how many times I called Cappadonna or Alaia, and my call had been ignored because Promise was watching something on YouTube.

"Somebody packed the kids up and drove here because he couldn't sleep with me being gone." Alaia cut her eyes at Cappadonna, who had no shame.

He kissed Promise's cheeks while looking at us both. "Capella's ass was in the front seat before I could get Promise and Rory strapped in."

We decided last minute to come out to the lake house to spend a few days. I missed my sisters, so spending a few days away from everyone and enjoying drinks out in the back surrounded by the lake sounded much better than a lounge.

"Cappy, you couldn't survive without your wife for a few days?" I joked, already knowing the answer to the question.

"Good morning," Erin yawned, with Capone trailing right behind her.

Before I could even say anything to them, the garage door

opened, and we all turned to see Capella strolling in with his shirt around his neck. "What the fuck I do now?"

"You mean to tell me that none of you could go a few days without your women?" I clowned them because they each had it bad for the women they loved.

Cappadonna pulled Alaia close. "My baby be needing me at night... she can't see in the dark, so I help her to the bathroom. You don't want piss on the rug, right?"

"Roy?"

Capp smirked. "Yeah, baby?"

"Fuck ya." She shoved him away from her and continued to make breakfast.

I turned my attention to Capone. "And your excuse?"

"Shit, Capp called and told me he was driving up here, so I grabbed Cee-Cee and Cooper to follow behind him." Capone shrugged without an ounce of shame. "She still breastfeeding."

"Oh bullshit... don't try and use my leaking breast as an excuse," Erin called her husband out, as I settled back in my seat.

I looked over at Cappadonna who was busy watching his wife cook. When he noticed me watching him, he smiled. "Chill out, you can still have your precious girl time... y'all can stay at your house. I can't be too far from my wife... sue me, Baby Doll."

Even though it had been well over a year since Alaia's brother had kidnapped her, she confided in me that Cappadonna still struggled with it. Some nights it kept him awake, which explained why he knew I was coming back into the country before everyone else. I didn't mind my brothers crashing our girl time because as much as I missed girl time, I craved family time, too.

"We about to be all coming up this way for the summer anyway... me and Aimee need to get some stuff for our crib." Capella shrugged.

Capri

The second the house next door to mine went up for sale, Cappadonna bought it for Capella and Aimee for Rory's first birthday.

"I'm excited about all of us spending the summer here... the last summer we spent here was a vibe." I smiled, thinking of all the memories we made here at the lake.

Capone kissed Erin on her head and swaggered over toward the garage door. "I'm about to break into our house."

"Thanks for reminiscing on the memories we had last summer, Capone," I called to his back, while Cappadonna kissed Alaia and took Promise upstairs with him.

Capella picked Rory up. "That summer was fucking tough."

"Sorry, Sugar Plum." I didn't mean to take away from the fact that he lost his aunt, and then his mother shortly after.

"You good, Pri... spending time up here with family helped me a lot, too. I'm just good being here this summer with shit being less heavy, feel me?"

I nodded my head. "Exactly. Do you know when my parents are flying back home?"

He shrugged. "You gotta ask them."

While everyone was supportive of me traveling for the last year, my mother wasn't a fan. She didn't understand why I had to take off and leave everyone behind. When I decided to leave, I had to do it for me. I felt like I was going to lose my mind and had put everything and everyone before me. Slowly but surely, I was losing Capri, and I needed to get away and do something for me. As much as she had been vocal about not understanding and not being supportive, I just wanted her to support it.

Erin nudged me with her shoulder. "You know how Ma is whenever she doesn't agree with something... how did you sleep last night?" she switched the subject because she could tell I was thinking about my mother.

"Like a baby. Before I went to bed I was talking to Quameer, and ended up falling asleep on him," I laughed.

Alaia sat a plate of eggs and toast in front of me. "I bet you missed him, huh?"

Both she and Erin eyed me suspiciously. "Why are you both looking at me like that?"

Erin bit into her piece of bacon. "You like that man, and you keep playing the friend card like you don't want to be more to him."

"We *are* friends," I defended.

When Quameer saw me off at the airport, I didn't think we would keep in touch like we had. I thought everything was talk, and he would forget about me by the time I came home. I had been with someone that sold me the river, and then handed me a damn bottled water, so it was hard to trust someone's word.

I accepted it because I didn't know any better and thought I could change him. Thought I could be enough to where other women wouldn't matter. With time to heal, I realized that no matter what I did or how I changed myself, I would have never been what Naheim wanted.

Quameer was different.

His words weren't just words, he put action behind them and was there for me. Quameer wasn't there because he had to be, he was there because he wanted to be. I don't think I would have lasted and probably would have come home earlier had it not been for his encouragement. Every time I felt myself breaking, he was a phone call or facetime away reminding me of my why.

"You like him though, Pri," Alaia accused as she stood with her hands on her wide hips, staring me down.

"Seriously, can I just be home and enjoy being back without thinking about a relationship? I want to date and have fun... not think of having feelings or not."

Alaia nodded her head. "Fair."

Capri

Erin clapped her hands. "Well, you have a birthday coming up and I think we should do what you wanted to do last year... shit went left so we never got to do it."

I stared at her confused. "Do what?"

"Roller-skate party."

"Erin..." Alaia warned her.

"What?"

"Tell her the truth," Alaia forced her.

Erin looked away. "I may have put a deposit down on the skating rink for your birthday party."

"What birthday party."

"Erin..." Alaia continued to pull it out of her.

"The surprise one me and Alaia were going to throw you," she mumbled, and shoved some eggs into her mouth.

Last year everything was so hectic with Cappadonna coming home that I never got the chance to fully celebrate my birthday. My attention was more on my brothers being together and finally celebrating their birthdays together, with Capp being free.

I had mentioned in conversation about wanting to do a roller-skating party and never followed up because life kept happening. When I was eight, I had a roller-skating party, and it was still one of the best memories that I had.

All I wanted to do this summer was have fun. I didn't want to think about anything or stress about nobody's nappy headed son. I had done that in the past and I was over that shit. It was time to get back to me, show them why they called me *Capri Delgato, make a nigga yell god damn.*

"You both were going to throw me a surprise party." I squeezed Erin and smiled at the both of them. "How did I luck up with the two of you?"

"You know Erin is a sucker for a party... especially a theme," Alaia teased Erin. A party hated to see Erin's ass coming because one thing sis' was going to do was plan a good one.

I jumped off the chair and clapped my hands together. "Fuck it, let's do it."

"Seriously?" Erin squealed.

"Yes. I want it to be fun... do you remember Passa Passa parties?"

Erin eyed me. "Yeah, but why the hell do you know about them?"

I smirked, knowing that I had done more than a few things that I shouldn't have done when Capone wasn't paying attention to me. "Anyway, I want it to be like Passa Passa and the movie ATL had a baby."

"I've always wanted to be New-New," Alaia smiled, her dimples mirroring Lauren London's dimples in the movies.

Erin already pulled out her infamous notes app and was taking notes. "We're about to have fun... I'm not pregnant either."

"Mommy," we all turned to see Cee-Cee, my namesake, rubbing her eyes and coming from the other guest room.

"Cee-Cee, can I have a hug?" I kneeled and she came running into my arms. "My girl... your cousins were acting funny."

"My baby acts funny because her damn father," Alaia defended Promise, who stared at me like I was a stranger trying to touch her.

I picked my niece up and kissed her while she giggled. "Your daddy is breaking into our house, Cee-Cee," Erin laughed while typing something into her phone. "Ever since Cooper was born, she has been a hardcore daddy's girl."

Erin and Capone named their son Cooper, Erin's maiden name. It was something special to honor her parents, and I thought it was the cutest thing. Even though she was a Delgato, it was a reminder of who she used to be before she married into our family.

"That's because Cooper is a mama's boy. Promise is a hard-core daddy's girl, and I cannot wait until our sons are born so they can be mama's boys." Alaia sighed.

Cee-Cee clung onto me as I sat back down in my seat, and I squeezed her. "I missed you, Pumpkin... you missed auntie?"

She nodded her head, with her curly hair all over her head. "Bacon, please." She held her hand out, and Alaia gave her a piece of bacon.

"Can Auntie have a kiss on the cheek?" Alaia asked, and put her cheek next to Cee-Cee, who kissed her before taking the bacon.

"Any particular people you want invited to this party?" Erin reached over and kissed her daughter while waiting for me to answer her.

"I'll leave the list up to you and will send you names of people to invite from college."

The garage door sounded, and Capone came back into the house with grass and leaves in his hair. "Got in that bitch."

"Daddy!" Cee-Cee nearly launched out my arms toward her father, and he grabbed her, kissing her on the head.

"Aye, where's my kiss?" he asked, and pointed to his cheek, and she placed her greasy bacon filled lips onto his cheek.

While Alaia and Erin went into planner mode while cleaning the kitchen, I went across the street to my own house to shower and recenter. I couldn't lie and pretend that it wasn't hard coming back to my lake house alone. The last time I stayed here had been with Naheim and NJ. It was like we had our own little family for the summer, despite Naheim being with Nellie.

It was that summer that I entertained the thought of possibly making it work with him. I thought I would have been able to make it work and pretend all the hurt we caused each other never happened. Had it not been for Nellie constantly calling his phone, I would have continued to have those thoughts.

Before I could get too deep into my thoughts, I went to shower so I could enjoy my day on the lake. I planned to take Capone's boat out and journal on the water while meditating.

Jesse came rushing into this Parisian themed café that was closer to her house in Hoboken. She was lucky that I had even drove all the way here to eat mediocre crepes and lukewarm cappuccinos. For the sake of my girls, I would do anything for them without a second thought.

I was a girl's girl all the way through and rode hard for my friends. If I told you that I got you, I stood ten toes behind that and meant every single word. Back in college while everyone was drunk and passing out, I was the one that made sure we all made it back to our dorms without a creep trying to accompany us.

Jesse plopped her Gucci tote onto the table and rushed around the table to hug me tightly. "Ugh, I missed seeing this beautiful face... don't ever go away again. Promise me right now," she kissed my cheek a million times before she finally released me.

She rounded the table, plopping down and tossing her phone into her purse, that was nearly spilling over with notebooks and magazines. I could only guess that it was nothing but bridal magazines and a checklist for the wedding.

Jesse had always been the checklist type. In college, she had a checklist for every damn thing, and it didn't change as we graduated and walked into adulthood. Even as a US Marshall, she still had a damn list for everything.

"I missed you, too. You excited to put your checklists away

and actually turn up for your bachelorette trip?" I flicked the clipboard that was partially hanging out of her bag.

She laughed. "Please don't get married... planning a wedding isn't for the weak. I wake up in the middle of the night blurting vendor's names."

"Don't have any plans on doing it again after the way it ended," I muttered.

Jesse realized what she said and quickly reached her hand across the table. "I'm so sorry... I didn't mean it that way."

It wasn't like Jesse knew everything I had been going through or had been there to hold my hand through it all. She wasn't the type that did check ins or worried herself about other people's problems. The only time I really heard from Jesse was whenever she had an event, or she needed me for something.

If I didn't reach out, I wouldn't hear from her. I purposely kept my college friends and life separate from my personal life. So, Jesse didn't know Tasha, or the fact that Naheim cheated on me with her.

She had only met Naheim a handful of times whenever we attended an event she was throwing. I usually attended most of our friend's events alone because Naheim hated them. It was easier than arguing with him about not bringing his gun or acting like he didn't have any sense. He also hated whenever I was around my college friends because I changed – slightly.

I had mastered the art of code switching, and Naheim hated it so bad. I was a lawyer; I couldn't carry myself any kind of way. With Jesse being a US Marshal, he felt uncomfortable, so I understood.

"It's alright, Jesse," I replied, even though it wasn't alright.

Had it been Blair, she wouldn't have allowed something to slip like that. Then again, Blair had always been mindful, and one of those friends that were good for your soul.

"Anyway," she quickly snatched her hand back, and pulled out the clipboard. "David's sister said Miami was too boring and we've done it so many times. Plus mostly all the rental houses and hotels are booked for those dates. She rented a beautiful villa in Anguilla... like this cost about twelve thousand a night," she whispered like somebody cared about our conversation.

I watched as she whipped her iPad out next and swiped through the different pictures of the villa. "This is beautiful. How much do we all have to pay so I can send it over."

"It's covered. She's covering the entire thing... you know she married well." She smiled and ran her hand through her pin straight hair.

Capone and Cappadonna had always instilled in me to never let anybody pay my way. I was always fine with picking up the tab. "Are you sure? It looks pretty expensive."

"She never had one so she's going all out, so don't worry about paying for anything. The villa is right on the beach, and the clubs and bars are only a few miles away. I want us to recreate our old bar picture from college, too." Jesse was speaking a million miles per second as she explained everything to me.

"I'm ready. Who else is going to be there?"

She looked away. "Brandi."

I rolled my eyes so hard that I didn't even know what to do. Last Jesse told me they fell out and hadn't spoken to each other in so long. "I don't think I can make it, Jesse."

"Stop, Capri. It's been years and you both never truly had a problem anyway... you just said she was stuck up."

"She was and you admitted it yourself. Brandi has always acted like she was better than all of us. Last I checked, she slept with your boyfriend which caused you to hate her. How did that change?"

"You know David is in politics and her husband is, too, so it was bound for us to run into each other. We were at some black-tie event last year and she cornered me by the bar and

Capri

asked for forgiveness. Turns out she goes to my Pilates studio, and we ran into each other again. I guess I'm nice and have a forgiving spirit because we've been pretty cool, and I invited her to the wedding."

"And you expect me to sit around her for four days?"

Jesse looked over the menu. "Come on... you love me. Brandi has changed... she isn't the same as she was in college. She even has a daughter now... oh, and she's not with Quameer anymore."

I snickered to myself because if she only knew that I knew all of the tea she thought she was spilling to me. "Are the dates the same so me and Blair can book our flights?"

"Same dates... make sure to email me the information so I can have them at the airport to pick you guys up."

Jesse waved over the waiter and ordered an acai bowl and an orange juice. I was fine with my croissant and half-eaten crepe that I wanted to toss across the restaurant at someone's head. She looked up at me with a sly smile on her face.

"I have someone that I want to introduce to you... you need to settle down and find a man. It's time, Capri."

"I don't want to meet anybody because nine times out of ten, he's gonna be a politician and I don't need that boring kind of life."

Jesse gasped as she playfully hit me with the napkin. "My life is not boring. Does work get in the way with the both of us? Yes... but I love him."

"I'm glad you found your forever with David. I, on the other hand don't want some square." Jesse didn't understand that I liked my men to be hood.

I may have had a degree, but I wanted a man that possessed the swagger and could defend me without getting the police involved. I wanted my man crazy about me and would do whatever just to prove a point. Whenever I thought of who I wanted, Quameer came to mind.

"How about you go on a date with him and find out. He's come from poverty."

I screwed my face up. "What the fuck, Jesse?"

Jesse always said the most fucked up shit and everybody always excused her because that was just Jesse. I was the one constantly correcting her. "I'm saying... he was raised in the hood. Like your ex-husband."

"I don't even know how to respond to that."

"Look, all I'm saying is that it wouldn't hurt to change your type. I'm involved with your type daily... always issuing warrants, bringing them in, and chasing them down. Maybe it wouldn't hurt to get you a guy in a suit."

Jesse didn't understand that I ran with real niggas and that was what I was attracted to. A man in a suit couldn't do anything for me unless we were working together. I could never see myself settling down with a man like that.

Since she was surrounded by men like that all the time, it was her type. Then again, she was attracted to a man with power, which is why she was even marrying David. Jesse knew her type was a hood nigga because that was who had broken up her friendship with Brandi.

Her boyfriend in college was on the football team and was from the hood. He was the only one in his family to make it out, and she was attracted to his power, and the fact that he wasn't like the other lames on his team.

No matter how much Jesse denied it, she wanted a nigga like her college boyfriend to pin her to a wall and knock the Mario coins out of her. Hell, I wanted the same thing. The only difference was that I wanted Meer's ass to be the one knocking them out of me.

Chapter 4
Quameer

No sooner than I pulled into the driveway and killed the engine, Ryder was pulling her seat belt off and rushing out the car. I shook my head and climbed out my truck, following behind her. She was always excited to visit her great-grandmother's house. Even though this was a random visit, I didn't doubt that my grandmother had snacks, drinks, and whatever else waiting on the kitchen table.

I hit the code on the lock and Ryder damn near crushed my fingers trying to turn the knob and enter the house. "Sorry, Daddy!"

I laughed. "You good, Peach."

I playfully pulled her crooked ponytails that I had done this morning. Ryder was tender headed as hell, so it was always a task trying to do her hair in the mornings. Shit, I don't know if I did them crooked or her day at school turned her every way but loose and they ended up crooked. Either way, as long as her hair was done it didn't matter if they were crooked or not.

From the foyer, I could hear my grandmother loving on Ryder. It had been a few weeks since I brought Ryder over here, so I knew they missed each other. My grandmother and

Jahquel J.

Ryder had been thick as thieves since the first time I brought her over here.

Gammy was Ryder's favorite person in the world. Even Quasim knew he couldn't compete when it came to Gammy and Ryder's relationship. I bypassed a few family pictures on my way to the kitchen.

"Hey Dumplin... I was wondering when you were going to make your way over here." My Gammy stood around 5'3, and Ryder was almost her height.

What she lacked in height, she had in mouth because that woman could cuss you out so bad that you would feel like you were her height. She wasn't no punk and let that shit be known the minute you met her. Her tolerance for bullshit was low, so everybody knew not to come to her with the bullshit.

Gammy practically raised me and Quasim, so naturally, that was where I got all my shit talking from. Plus, my tolerance for bullshit was so low that I might contemplate killing yo' ass if I sat and thought about it long enough. Gammy allowed shit to roll off her shoulders, and I was the type that broke your fucking shoulders.

We were the same, and different at the same time. That was my girl, and I would always do whatever I could for her. I'd lay down and die for my grandmother because I knew the sacrifices she had made for our family throughout the years.

I bent down to kiss her cheek. "Got caught up... I'm here now and brought your favorite."

She smirked. "I don't have favorites."

"Like hell you don't, Gam... you replaced me with my own daughter."

Ryder stood there smiling right along with her great-grandmother. "Don't be so pressed, Dad... Gammy just knows perfection when she sees it."

"Who the hell you been hanging around, Peach?"

She giggled as she grabbed a fresh baked cookie from the

Capri

cooling rack and bit into it. "These have to be your best cookies yet, Gammy."

"I think so... I have about three more batches before they're done... don't eat those back there," she snickered.

"Which means I can have one of those," I went to grab one and she slapped my hand. "I'm grown as hell, Gam... the hell you mean I can't have one."

"I will package some up for you."

Gammy was known for her cookies everywhere. She was always baking cookies for some fundraiser or because a friend had requested them. As much as I grew up on her baking, my favorite had to be when she started making edibles.

A nigga didn't have a regular grandmother, I had a cool grandmoms 'cause she could make the fuck out some edibles. Last time she made me cookies, that shit had me stuck on the couch for three hours.

"Yeah, you right. Last time had me stuck on the couch looking into the air."

Gammy chuckled as she poured some milk for Ryder, who took her cookies and milk into the living room. "Get your homework done so it's one less thing you have to do later," she called behind her.

"Got you, Gams."

She turned her attention back to me as I slumped into the kitchen chair. "I told you those cookies ain't no hoe... you never want to listen to me."

"I need about six to hold me over... you know I'm good for it," I pulled a knot of money out and sat it in the middle of the kitchen table.

She snatched the money and placed it back into my hands. "I don't need your money, Dumplin. You, your brother, and father already do more than enough for me and your mother."

I took the money back knowing that I would find some place to stash it like I usually did. It was always like pulling teeth when it came to trying to do something for her. The only reason she accepted this new house we bought was because she knew it was needed.

"We can never repay you for what you do, Gammy... you know that shit, right?" I stared at her, as she removed cookies from the cooling rack.

"I don't do it for the payment. She may be your mother, but she is my daughter. A mother always takes care of her baby. You know... there's nothing in this world that you wouldn't do for Ryder as her father."

"Damn right." I paused, looking around the kitchen before our eyes met. "How has she been?"

She turned to smile at me. "Some days are always better than others. Today happens to be a good day. It's good that you bought Ryder over so she can see her."

"Yeah."

"I know you struggle with visiting her, Dumplin." She came over and kissed my head, then went back to mixing up another batch for the cookies she had to bake.

The day I woke up to our apartment smelling like it was on fire was something that I still had nightmares from. I wore the souvenir of the day on my face and the left side of my body. It had been over twenty years since my mother had set our apartment on fire, and I had been caught on the inside.

I tried everything to get out that room and burned the inside of my hand because the knob was scalding hot. When I finally did get the door opened, a burst of flames hit the side of my body, causing my face and torso to suffer burns. As I laid on the floor, I looked at my Michael Jordan poster, knowing that it would be the last time I saw that shit.

My father didn't give a fuck who felt a way. He ran into our apartment and burned himself in the process getting me out. I could have died had he not went in and didn't listen to what the fire fighter had told him.

Capri

As rough as our relationship could be at times, he was still my fucking hero, and I would do anything for him. I remember being rushed past my mother on the gurney and seeing how spaced out she looked. She sat on the back of the other ambulance with a blanket draped over her. It was like she didn't know what she had done, or she didn't care. Quasim stood there talking to her, asking her what happened and all she could do was stare into his eyes, never saying a word.

We later found out that she had put on oil to fry chicken and walked away, forgetting that she put it on. It was a good thing we found that shit out because I thought my own mother tried to line my ass up. She was always forgetting shit, and we chalked it up to being who she was. Moms would lose her fucking head if it wasn't attached to her shoulders.

I remember she had forgot me at the mall, and my father had to come back to the mall and pick me up because her ass had already made it home and was cooking dinner like she hadn't left her damn child behind.

Moms had always been a little different and we all accepted her like that because we didn't know her any different. She had always been eccentric, as Gammy liked to call her, and we accepted it. Pops said that was the reason he had fell in love with her. She wasn't like every woman that tossed herself at him.

She was different.

Every time he spoke about how she used to be; I could see the sadness enter his eyes. He missed who she used to be before her light was dimmed and she had become a shell of herself. It was hard coming to grips that your mother was diagnosed with early onset Alzheimer's. At forty, she had been diagnosed with it, and our entire life had changed.

All the forgetfulness, poor judgment, changes in her mood was all signs that we all missed. We were too busy making it her personality and she was suffering on the inside with these changes. It was hard seeing my mother because it reminded me of the woman, the mother she used to be. The grandmother that she would never be.

I missed her fucking laugh so much.

It was so goofy, and we always made fun of how she made this whistle noise with her nose before she broke out into full laughter. How she used to mess around with us, always with a joke. Aside from her being so forgetful, she was a good mother. A mother who cared and never took herself too seriously.

When she was first diagnosed, she was more active. I could have conversations with her, and we heard that laugh occasionally. The more time that went on, she went from being so lively to now sitting in her favorite chair and offering some conversation before she eventually retreated back into her head.

The only time you saw some kind of life in her eyes was when she saw my father. When he walked into a room, she snapped out her trance and was there with him. Each time I saw my parents together the shit broke my heart. It broke me because they were the definition of true love, and loved each other, even though life hadn't been kind to their marriage.

They were the reason that I believed in love and wanted that shit so much. It was clear that my father could never have the marriage he intended to with my mother. You couldn't tell him shit about his wife and he came to visit her every day. He would sit with her for hours before she went to bed, and then he left, giving her a kiss on the forehead.

Shit was heartbreaking.

Ryder had only known her grandmother as the woman who sat in her favorite chair and stared aimlessly out the window, only getting excited when she saw her grandfather. She would never know the woman that would have picked her up, tickled her, and then fed her sweets despite what her parents told her.

My father had always been the disciplinarian while my mother was the fun. Half the time, it was me and Quasim

Capri

looking after her ass. Whenever Pops was away, we knew we could get away with murder. Homework was never finished; we ate whatever we wanted and there wasn't a bedtime. Naturally, Quasim stepped into a parental role because my pops couldn't be in two places at once. Had it not been for Quasim, my ass probably wouldn't even considered college.

When my mother was diagnosed, my father stepped back and Quasim took his place as the head of the Inferno Gods. Even though he was young, niggas respected him. He was the heir to the Inferno throne, so niggas knew to respect him, or we would be paying our respects to their families disrespectfully.

I thought being the second son of Papa Inferno meant that I was up next. Boy was I fucking wrong. If standing on business was a person, it was my fucking older brother.

Quasim was serious when he stuck his fucking nails into me and told me that I needed to go to college.

His ass told me once I graduated, I could become IG, so my ass did what the fuck I had to do. It took a minute before I officially became IG because I was so caught up with Brandi's big-headed ass, and trying to please her. Even with Quasim being my older brother, his ass was like a second father, too. Always one call away whenever I needed him. When me and my pops went through it, I knew I could always turn to him for advice.

Half the time his ass offered it without me even asking.

"Cabeça nas nuvens," Gammy pulled me out my thoughts, as she scooped dough onto the baking trays.

"O tempo todo hoje em dia," I replied, sitting my phone on the kitchen table, and leaning my head back against the wall.

"Sobre aquela mulher? Seu amor?"

I chuckled. "Why you assume that she's my love, Gams?"

She put her hand on her hip and gave me that knowing look. You know the look every grandmother has when they're staring at you. It was like the moment you became a grandparent, that look was downloaded into your memory, and you knew exactly when to use it.

"You've waited a whole year for her to return back from her travels, which I think is great. More women need to travel alone and learn who they are." She held the spliff between her lips and sparked it. "Não entre aqui meu amor... estou fumando!" she called out to Ryder.

"Eu não vou," Ryder replied.

Ryder was bilingual and it was because Gammy made sure she knew Portuguese like she did with me. I spoke it fluently while Quasim knew a few words but understood it. My grandmother was Portuguese and Black. Her father was stationed in Portugal when he met my great-grandmother, and the rest was history.

My great-grandfather passed before I was born, and my great-grandmother passed when I was five. Quasim remembered more about her than I did, and she used to speak to him in Portuguese. Which made it that much worse that this nigga didn't speak the language as fluent. When Gams met my grandfather, she continued to blacken up our blood line, washing the Portuguese on out.

She still held on close to her roots by making sure that we knew the language.

"Who said I waited for her, Gams?" I chuckled, as she passed me the spliff. I took a pull, closing my eyes. "This some good shit," I choked.

She went back to transferring the cookie dough onto the baking sheet. "Zahir came over to see us and brought me a special delivery." She spoke of my cousin, Za, who had the best weed out there.

He owned a bunch of dispensaries throughout the city, and those shits brought in bank. New York fucked up when they made weed legal, cause that nigga got to the bag. Aside from his

Capri

dispensaries, Za had his hands in every damn thing. Most of his paper came from the investments he made. Unlike most, I never got jealous, I paid attention and learned from him. He was a millionaire because of his smart investments and businesses, why the fuck wouldn't I shut up and learn from him? We owned a couple of businesses together, and he had told me to invest in a few companies that had me and Peach set up.

"He don't bring me no shit like this," I took another long pull before passing it back to Gam, who tucked it in her lips while continuing with her cookies, never breaking her stride.

"You're not his favorite grandmother." she snickered. "Stop switching the subject, Dumplin... you like this woman?"

"I do."

I couldn't deny that I liked Capri, may even love her ass. The feeling I felt for her was so strong that the shit made it difficult to think logically when it came to her. Soon as she mentioned another nigga, I was already thinking of ways to cut his brakes and put him in a wheelchair for the rest of his life.

Maybe even have his mama pull her black dress because the car toppled over a cliff, and he didn't make it.

Shit was never normal when it came to Suga, and I learned that the minute I watched her board that plane without me.

"Then what is stopping you from letting her know that?"

"A lot, Gams... I can't just make a move because a lot comes with that, and Quasim has already reminded me."

She heaved a sigh. "Simmy knows more than anyone how short life is and how we need to live in the now, make moves because we never know when God will pick up that phone and call us home." She sat a cookie on the table next to me.

"I hear you."

Gams was my best friend and the person I always came to when I didn't feel like going to Quasim. I knew I could get the real without any sugar coating when it came to her. She was going to give you the real, and only if you were real, you could appreciate it.

I sat there for a couple minutes before I went down the hall to my mother's bedroom. Like I expected, she was in her favorite chair, but she was asleep. When she heard the door creak, she looked at me before turning her head back out the window.

It was expected.

I wasn't my father, the love of her life, so no matter how much I favored him, she knew the difference. "Hey Mommy... what's going on with this hair, lady?" I walked over and dropped a kiss on her curly hair.

It was funny because Ryder had the same texture hair as my mother, and she resembled her. Especially now, as my mother sat here with bed hair. I could tell Gam had probably got her up from her mid-noon nap before we came over.

"Quinton is here?" she asked for my father, and I stared down at her and smiled.

As life moved on, she declined. She went from laughing and being able to have conversations to only saying a few words, and one of them was my father's name. I heard the door behind me and saw Ryder standing there.

She slowly walked over and kissed her grandmother's cheek. "Hey Nanny... I love you."

Shit always broke my heart watching my daughter with my mother. Even as time went on, it never got easier having to witness my mother deteriorate into the person she was now. It was the reason that I never spoke about it.

It was our family's business, so I never felt comfortable talking about it to anyone else. There had been a few times when Capri had tried to pull shit out of me and had become frustrated. The last time I opened up to a woman, she broke me in ways I didn't think was possible.

Capri

Suga had the power to do that to me again, and that was something that wasn't lost on me. I understood the power that she had over me. I knew she had the ability to break my heart and that was the reason I was cool with being friends with her first. It was my way of easing into a situation where I knew the outcome could end with heartache again. At least this time, I had nobody to blame but me, because I knew what I was getting myself into, and still pursued her.

My week with Peach went by too damn quick.

By the time we got settled into our routine, it was time for her to return back to her mother. When we met up this time she was with her husband, so her ass tried to play it cool. Even though I could tell she was still salty about our last conversation. Her ass was real careful with how she was chatting because she knew I didn't give a fuck what came out my mouth. Brandi's ass wasn't trying to poke the bear.

At least not when her husband was standing nearby.

I knew Brandi long enough to know that she was very much still in her feelings about our conversation. It was probably eating her alive that Capri even had my number. Especially since she used to catch an attitude whenever me and Capri would run into each other on campus. If she knew that was *my* Suga, she probably would have exploded right in front of me. The minute I dropped my daughter off and kissed her goodbye, I didn't think about Brandi's ass again. She wasn't a second thought, and if she knew what was good for her, she would mind her business and stay the fuck out of mine before I shot at her husband.

Goon: *Your girl up in the spot tonight… she with Blair.*

Jahquel J.

After I dropped Peach to her mother, I don't know why my ass even came over to boring ass Quasim's crib. The nigga didn't even offer me something to drink, and I had been here a whole damn hour. The whole reason I came over here was to convince him to get out the house tonight. I had given Suga her space since I was busy with my daughter, and she needed to spend time with her family. Only I knew how much she missed them, and how much she needed to be around them right now.

"He a fucking fool," Quasim laughed at an episode of the Wayans brothers. "This shit hit different when you're older and understand the shit fully."

"You know what I never understand fully."

"What, Blaze? I already know you a little slow, so go ahead."

I chuckled. "Why the fuck you in the house on a Friday night... we should go get a drink at *Fern*."

"You just want to go because Capri is there with Blair."

I looked at his ass like he had two heads instead of one. "How the fuck you know she there?"

Quasim smirked. "I keep tabs on Ms. Delgato like you do... she's a fucking Delgato for crying out loud."

"Fuck all that... you keeping tabs on Blair. You keep tabs on her, but you won't make your move on her? The fuck is up with you?"

"Why the fuck do you keep trying to push me with Blair. How do you even know I'm interested in her?"

Quasim may have been able to convince himself that he wasn't into Blair, but anybody with eyes could see that he was crushing on her ass bad. It wasn't like the feeling wasn't mutual, Blair was very much into his ass, too. Sim was just being fucking weird and running from her ass like she had cooties or some shit.

"Capp did mention that you were gay or some shit like that.

Capri

He was ranting about celebrating pride for you because you're in denial about it."

Quasim did a deep sigh before he turned the TV off and stood up. Thankfully, his ass was actually dressed today and wasn't still sitting around in pajamas. "We out."

"Now you want to be out because we starting to think you gay," I mumbled.

> Me: On my fucking way.

Sim turned to give me that look before he snatched his keys and wallet to head out to the garage. I could hear the sound of his motorcycle before I left the living room and followed him out the door. After dropping Peach with her moms, I went home to grab my bike and park my truck up. If you saw me, I was usually on my bike. The only reason I had a truck was because I needed something safe for my daughter. Even though Peach had rode on the back of my bike more times than a few. Her moms always acted like a bitch about it, but I had been teaching my daughter bike safety since she could walk.

Quasim didn't live too far away from *Fern*, so it didn't take long for us to arrive. Soon as we pulled onto the block, it was covered from side to side with motorcycles and cars parked or double parked. It was Friday night, so everybody was out here trying to chill and see where the night took them.

The smell of barbeque invaded my nostrils and made my stomach growl. I already knew Dugg was in the back going crazy on his makeshift grill that he made out of a damn steel drum. Soon as Quasim pulled onto the block, one of the Gods hopped on his bike, making space so he could pull right in. I followed behind and parked beside him before climbing off my bike.

Goon didn't even need to tell me Capri was in there. I

knew my baby was here because I could smell her ass in the air. "Why the fuck are you sniffing the air?" Quasim questioned.

"Fuck you meannnn... were you around the fucking block when I texted you?" Goon came out and dapped both of us. "How in the fuck you got this one out the house?"

Quasim laughed. "Came to check on business...make sure we making money and you niggas ain't drinking it all."

"Yeah, ight... if business name rhymes with hair." Goon clowned his ass because we both knew that was the only reason his ass was out here tonight.

While Goon and Quasim kicked it, I left them and headed into the bar. Fern wasn't all that big, so soon as I stepped in the spot, I spotted my Suga instantly. Just as the happiness filled my chest, the shit was sucked out because my eyes had to be fucking with me. She was sitting at the end of the bar twirling her freshly straightened hair around her finger while talking to some corn ball. How did I know he was a cornball?

I had a feeling about niggas like him.

He was respectful, careful not to touch what was mine and was just talking. It was Suga who had all her damn teeth showing as she flirted with him. I could read her fucking lips from where I stood.

Did I go over there and slam homie's head into the bar top, or did I play it cool? These were legit questions because I was about to grip my gun and put the shit to his head for even being near mine.

"I see that crazy ass look in your fucking eye... chill the fuck out," Yasin squeezed my shoulder, pushing me over toward the empty spot at the bar.

Shante slid me a drink. "You got it bad for her... every man that has come through those doors has stopped to talk to her."

"Oh yeah? Which ones?" I asked, taking back my shot of Don Julio, while waiting for Shante to point out the niggas I needed to beat the fuck up.

Capri

Yasin shook his head. "Last I checked you both single as fuck."

"Shante," I replied, ignoring him talking about some shit that didn't pertain to me. All that single shit went out the window when another nigga was smiling up in her face.

Yasin looked at Shante. "Don't you even point them out... we cool tonight."

"You fired, Shante... go to the back and grab your shit."

Shante laughed, sliding me another shot before she went to tend to the other end of the bar. "Capri got you out here wild. I don't even remember you being like this with Brandi's ass."

Brandi wasn't the one. While I thought she was and was fully prepared to marry her ass, time and her actions let me know that it would have been the biggest mistake in my life. Shit was different when it came to Suga.

When I spoke to her, I could see my entire future within her eyes. I could see us walking along the beach with our kids running and playing ahead of us. I could feel myself holding her heart knowing that I could protect it, and it would never ache again.

Before I felt her arms around my neck, I smelled her approaching me like a fucking pale ass vampire from that teen movie. Capri had me out here feeling like I was immortal over her fine ass.

"Hey Meer... why didn't you tell me you were coming out tonight?" She released my neck, and I pulled her between my legs, away from anybody that could possibly touch her.

I needed every nigga in this bitch to know that she wasn't to be touched. "I could say the same about you, Sug... why the fuck you out tonight? Ain't you supposed to be at the lake?"

She playfully mushed me. "First of all, why you clocking me?"

"I'm always clocking you... why you out here tonight?"

She pointed over toward the bar where Blair was on the

phone. "I haven't seen Blair since I been back, so we came out to get some drinks. Plus, I needed to grab more things from my house since I'm gonna be staying at the lake for the summer."

Even though she was dressed down, she could still turn heads. She wore a Yankee dad hat, plain white baby tee that exposed her stomach, and baggy jeans that fell at her waist. Even with the jeans being baggy, there was no denying her fucking shape.

"Blair going back to the lake house with you?"

"I wish. She has a man now so she's going to meet him for a late dinner," she fake sulked, then smiled at me. "I just knew me and her were going to tear the summer up being single together." Capri shrugged, looking back over toward Blair.

I paused. "A man? How the fuck is that possible? She don't know she's my fucking sister-in-law?"

Capri broke out into laughter. "Calm it down, Crazy Pants. I just found out that she has a boyfriend and she's been keeping him a secret until she was sure about him. After the whole Tookie situation, I don't blame her for taking her time to make sure he's the one."

"He ain't the one because his last name ain't Inferno. Tookie's ass is lucky the law got his ass before I did, because I was gonna buck fifty the other side of his face."

Tookie's ass had got caught up and now his ass was serving time up north. Even being in prison wasn't going to excuse the pressure I was gonna put his ass through the minute he stepped out of prison. If he thought I was going to excuse that shit he did when I was with Suga, his ass had another thing coming.

"This is all your brother's fault, Meer. Had he made a move, she wouldn't have moved on." I couldn't even front like Quasim's simple ass didn't fumble this shit.

Capri has always been team Quasim and wanted them to be together more than anybody. "Will you talk to him? I think he might still have a chance."

Capri

"If Blair is about to leave, what you about to get into?" I ignored her question because I wasn't about to get involved in a grown man's personal shit. I knew the reason Sim was being so distant and acting scared of Blair. It wasn't my place to talk to him or Blair, I had to sit back and allow time to do its thing.

She shrugged. "Was going to have another drink before going home, then driving back to the lake... I can tell she wants to hang with her man, which is fine... I'm not pressed she's leaving."

Her phone chimed and she looked down at it before smiling. "Why the fuck you showing all your teeth in your mouth, Capri?"

"Since when I became Capri? I was just Suga a second ago." She realized I wasn't laughing and furthered her explanation. "I was texting a guy I met earlier. He left because he has a game in the morning. Apparently, he plays football... you heard of Mason Jackson?"

I chuckled. "Yeah, I know his ass... he might end up with an injury this season, too."

Mason Jackson played for the New Jersey Black Jackets, and if his ass wanted to continue to play for them, he needed to leave my Suga the fuck alone. His ass was cool with a few of the Gods, and he paid them to look out for him when he wanted to do his own thing without the stress of the media in his face.

Being a celebrity meant everybody was on his dick and he just wanted to chill out and be regular – whatever that fucking meant. The few times I met him, he was cool people, and we kicked it together if we happened to be at the bar at the same time. However, that didn't mean I wouldn't Peter roll his ass when it came to Capri. "How do you know tha... Quameer!" she pinched me once she realized exactly what I meant.

"What you mean? I'm good at predicting shit like that."

She got close to my ear. "My brothers are Capone and

Cappadonna; you don't think I know how to read between the lines? Leave that man alone, Meer."

"Then tell him to leave you alone." I stared her right in the eyes. She stepped back and I pulled her back until she was standing directly between my legs. "Come take a ride with me."

Before she could reply, my brother finally made his presence known by walking behind the bar. I watched as he poured a drink, and then looked at me and Capri. "Welcome back, Capri... happy to be back home?"

"I am... I didn't think I would miss home so much."

As he was about to reply, Blair came rushing over with her phone to her ear. "I'm going to head out, Capri... let me know when you book your flight for Jesse's birthday trip."

"What up, Blair?"

I almost snapped my neck with how fast I turned to look at Quasim. Part of me just assumed that his ass wasn't going to even acknowledge her. "Hey Quasim... how are you?"

Me and Suga looked between the both of them and the attraction was so damn thick I might have choked on the shit. Just from sitting here, you could tell they both were feeling the other. Neither of them were gonna make a move though. Blair damn sure wasn't about to make one now that she had a man, and when it came to my brother, who the fuck knew when or if he would ever make one.

"I'm straight." He took back his shot and then walked further down the bar, leaving me to look at Capri and Blair.

Capri looked at me before she switched subjects. "I think I might charter a jet for us... a wedding gift for her." Capri shrugged like it was nothing. In fact, it wasn't nothing for her to charter one.

The only reason Capone never bought a jet was to avoid all the added attention. He didn't want anybody questioning how a man who owns a trucking company could afford a multi-

Capri

million-dollar jet, even though Delgato's trucking was highly successful, with government contracts.

From the way that Blair quickly ended the call she was on, I could tell she wasn't feeling Capri's idea of a wedding gift. "You've already come home early to attend the wedding festivities. Not to mention, you've been complying with all her expensive demands, like buying that three-thousand-dollar bridesmaid dress. You've done more than enough, Capri. I don't want you going all out for Jesse because we both know how she is."

I understood where Blair was coming from. I've been around Capri enough to know that she gave too much to people and often never got anything in return.

"I can't believe you still friends with that bitch," I blurted, and Capri pinched me, while turning back to Blair to finish their conversation.

Jesse Anderson was some mixed bitch that thought she was the shit. I think she was black and Cuban or some wild shit like that, so being mixed was entire identity in college. She used to hang with Brandi hard back in the day, until they fell out.

Brandi never told me the full story on why they fell out, but my Spidey senses told me that Brandi fucked Jesse's nigga and that was how they fell out. I never had the proof and never looked fully into it, but something always told me that Brandi was out there fucking other niggas.

Quasim used to tell me to use my head, and I couldn't because my heart was so wrapped into her. I refused to believe she would ever give a nigga my pussy. Once you refuse to believe something, just go on and accept that it was happening.

"So, you understand why I feel the way that I do?" Blair stood with her arms folded, ignoring Capri and looking straight at me.

"Suga struggles with giving too much to the wrong people

and never getting anything in return... we working on that, right, Sug?"

I learned that about Capri before even fully getting to know her in the past year. She was the type that would go above and beyond if she cared for you. So much that she ended up being the only one hurt in the end. In her marriage, Naheim had done wrong, and Sug got her lick back, but she still stuck around to help him raise another woman's baby.

There weren't too many women that would stick around and make sure the man who did her dirty remained untouched. She was and still was the driving force behind making sure Naheim remained untouched by her brothers.

"Sadly, this is a problem she had in college, too. Remember when you spent nearly two bands for her birthday dinner, because none of the niggas that she invited wanted to pay. Everybody was debating on how many drinks they bought, and Capri just swiped her brother's credit card to avoid conflict."

"Well damn, Blair. How about you tell all my business."

"I'm your friend before I knew how powerful your family is. I hate to see people take advantage of my friend, and Jesse takes advantage of you. She knows that you're a real friend and there's no limit to the shit that you would do for the people you care about, Pri."

I held onto the belt hoop of her jeans while looking up at her, and she briefly looked at me. "Leave me alone, Meer."

"I'm just saying... we bout to go get that fucking money back from that birthday dinner. What niggas come to a dinner and don't pay for everybody's meal?"

"College guys, Meer. They didn't have money like that."

"Then those are niggas you don't need to be around. I was paying Brandi's bills when I was in college. You not chartering a jet for that bitch's bachelorette party... if she want a jet, then she need to ask her fuck ass husband."

"Mee—"

Capri

"Conversation over, Suga... come on, Blair... let me walk you out." I grabbed Capri's hand and pulled her behind me as she sulked.

She was so used to going above and beyond for everybody and that shit stopped now. I don't know how many conversations we had over this year where I told her that she needed to be selfish. Capri deserved to be selfish more than anyone I knew.

It was always her having to take the high road and be the bigger person. Always having to take everyone else's feelings into consideration before her own. Naheim cheated on her with her enemy and his ass was still walking around to talk about it because Capri cared about what happened to him more than her own feelings.

More than the hurt that he caused.

Even if I never became her man, long as I was around that shit was going to end. We walked Blair outside to her car and watched as she pulled away, Capri flipping her middle finger at her. I shook my head because she was mad that Blair was actually a good friend and didn't want her used.

Jesse was the type of bitch that would use you for whatever you could offer her. She only fucked with niggas on the football team according to Brandi. I didn't know what she was up to or who her new man was, but I was almost certain he was getting to the money because she didn't go for broke niggas that couldn't offer her shit.

"How do you know I'm ready to head home?"

I walked her over toward my bike. "Blair is gone so there's no reason for you to be in there alone. Your boyfriend gone, too... didn't you say he had a flight to catch."

"He's not my boyfriend. Just because we exchanged numbers doesn't mean he is my boyfriend." She rolled her eyes, and then our eyes connected again.

Capri had these eyes that you could get lost in. Although

they were big, beautiful and brown, she did this thing when she lowered them and gave you those fuck me hard eyes.

At least, that was what I felt whenever she looked at me with them. It was when she lowered her eyes, looked up at me and then bit her bottom lip. It was like she was begging me to put my hand around her neck and give her this dick on the bike.

"Come take a ride with me, Suga," I said, handing her my helmet. "Or do you wanna confirm with your boyfriend?"

She snatched the helmet and laughed. "You playing around until I'm becoming the girlfriend of an NFL player. My mother would really be proud then."

I held her chin. "She's proud of you now... you don't need to marry a nigga for her to be even more proud, Sug."

She stared up into my eyes. "Yeah, right. She was never a big fan of me traveling this year, and she's the hardest on me. Capone and Cappadonna can get away with murder because they are her boys." She scoffed. "Me? I'm still getting shit because I decided to end my marriage and not listen to her and work on it."

"She wanted you to stay married to him?" I met Jean Delgato more than a few times and she was always sweet as shit. The glue that held the Delgato family together. You could feel how much she loved her family, and there wasn't nothing she wouldn't do for them.

It was crazy to hear how Capri spoke about her mother being so hard on her and punishing her for the decisions she decided to make with her marriage. The shit was the complete opposite from the warmth I experienced every time I was around Jean.

"My mom is the kind of woman that believes that marriage is through thick and thin. You get married and you stay married." Capri shrugged.

"I believe in that too, Sug."

Capri

"I did too... once upon a time."

I continued to stare down into her eyes. "Maybe one day you will again... huh?"

She smiled while sliding the helmet onto her head. "Maybe."

I got on first and then helped her get on behind me. She held on as I started the motorcycle and sped away from the bar. As I zipped down each street, she held onto me tightly. The wind blew through my locs as I was careful with how I flew down each block.

This wasn't the first time that Capri had been on the back of my bike, but this was the first time she was on the back of my bike with me having the feelings that I did. When she held me tighter, that shit felt like she had my heart in a vice grip.

Everything was a blur as we sped over the bridge into Staten Island heading toward my favorite spot. She released me as I pulled into a parking spot, and I got off to help her. She took the helmet off and placed it on the seat of my bike.

"We are not going to a dark park at night."

I grabbed her hand and strolled into Clove Lake Park. It was my favorite spot since I was younger. I went to the middle school up the street, so I always frequented this park after school. It was the place I had my first kiss, sparked my first spliff, and nearly split a nigga's head open. The park held a bunch of memories for me, and whenever the world got too loud, I came here to silence it.

"If you scared just say that."

She laughed. "I am not scared... just want to know why you wanted to come to a park at night."

"Everything is always quieter at night... you agree?"

She still held my hand as she looked up at me. "Almost too quiet."

I looked over at her and she was staring into thin air as I led us to my favorite spot. It was a bridge that took you to the other side of the park. During the day you could see the turtles that kept near in case someone dropped some food to them.

While Capri leaned over the bridge staring into the dark pond, I chose to hop up and sit on the edge. "You still having trouble sleeping, Sug?"

She shrugged. "I get four hours in... it's better than when I couldn't sleep at all."

"Why you not sleeping though?" I sparked my spliff, taking a long pull while blowing the smoke in the opposite direction.

She turned and leaned her back on the bridge and looked away. "I took the year to heal and now I'm back home and it's like now what? I love my brothers, but I see what they have and want the same... I want to be happily in love."

Taking a pull, I slowly nodded my head. "Yeah. I feel you."

"What's stopping you from finding someone? I know you joke around about being with me, but we both know that can't happen, Meer."

Her question caught me off guard. "Why can't it happen, Capri?"

Our eyes met. "You're my best friend. The person that I can tell anything to, and I know you won't judge me. I'm afraid to lose you if we ever crossed that line. I crossed it with Kincaid, and you see how that ended up."

Kincaid was my nigga, and I would always ride for him. However, Capri wasn't all to blame in how shit went down with them. He should have never crossed that line with her. From the way Capri told it, you could clearly see that she was spiraling over her husband and marriage. He should have never allowed it to get that far with her.

It was the main reason I've never made a move on her. As hard as it was to watch her leave, I knew it was needed because she could never be any good for me if she wasn't healed. If she never took that time to become the woman I needed.

We needed.

Capri

It wasn't just me that I had to consider. Ryder was just as important in this as I was, and I didn't want a broken Capri. I wanted her to see the world, learn how to exist in this world without someone.

I could tell she was different the moment I saw her at Jaiden's game. There was a different aura about her, and it was probably why I was going crazy over her. I've always been able to keep it cool when it came to Capri.

Lately, I found myself ready for anything whenever she mentioned a nigga that wasn't me. I didn't want her with anyone else. Nobody else deserved the woman that she was today. I was the nigga that had been there, listened to her cry, felt her pain from thousands of miles away.

"I'm not Kincaid, Suga... I'm *your* Meer... the man you know would never hurt you." I passed her the spliff and watched as her thick lips curled around it, taking a deep pull that caused her to choke. "Told you to stop choking it down... easy and slow," I got down from the bridge, and stood beside her, removing it from her lips and taking quick pulls while staring down into her eyes.

"Why are you keeping your daughter from me? I want to meet Peach, and you act like I'm not good enough."

I chuckled because her ass had always been good with switching the subject. "You want to meet her?"

She pinched me. "You know that I do. Both of you should come spend the weekend with me at the lake house. I have a pool, and we can even take the boat out on the lake." Suga was so excited that I couldn't turn her down.

"Let me think about it."

"Meer... you owe me," she whined as she hugged me, knocking me back a few.

I held her with one arm while I continued to smoke. "How you figure?"

She looked up at me. "You know I dreamed about giving you a hug since our last hug at the airport."

"You can't say shit like that to me, Suga."

"Fair… you coming to my birthday party, right?" she looked up at me.

Those eyes. When she looked up at me with her eyes, I knew I was in trouble. I suppose I had always been in trouble when it came to Capri Delgato. Ever since I tasted her back in college, she had always been bad for me.

"Wouldn't miss it for the world." I kissed her forehead, as I finished the rest of my smoke.

Chapter 5
Capri

THE GLASS MUG BROKE INTO PIECES AS I SLAMMED IT ONTO the kitchen floor, looking at my husband as he got ready to leave out. I wanted him to pay me some attention and continue the conversation we were trying to have. Naheim hated to have the hard conversations.

When he was in prison, he wanted to talk about everything under the sun. Now that he was home, it was like pulling mud through a straw to get him to have these tough conversations. I always tried because I was in this through thick and thin. I was serious when I married Naheim and took our vows seriously. Even though everyone thought I was too young, I knew that I could be the perfect wife.

"Why else would she find my school and put this on my car? She's telling me that she's fucking you and you want me to pretend that I never saw the letter!" I screamed, holding the letter in my hands.

No woman is going to go through all that work if she was lying. This woman left me a damn letter on my windshield and I'm positive she was the one calling my phone from a blocked number. Why else would she go through all of that if he didn't fuck her.

He put his watch on. "Muffin, I told you I'm not fucking nobody but you. Why the fuck you so worried about what the next bitch is saying... she jealous of you and who your brother is."

I laughed manically while looking for something to toss at his head. "Nobody even knows who my brother is, or who I am... Capone and Cappadonna have made sure of that. Try the fuck again, Naheim!" *I screamed.*

He shook his head. "Now you want to be the concerned wife? Stop with the shit, Capri. I'm surprised you even saw the letter with how far your face be in that damn textbook."

I was gagged – literally.

"You're fucking around on me because I've been busy with school? Please help me understand what you mean, Naheim."

"When the last time we fucked, Capri? Every time I want some pussy you always too tired or sleep at the fucking kitchen table... when the last time my needs were met. It's always about what you need or want, but did you ever consider what the fuck I need too?"

I plopped down on the edge of our bed and looked across the room at him. "Just tell me if you are cheating on me and we can fix this. Mommy said that we can always come back from anything in our marriage if we're honest. I swear on my parents, Naheim. If you tell me the truth, we can fix this, and nobody will ever know." *My voice shook as I looked at him.*

I abandoned the bed and walked over toward him, grabbing his hand while pleading with my eyes. Begging him to let me in. "Get that shit out your head, Capri. I'm not fucking anybody, not even you. Drop the fucking subject."

He was lying to me. I've found the condom wrappers in his laundry. Despite him lying to me, I stared into this man's eyes, wanting to believe everything he was saying, knowing that it wasn't the truth. Naheim was staring down into my eyes while lying right through his teeth.

Capri

"Let me in, Heim... you can tell me what's going on with you. I'm your wife, we can fix this... I won't study when you're home."

He chuckled and removed his hand from mine, which felt like a punch to the gut. "I'm out, Muffin... go study or something." I watched as he checked his wallet, not noticing that I could see him through the mirror looking through the money and the two condoms that was sandwiched between the money.

I snapped out of my head and drove up the hill to Meer's house. He lived up a hill on a dead-end street. All the homes were older, all single-family homes, then you got further down the block and saw this three-story house that didn't match the block at all. It stuck out like a sore thumb, but you would only see it if you came all the way down the block.

His home was a three story all black and gray modern home with beautiful large glass windows everywhere. The front door was made out of glass, and you could see straight through to the kitchen as I pulled into his driveway.

He was still awake because I could see the lights throughout his home, and Meer was a night owl like me. There were plenty of times I called him in the middle of the night, and he would be wide awake in his office on the computer.

I saw movement in the front and knew that he already clocked that someone pulled into his driveway. It was hard to sleep, so I figured I would take a drive, and then I ended up here at his house. I didn't know where else to go. When I was in Singapore and got lonely at night, he was the only person I called. Meer always picked up the phone for me.

Killing my engine, I grabbed my purse and climbed out of my truck. Soon as I started to climb the steps, he appeared in the doorway. I saw his gun in one hand, as he opened the door.

"The fuck you doing out here at this time, Sug?" His locs were pulled up into a bun, and he wore a pair of eyeglasses.

"Why you so paranoid... nobody even knows where you

live besides me." I walked past him, while he did his survey and came in the house behind me.

This was my first time coming to his house. I only knew his address because he forced me to send him and Peach a bunch of different ramen flavors that they didn't have in the states. I memorized his address for whatever weird reason.

He closed the doors and hit a button on the touchpad next to the door, and the doors and windows became frosted. "Why you didn't tell me you were coming over here?"

I watched as he crossed the foyer to a modern accent table and slid his gun into the drawer. "You got a girlfriend over or something?" I teased as I pretended to look around, as if a girl was going to pop out from somewhere.

The only reason I was comfortable with coming over at this time was because I knew my friend. Meer would never bring a woman to the same place his daughter laid her head at.

"Yeah... I was about to give her some dick... you fucking up the mood."

"In a bun with glasses on? Why didn't you tell me that you wore glasses," I continued to tease him, sitting my purse on the same table he had slid his gun into.

He stood in front of me with his arms folded, staring down at me. "Why you out at this time? Capp and Capone know you over here?"

I rolled my eyes while shoving past him. "I am a grown woman, Quameer. My brothers aren't in charge of me."

"Tell that shit to them," he muttered and followed behind me.

Despite how big the house seemed on the outside; it was cozy on the inside. Everything had a modern touch to it, and minimal furniture. The enclosed stairs were off to the left of the foyer, and straight ahead were glass windows on both sides of the doorway that led into a living room with a hunter green

Capri

sectional. It was the only piece of color within the entire living area, which was mostly taupe or gray.

I smiled when I noticed the wall with different pictures of Peach. They were all taken at the same time because her outfit was the same. Each picture captured her personality perfectly. Cool, sassy, and silly. We hadn't met in person, and I could already tell she had her father's personality.

"What are you doing up so late anyway?"

"Had to look over some investment shit that I had been putting off." He walked further down the hall and ducked into a room.

I followed behind him, looking at the different black art that lined the walls to his office. The color washed walls were nougat, and each wall had a different piece of art on the wall. When I rounded the corner and entered his office, he was behind his desk looking at something on the computer.

He had an incense lit with Teddy Pendergrass playing softly from the vinyl player across the room. The lights were low enough where he could still see, but not enough to kill the ambiance of the room. I spotted the bottle of bourbon and the empty glass sitting beside his computer.

"You're my latest and greatest inspiration," Teddy crooned as I slowly slumped into the chair in front of his desk.

Just being in his presence, taking in his energy made me feel better already. "Any good investments lately?"

His face relaxed from whatever he was looking at on the screen. "A few." His eyes wandered from the screen over toward me. "What you need from me, Suga?"

I smiled. "Just being here with you is all I need, Meer Cat."

He nodded his head as he pulled out the drawer in his desk, placing the box of Uno cards onto the desk. "You up for getting your ass spanked?"

I wanted him to spank me in a different way but pushed that out of my mind. Meer was my best friend, and we couldn't cross those lines with each other. It wouldn't be right, and I would regret ever losing him because I couldn't keep my legs closed – again.

He abandoned his desk and went into the beverage fridge built into his bookcase and produced a bottle of wine. "Walk with me, Sug."

I followed behind him into the kitchen where he grabbed two glasses before sliding the door to the back terrace open. When I stepped out, I felt instant relief looking out at the New York skyline. It was the one thing that I missed about living in this area. How crazy was it that we lived within the same area and had never run into each other, other than whenever I was with my brothers or doing something illegal.

Living in this area brought back the good and bad memories. As much as I missed living in this area, it reminded me of the woman that I had lost when I lived here. How I would sit on the balcony of our condo and stare out at the same view with tears blurring my vision.

Quameer was dressed down in a pair of Essentials sweatpants with no shirt on. His body was perfect. His six packs bulged as he sat the bottle onto the table and popped the cork. His arms were muscular like he lifted weights a few times a week, despite hating the whole idea of going to a gym.

I saw his burn on the side of his stomach. The burn that I still didn't know much about, even when I asked him. Quameer had mastered the art of telling me just enough without telling me nothing at all.

While I knew all the simple things about him, I didn't know the deep things. I craved to know the deep things about him. What made that heart of his so cold and warm at the same time? He had been hurt, wronged when it came to the love department. Even with him being burned when it came to love, he was still so open to experiencing it again.

"The guest room is upstairs... you not driving home." He let me know as he passed me the glass of wine, which I took a huge gulp of.

After nearly guzzling my glass of wine, I sat it on the table next to us while pulling my legs to my chest and shuffling the cards. Meer sat on the opposite side, facing me, and slowly tasted his wine.

"What has you up, Sug?" He took the cards I dealt him and looked them over before waiting for me to put down my card.

"Why does it have to always be something keeping me up? Maybe I like to be up at night, Meer." I sat down a draw four card and he sucked his teeth.

"Cheating ass."

"How? You literally watched me shuffle the cards in front of you. I think Peach is right... you just suck at Uno."

He smirked, as he took me in with his naturally low eyes. "Stop side stepping the question and be real with me. I'm your Meer... we acting funny now that you back on US soil?"

I laughed. "I feel like I'm always putting all my shit on you. You never tell me when you are going through something, Meer. You avoid all my questions... how is it that we're best friends and I don't know what's going on in your world. I know you say Quasim is private and doesn't open up, but you're the same way."

He cocked his head to the side and chuckle. "You know everything about me... the rest of the shit is heavy."

"I want to know the heavy stuff."

"In time... I got you."

He put down some cards, and my eyes remained on him. I watched as his eyes lifted from the cards until they were locked in with mine. "Don't lie to me."

"Would never lie to you, Sug."

"Okay."

We played a few hands of Uno before I tossed the cards into the middle of us and pulled my legs closer to my chest.

Jahquel J.

Meer positioned himself until he was sitting right beside me, as we both looked out at the view.

"Tell me what's on your mind?"

"Naheim called me... said he wants to see me."

I don't know where he pulled a cookie from, but he started eating really small pieces of the cookie while listening to me. "Oh yeah. How you feel about that?"

"Like I don't know if I want to see him or not. It's been easy not seeing him or having anything to do with him. He mentioned NJ, and now my heart is confused on what I want to do."

"Your brothers stopped inviting him to family shit, too. Capone said that he needed to respect you, and having your ex-husband and his new bitch at family events didn't sit right with him."

"Yeah. I've heard. At least Naheim has gotten closer with his own family since his mother passed... that makes me feel better. I don't mind him coming around, it doesn't bother me, and he is family."

"Hmm."

"I haven't seen or reached out to him since I been back. Think he's wondering if we're on good terms, so meeting up with him might soothe the tension."

Meer turned his face up. "Stop being so fucking accommodating for a nigga that didn't accommodate you. He was your husband and didn't give a fuck about your feelings, Suga. I don't even like bringing this shit up because I know how much it hurts you, but that nigga didn't give a fuck when he moved the way he did. Punished you for putting your education before him... I don't got no remorse for the nigga. You don't have to see him unless you want to. Fuck soothing tension... it's all tension when I see that nigga." It was how ominous and calm he was as he spoke about it being tension whenever he saw Naheim.

"You think I should?" I peeked over at him.

Capri

He took another small bite of the cookie. "That's a choice only you can make, Darling."

I snorted. "I guess you're right."

"Tell me what's going on in your head... I can see your mind going from over here."

He got comfortable, putting his head on the back of the couch. "He hurt me so bad. Tasha's shit was the straw that broke me." I paused. "I knew he was messing with other bitches and that shit hurt, but I figured it was my fault. I started feeling like I wasn't enough for him, wasn't experienced enough for him... he had to get it out his system, you know?" I sniffled, as the tears fell down my cheeks.

"I don't know... not that kind of man so I could never relate to some shit like that. You are enough... always have been." He reached over and swiped my tear away.

"When I cheated with Kincaid, I wanted him to hurt like I was hurting." I winced, as I held onto my chest. "I wanted him to feel the pain I felt in my chest every time the proof would be staring me in the fucking face. I didn't intend to fall for Kincaid, and I felt bad for using him. Then again, he was using me to get over his own hurt."

He took my free hand into his and rubbed it with his thumb. "You both used each other to get over that pain you both were suffering from. Do I agree with the way you both went about it... nah. I can't judge because I wasn't in you or Caid's shoes at the time, feel me?"

"Yeah. I guess I always knew that me and Kincaid could never work. I didn't meet his mother for crying out loud... then when I spoke about kids, he acted weird. Funny he's a whole father now." I laughed to keep from continuing to cry over two men that I shouldn't have been crying over.

"You told me that you don't want children."

I wiped my face. "Do you know how it feels to lie and say

you don't want kids because your husband went and had one with your ex-best friend?"

"Shit is wicked."

"I wanted kids. I wanted marriage. I guess in some way I *still* do want those things. I want a life like my sisters and now I'm reduced to being asked *what you doing* or *what's my favorite color* questions." On cue my phone lit up, and I looked at the football emoji come across the screen.

Quameer peeped the call, and his jaw tensed. "Who says that you won't ever have those things? Stop counting yourself out... you deserve happiness, Suga. I don't say that shit because it's encouraging, I say it because you do. You've put everybody before you, and I think it's time for you to get what you deserve."

"From whom? I don't take any man seriously because my trust is all fucked up. Mason has been hitting me up back-to-back, and I keep ignoring him. A whole running back worth millions and I'm ignoring him because I can't trust him with my heart."

"Me," Meer replied lowly, looking over at me.

"Be honest with me, Meer."

"Always honest with you, baby." I turned to face him, as he stared me in the eyes. His eyes were lower than before as he stared back at me. I removed his glasses and pushed my lips onto his. He hesitated a bit before he grabbed me and put me onto his lap. Straddling his lap, I softly kissed his lips while loosening his bun and allowing his locs to fall.

"I know I don't ever ask... and you don't have to tell me." I paused. "Are you still celibate?" I asked between kisses, while looking directly into his eyes. His low glare sent chills down my back as he held me tightly.

"You already know the answer to that question, Suga." Meer pulled on my bottom lip with his teeth, as I continued to look into his eyes. "The questions is if you believe me?" he asked when he released my lip.

I nodded my head slowly before kissing his lips again. It just felt so right feeling his lips on mine. Before I could kiss him again, he nuzzled his head into the crook of my neck. "Fuckkkkk." Then, he quickly removed me from his lap and jumped up like he caught the Holy Ghost. "Fuck... I can't do this... shit," he cursed himself as he paced the terrace, as I looked on confused.

Feeling slightly embarrassed.

"You don't want me, Meer? I'm...I'm sorry that I read into that wrong," I quickly apologized while trying to think of all the damn hints he had been throwing down.

He snapped his head in my direction. "Suga, I want you more than you fucking know. I gave somebody my word... and I don't want you like this, feel me?"

He was talking in circles and his eyes were wide as hell. "Um, okay." I climbed off the couch and then looked up at him. "Are you okay?"

"I'm straight... cookies my Gams made me got me tripping out."

I picked up the half cookie and looked at it. "Why?"

"Edibles, Suga." He laughed and took it from me, pulling me into the house. He put the cookie on the counter and turned to face me. "Don't ever think I don't want you. I waited a fucking year for you to return... I want you. Shit... I may even need you at this point. You hear me?" He pulled my chin up, placing a kiss on my chin.

"Are you going to bring Peach to the lake house?"

He stared down at me, biting on his bottom lip. "Yeah."

"Are you just saying that because you high as hell, Meer?"

He laughed in slow motion, if that was even possible. I was starting to believe I had ate the cookie instead of him. "We coming... I got you."

Jahquel J.

I smiled. "I really want to meet her."

"She wanna meet yo' ass, too... always asking whenever she hears us on the phone." He pinched my cheek.

It didn't matter how high he was, he secured the house before showing me the guest room upstairs. It was down the hall from his bedroom. I wanted to go to his room, see if it smelled like him. A woodsy scent of vanilla. If you smelled him long enough, you could pick up hints of weed too.

I loved inhaling his scent and hadn't forgot it since I had been gone. The knock at the door pulled me from the window seat with the same view from the terrace. Opening the door, he stood there with a T-shirt in his hand.

"Figured you might want to shower... if you not tired, you can come watch a movie with me in my room."

"Okay."

I quickly changed out my clothes and met him in his room. Quameer's room was pretty simple with a black tufted bed, black artwork and white walls. I was surprised the room wasn't the same color as most of the house.

There was a sectional in the corner of the room with a huge TV on the wall. I looked around and noticed his rolling papers, and the bar in the corner. "I don't know what I thought your room would look like... this seems so simple."

"I'm in here to sleep.... spend most of my time on that couch or downstairs in the office. Shit, I'm barely home most of the time."

I climbed on the couch, cuddling up with the pillows while he put on a movie. My eyes had become super heavy the moment Quameer plopped down beside me. He pulled a throw blanket over the both of us while he loudly munched on chips he pulled from the coffee table.

"You got the munchies... don't you?"

He tossed more chips into his mouth while laughing. "Shut up and watch this boring ass movie."

Capri

The sound of the TV, his scent, and chewing sounded like white noise to me and before long, I was fast asleep. Before I fell into a deeper sleep, I felt Quameer's cool lips against my forehead, and the blanket being pulled up onto my shoulders a bit more.

WHENEVER THE SUN STARTED TO RISE OVER THE LAKE, IT seemed like that was when my eyes wanted to grow heavy, and my body was finally ready to sleep. Nights were never easy for me, and it didn't matter the house or country. Sleeping just didn't come easy to me anymore and it was something I hated. No matter how many sleepy teas or melatonin gummies I popped, it never worked. None of that ever compared to a warm body beside you.

I found myself more wired than sleeping after doing both of those things. Since I was helping Aimee's father on overturning his conviction, I usually stayed up and looked over the notes from the other lawyers working on this case.

In college, it was fine because I had never experienced having someone share a bed with me. After Naheim, I was spoiled and craved a pair of arms holding me at night, kissing my neck and muttering they loved me while asleep.

I stared out the huge bay window that overlooked the lake and took in the sun. The light pink and orange hues in the sky looked so beautiful. I softly closed my laptop and sat it on the empty side and climbed out the bed. It had been a week since I spent the night over at Quameer's house.

Brandi had surprised Ryder with tickets to Broadway, and asked Meer if he was fine with switching days with her. They were driving up this afternoon and I was excited and nervous to meet the infamous Peach. Quameer didn't show much emotion, however, when it came to his daughter he was like putty. It was like experiencing a different him and I loved to witness him in daddy mode.

Checking the time, I quickly did my morning routine and switched into an athletic set, while rushing out the house. Just as I hit the porch, Cappadonna came running by with Alaia on her bike. She wanted to get in shape after Promise, so Cappadonna was acting as her personal trainer. With the way the both of them were like horny teenagers, I don't see how much training was getting done. I stretched quickly before running behind them. I got in good pace with Alaia as she listened to her music in her headphones.

"Good morning... brought you water," she pointed to her basket filled with water and I smiled. Alaia was like Mary Poppins. If you forgot something, she was going to be right there with whatever you were missing in her bag.

"I almost missed you both."

"You need to get some sleep, Pri... the circles around your eyes are crazy." She focused back on keeping the bike steady while Cappadonna was far ahead of us.

"Why do you even come with him... he leaves you every time."

She smiled as she admired my brother's back. "He doesn't leave me. He does the first lap around the neighborhood alone and then comes back to run slowly beside me... Capp would never leave me."

"Relax, Love Bird."

"Is Quameer and his daughter still coming to stay the weekend with you?"

I smiled. "Yes. I need to go grocery shopping and grab a few things because my fridge is bare."

"When are you going to tell him that you like him, Capri? Soon as his name is mentioned you light up... he does the same."

"He does?" I eyed her down while trying to keep a good

pace, and not fall on the pavement. As we passed all the other lake houses in the community, I couldn't help but to feel this sense of gratitude.

"He is smitten with you. Erin has said the same thing and we both like him for you. He's close to the family, trustworthy, and he doesn't have baggage."

"A daughter isn't baggage?"

"Your brother didn't seem to think so. In fact, he gets upset when I would refer to Promise as baggage." She shrugged.

"We kissed, Alaia," I whispered; however, she heard me loud and clear like I had screamed it out in the neighborhood.

I could tell she was excited and want to scream, but she was too focused on keeping the bike from crashing into someone's mailbox. "Yess! How was it? Did you like it, or did it feel like it was too soon," she asked a million questions.

"It was fine... I wanted more and then he jumped up off the couch like I was a disease or something." I sighed, slowing up.

Alaia hit the brake on her bike, and we stood in the street. "He's probably scared of crossing that line with you. It's understandable, Pri... you both have been connected at the hip while you were away."

"Yeah... that's my fear, too. He said something about giving someone his word."

Alaia smiled. "Well, you're a Delgato, he's an Inferno... crossing those lines are different and involves the family. Probably doesn't want to take that step until he speaks with your brothers... it's a respect thing and those Inferno brothers ooze of respect when it comes to your brothers. It goes both ways."

Like Alaia said, my brother came running down the street, slowing down as Alaia puckered her lips out. "Came back for you."

"Always."

"E-nough you two." I playfully rolled my eyes, grabbing a water from the basket, as Alaia decided to walk the bike.

"Damn, what the fuck is that on your face, Baby Doll?"

I rubbed my face, sure that I got all the crumbs from my late night snacking off when I washed my face this morning. "What? Is it a pimple?"

"Nah... look like a little bit of hate right there on the side of your face."

Alaia busted out laughing. "Your man not all that funny."

"He laughs these panties right off," Alaia snickered as Cappadonna kissed her lips a few times. "See you later, baby."

They did their handshake and sealed it with a kiss. "Later? Where are you going?"

"Got to run a few errands... you straight?" he came over and kissed me on the head before getting ready to dart down the street.

"Perfect... Quameer and Ryder are coming up for the weekend."

"Hmm."

"What, Cappy?"

"He staying with you?"

I put my hand on my hips. "Where else would he be staying, Cappadonna? We're friends and you know that... so please stop. His daughter is gonna be here, too."

"Kids eventually go to sleep, Baby Doll... I know that because my own kid goes to sleep, and I be all in... just know Promise ass goes to sleep and I'm up with her mama."

"First of all, ewe. Second, I ne—"

"Roy, as much as you don't like it your sister is a grown woman, not your daughter. She's not your child and doesn't have to ask your permission for anything. Quameer has always been respectful when it has come to her, so why do you think anything would change?" Alaia stared up into his eyes.

"Corrupting my wife... I see how the shit is." He grabbed Alaia's face and kissed her lips again. "You talking all this tough shit... let me see this tough shit later."

Capri

Alaia whimpered and that was when I had enough. "Later... thanks for the half a run," I said before taking off jogging back to my house.

I had enough things to handle anyway. "Sorry, Pri," Alaia replied while Cappadonna took the bike from her and walked it.

It didn't take a genius to know what the hell they were rushing back to their house for. I pushed it out my head and continued to run back toward my house so I could shower and head to grab some groceries and fun games for us to play.

> Meer Cat: We about to leave in a little while. You need me to pick shit up?

> Me: Nope. I'll handle everything.

> Meer Cat: Bet.

As I pulled onto my block, I saw Meer's big ass truck parked in my driveway. He drove a Ford Shelby F-150. It was black on black with huge mud tires and black rims. You had to literally climb onto the wheel to get up into the truck.

He was across the street leaned up against Capone's car talking to him. I quickly pulled in on the other side of my driveway and hopped out my Bronco. I had gone to the grocery store and some other stores to grab games and fun stuff for Ryder for the weekend. I wanted her to feel comfortable with me. It wasn't like Meer was introducing me as his girlfriend or anything.

We were friends.

"Suga, why you got those little ass shorts on?" Meer called from across the street as I rounded my truck to open the trunk.

He had on a pair of sweat shorts, Jordan 1's and white T-shirt. His locs were pulled back, being held with a rubber band, and his beard was freshly lined up.

Shit.

Erin had come out the house and Capone held the passenger door open for her. "I'll be back later on. Capp should be too, so come through later." He dapped Capone up, then came across the street. "Those shorts are too short, Pri... the fuck?" Capone yelled out the window as he pulled past my house.

I flipped him the middle finger. "Mind ya business, Winston."

Erin leaned over her husband. "They some haters... you look cute, Pri... the body is bodying," she winked.

"Why you encouraging this shit, Gorgeous?" He sucked his teeth and rolled his window up, cruising up the street since the kids were out playing. Meer came over to where I was standing with the back door to my trunk opened and pulled my shorts down.

With his teeth biting down on his lip, he looked down at me. "I ain't feeling those shorts, Sug... burn 'em."

Looking down at my shorts, I didn't understand why he didn't like my shorts. They were a simple pair of Nike shorts, and I wore a sports bra with it. Anytime I had errands, I always tossed on the same thing.

"They only like this because I was sitting in the truck. What is wrong with my shorts, Meer?" I laughed, attempting to pull the bags of groceries out.

He gently moved me to the side and grabbed all the bags. "You showing a little too much... you don't got that little booty you left here with. All that damn rice and ramen got you thick." He pulled at my shorts with one hand, and I slapped his hand away. "Those grown woman curves coming in for me."

I was gagged. "You tried it... my ass was never smal—"

"Sugaaaaaaa!" I felt a little body crash into me before I could fully comprehend what was going on.

When I looked down, the infamous Ryder Inferno was staring up at me with her father's eyes and face. I could see

Capri

small hints of Brandi in her, but for the most part she was all Quameer. His toasted almond skin, low eyes, and curly hair. Even though Quameer had locs, his hair was curly, especially when he was in between a retwist.

"Hey Peach!" I hugged her tightly and looked at Quameer, as he continued to grab all the bags out the trunk.

Our eyes met and I smiled. "You both finally meeting each other. Now you can both stop getting on my nerves." Meer smirked and headed toward the garage I had opened when I pulled into the driveway.

"I couldn't wait to meet Daddy's best friend." Ryder continued to hold onto me and my heart melted.

"I told him that I couldn't wait to meet you, too... we're gonna have fun this weekend, are you ready?"

"Omg... I'm so ready." She cheered as she continued to hold onto me while we followed behind her father.

I let us into the house and Quameer put the bags down on the counter while Peach ran into the house behind me, taking in my house. While I was away, I had Capone overseeing the renovations of my lake house. I wanted everything brand new with no traces of my past in the house. Since selling the house wasn't in the cards, being that my family lived on the block, I needed to gut everything.

The white oak wooden cabinets brightened up the kitchen along with the white marble quartz countertops. My favorite was the rattan pendent lighting over the counter, with matching stools. I had them knock out a bunch of space that the previous kitchen had, and now I had a clear view of the lake, and the plants that I had them add. My kitchen reminded me of a little slice of Tulum, and after being away, this was a pleasant surprise to come back to.

"This shit nice... you were right about that big ass window."

I smiled. "Let me hear that again."

Quameer had seen my kitchen while in the process because

a few of the times the contractors would ignore me. If Capone couldn't get to them for whatever reason, Quameer took the drive to Lennox Hills and hemmed his little Italian ass up. After meeting Quameer, he answered the phone on the first ring for me.

"Can we swim in the lake and then jump in the pool?" Ryder ran from the back door over to where we were standing.

"We can do whatever you want this weekend." I smiled as she rushed into my arms.

It was funny how this was the first time we were meeting in person, but I felt like I knew this little girl for years. "I don't know about whatever you want." Meer rubbed her curls, and then went to the fridge.

"There's nothing in there... I plan to cook tonight."

Meer leaned against the fridge. "Let me cook."

Ryder grew excited. "Seriously, Daddy? His food is always so good... he just likes using the UberEATS app more," Ryder called her father out.

"I thought we discussed not telling my business, Peach. Damn, you my homie or hers?" He faked like he was so hurt.

I smirked as she hugged me tighter. "Hmm... will you let me stay up late tonight, Capri?"

"Um, how else are we supposed to watch scary movies?"

Ryder laughed as she turned my way. "She's my homie today... we shall see how the rest of the weekend goes."

"Oh, you foul for that one. When you hear a noise after watching those movies, don't call me."

I was a scary cat when it came to scary movies and knew I would be hearing all kinds of things after watching whatever movie we chose. "We have to keep him on our team because he's a man or whatever." We shuffled over toward him and pulled him into our small huddle.

"Yeah... he does check my closet and bed," Ryder whispered, and we both snickered like two friends in school.

Capri

I looked up at Meer, and he was just staring down at the both of us. It was no mistake that there was love in his eyes. "You ready for me to show you the guest rooms?"

"Yesss!" Ryder jumped up and down and pulled my hand to the stairs.

We went on a quick tour of the house, and I showed them the guest rooms that were separated by a Jack and Jill bathroom. One had two twin sized beds and the other had a king-sized bed with a balcony.

"Can you sleep in this room with me?" Ryder asked.

"Of course... I hate my room anyway." I opened the curtains up to let the light into the room. The room had the perfect view of the lake and the pool at the same time.

Ryder's phone buzzed from the little purse she wore around her. "Mommy's calling."

"Go ahead and talk to your mother," he told her, and she ran out the room. I could hear her answer for her mother as she walked down the hall.

"Does her mother know that you guys are staying here for the weekend?"

"I told her that we're staying at a friend's lake house. That's all she needs to know." He leaned in the doorway. "You know you don't have to tell her yes to everything. Peach gonna like you even if you say no."

"No, I want to. I've only had a nephew and all he wanted to do was watch Sonic all the time. Then I got another nephew that was too damn old. When I finally had two nieces, they're too young to do all the fun things with... I want to have a mini sleepover with her. She's giving me practice for when Promise and Cee-Cee are older."

"I hear you. Show me around the new and improved kitchen so I could cook tonight."

I smiled. "You failed to mention that you know how to cook."

"I mentioned it. You just always clowned me that I didn't know how." He looked me over, like he was drinking me with his eyes.

"Are we going to acknowledge what happened at your house or pretend that it never happened."

He abandoned the doorway and made his way over toward me. Taking his finger, he lifted my chin. "Not gonna acknowledge it this weekend, but definitely not pretending it never happened... we good, Suga."

"Okay." I smiled.

"Can I get a hug now?" I wrapped my arms around him while he rested his chin on the top of my head. "Later I have to run out to handle something... you good with holding Peach down for me?"

I lifted my head. "You trust me to be with her alone?"

"Stop playing with me. Aside from my own family and the Gods, you crazy ass Delgatos are the only people I trust around my daughter."

I blushed. "She'll be well taken care of while you go handle whatever."

"Lemme see what you bought from the grocery store." I headed toward the door and turned back around when I noticed Quameer about to bite his lip off.

"Yeah, give me those shorts after you take 'em off... I'm burning them shits."

"Oh please... come on." I rolled my eyes, and we went back down to the kitchen so he could see everything that I bought.

Chapter 6
Quameer

"This ain't Juniors but I guess it's cool." I ate a piece of the cheesecake that Suga had bought from a local bakery in the area. She laughed as she drizzled the caramel sauce she made over the cake. "See if you got to do all that shit, it ain't good cheesecake."

"Since when did you become the Gordan Ramsey of cheesecake?" she dipped her spoon into the cake and took a bite. "See, yummy... it's so good."

"Suga, it's not Juniors, but it's good," Peach told her, and Capri paused before she started hysterically laughing.

I always laugh to myself whenever Peach called Capri Suga. She always switched between Suga or calling her Capri. Once in a while she might call her Pri, but that wasn't all that often. As we sat on the couch with Annabelle playing in the background, I knew this shit was a mistake. Peach liked to watch scary movies until it was time to go to bed.

Then she had a million fucking excuses as to why she couldn't go to bed right away. She made excuses until I gave in and allowed her to sleep in my room. Even then she would be asking if I heard something or if the statue in my room always been in that position.

"Not the both of you ganging up on me."

"It's Daddy's favorite... every year me and Grandpop get him one for his birthday." She beamed at the tradition that she and my father had.

Peach sat in between us slumped down with her cheesecake and a bunch of throw blankets. Capri had went as far as to get them both matching pajamas. I knew there had to be a reason she was asking me what Peach's size was.

We were halfway into the movie and Ryder's ass was sprawled across both me and Capri knocked out. I watched as Capri pretended like she wasn't scared but kept gasping and using the pillow to cover her eyes. A few times I peeped her kiss her fingers and make a cross while saying amen.

"Hey. I was watching that." She snapped her head in my direction when I finally had enough and turned it off.

"You just as scared as she was... you not finishing that damn demonic ass movie."

"Well, you were the one that agreed with it."

"I don't watch movies that are based on true stories. Since I was outnumbered, I didn't put up a fight."

She took a deep breath. "I can understand why. I need to say a few prayers before I close my eyes tonight."

Sim: I'm here.

Pops: Here too.

I looked at my phone and then at Capri. "I won't leave if you too scared."

She smiled. "We're going to be fine. Just carry her upstairs because she is almost my height."

"Got you."

I rubbed her hand that was resting on Peach's back. "You never gave me your rating."

"On?"

"Stop playing with me."

Capri

"It was good... I don't think I had shrimp scampi as flavorful as yours, and I had some in Italy."

"Chicken bouillon."

"Oh, you giving me secret ingredients."

I smirked, standing up to pick Peach up. Capri turned everything off downstairs as we climbed the steps, and I placed her on one of the two beds. Suga climbed into the other bed and turned on the news.

"You sure you good? Do I need to check under the beds and the closet?"

Capri laughed. "We're fine. I'm not even scared anymore... I had to pretend for Peach." She tried to convince herself because I knew her ass was scared as shit.

"Alright... I won't be long. I got the code to the door and security."

She stared at me from the bed, making a nigga blush. Capri had this shit with her eyes that she did and didn't even realize it. Her eyes were low, seductive, as she looked over at me. I wasn't a nigga that would ever admit to a woman making me blush, but that one. That one in the bed across the room could blush the briefs off my ass.

"Okay. I may just go into my room to pack for a little bit until I get tired. Jesse sent over a full PowerPoint of the colors and vibes for each day of the trip."

"I don't care if she had a lobster suit on that PowerPoint, long as you didn't charter a jet, and don't have your ass hanging out, we good."

She laughed, removing her hair from her ponytail. "I didn't charter a jet, and I am grown. You can't make request like that, Meer."

I turned to leave the room. "Yeah, not just yet."

"What's that?" she called behind me.

"I'll be back, Ms. Delgato," I smartly replied as I headed down the steps and out the house.

Jahquel J.

I wasn't even going far. I crossed the street to Cappadonna's house and rang the doorbell. Alaia opened the door while holding their daughter on her hip. She had a piece of chicken in her hand and was going to town on it with her one little tooth.

"Hey Quameer... you hungry?"

Alaia was this warm presence that always made sure everybody was taken care of. If you didn't know her and Cappadonna well, you would have assumed she was this sweet little housewife. Her ass was just as twisted and wicked as her damn husband.

"Nah... I cooked for us tonight."

Alaia damn near dropped her baby. "Y...you cooked for, Pri?"

I was looking around her because the expression on her face was giving stroke. "Yeah... Alaia, the hell wrong with you?"

"I don't know... I'm just shocked that you cooked for her." She finally welcomed me inside. "You know, I have a feeling about you two... I think she's gonna be your wife one day."

I looked down at her and pinched Promise's cheeks. "Think? Come on, Alaia, I know she gonna be that."

"I know that's right.... Ain't that right, mamas," she tickled Promise as I made my way to the back where everyone was.

When I told Cappadonna that whenever Capri was ready, I would give him and Capone the respect and speak with them before ever making a move, I meant that. I was a man of my word. When Suga kissed me and straddled my lap, my high ass was ready to do everything I had been dreaming of doing since I first saw her ass.

Nobody knows more than God how much I wanted to bring her upstairs to my room. Capri deserved better. She deserved more than just sex from me, and that's what I wanted to show her. She kissed her fair share of frogs and even married one, and I wanted her next kiss to mean something.

I *needed* it to mean something.

Capri

This whole journey she had went on alone would mean nothing if I didn't come to her like a real man. Showing her my intentions and how I wanted to love her until I had nothing left to give. Suga deserved someone to put her first for once. A man that was going to come behind her with pure love and devotion. We both had been hurt, our hearts broken, and together I felt like we could heal each other.

"About time you showed the fuck up... you are staying across the street at my sister's house. Don't take that long to come over here." Cappadonna's smart ass was the first one to speak with a smirk.

Capone and Desmond were seated across from him. My father and Quasim were seated on the single armchairs. Quasim had a plate of food while my father was nursing a drink.

"They suckered me into watching a scary movie... my bad." I was nervous as fuck.

I've always been the kind of man that moved to the beat of my own drum. Not too many people could tell me what to do and I would listen. Respect had always been big with me, and it had been instilled in me since a child. I didn't fear anyone because the next man bled just like I did. This wasn't that though.

These men had the power to determine my happiness, and I had respect for each of them to put their word before my own happiness.

"Shit... this must be serious for him not to say some wild shit." My pops chuckled and took back the rest of his drink.

He sat the glass down and poured more from the decanter into his cup. "Tell us what's on your mind, Blaze." Quasim nodded, biting into his chicken.

Capone and Cappadonna both sat back messing in their beards. Niggas was sitting there stroking their beards while looking like the twins out The Shining movie. I looked at

Desmond and he was leaned back with his leg crossed at the ankle staring at me.

"How you doing, Des?"

"Better if I knew why I'm being pulled away from the bowling tournament that's on right now," he replied, and I laughed.

"Don't worry, Pops... you the only nigga watching that shit." Cappadonna snickered, and everybody laughed while Des tossed the throw pillow at his eldest son.

"I ain't never been one to beat around the bush."

"Then don't start now," Capone replied.

I held my middle finger up as I sat on the arm of the chair that my father was seated in. "I told you in Miami that whenever Capri was ready that I would sit down and have that conversation. As a man, I couldn't have that conversation without including her father and mine. I know how close Capri is to her father, and how our families are close with one another. This shit is bigger than the both of us... it's not lost on me."

Desmond was now interested in what I had to say. "I'm listening."

My father reached up and squeezed my shoulders. "Cap, when I told you that Capri wasn't ready for what came with me in Miami, I meant that. She wasn't ready. She had a lot of pain and hurt she had to sort through, and she needed to find her happiness. Happiness without depending on a man. I wanted her to find happiness and who she is without feeling the pressure of entering another relationship. I created a safe space for us to become friends. I wanted her friendship more than anything."

"You damn sure got it.... Baby Doll don't even call me anymore... it's always Meer this... Meer that," Capp was the first one to respond.

"Capp, she's my best fucking friend. The person I always

Capri

want to talk to and end the day talking to. No funny shit, my day don't go well unless I hear her slurping coffee in my damn ear. I told you she wasn't ready because she wasn't ready for the love I wanted to give her. The woman I've witnessed over this past year... the woman that you see as that little girl, was a woman that was suffering. Her heart was broken, and she was holding the pieces together trying to be whole for her family. That's the kind of person my Suga is."

"Suga?" Des spoke.

"I call her that... I'm Meer Cat and she's Suga."

He smiled. "I call her Suga Cane... always called her that since she was a baby. Her favorite thing to have in the summertime was sugar cane. Always had so much that I would tease and tell her she was going to turn into one."

"Shit, they never told me."

Capone leaned up. "Wasn't trying to encourage whatever was brewing between the both of you. Keep it real, what you trying to say or ask."

"I ain't never asking nobody for shit because I'm a grown ass man." I stood up, looking them all in the eye. "But, because of the respect that I have for your family, and my own, I'm asking all of you to give me your blessing to date Capri."

"You called that shit, Qua." Capp looked over at Quasim who had finished his plate and sat it on the table next to him.

"Let's be real, Quameer's a fucking asshole most the time... nigga never feel like he owes anybody shit. Blaze, I respect you for humbling yourself and coming before her family and ours to get our blessings. I see how you are with Pri, and I know she's in good hands with you. You have not only my blessing but my respect as long as Pops, Des, Cappadonna, and Capone give theirs."

My pops looked over at me. "Des, we laughed about sitting on a porch somewhere joking about your cab stories, and my

Jahquel J.

bike stories... didn't think we would sit on that porch discussing your daughter and my son."

Des leaned forward, honing the same expression that his sons wore on their faces. "She's my baby."

"I know that."

"The last man hurt her more than I care to admit... broke her. I don't speak often, and it may look like I'm in my own world most of the time, but I saw how lost my Suga Cane was before she left. The lights were on, but there was nobody home... she was on autopilot."

I knew exactly what he was talking about because I experienced it. It wasn't until midway through her travels that I saw the true spark in Capri's eyes. The one I was kicking it with in between all the bullshit we had going on wasn't the real Capri.

"She was... I'm not taking credit for her journey and how she has healed. I am taking credit for being there. A phone call away when she was struggling mentally. I was there. I saw it all, and always feel honored that she trusted me enough to allow me in. I'm never going to get deep into her shit because that's for her to discuss. I do know that I stood ten toes behind her as a friend, and I want the chance to continue as her man."

Des stood up and extended his hand. "You have my blessings, Quameer. There's something about you that I see... something telling me that you gonna stand by your word. I don't need to give you the speech on what will happen if you break her heart because I know her brothers and yours will." I shook his hand, falling into a hug. "Protect her. Love her... she deserves that," he whispered before he stepped back.

"Blaze, you got my blessing. I never thought I would see the day you would open your heart again. Did I think it would be with a Delgato, nah." My father rubbed my shoulders, and I turned around and hugged him.

Pops and Des left us while going back into the house. I

stood there watching both Capone and Capp's expression, and they were staring at me. Sizing me up like they wanted to get in my mind.

"I ain't been the best when it comes to protecting Pri like I should have. Like kids, little sisters don't come with manuals. I never knew how much was too much, or how much wasn't enough when it came to allowing Pri to have her own life. It's some shit that I will always regret." He stood up. "You got my blessing... don't fuck this up," he whispered as we hugged.

"On my seed, I'm not."

Capp remained leaned back as he stared at me. "All of this lies in Baby Doll's hands...she has to make that decision; I can't make that for her."

"Which is true."

"Quameer, that gir—"

"Woman," I corrected.

He smirked. "Woman... she means the world to me. Things I've done that I thought were protecting her ended up hurting her more. All I want for her is what I have with my wife... what Capo has with his. We want her to be in love, feel love, and have the fairytale life she has always imagined... she fucking deserves that shit, feel me?"

"I need you to do me a favor."

Cappadonna remained leaned back. "Nigga, you want blessings, respect, and now a fucking favor?"

I laughed. "This one is more important that the blessing."

"What?"

"I'm asking," I looked at both of them, "the both of you to give me the respect that you both have when it comes to your own relationships. Give that to me when it comes to me and Capri."

"Wait a minute. You in a relationship with her already? I'm fucking confused," Capone questioned.

Jahquel J.

"Nah... I'm talking about if we get to that place. I watch the both of you with your wives... nobody can tell you shit when it comes to Erin, and nobody damn sure can't tell you shit when it comes to Alaia. Your relationships and marriages are off limits. Not up for discussion, which I respect. Shit, you both don't even intervene with each other's marriages." I paused. "I'm telling you not to do it with mine. Capri is grown... allow her to have her shit. Be there as her brothers... she doesn't need more fathers, she got one already. I'm stepping forward and taking responsibility for her... that's mine. I got her, and you know when I give my word, that I take that shit seriously. I've told you since day one when you asked me to hold her down, that I had her...I've stood on my word and came through on that shit."

Capp sat there and I could tell he was digesting everything that I had said. He was the type that let shit absorb before reacting or responding and it was something I respected about him.

"Quasim, when the fuck did pissy ass Quameer become a man?"

"Nigga, I ain't never pissed the fucking bed in my life," I replied, cutting that shit right now. These niggas weren't about to be calling me fucking pissy.

"It always been in him... nigga built like the rest... I have no doubt that he'll be the man that Capri wants and needs by her side. Big Pri not some baby... your sister holds her own and has held her own numerous times. Give her the space to hold her own when it comes to her personal life."

"I've witnessed you do some ruthless shit in the streets without blinking an eye. With Baby Doll, you are different. You soften whenever she's around, and I've watched you follow her around whatever room she's in. It reminds me of how I feel with my wife... I'll murk a nigga and put on a damn seaweed mask if she asks me. I'm soft and vulnerable for my wife. How you protected her in Baltimore, I know you'll protect her. In

Capri

Miami, when you kicked that nigga in the face, I know you'll spill blood behind her."

"He fucking what?" Quasim blurted.

Capp stood up. "You got my blessing to pursue Baby Doll. Protect her and her heart... that shit is made out of gold," he patted me on the back as we hugged.

"You got my word."

"Whenever you're ready for marriage... I want you to meet me in my office and ask me like the Godfather."

"This nigga," Capone snorted.

Quasim took the cup my pops had and poured him more liquor into the glass. "So, both you niggas know you just gave this lunatic permission to crash out behind Capri, right?"

Capp smirked. "I'm the biggest crash out when it comes to my wife.... it's every man for themselves out there. Only the stupid would go against this nigga when it comes to Baby Doll."

I sat and had a few drinks with my brother and Capone, before this nigga Cappadonna turned his fucking back porch light off. Even then, we were still chilling, and this nigga gonna yell from his room's patio to wrap it up, we laughing too loud under Promise's window.

When I made it back across the street, Capri had showed me how to secure the house, so I made sure everything was straight before I grabbed my duffle bag and climbed the stairs to the guest room.

The door was closed to my room, so I assumed Capri had closed it after I left. I pushed the door, and it felt stuck. Shoving the door in a bit more, I was able to get it opened and turned the light on.

"Ahhhhhhhhh!" Peach and Capri both screamed holding onto each other.

I noticed the terrible job of trying to barricade the door with the closet door behind the door. "What the fuck?"

"Oh... it's your father. We're good, Peach," Capri did a

nervous chuckle as she and Peach were in the bed that was supposed to be mine. "We heard a noise, and both got scared, so we came in here... then we heard footsteps, so I tried to barricade the door."

Tossing my duffle bag into the chair in the corner, I turned to look at them both. "I told you that movie was going to scare the both of you."

"Um, Daddy... can we share your bed with you?" Peach asked, still scared from watching a movie her ass shouldn't have ever watched.

"Yeah."

She turned to Capri and whispered. "Ask nicely, he always folds."

"Meer don't make me go down the hall alone... please," she damn near begged.

I laughed. "You can sleep in here with us."

Peach clapped while yawning. "Perfect... I'm going back to bed."

I shook my head because my daughter had too much personality. One day, she was going to go out into the world as an adult and give those people hell. The minute somebody had a problem with it, I was gonna bust some heads behind my baby.

Capri fixed her bonnet as she looked over at me. "Everything alright?"

"More than that... I'm about to shower."

"Okay." She pulled the cover up over Peach who was tossing and turning until she found the right spot. She had been doing that since she was a toddler. It took her ten minutes to get the right spot before she eventually went into a deep sleep.

As I showered, I thought about the conversation I had with her brothers. The conversation that could have either made or broke my night. Being real, I would have been fucked up if I

Capri

had to abandon all thoughts of being that man for Capri. Having to witness her be with someone else would have torn me apart. I didn't want to see her with somebody else, I wanted to see her with me. By my side, being loved the way she deserved to be, taking this dick the way, I knew she wanted it. I wanted to change that name from Delgato to Inferno, and I had no doubt in my mind that we would make it to our twenty-year anniversary with our kids by our side. When I looked at that smile, heard her smart ass comebacks, I saw all that shit in our cards.

Brandi fucked me up to the point I never saw myself with anyone. I was cool with fucking bitches and getting by, never needing a bitch for anything other than pussy or head. I had convinced myself that love was overrated, a man didn't need love to live. When Capri popped back in my life, I started feeling things that I never thought I would feel again. I forced myself to push it out of my mind because she was Capp and Capone's little sister.

Off limits. Our past didn't matter to them, all they knew is that she was their baby sister.

Quasim and Capp were close, so I would never cross those lines without having his blessing. I thought the year with her being gone would change things. Maybe we would become distant, move on with other people. All it did was make me closer to her, craving her more than I did before she left.

I went a year without pussy, and I loved pussy like the next nigga. What bugged me out was that I didn't even miss the shit because the only pussy I wanted to be in was thousands of miles away from me. All the bitches I was fucking with I had cut off without an explanation.

Instead of worrying about the next bitch, I focused on myself and my daughter. Took up hobbies, invested a shit ton of money into smaller startup companies. Every time I got the urge to fuck, and it usually happened when I was talking to Capri, I went and invested money.

Niggas took a cold shower to relieve their stiffy, I jumped my ass on my computer and spent money. Nothing made my dick softer than seeing a bunch of money leaving my damn account. It was because of my investments that I was now sitting on money for me and Peach's future. Shit, I had money for Peach's kids, and even her kid's children in the future

When I came out the bathroom Capri wasn't in the bed. Peach was sleep across the bed, so I kissed her head before covering her up. The girl slept wild as shit, which is why I was always hesitant to have her sleep with me. I always woke up with my back sore because her damn feet was in it.

Soon as I hit the bottom step, I peeped Capri on the couch with her phone to her ear. "No, it's not that… I'm not near the city right now," she paused while the person on the other end of the line spoke. "I'll think about a date… okay? Night, Mason."

I was grinding my teeth together so hard that I'm sure they were about to crack. Mason's ass wanted to be out for the season, and I meant that shit. Now that I had her brother's blessings, I wasn't letting another man take any chance to slip in.

Before she could fully hang up, her phone started ringing again. "Hey Jesse… no, I wasn't sleep. Yeah… uh huh… yeah… no, I don't wanna meet him… there's nothing wrong with being single."

I made myself comfortable on the bottom step as she held a conversation with Jesse about whoever she was trying to introduce her to. "Fine… I will meet him, but just so I don't have to hear your mouth anymore. A chill kickback? Girl, you are engaged to a politician… he don't even know what a kickback means." She put her phone on speaker as she checked her messages at the same time.

"He has a business conference in California, so I figured we

Capri

could go out and chill like the old times... I really want you to meet him. He's perfect for you, I promise." Jesse's fucking voice pissed me off.

"Uh huh."

"Capri, are you even listening to me?"

"Yeah... Mason sent me two pictures of different jets and wants to know which one I want to take on our date."

"Mason who?"

"Mason Jackson."

"The NFL player?" Jesse squealed. "Bitch, you didn't tell me that you were talking to him... when did that happen?"

"We're not talking... I met him and we just been texting and talking whenever I answer."

"Whenever you answer. Girl, he is Mason Jackson... don't be crazy. The man wants to take you out and asking which jet you prefer... text him back now."

I shook my head because Capri wasn't moved by that shit. Her family had money and jets wasn't something new to her. If she wanted to charter a jet right now, she had the money to do it. Jesse was used to chasing niggas with money, so that shit was impressive to her basic ass.

"As if you don't have me packing for this trip and doing everything else... when is it?"

"I'll text you the information... it's the turn up before the actual turn up. It's gonna be fun... like college, Capri. We used to have so much fun, and I just wanna do that before officially becoming a politician's wife, and resigning."

"Wait, you're going to resign from your job?"

"David wants a stay-at-home wife... wants to try for a baby right away, too. He's older, so it makes sense, and it's a good look for his career. Family man, you know." She sounded depressed while explaining her stupid ass life plans to Capri.

"What about what you want, Jesse?"

Jesse did a fake yawn. "I'll text you the deets. Night... get some sleep, okay?"

"K."

I stood up and made like I had just came down as she ended the call. She smiled when she saw me stroll into the kitchen and grab some water out the fridge. "I thought you would have been knocked out."

"You know me... I don't get tired until the sun starts peeking." She giggled and patted the spot next to her. "Come sit."

I crossed the kitchen into the living room and sat beside her. "What up with you, Suga?"

"Honestly, nothing. I'm really just chilling."

"Why you not sleeping?"

She shrugged. "Guess I forgot how good it feels to have someone in the bed with you. It feels lonely climbing into bed alone... you know?"

"Yeah."

She turned toward me and tucked her feet underneath her. "Is this friendship just one-sided?"

"Where the fuck did that come from?"

"It feels like it sometimes. Like I'm not pouring back into you the way you pour into me. Meer, you don't offer much... so, is this friendship one-sided?"

Capri had tried to pick my brain so many times and I always found a way to get the subject off me. I've always been that person though. Never wanting to burden anybody with my personal shit. With Brandi, it worked because she was so self-centered that she didn't notice when life was crashing around me. It was always about her and the stupid ass superficial problems that she had going on.

"I don't enjoy putting my shit on other people. It ain't one-sided. I recognized that you needed me more, and I adjusted."

"That's not what a friendship is, Meer. I want to know more... I need to know more. Sometimes I feel like I'm going

Capri

crazy because I feel like I know everything about you, and nothing at all."

"What you want to know?"

"What happened between you and Brandi? You can rewrite history now and hate her, but I knew you both when you were together."

"Before or after I ate your pussy?"

She blushed and looked away. "We're not discussing that."

"Why not? You want to talk about the past... let's get it all out."

Capri put the pillow over her face as I laughed while staring at her. "You and Brandi were broken up... that's what you told me. You were at the dorms to win her back."

"And you and Jesse were covering for her... be honest with me, Capri."

She tried to sit up and I pulled her ass back down onto the couch, pulling her onto my lap. "This ain't my business, Quameer. It happened years ago, why are we even speaking about this?"

"Cause I need to know."

"What do you want to know?" she asked, her cool breath hitting my bottom lip like brisk air. Neither of us said anything as we both were lost in each other's eyes.

"She was fucking other niggas when she was with me?"

"I don't know, Meer."

"Suga, don't lie to me... promise me that one thing. I dislike liars, and you can't come back from that."

"Why am I being forced to tell you this. Shouldn't she answer the question?"

"Capri."

She stared into my eyes. "Brandi messed around, yes. It wasn't my business, so I never said anything."

"Thank you." I released her, and she climbed back over

toward her side of the couch. She messed with her nails before looking up at me.

"Meer, what happened?"

"Life, Sug... that's what the fuck happened."

She sat on her feet and stared at me with those damn eyes. "What do you want?"

"You, Sug... I want you."

"How can you ever have me if I don't know *you*."

I looked away. "Don't even do that... you know me. Just because I don't want to give Brandi any more attention doesn't mean that you don't know me."

"I've cried to you about Naheim... literally told you things that I haven't even shared with my brothers. Why is it so hard for you to be honest with me about your past with her and how it ended?"

Fuck.

I knew eventually I was going to have to talk to her about the shit. Eventually she was going to want to know, and I wouldn't be able to talk my way around it. As she stared at me, wanting – needing – to know about how me and Brandi ended, I knew I couldn't leave her hanging. If I wanted a future with her, then I needed to be honest.

"She fucked me over, Suga. Broke my fucking heart, and I promised myself I would never talk about the shit with nobody."

Capri grabbed my hand. "I'm not nobody... I'm *your* Suga. Our secrets are safe with each other... remember you told me that."

I smiled. "Yeah, I remember."

"So, tell me." She patted her lap, and I laid down on her lap as she massaged my scalp. Capri's scent was driving me crazy. She always smelled like pears and patchouli, and a year away didn't change it.

"I was going to marry her... wanted her to be my wife, and

Capri

she allowed her family to get in the middle of that shit. She chose her family over what we could have had together."

"Wow. I was thinking you weren't the marriage type."

I looked up in her face. "Why the fuck would you think that?"

She shrugged. "Meer, you joke around about it, but I never took it as anything serious coming from you. Let's not act like you didn't get around... so marriage didn't seem like it was in your cards."

I laughed because she had a fair point. The way I moved after Brandi, I wasn't interested in nothing serious. Most of the bitches I messed with barely knew I had a child, so she had a point. I never kept the same woman around for more than a few months. Once you get comfortable and learned my pattern, you had to get the fuck from around me.

"I take it seriously."

"Brandi didn't want to fix things."

"Nah. She played fucking games with me, and then used my daughter in those games." I could feel the heat radiating off my body thinking about all the games she played with me. "She broke my heart in more than one way. Played games with me trying to be there at the doctor appointments, and then moved to Atlanta midway through her pregnancy and had Ryder down there. Shit had me depressed going through a lot and then had to fucking play games with where my baby was. I missed the first six months of my daughter's life because her mother played games with me... I didn't get to see her take her first breath because her mother was being an immature bitch." I bit the inside of my cheek as I thought about the shit.

Brandi took that away from me. She took the chance to witness my daughter growing in her womb. I didn't get the chance to see Ryder be born and have those memories. All of that shit was stolen from me like the marriage I wanted with her. Even to this day, she would never admit the wrong she has done to me.

It was swept under the rug like the shit never happened. Brandi loved to rewrite history, so I'm sure she probably has her own story for why she moved the way she did. Either way, I knew what happened and felt the hurt of her calling to tell me that I had a daughter, but not telling me where she was. I wouldn't wish that hurt on my worst enemy.

"What made her come around?"

I smirked. "I sent her a picture of her father out with her grandmother. Told her that I would pop that nigga in the head in front of her grandmother."

Capri looked down at me horrified. "Meer, you did not."

"Bitch fell in line right away." I shrugged. "I got to meet my daughter a week later and been glued at the hip with her since."

She broke out into laughter. "I mean, I get it… it's not like she didn't ask for it."

"What you mean? She your best friend." I stared up into her eyes as she screwed her face up at me.

"If you don't quit saying that… we hung around because of Jesse. Back then, we all stuck together because the men on campus were all gross," she rolled her eyes, reminiscing about how her college days were.

"Had those niggas on campus going crazy for yo' ass… still got them going crazy for you." Every nigga and his brother wanted Capri Delgato. Shit, there was a few Gods that wanted her, and knew I'd fuck them up if I ever found out they stepped to her.

Before I could get to, they ass, they needed to be worried about Capp getting to them first. "Stop acting like you don't got a bunch of hoes hiding somewhere, Meer."

"I don't."

She screwed her face up like she didn't believe me. "Stop lying. You didn't date or mess with nobody while I was away?"

Capri

"I run a tight ship over here, Sug. Ain't no bitch gonna be coming to you as a woman... I shut that shit down. I told you I ain't had no pussy and I meant that shit... just me and this hand." I placed it over her face, and she squealed.

"Eww, Quameer!" she shrieked, while laughing at me.

We both settled down from laughing and I stared up into her eyes as she looked out at the lake. "INY, Sug," I admitted.

If she only knew how hard it was for me to admit that to someone, she would know how special she was. I hated to need anybody, and I damn sure wasn't going to tell anybody that I needed them.

"I need more, Meer. I've been with somebody who refused to let me in. I don't want to give somebody my heart again and end up with the same situation. Why is it so hard for you to talk to me?"

"Because it is, Suga... that shit don't come easy when I've spent the last few years protecting my heart. I can't just open my mouth, and all my shit just comes out."

"Then you can't have me."

My eyes popped open as I looked into hers. "The fuck you mean?"

"I mean, you can't have your cake and eat it, too. It shouldn't be this hard to talk to me... I'm your Suga, but you're acting like I'm a stranger. You know me, Meer... you know who I am, and how I am. It shouldn't be that hard. If you can't give me this and we're friends, I don't want to be in a relationship. You have to let me go, and allow me to find someone that is gonna let me in."

I leaned the fuck up because she had my heart beating all fast. If I was hooked up to a monitor, I knew for sure they would have been trying to calm me down.

"What the fuck you mean, Capri?"

"Exactly what I said," she stared me in the eyes with a

serious expression on her face. I could tell she was deadass with the way she held my gaze.

"Let me see you with another nigga, Suga... you ain't seen shit yet," I threatened, and she shrugged, as if I didn't just warn her that I was going to lose my mind if I saw her out with another nigga.

Before I had no choice but to tolerate the shit because I didn't have Capp and Capone's blessings. Now that I had it, Capri might as well had been my fucking wife.

At least in my head.

"Kiss me, Suga," I demanded.

"Friends don't do that, Meer."

As I was about to say something, both our heads turned toward the steps. "Suga, can you come lay down with me?" Peach stood on the steps.

Capri smiled. "Yes. I'm tired anyway. We can give your daddy back his bed... back to just us girls, cool?"

Peach nodded. "Yes... can we share the bed though?"

"Of course." Capri laughed.

"Suga," I said under my breath, and her ass heard me, but stood up trying to walk past. I grabbed the hem of her sleep shirt. "You hear me."

"Oops, got caught on something... coming, Peach." She snatched her shirt back, and smirked. "Night, Meer."

I leaned back on the couch. "Fuck," I muttered.

Why the fuck was it so hard to open up to her? I trusted Suga with everything, but every time I came to opening up, I shut down. I talked so much shit about Quasim, and that shit was in me too. I wish I could solely blame Brandi for the way that I am. I had this fucking fear that the minute I opened up and allowed someone into my world, shit would go wrong.

I felt like a bitch whenever I thought of the way Brandi played with me. Felt like I let that shit happen, so I vowed to never let somebody play with me like she did. Yeah, I know

Capri

Suga was different. It still didn't stop me from feeling that way and bringing her into the folds of my life. Shit wasn't sweet my way.

My mother wasn't who she was, and that was a whole situation in itself. We didn't talk about the shit beyond our immediate family. Introducing her into my life meant that I had to open up and bring her all the way in.

What if she fucking went running? Her phone beeped, and I grabbed it before heading upstairs to bed.

Chapter 7
Capri

NEVER ALLOW JESSE TO SET YOU UP ON A BLIND DATE. I marked in my note's app as we sat at the bar of this small club/bar in Jersey. Jesse's so-called blind date for me never showed up and she had been calling his phone damn near all night. I was cool with it just being us because I didn't want to meet nobody anyway.

Blind date aside, Jesse was boring as shit. We had been sitting in this bar watching all these new wannabe rappers, and the shit was boring. If this was her idea of reliving our college years, I was going to need her to tap back into that and actually remember how we used to turn up with our other friends. Instead, she was in here acting like she couldn't have a drink, and then turning her nose up at every chick that walked in here like she was better than them.

I knew going out with her was a bad idea. We were more brunch and light shopping friends. Anytime we went to parties in college, it was never her who planned the outings. Come to think about it, I didn't even remember Jesse ever being the life of party in college.

Because I didn't think of this before coming out, now I was stuck watching her run her hand through her hair multiple

Capri

times. She kept checking her cup like someone had come between us and slipped something inside of it. If she spoke about her fiancé one more time, I knew I was going to scream.

> Mason: I'm here.

Do you know how bored I had to be to invite Mason out? It wasn't that he was boring or unattractive, I just wasn't feeling him like that. He liked to toss money around too much like it impressed me and it did the opposite for me.

I wasn't moved by how much money he had or what he could do. If I wanted the same things, I could have them with or without him. When he shot me a text to see what I was doing, I invited him out to see if he would take the bait. If he was really interested in chilling, then he was going to come out with me tonight and actually chill.

After me and Meer's conversation, I was even more confused. It was like he wanted to tell me everything, and then he held back at the same time. In one breath, he was telling me he wanted me, then his actions were showing something else. When we sat on that couch, it felt like he was in internal battle with himself. Trying to figure out how much was enough to tell me, and how much was too much. He was careful on how he spoke, and I didn't want that in a relationship. I've spilled my heart to him – sobbing in the process. I wasn't settling for the bare minimum anymore, even when it came to Meer. He either needed to tell me he wanted me, and give me what I required, or we could remain friends.

The ball was in his court.

"Mason is outside... wanna ditch here?"

"Jesus, yes." Jesse damn near beat me outside.

She was the one that wanted to come here and now she was acting like I dragged her out here. We made it to the front and

Mason was leaned on his Bentley, which pissed me the fuck off. Why in the hell would you come to the hood in a Bentley.

Then, he had the nerve to have security with his ass, and a damn driver. All of this shit was too showboat material, and I was regretting even calling his ass. "What up, Capri? Finally get to see you." He pulled me into a hug and kissed my cheek.

"Hey Mason," I smiled. "This is my frie—"

"*Best* friend, Jesse," she quickly shoved her hand into his and was showing all thirty-two of her sparkly white teeth.

I was trying to figure out when she had become my best friend, and when she was going to tell me. The only person I considered a best friend, aside from my sisters, was Blair. Since reconnecting, we had become closer. That was my right hand, I just needed her to realize that I ran with some real gangstas, and shit was gonna happen every once in a while.

Other than that, that was my girl.

"Nice to meet you, Jesse. My bad intruding on girl's night... when this one hit me up, I wasn't going to miss the chance to see her."

Jesse was all blushing like he was talking about her. "No, don't worry about it. I'm actually going home anyway. I have an early morning with my wedding planner."

She surprised me when she spoke about her fiancée since she was acting flirty as hell. "Congratulations... whoever homie is, is very lucky."

"Awe, you're so sweet... Capri, I will call you in the morning for a full report." She hugged me and gave me a double cheek kiss like this was something we often did.

I watched as she quickly walked down the block to her car, since we both drove separately. I wanted to drive my own car in case I wanted to leave, and didn't want to wait on her. "What we doing tonight, Ms. Capri."

Mason was fine as ever. He was the perfect man on paper, and in the media. The man was worth three hundred million, and had endorsement deals out the ass. You couldn't pass a billboard without seeing his face on it holding some sports energy drink or dressed in athletic wear.

His brown skin glistened under the streetlights, and his million-dollar smile had the same shine. I watched as he stared down at me. I looked away because he was so damn handsome. When he smirked, he had deep dimples. The man checked every box physically.

Mason had the height, perfect teeth, and his waves were on swim for sure. Even his swagger matched the criteria, and that was because he often hung around the hood and was born and raised there.

It was his need to always brag that always fucked up his chances with me. "I was going to get something to eat."

"Bet. What you in the mood for? I could have any restaurant in the city stay open late for us."

I smiled. "Thanks... but no thanks. Let's grab chicken from the chicken spot down the way. They stay open late and have the best chicken."

He stared at me strange, probably taken back that I wasn't impressed nor wanted to go sit in a fancy restaurant. I've been to plenty, and all I ever did was leave even hungrier than I arrived. Mason was with chicks that would have jumped at the chance to be seen with him dining at a popular hotspot in the city.

It would never work with Mason because I didn't want my face splashed across blogs for the world to see. My life was complicated, and I couldn't afford for that to happen, and Mason wouldn't understand. Or maybe he would, but I damn sure wasn't about to explain my life story to him. He was fine to chill with tonight, but after tonight I was going to have to let him down easy.

"Ma, I can take you anywhere and you want to eat some greasy ass chicken?"

"It's not greasy and I know you can take me anywhere... wanna know something else?" I asked while fishing into my purse for my keys.

"What's that?"

"I can take you anywhere, too. Mason, I'm not one of your groupies... not easily impressed by dinners and cars. My brothers have Rolls Royce's... do you hear how that sounds? So braggy."

"You a tough one, huh?"

"The toughest... you can come with me to grab chicken, but you need to be in my whip. I don't want all that flashy shit while we're trying to get chicken. That's the easiest way for someone to line you."

He was thinking about it while I started down the block to my Bronco. "Bet... I'm gonna come with you."

Mason spoke to his security before he jogged down the block toward me. He held the door open for me as I climbed up into my truck and he got in on the passenger side. "I can't say I ever had a chick ask me to take her to get chicken. Maybe in college, but not as of recently."

"Wait until you find out that I'm going to buy the chicken, too," I giggled.

"Oh shit... you a sugar mama now?"

The word sugar, though not the way *my* Meer says it, had me missing him. When he and Ryder left after our weekend, we hadn't spoke, which wasn't like us. We were always texting or on the phone, but I figured he had been busy. Busy with his super private ass life.

"Don't push it now... I still love for a nigga to trick on me," I winked, and he licked his lips while staring at me.

The chicken spot was jumping like I expected. Everybody leaving the bar was heading down this way to grab food to end the night. Everyone knew getting chicken out the hood spot after drinking all night was the move.

Capri

There was nothing like having greasy ass food to soak up all the alcohol you had consumed. I found a spot and double parked before we climbed out my truck. Everyone was either too busy talking or drunk to even notice who Mason was, which I thanked the lord for. The last thing I needed was someone shoving their phones into our damn faces.

Mason stood in line with me, and it moved pretty quickly. He allowed me to order our food, and we stood to the side while leaning on the window and waiting for our number to be called.

"You going to have me working extra hard in the gym tomorrow morning."

He looked down at his phone. "You okay?"

"My security on their way... he feeling uneasy about me being out alone at this time... typical shit."

"At least you got a few minutes of freedom." I nudged him and smiled.

He chuckled. "Word... shit gets depressing sometimes. I mean, I love the money and shit, but I miss being able to go somewhere and just chill."

"I can see where that is annoying. My nephew is soon going to enter the league, so I worry about him when it comes to his privacy and our family's privacy."

"Tell him to have tough skin. This life isn't for everybody, and to protect the family. I keep my family out the media because I want them to have a regular life. I asked for this, not them." He removed a loose strand of my hair and tucked it behind my ear.

"I respect that."

> My husband. My world. My everything.: Aye, Suga... what you doing?

When the long ass contact name popped up and I opened the text thread, I shook my head and squeezed my phone. When did this nigga switch his contact's name in my phone?

> Me: In bed scrolling through videos... wby?

Call me petty, but I felt like lying to him about where the hell I was because he didn't tell me everything about the moves he made. Yeah, I know I needed to grow up, and I would one day. Tonight, I was going to play his game.

They called our number, and Mason went to get our order. I asked them to bag them separately because I wasn't about to eat this damn chicken in my truck.

> My husband. My world. My everything: Oh ight... I'm stupid now, huh? Born last fucking night huh, Sug?

I looked around the small restaurant and then scoped the window. Was he at the lake house and knew I wasn't there? My security system would have alerted me if he pulled up. Maybe he was visiting Capp or Capone and didn't see my car parked in the driveway and noticed all the lights were off.

Before I could even respond, another message came through from him.

> My husband. My World. My everything: Get the fuck out that chicken spot before I send a bullet through that nigga's three hundred-million-dollar knee... you cool with him being out this season, Suga?

My eyes nearly popped out my head because if it was one person you didn't want to test, it was Quameer's crazy ass. It was clear he was nearby and could see me with Mason. Or, knowing him, he had eyes everywhere, so someone had probably saw me and put him onto game.

Capri

Mason came back over with his phone to his ear. "Yo, Capri, I hate to even leave you... I gotta dip though... something came up."

I smiled, secretly thanking God because he was giving me a way out of all of this. "You're fine... we can link soon."

He went to hug me, and I gave him a stiff church hug, which caused him to look at me strange. "Let me walk you to your car."

"It's double parked... I'm good, Mason."

"Text me when you get home."

"I will," I lied, as he handed me my food, and I quickly left the restaurant and climbed into my car. Before I pulled away, I checked my messages again, and Meer hadn't sent another. As I pulled away from the block, I looked to see if I saw his bike, or even his truck, and I didn't see them. His ass probably had one of this friends report back to him, and that was how he knew I was here.

As I jumped onto the highway, I turned on music to make the ride back to the lake house go by quicker. I was slightly fuming over the fact that Meer texted me and had the nerve to demand me to leave like he was my man.

I left though.

As far as I was concerned, he never asked me to be his girlfriend, and we were friends. He said we weren't talking about what happened that weekend and we both kept our word. It had been about Ryder the weekend and doing everything to make sure she had fun.

My phone rang and I saw the ridiculous contact's name he changed his to and clicked the red phone icon on my car's screen and continued to listen to my favorite Brent song as I drove, pushing his stupid ass shenanigans out of my head.

"You ignoring my calls now?" my eyes looked in the rearview mirror, and Meer was climbing his tall ass over the fucking seat from the trunk.

"Ahhhh!" I damn near drove my truck off the road when I looked in my rearview mirror. He was now leaned in the back like he was being chauffeured.

"Pull the fuck over," he sternly but calmly replied, still cool as fuck in the back like this was normal.

I pulled onto the shoulder of the road and put my hand on my chest. My heart was going haywire, and he was still calm, allowing me a minute to get my thoughts together.

"What the fuck, Quameer?"

"You trying to end that nigga's career, Suga... shit is foul."

"W...what are you talking about?"

He pulled a spliff from behind his ear and lit it up, getting out the back of the car. I watched as he opened the door. "Move over."

Since I was in no shape to drive after he damn near scared me off the road, I climbed into the passenger seat as he adjusted the seat and then jumped in, pulling off while smoking his spliff coolly.

Almost too coolly.

"What the fuck are you doing in my car? How did you even know I was there to begin with, Quameer?" I had steadied my breathing and calmed down, and now I wanted answers.

"You supposed to share locations with your husband." He pulled on his spliff, as he sped down the highway toward the lake house.

I stared at the side of his face as he continued on like all was great in his world. It was probably great in his world because his ass was the one causing the mayhem.

"You are not my husband, Quameer... you had no right to switch my contact's name, stalk me, and then climb in the back of my truck. Hell, you don't even have the right to threaten Mason's career like you are doing. For what? We're not even together and you made that very clear."

"How did I make that clear, Sug?"

Capri

My eyes nearly popped out my head when he asked that question. I don't know if it was the fact that he was so calm that pissed me off, or the whole situation in general. "I haven't heard from you since you and Ryder left my house. Not a call, text message, or nothing."

"Did you call or text me?"

"Well, no, I thought you... never mind," I folded my arms and leaned back in the seat, looking out the window.

He had a point. I was so busy being petty because I felt like he was being petty, and I could have sent him a message and checked in on him. Neither of us had anything to say for the rest of the ride.

By the time he pulled into the driveway, I was tired and ready to go to bed. "Thanks for nearly killing us... night."

Quameer hit the alarm on my truck and followed behind me as I hit the code into the keypad. I started to close the door behind me, and he stuck his foot in the door. "Stop playing with me, Suga... my fucking back hurt, and you playing kiddie ass games."

"Nobody told you to get in the back of my truck, Crazy."

"I'll be whatever the fuck you wanna call me when it comes to you... why the fuck you out with his ass?"

I put my purse on the foyer table and kicked my heels off as I made my way into the kitchen. "Does it matter, Meer? Why are you texting me and demanding that I leave places."

"You left."

"Only because I got my food."

He hopped up on the counter and looked over at me as I pulled my food out the bag. "Not the way you were running out of there and looking around like somebody was gonna jump out on you."

"Whatever. I assumed you wanted space, and I gave you that... that's why I didn't reach out to you."

"You assumed. A simple call could have answered your

question. Even a text message... this the shit I be trying to get you to understand... I'm a grown ass man... communicate with me."

"Oh, that's real grand coming from somebody who refuses to communicate with me," I raised my voice, as I placed my hand on my hips.

"I communicate. Just say you don't like that I don't communicate everything with you. You lied to me, Sug."

"I don't have time for this." I tried to walk past him to get to the pantry and he snatched me between his legs. I was able to remove myself again and push away from him. "I'm Big Mama... Meer, niggas want me. I'm not about to play these back-and-forth games with you."

He got down from the counter and snatched me up. "I'll kill every nigga you think you 'bout to fuck with, Capri... I'll dead any nigga that thinks they got you... feel me, *Big Mama*?" A chill did a slow wine up my back as I stared into his eyes, seeing the seriousness in them. "You always have time for me always... you hear me?" He held my chin up to look him in his low eyes. "Don't even say no shit like that to me. 'Cause when it comes to you, I'm always going to have time for you. Have I not proven that?"

"Yeah," I muttered, trying to look away and he brought my face back toward him.

"I can't hear you, Capri."

"Yes, Meer," I replied.

How did I go from being terrified on the side of the highway to turned on by this man. "I want you, Suga. I ain't never wanted someone as bad as I want you. I told you that you were bad for me because of how you make me feel. I sat in your trunk considering if I was gonna blow that nigga's knee out over you."

I removed myself from him. "Why are you making it so complicated then, Meer? I've let you in... all I'm asking is for

Capri

you to let me in now. I don't want to feel like I'm in the dark when it comes to your life... your family."

"You met my father."

"You never talk about your mother... never. Even when Peach started to talk about her, you shut it down before she could even get a word out." Like I expected, he shut down and I turned my back and continued fixing my plate. "Kincaid never spoke about his family to me. When he got shot, I realized how much he knew about me and how little I knew about him. It hurt knowing another woman knew more about my man. Same situation, different man," I sighed while I sprinkled hot sauce and vinegar onto my chicken.

I felt his arms around me, turning me to face him. He pinned me between the counter and the stove. "Not the same situation, Suga... I promise," he kissed my neck, and I whimpered.

"Meer... we can't do this."

He lifted his head and kissed my lips. "My moms has Alzheimer's, Suga. I don't talk about it because it fucking hurts to admit it to someone other than my family. I went ghost because my Gam's had surgery, so me and Sim took turns staying over the house with my moms and the aid."

Meer turned his head to avoid looking me in the eyes, and I pulled his face back in my direction and down to look me in the eyes. "I'm sorry, Meer. I know how hard a disease like that is."

"Shit tough. My family means everything to me. We been through shit that was supposed to break us. I still don't know what lesson God trying to teach us, but I carry this shit with me every day. I've learned not to put my shit on other people. I do me."

"Meer, you told me that I can tell you anything and you would never judge me... that you will be the shoulder that I need."

"I know what I said." He smirked, exposing his grills.

"Then let me tell you... you can tell me anything and I will never judge you. I want to be there for you. I want to be the person you can come to when things are tough. You can only be so strong until you break... I've broke before, Meer, and I don't want that for you," I softly kissed his lips and wrapped my arms around his neck.

Meer moved my food to the other side of the counter while hugging me. He picked me up and sat me on the counter. "I don't want you with no other nigga, Suga... do you hear me?" he said in my ear, his lips and beard brushing against my ear.

My body felt like he had shoved a quarter inside of me and I had come to life. All the hair on my body was at attention when he kissed on my neck. "You can't make that demand, Meer."

He bit down on my neck. "Do you fucking hear me?"

"Uh hmmm," I moaned out, as he held my face and kissed my lips a bunch of times.

Meer kissed my neck once more and stepped back while taking me in. I looked at him, and he blushed. "Why you looking at me like that, Suga?"

"Like what?"

"Like you wanna get fucked every way from today to Sunday." He bit down on his bottom lip, as I pulled the strings of the halter dress that I wore tonight.

"I do."

"Suga, ain't no going back once I'm in that shit... if you thought me tracking you down and getting in your trunk was crazy... once I mark my territory, all bets are fucking off."

I pulled him closer to me. "There's no going back once you're in here... you can't leave me, Meer."

He softly kissed my lips and stared straight in my eyes. "I ain't letting you go nowhere."

I roughly kissed his lips, teasing my tongue inside of his mouth while he pulled the rest of my dress down. Moaning in

Capri

his mouth, he got tired of the counter and picked me up, tossing me over his shoulder while slapping my ass.

"And you ain't got no panties on... you was really trying to make me crash the fuck out, Suga."

"All my thongs were showing my panty line," I squealed as he took a handful of ass in his hand and slapped it a few more times.

I thought he was going to the bedroom, but he tossed me onto the couch, and I moaned, as I watched him loosen the sweats that he wore. He took his vest off, and then his T-shirt, showing his body.

Leaning forward, I kissed his burns while looking up into his eyes. "Suga, fuck," he groaned, as I continued to kiss them.

They were apart of him, so I wanted him to know that I accepted every part of him. He pulled me on top of him, and we just stared into each other's eyes before I kissed the side of his face. He held me tight, as if he never wanted to let me go.

His touch made me feel warm all over. Like this wasn't just sex between the both of us, this was something much deeper. A connection that we both were a part of, and now that we were together, we were a force.

"I want you, Meer," I whispered in his ear.

He didn't know how much I wanted him. How much I needed him, and how much I never wanted to let him go. I've waited my whole life to feel like I felt with this man and kissed a few frogs in the process.

Quameer Inferno made me feel seen. He heard me, understood me, and was patient. I felt protected whenever I was with him. My heart felt safe in his hands. He didn't beat around the bush with how he felt about me. I knew from day one that he wanted me, and he had showed me that being my friend was more important first.

Without the friendship, I don't know if we would have ever

gotten here with each other. "You want to break your celibacy with me, Sug?"

"Yes." I gyrated on his hardened member, as he leaned back looking at me with this sly smirk on his face. As if he knew he had me, and I had to admit... he did. "I want you, Meer."

"You Big Mama, huh? That's what you were saying, right." His cocky ass had the nerve to ask.

"I am," I twisted his loc around my finger. "You seem to think so, too.... Had you in my trunk, didn't I?"

Quameer broke out into laughter, all while I was feeling myself. While I was in the midst of mentally gloating about my come back, he flipped my ass over, and now he was leaned over top of me. Both his locs and gold chain dangling in my face.

"Yeah, ight. I wanna hear all that talk when Big Pa blowing that back out... you hear me?" he asked, as he easily slid the rest of his sweats off and separated my thighs with his knee.

AFTER NOT HAVING SEX FOR A YEAR AND BEING REDUCED to my vibrator that broke midway through my travels, I wanted this more than that damn chicken on the counter. My entire body was warm because I knew what was about to come. Meer wanted this as bad as I did, because his dick was shiny with pre-cum, waiting to enter me.

My legs were wide opened, waiting on him as he kissed me softly on the neck. I wanted to feel him inside of me. Quameer bit and pulled on my nipples as I tossed my head back, feeling like an electric current was brewing at the base of my back.

"There ain't no going back from this, Suga... tell me now and we can stop... I can wait," he said in between kisses.

"Meer," I moaned in his ear.

"Talk to me, Sug... what up?"

"Fuck me, please," I breathlessly pleaded.

That look flashed in his eyes and a smirk rose onto his lips,

Capri

as he bit down on his bottom lip, and roughly opened my legs further. "Don't run from me, Suga."

I couldn't make any promises because I knew he was about to put me through. Meer held onto the arm of the couch above me, as he slowly pushed himself inside of me, and I adjusted my body.

His body shuttered the further he entered me. "Meer," I cooed in his ear, as he held the arm with all his might. "Look at me, Meer."

He finally looked down into my eyes, and the look he gave me was one I had never experienced before. No man had ever looked at me the way he was looking into my eyes. It was like he was looking beyond me.

"Shit feel too good... ain't no fucking way you better have another nigga around you," he said through gritted teeth as he thrusted in me. "You hear me, Suga?"

His hand found its way around my neck, and I felt like I was about to cum once he applied pressure. "I...I hear you, Meer!" I screamed.

"Nah... I need to hear Big Pa... remember all that shit you were talking, right?" He lifted my leg while holding my neck and slammed his dick into me, and I whimpered because it felt that good. "I don't hear shit, Suga... where all that mouth at?" He grunted, pulling his dick out and teasing me before slamming himself back into me.

Each time he pulled out, I felt like a tub that had a stopper removed. Easing back on the couch, he pulled me back to him while my legs were shaking. "Pa, I hear you."

"You feel this shit in you, right?" he released my leg and got closer to my ear. "This shit big inside you, right, Suga?"

"Soooo big!" I sang out when he lifted me up while still inside of me. He held my waist as he slammed me onto his dick while we sat in the middle of the couch. My breast hit my chest with force with how fast we were going.

Sweat was coming from every part of my body. My hair was stuck on my forehead as I tossed my head back while holding onto his neck. I was seconds from tapping out while I held onto him with all of my might. "You can take it... you got this, Sug... take this dick," he said while biting down on his lip.

"Meeerrr," I moaned while biting down on his neck, and he wasn't letting up. "Ahh... Meer... I'm about..."

"I can't hear you, Suga... where that mouth at, huh? Let... me... hear... all...that... mouth...Big Mama," he slammed me on his dick with every word.

"Hmm ummmm," I whimpered because the pressure was building, and I was about to explode.

"Stay still for me, Suga... stop running from me... right... fucking...there... shitt... I can't hear you, Mama... let me hear you. Who do you belong to, Suga?"

"Y...You?" I screamed while bouncing up and down on him.

"Aceite isso como uma boa menina, meu amor," when he spoke Portuguese in my ear, I just about lost it and the dam broke, releasing everything I had inside of me.

"Me...Meer," I cried out because my body felt so good.

He slowed down, hugging me into him while he bit my neck, and I felt his dick pulsating inside of me. "I swear to God I will kill a nigga behind you, Capri."

I was too spent to reply, and he knew it because he laid me back on the couch, and got behind me, pulling me into his arms. "Meer, hold me tighter."

He did as I asked. "I ain't never letting go, Capri."

"Promise?"

"Look at me." I turned slightly until I was staring in his eyes. "I put that on my life." He kissed me on the neck, and pulled so close that I was certain that we would merge into one person.

"I don't have to sleep with your lighter tonight because

Capri

you're right here." I yawned, my eyes becoming heavier, as he traced my fingers with his.

He kissed my temple. "Didn't know you still had it."

"It's broken because I flicked it too much," I admitted, remembering the nights I sat on the balcony staring out at the view from my condo flicking the lighter like a lunatic. My eyes eventually closed, and I scooted back trying to get even closer to him.

"I love you, Suga," I heard him whisper as I was slowly drifting into a deeper sleep.

Chapter 8
Aimee

When my aunt told me that my memaw was in town, I decided to stop being bitter and come over to see her. It had been well over a year since my brother and mother's funeral, and the infamous wig shift, and I figured it was time to put everything behind us. As much as Capella's family treated me like family, they weren't my biological family. At times I felt alone in this world, even with having Capella and Rory.

It felt like something was missing from my life and I couldn't figure it out. We would always have Capella's family to spend holidays with, but what about mine. When it came to making rounds during the holidays, we would never stop at my family's house, so I needed to make things right.

Did I want to come groveling to my grandmother and apologize for my boyfriend shifting her wig?

No.

Her wig *was* crooked, and it desperately needed to be shifted. It had needed to be shifted for years, and nobody was bold enough to do it. Leave it to my man to shake the table and do it.

"You got there?" Capella's voice pulled me from my thoughts as I paralleled parked in front of my aunt's house.

Capri

I put my truck in park and leaned back in the driver's seat. "Just finished parking."

"I don't know why the fuck you want to go over there," he replied, not understanding how badly I wanted my family to accept me.

I knew he felt it was stupid of me to even show up when my family wasn't worth shit. There was still this part of me that wanted to be accepted, and I couldn't help the feeling. During the holidays when we all gathered, I felt the most alone because I didn't have any family. No grandmother to call and wish me happy holidays.

"You wouldn't understand." I sighed.

"Then try me, Aim... I get you feel lonely with your mother and bitch ass brother gone...fuck, my bad, Aim."

"It's alright, Honey," I replied, watching an Audi R8 speed in front of me and double park. I nearly choked when I saw my cousin Rowland get out the driver's side and stroll around the car. He was too consumed with his phone call to even notice me or pay attention to his surroundings.

Rookie mistake.

"Let me meet you over there... I'm not that far from you."

I laughed. "Capella, are you watching my location?"

"You damn right... I'm about to head to you."

I shook my head. "This is something that I have to do alone. You know my memaw still not over the way you acted at the repass... I have to slowly bring you around."

He wasn't a fan of me being here alone and his silence spoke louder than his words. Before he changed his mind and came over here, I decided to end our conversation here. "Aim, call me if they start that shit again... you hear me?"

"Okay... I will."

"Alright... love you, baby."

"Love you way more, Honey."

"Fucking impossible... you got your shit on you?"

"Always." I patted my purse that held my nine inside of it.

Once I finished my conversation with Capella, I hopped out the car, slinging my crossbody Glamaholic bag around me, and jogging up the steps to my aunt's house. I was nervous like I was meeting them for the first time.

My fingers hesitated over the doorbell for a bit before I eventually pushed it, turning around to do some light breathing. I needed something, anything to calm these damn nerves. When I heard the locks turn, I turned around at the same time that my aunt opened the door.

I half expected to see a sour expression on her face but was relieved when she smiled at me. "It's been way too long, Aimee," she pulled me into a hug and kissed my cheek.

Even when my brother and mother were alive, she never ever pulled me into a hug or showed any love to me. It bugged me out why I wanted to be accepted by them when none of them ever showed me love.

She ushered me into the house, and I could smell the food that she was cooking. "It has been too long."

I hadn't seen or spoken to them since the funeral. They were missing out on my little boy growing up. It was already a tough pill to swallow knowing that my mother would never see Rory grow up.

When I entered the kitchen, Memaw was sitting at the kitchen table smoking a cigarette. The smell of cigarettes always made me feel sick. "Get on over here and give me a hug... missed you girl."

I went and got a big hug from my grandmother, one that I had always craved. She kissed me a few times on the cheek as she looked me over. "Hey Memaw... how are you doing?"

"I'm getting on with life like everyone should be doing. This life isn't promised, and your mother and brother have shown us that."

Capri

I was hoping she would wait before she started to bring up Ace and my mother. Hell, I was hoping she wouldn't bring them up at all because I wanted to pretend they didn't exist – just for a moment.

"Yeah," I replied, taking a seat at the kitchen table.

Memaw lived in Delaware and rarely came to New York. So, I was surprised that she was even here. Aunt Tiny fixed Memaw a plate of food and sat it in front of her. I declined and just accepted some iced tea that she had freshly made.

"What is new with your boyfriend? I see that truck out there... must have cost a pretty penny."

I was humble when it came to discussing any of the blessings that I had. Even when I arrived at school, everyone was always pointing and asking me about my Mercedes G-wagon. They wondered how a college student could afford a truck like that, or the designer things I wore. All I had to do was mention I wanted something, and Capella was going out his way to make sure I had it.

The little income I made for hacking into stuff for friends or acquaintances didn't touch the surface on the things that Capella did for me. When he told me he would take care of me, he meant it with every word.

"My boyfriend is very generous," I smiled, hoping they would drop the subject and bring something else up.

"Very generous... I see. I know that's a limited edition or something," my aunt sipped her drink, eyeing me down.

"I think so... not sure."

My memaw continued to eat her food, stealing glances at the ring that Capella had on my ring finger. It was a princess cut diamond ring that he promised would be bigger when he finally popped the question.

"That ring real pretty, Aimee." Memaw reached over and grabbed my hand, admiring the ring.

This went from being a visit to catch up and hopefully mend our differences, and now I felt like they were more concerned with the things that I had. Why was what kind of car I drove or ring I wore important to them?

I was feeling uncomfortable, and wanted to leave, but the people pleaser in me didn't want to hurt their feelings. That was the thing about being a people pleaser. I would make myself uncomfortable just to make those around me more comfortable and spare their feelings. The shit was wicked and one of the things that Capella hated.

He hated how I always went along with things because I didn't want to cause any friction. Like at the funeral, I was so uncomfortable, and he noticed and stepped in right away. "We're going to get married before our house is finished being built."

Stupid.

Why in the world would I even mention the house we were building? It wasn't a secret, but I felt like letting these two know wasn't the smartest thing in the world. My aunt's face perked up at the same time as Memaw's.

"A house? Wow, your man truly loves you. I hope we're invited to the wedding, too... we are your family."

Capella would rather jump into a tank of dolphins naked before he allowed my side of the family come around. "Um, yeah. We haven't planned anything, and he hasn't really proposed yet."

My aunt didn't give a damn about the wedding and quickly waved that away. "Speaking of houses... your memaw just lost the house in Delaware."

"Oh, no... I'm sorry. What happened?"

"It went into foreclosure. We couldn't afford to make the payments on it anymore, so the bank took it. You know how special that home was to her."

On cue, my memaw had this somber look on her face as my

Capri

aunt did all the talking for her. "Your mama brought you home from the hospital in that house." She sighed, pushing her potatoes around the plate.

"She's been living here for now... the bank has offered us to buy it back if we can come up with a hundred thousand dollars." Aunt Tiny continued to pour it on like she was so distraught.

"Oh. Maybe it's best for you to stay here in New York close to family. Memaw, you are getting older and being all the way in Delaware isn't really good for you."

"You know I hate to burden anybody, Aimee. I like my space away from everyone."

"Maybe you can find a condo or smaller house close to auntie... that way we can all check in on you and you can still have your independence."

Memaw heaved a sigh. "All of that cost money. I found a cute single-family home in Queens. It cost a little bit over two hundred thousand."

"It's so cute and quaint," Aunt Tiny chimed in. "I could probably quit renting this house and move in with her, too."

I stared off and then looked at the both of them. "I thought Memaw wanted some independence though?"

"Will you ask your soon to be husband to help you buy the house for me?" Memaw quickly asked, and I took a quick breath.

They both stared at me with these sad eyes, waiting for me to grant them a wish that I couldn't grant. Capella wouldn't give me that money to help them. It was a drop in the bucket for him. Even if he would, I didn't feel comfortable giving them that kind of money when they didn't give a damn about me for the last year.

"I don't think I can do that, Memaw. Capella isn't the biggest fan of lending people money."

"*Lending?*" Tiny blurted. "This is your grandmother... she

shouldn't have to pay you back for anything. Why is it so hard to just ask him? What's his is yours, right?"

Every member of the family had the black American express and could use it whenever they wanted. Aside from that card, I was an authorized user on all his personal cards and bank accounts. I could take whatever I wanted, and he would never question me.

This didn't feel right, and I was starting to think that was the reason they called me over here. Acting like family under the guise of wanting me to bail them out of the situation they found themselves in.

"She is *my* grandmother. Not my man's grandmother, so he doesn't have to do anything for her," I replied.

Why did she think I owed her anything? "Ace took care of her and paid all the bills until his last breath."

I was over the conversation and found myself feeling more uncomfortable by the second. "I am not in the position to pay for a house for her. If you need some money, I can help with that. Asking for two hundred thousand dollars is crazy."

Tiny had this look of hate on her face. It was a far cry from the welcoming aunt that had hugged and kissed me on the cheek. "How much can you help me with?" Memaw questioned.

"You have all this jewelry on and driving that nice ass truck and you can't help your own family. Aimee, I heard about the family you're going to marry into, and they are not hurting for money."

"Alright, Mama... I'm out." I turned to see Rowland standing in the doorway. He had switched out the clothes he was wearing when I saw him pull up.

"Alright, Baby... let me know if you're going to make it over here for dinner tonight." She abandoned the table and reached up to kiss him on the cheek.

The relationships between the women and sons in this

Capri

family made me sick. I promised myself I would never be like that with Rory, and I planned to keep that promise. "What up, Aimee... good to see that you not kissing ass for the Delgatos." He snickered.

"Leave me alone, Rowland."

Tiny grew excited that there was friction between me and Rowland. "It's Row."

"I don't care." I cut my eyes at him and prepared myself to leave. "Memaw, let me know if you need anything from me."

"She needed something, and you can't even help her, so what would calling you do?" Tiny folded her arms.

"What you mean? You won't help Memaw?" Rowland now wanted to be involved.

"It's none of your business."

"Memaw lost her house, and she won't help buy her a new one... knowing she has the funds." Tiny decided to lay everything out on the table with a smirk on her face.

"Alright, I'm going to go."

"You fucking that nigga, and he can't even help you with your family... bird ass shit," Rowland spat, feeling like he was the man.

I laughed. "Where's your money, *Row*? Match my hundred thousand and then I'll buy her the house... you got the bread?"

Just by looking at his face I knew his ass didn't have a hundred thousand dollars to match mine. The car he pulled up in had out of state plates, which meant the shit was a rental that he was flossing in. Tiny moved to New York when he and Ace were teens, so this nigga thought it was cool to cosplay as a New York nigga.

He was pathetic.

"You the one coming through with all this shit... pay for it yourself *without* a nigga's money."

"Okay." I shrugged.

He looked like he wanted to shit his pants. Just in the bank account that Capella opened for me alone, I had half a million just sitting in it. Like his father, he was always preparing for the future and made sure the money in that account was in there in case something ever happened to him. I hated to even think that way, but I was grateful that I was with a man that thought about us before himself.

"Okay?" Memaw asked.

"Yeah... wanna go to the bank now or..."

"Man fuck you... always been a lying ass bitch. That nigga got you feeling yourself a little too much... nigga ain't invincible. I ain't run up on his ass after that stunt because he ain't worth it."

Row knew the main reason he didn't step to my man was because Tiny's ass would have been burying him. "Don't get mad at me because you broke, living with your mama, and fronting in a rental... like I said, I'm here if you need me, Memaw."

"Bitch, I'll knock—"

He and his mother jumped back when I pulled my gun out. "Put your hands on me and I promise your mama gonna have to do CPR. Don't ever threaten to do anything to me." I moved past them until I was in the living room near the front door.

Tiny was shaking in her damn boots as she stared at me holding the gun. "She pulled a gun out on us," she shrieked in disbelief like I was aiming the gun directly her way.

"You got it, Gangsta... I promise you won't get a second chance to pull a gun on me and my mama."

"Is that a threat, Rowland? 'Cause my son's father and grandfather don't play 'bout me... you sure you want your name on their radar?"

"The only man I fear is God... fuck you tossing they name around like I'm scared."

"Okay."

I left the house because I needed to get the hell away from

Capri

my so-called family. Capella was right when he told me I was wasting my time. They didn't want anything from me unless I was giving them money and helping them out of their problem.

Should have been smarter than that. My mother was the same way, and the apple never fell too far from the tree.

Chapter 9
Capella

"Let me ask you something... if we're supposed to be keeping a low profile, then why the fuck would you pull on this block blasting music at four in the morning?" I asked, while squeezing this little asshole's neck tighter with each word that left my mouth.

He stammered while trying to avoid the eye contact I was giving him. I was so close to this nigga that my eyeball was damn near touching his. "I...I was drunk and didn't think."

When Quasim called me last night and told me what this ass monkey had done, it took everything in me not to get in the car and drive to the city right then and there. Forty told us not to open any new traps and to abandon the traps that we used to have.

Aside from the warehouses, we had a few houses with the IG's that we had been using for the past year and everything had been moving smoothly. We didn't move sloppily, and shit was on the up and up.

It always took one asshole to do some stupid shit. Not only was he fucking with everybody's money, but he was also putting IG's shit in jeopardy too by trying to showboat and

Capri

cause a scene. The chime to the front door sounded, and I turned to see my pops walk through the door.

As much as my father wanted me away from the streets, this shit was in me. I had gotten a taste of the shit, and he knew he couldn't keep me away from it. He, however, made sure I moved smart so that I never ended up in an emergency room again.

I couldn't in good consciences sit and allow my father to take care of me and my family. Even though he was against it, he respected my decision and knew that it was important to me to take care of my family. Aimee and Rory were my responsibility, and I was going to make sure they were taken care of, like he would do the same with Alaia and my siblings.

"Gun shots, my guy... you were out there turnt up, huh?" Cappadonna laughed, shaking off his sweater and laying it on the back of the chair.

Homie looked like he was about to shit his pants when he stared up into my father's eyes. "I drove over two hours here to meet you... why you so quiet?"

I watched as he pulled his phone out and showed him the security footage of this nigga getting sturdy in the middle of the block while blasting music. He had some hoes with him, which was a fuck no, and then had the nerve to let out some shots in the air.

Shit would have been easier if he had done that in the middle of the hood, not a quiet suburban neighborhood in fucking Brooklyn. A neighborhood where they called the cops for every damn thing.

"I think they put some shit in my drinks, Capp... I don't even act like that." He made up an excuse for his stupidity, like it would make a difference.

My father put his phone away. "I know, I know. I said that's not even like Kareem... told them they had to be fucking with me."

Jahquel J.

Whenever my father spoke in that tone, one that I knew meant he was about to go off the deep end, it never ended well for whoever he was talking to. Kareem was so busy being relieved thinking that he was good that his ass didn't notice the switch in my father's eyes.

"Thanks, Capp... it won't happen again."

He smirked. "I know... you good peoples, Kareem." He held his hand out and like a fool this nigga dapped him up and squealed like a bitch when Capp twisted his hand, breaking his wrist. "Oh, I know you won't do that shit again because this hand gonna be out of commission for the next year, Ja Morant."

Kareem dropped to the floor holding his limp wrist while Cappadonna casually stepped over him. "You gotta stop stepping in... I told you that I had it."

"Never doubted that you couldn't handle it. I had to come to the city to handle something anyway."

"And you so happened to come here after I spoke to you this morning... come on, Pops."

"Don't I make fucking money in this bitch? Why the fuck wouldn't I come and check in on how shit is... you don't think I got the same call you got? If I was pressed, I would have been here before you... Relax, Capella." He patted me roughly on the shoulder and walked to the back of the house.

I stepped over stupid and continued on with my fucking day. Why did it always have to be one rotten apple to ruin the bunch? All he had to do was handle business like his ass was being paid to do, and he wanted to be letting his shit loose like shit was all good.

By the time I made it back to the lake house, Aimee was up in bed on her laptop. She had her textbooks, flashcards, and notebooks everywhere on the bed. I knew I had to get in where I fit in, because her ass wasn't going to move them.

Rory was asleep in Promise's room. The two of them were close, so they slept in her crib together most nights. I don't

Capri

know what the fuck was gonna happen when we eventually moved into our own house.

"Why you look like that?" I asked, the minute I noticed the look on her face. Aimee couldn't play Poker to save her life.

If she was going through something, you were going to see it right away. Since I was busy most of the day, she was able to slide under the radar by pretending over text message. She wasn't stupid though. It was the reason she had all her shit all over the bed, so she could pretend like it's school that got her ass stressed out.

"What do you mean? I'm just stressed with school and trying to figure everything out," she lied while quickly looking away from me.

I remained quiet as I settled in the doorway. She continued doing whatever she was doing on her computer, then slammed it shut. "I had to pull my gun out around my memaw."

"You fucking what? The fuck you do that for, Aim."

"Rowland tried to put his hands on me. My grandmother and aunt only called me over there to talk to me about buying her a new house... she lost her house in Delaware." My fucking chest was tight watching how this shit fucked with her.

"I told you I didn't trust those bitches... I knew it was fucking something with them." I started pacing the room.

"He got all big chested about me having the money, so I told him I would put up half if he put in half, and then he got in his feelings and tried to put hands on me."

I paused. "Oh yeah."

"Capella, I don't want you beefing with my cousin."

"Baby, this ain't a fucking beef. Nigga gotta have something to go toe to toe with me for it to be considered a fucking beef. If you think I'm letting this shit go, you got another thing coming."

She put her face in her hands. "Capella, please."

"Please what? I wanna see him lunge at me." I sat down in the corner chair and removed my boots.

"I'm out." My pops stuck his head in the room. "The fuck happened now?" he looked between me and Aimee.

"Her cousin tried to put his hands on her."

"Capella!" Aimee yelled.

"He tried to do what?"

I sighed. "She had to pull her gun on his ass... I ain't letting shit slide."

Aimee shook her head. "Good shit, Aimee. There's gonna be a lot of people that don't like you because of your last name. Alaia and Erin walk around with bitches mad at them every day because of that shit. You let that shit roll off your shoulders, and if it comes to it, you let your shit bang."

"Thanks, Capp."

"Family doesn't always need to be blood... trust me, you better off without them." He walked back toward the door. "Handle that shit, Capella."

"Already handled."

WHEN MY BABY TOLD ME THIS NIGGA TRIED TO STRONG-arm her, I didn't take that shit lightly. I had a problem with this nigga ever since I saw him at the funeral. You don't try and put your hands on mine and think you wasn't going to hear shit from me. Luckily, I taught her how to protect herself.

Every woman in our family knew how to handle a gun and even though she wasn't a Delgato yet, I would be damned if she didn't know how to handle herself. I took time teaching her how to use different guns and making sure she knew to keep that shit on her wherever she went. Aimee was horrible about remembering her gun and always made excuses about not bringing it with her to school.

Pops had got her truck fitted with the gun safe we all had in our whips, so she couldn't use that excuse anymore. I was glad

Capri

that all my nagging had finally paid off because she brought her gun with her when she went to visit her family. Deep down Aimee knew her family wasn't shit, but she had to witness that for herself.

I could holler that her family wasn't shit until I was blue in the face. It was up to her to believe it, and Aimee had to see it for herself. They only wanted what she could offer them but spent most her life calling her a liar and believing the man that abused her.

When she told me that she wanted to fix things with them, I knew the shit was a bad idea. Nothing good could come out of trying to fix things with her family,vand I hated to be right. My baby was missing a piece with her mother gone and now I understood what Pops was saying.

That shit would have broken me knowing that I was the one responsible for taking her family away. Aimee had been silently struggling with moving on with her mother gone. She was trying to make sense on why her mother would kill herself. I felt like I was lying to her because I knew her mother didn't kill herself. The only person she had was her father, and even then, that wasn't enough.

Mother and daughter relationships were complicated. As much as I thought her moms wasn't worth the skin she was in, Aimee felt differently because that was her moms. She was familiar to her and the person that had raised her for most of her life. The bitch could rest in piss for all I care.

I whipped around the block with Goon and Yasin trailing behind my truck. Soon as I got the drop on where this nigga chilled at, I made it my business to give him a visit. When it came to Aimee, I didn't play those games about her.

You didn't make my baby uncomfortable and make her feel like she had to protect herself. When she told me he lunged at her, I damn near broke the mirror in our room because who the fuck did he think he was?

Jahquel J.

Nigga had to be slightly off the rocker, but I was gonna show him what it meant to not even be near the rocker. I felt heat in my hands as I whipped into the empty spot in front of the Chinese restaurant.

There wasn't shit like Chinese food in New York. No matter where I had been, Chinese food in New York was always top tier in my opinion. Hopping out my whip, he watched me, as I walked into the Chinese restaurant and put in an order for fried chicken and shrimp fried rice.

"Don't be cheap with the fucking shrimp, either," I barked, and left out and walked over toward Row, and snatched him by the neck.

The nigga didn't know what to expect as I continued to walk his ass to the rented ass Audi. I knew a fucking rental when I saw one. The no smoking stickers on the back of the window was a dead giveaway.

"Let me make something real clear with you. I thought I was clear when we was at yo mama's nasty ass house... don't make me prove a point because I would hate to attend another repass with salty ass chicken. Try and put your hands on my wife again and I got a bullet with your name on the shit."

"Twelve just pulled up," Goon told me, and I watched as him and Yasin stood by the restaurant.

"Everything all good here?"

I don't know why the officer thought I was scared or would fold. He must didn't know me if he thought I was about to fucking fold on what I said. "Yeah... I heard he tried to hit my wife... just informing him on what the fuck would happen if he did the shit again... right, Rowland?" I released his neck, and he stood up, straightening his clothes.

"Are you alright, son?"

"Yeah. I'm straight... we're clear. Shit won't happen again." Aimee told me that Rowland had a record, so his ass wasn't

Capri

trying to give them anymore reason to sit here and ask more questions.

"Alright, move around... all this loitering in front of the store isn't good... if you not getting food... you need to move on," the other officer said, and Rowland quickly rounded the front of the Audi.

"I didn't stutter." The officer looked in my direction.

I couldn't stand a cop that got mad because you weren't scared of them. He expected me to cower and answer him with sir and fear. That shit wasn't me and unless I was breaking the law, I was free to stand here and wait for my food.

"I heard you loud and clear."

He gritted his teeth. "Then why the fuck are you not moving around like the rest of them?"

I stood firm. "Cause I'm getting fucking food, Dick Breath."

The bitch didn't like my response because he got closer to me. We were around the same height as he stared into my face, expecting me to bow down. "You got something you want to say." His ass purposely spit when he spoke to me.

"Yeah... your breath smell like donuts and rotten pussy. Instead of being in my face, head down the block and get you some fucking gum. Kind of partner, are you? I know he been melting the side of your face all damn day."

The other officer turned, and I could see the smirk because he knew what I said was true. "That's it."

He yanked me up and I shoved his ass off me. "Get the fuck off me."

"Resisting arrest... he's resisting arrest." He pulled his billy club out and hit me in the torso, sending me over.

I wasn't stupid and wasn't going to put my hands on him. I peeped Goon say something to Yasin before they did the IG handshake, and Yasin pulled his phone out and started recording.

"Fuck you mean.... yo, stop fucking hitting him like that...

chill out!" Goon yelled while yoking up the officer that was about to swing and hit me again.

"Aye, back the fuck up... back the fuck up."

"Fuck all that shit... he beating his ass with that club and he ain't did shit," Goon shoved the officer and came back over toward where the officer was beating the shit out of me with his stick. I couldn't even see him really, just heard his voice.

All I felt was the back of the damn club hitting me in the back as I fell onto the hood of the car and my arms were pulled behind my back. The other officer slammed Goon across from me and put his hands behind his back.

"Pussy niggas knew we would have given it up if they weren't in they funky ass uniforms." Goon spit. "You know you fucked up, right?"

"We straight, Goon... yo, Sin... call my aunt and pops!" I hollered to him as they shoved me in the back of the police cruiser. "Get my food, too... I'll be out in time to enjoy it."

"I wouldn't count on it." The officer shoved me roughly while slamming the door.

Before he could pull off, another two cars pulled up, and they shoved Goon into the back of another squad car.

I could see Yasin already on the phone already putting out word on what happened.

Chapter 10
Capri

"It makes me sad even coming down here anymore... look at the buildings and all these stores. Capri, there's a damn Apple store and Whole Foods in the middle of downtown Brooklyn!" I listened to Blair become worked up as we waited in line in Juniors.

Ever since Quameer mentioned his favorite cheesecake was Juniors, I was determined to get him a slice. I knew he could get his own slice whenever he wanted, however, I wanted to do something special for him.

He was always doing sweet things for me, so I figured I would do something that he would like for a change. Even as I stood in this line, listening to Blair rant, I couldn't help but to notice this one man off in the corner.

It wasn't out the norm for someone to be standing in Juniors, waiting on their order to be done. Hardly anyone ever ate in the restaurant part of it, so I knew he had to be waiting for an order from the bakery. Some would call me paranoid, and my brothers would say I was on point. While Blair was going on about the men selling incense and buying her dollar doorknockers from the different tables, I watched the man continued to keep an eye on me and Blair as we waited in line.

Jahquel J.

He wasn't paying attention to anyone else that came into the restaurant, just the two of us. I would say he was admiring our beauty; however, I was smarter than that. Three women walked in after us showing a whole lot of ass, so why was his focus on us?

It was so busy they were doing a number system, so when I heard my number, I moved to grab the bag from the lady. "Your lashes are really pretty," she complimented.

"Thank you. Can I have more napkins and plastic forks?" I asked, while pulling my phone out, and getting Aimee's name up on my screen.

She opted to stay in the car since we were only running in to grab the cake. I purposely asked for more napkins and utensils as I watched him in the mirror picture near the register. He was preparing himself to leave right out with us, with no order in his hand.

"Here you go... enjoy your day."

"Thanks... you too."

Blair was still going on, as I pushed her in front of me as we headed out. I turned and noticed he abandoned his post and was making his way through the people in line waiting to place their orders.

"Blair, I'm gonna need you to match my pace... alright?"

"What's going on?" I could hear the hysteria in her voice, and I sighed, wishing one of my sisters were here with me instead of crying ass Blair.

I loved her down, but I needed sis to realize the kind of life that I lived, and that anything could happen. One second, we were driving over the Brooklyn bridge singing out loud, and now we might be in danger.

We walked past the makeshift outside dining as we walked down the block to the car. Soon as I hit her contact's name in my phone, Aimee answered.

"Let me guess... they didn't have the chee—"

Capri

"Think somebody following me, Aimee." I turned and sure enough he was behind us, trying to walk casually like he hadn't followed us out the restaurant.

Had he been following us the entire time? He did walk in after we did, but I brushed it off because so many people loved Juniors. "Tell me what you need me to do."

"Soon as you see us, hop out and let Blair in the back," I replied, wishing I hadn't taken my challenger out today.

"Aye, let me speak to you for a minute," I heard his deep voice, and paused.

"Go to the car, Blair," I replied to her, and she looked at me like I had lost my entire mind, but didn't question me.

"Why the fuck are you following us? We're not interested... move the fuck on." I turned, keeping my hand wrapped around my gun in my purse.

He chuckled, his locs shaking in the process. "I got a whole wife and kids... I don't want you bitches. My boss makes a requests and you know... you should know where I'm heading with this. You take something from us... we return the favor."

"You want me to willingly come with you?" I broke out into laughter in his face. At what point were these niggas ever going to become tired and realize that they couldn't fuck with us?

"If I wanted, I could put a hole right in your head right here." He pulled his gun from behind him, and I froze slightly, before shaking off the feeling.

"Then I'm gonna put one in your head next... wanna play?" I heard Aimee, and noticed she was behind the man. She must have slipped out the car, and came around us as he was busy talking about what he was *gonna* do.

Pussy wasn't going to do shit.

She held her gun, and stood firm, as he turned around, realizing that he could get done the dirtiest and there wasn't shit he could do right now. A Mexican woman nearly choked when she saw Aimee holding out her gun, and quickly rushed down the remainder of the block.

"Oh, you bitches think you tough, huh?"

"Think is an understatement and a little disrespectful." Aimee walked around him; her gun still trained on him.

"Know is more like it," I pulled mine out, as we walked backward back to the car. "Tell your boss I don't really feel like dying today... so thanks, but no thanks." I winked, as my ass hit the back of my car.

He stood there, and then turned to speed walk down the block. "Let's fucking go," Aimee whispered, and hopped in the passenger side.

"Who the fuck was that? Why is it always some shit?" Blair bombarded us with questions soon as our asses got into the car.

We both ignored her as I revved my engine and took off down Dekalb Avenue beeping my horn at traffic once I got onto Bond Street, then Livingston. Who the fuck did we take? And what did that man think he was going to accomplish in busy ass Brooklyn.

"Who the fuck was that?" Aimee asked, sitting her gun in the cup holder and looking behind us, like she was taught.

"I don't know... clearly we must have done something to his boss... that's what I got from talking to him."

A motorcycle pulled up behind us, and I sucked my teeth. I hesitated for a minute, deciding whether I wanted to get caught up in traffic going over the Brooklyn bridge, or just take the Brooklyn-Queens expressway.

Soon as the traffic cleared, I made a sharp left toward the BQE, and watched the motorcycle follow closely behind me. I was a bit rusty, but knew I could get the job done. Cracking my neck, I looked at Blair and she stared back, fear in her eyes.

"I'm already knowing... get down," she sucked her teeth, and got down on the floor while Aimee was already cocking her shit back. Soon as we turned to get onto the BQE, I noticed the mustang behind the motorcycle as I yielded until traffic cleared enough for me to merge onto the expressway.

Once I got the clearance, I took off, zipping in and out of traffic while the motorcycle stayed close behind me. "He's not IG," Aimee took the words out my mouth.

Every God had a small badge of flames on their bike in the same place, and I didn't see one on his. The mustang swerved around the cars until he was right on the side of us, and I merged onto the shoulder, going around a slow-moving Mini Cooper.

"Dammit, Erin," Aimee said, and we both broke out into laughter. I needed that laugh while I pulled Quameer's name up and hit his contact. "My husband. My everything. My world?" Aimee questioned.

"Long story." I sighed, knowing I needed to change his name, and he was going to give me shit for it. Even though this man was knocking the coins out of me, we hadn't told anybody about us just yet. I wanted more time in the world knowing that only we knew about us.

We were heading near Staten Island, and I knew he was out there today. Soon as the call connected, I quickly merged in front of the mustang to the point that he had to stomp on his brakes.

"What up, Sug?" he sounded relaxed.

Knowing him, his ass had probably smoked the biggest spliff and was chilling out. "So, do you happen to know who my brothers killed and why they would want my soul?"

"The fuck?" his voice remained calm.

"I'm on the BQE, about to head toward the Verrazano, and a motorcycle and a mustang are following me."

"They fucking crazy?" It was how calm his voice was with the mix of malice laced within his words. "They touched you?"

"No."

"Swerve now!" Aimee hollered, as I caught the nigga in the mustang pulling his hand out his window about to let off shots.

Soon as he saw me swerve, he pulled his hand back into the window. If he and the nigga on the motorcycle was together, they damn sure wasn't acting like it.

"Oh, niggas stupid fucking with mine," I heard him mutter. "I'm on my way, Sug."

"No... I'm heading your way. How fast can you get to the exit off the Verrazano?"

He laughed. "I'm about to put these niggas through it... come to me, Suga."

"Copy."

Pow! Pow! Pow!

We both ducked down while I switched lanes and avoided the cars frantically swerving. We merged toward the Verrazano bridge sign. The nigga in the motorcycle pulled his gun out and sent bullets into the mustang. "Who the fuck is that? He's shooting at the nigga in the mustang...ain't they together?"

"What?" Aimee turned to look, as he sped up and motioned for us to go ahead of him. "Who the hell is this nigga?"

I didn't know who he was, but it was clear he didn't want any smoke with us. He slowed down in front of the mustang and each time the mustang tried to get around, he would move his bike in front.

While he was doing that, I sped up until I saw that infamous bridge in our view. The motorcycle did his best to keep the mustang back, but when the lanes opened on the bridge, the mustang was back on my ass.

Pulling my gun out on a bridge with all the cameras around was stupid. I hit the button, covering my license plate. My windows were all tinted, so I wasn't worried about anyone seeing inside of the car.

Motorcycle man hung back as the mustang continued to

Capri

ride our ass across the bridge. Quameer's call came through as we went through the tolls.

"Where you at?"

"Taking Hyland Blvd exit... where should I meet you?"

"There's an old motor lodge near the highway... can't miss the shit, Sug. Pull in there... I'm coming down the expressway now."

"Okay."

I rushed past the toll plaza and down Hylan Blvd., while looking out for this motor lodge that he claimed that I couldn't miss. "Right there," Blair pointed out.

I quickly hit a sharp right, and then headed down the street, hitting a U-turn to get on the side where the motel was sitting. The mustang had did the same, and I took a deep breath while I watched Aimee prepare herself.

"You got me, and I got you... we family, Pri." She nodded.

"Shit go left..."

"We bringing that shit back right... never get it twisted." She smiled, as I slowly pulled into the empty parking lot.

It looked abandoned, but I could see the open vacancy sign clear as day. Which told me that someone clearly worked here. I backed into my spot and watched the mustang do the same, opposite of me.

I grabbed my gun, cocking my shit back, while preparing myself for anything. Before he could come to me, me and Aimee both hopped out the car, as he did the same. In the distance, I heard motorcycles and knew my baby was coming.

Homie pulled his gun the same time as we did, and he looked to Aimee, and then back at me. "Capella gonna kill me for not calling him."

"Worry about that after we make it back home."

The same motorcycle came into the parking lot, with Quameer behind it. Meer didn't even let the bike slow down before he dropped that shit on the floor and power walked to homie. Before he could react, he grabbed his ass by the neck and marched him over toward the hood of his car, slamming his head onto the hood.

I could see he was high and heated at the same time. If you knew my Meer, then you knew he hated for anybody to blow his high. He pulled his gun out and pointed it at the nigga on the motorcycle who still had his helmet on.

"Once I'm done with this nigga, I'm gonna get with you next," he said lowly, while slamming the other nigga's head back onto the hood of his own car.

I saw him looking past all of us, and the employee looked at us through the blinds of the office. Meer nodded his head, and he returned a nod before closing the blinds and going about his business.

I figured it had to be a reason he wanted me to meet him here. "Who the fuck sent you?"

He didn't allow him to finish before he walked him over toward one of the first-floor rooms, using his boot to kick the door off the hinges. I watched as he dragged this nigga like he was a rag doll.

Me and Aimee turned our guns on helmet man while slowly backing up toward the room. Helmet man stood there with his arms up. "Keep an eye on him, Aim."

"Got you." She remained trained on him, while I went into the room.

Quameer had this man's head in the toilet while asking him questions. "You must have been doing that good shit to come after my Suga... you don't know she got more than a few niggas that don't play about her.... especially me. I'm a few screws loose behind that one... feel me?"

I blushed while I watched him dunk this man repeatedly. "Yo... I...I can't breathe... Shmurda wants somebody to pay for taking his sons." The man struggled to breathe. "LaLa and

Capri

Cho...Choppa," he gagged because that toilet was disgusting. Was housekeeping on vacation or something?

I could see the murder in Quameer's eyes. "Why this Teletubby ass nigga coming back from the dead and giving more fucking problems." He slammed the man's head into the toilet and then held him in the toilet water while he was kicking his feet.

It was then that I noticed this nigga had lodged towels into the back of the toilet, causing the water to fill in the toilet bowl. He flushed the toilet, causing the water to spill out the toilet. I leaned in the doorway watching him shove him further and further while the man fought with all his might.

Eventually his attempts grew weaker, and he gave up altogether. Quameer felt his neck to confirm he was gone before sliding his fingers across his nose and spitting on the man. He turned toward me.

"You good, meu tudo?"

I nodded my head. "I'm good... I should probably call my brothers."

"You called me... I'm responsible for you."

He pulled me behind him as we exited the room, and he lowered Aimee's gun. "Who the fuck are you? You Daft Punk looking ass nigga."

With his gun in one hand, and holding my hand with the other, he looked at helmet. He was tall, even taller than Quameer, and Meer was already over six feet. We watched as he pulled the helmet from his head, and that's when me and Aimee both gasped at the same time.

"What the fuck is going on?" Quameer was the first to blurt, as we looked at the man standing before us.

The man that stood in front of us resembled both Capone and Cappadonna with a mix of my father. He had a tire mark tattoo tatted on the side of his face, as he looked down at me. Our eyes were the same chocolate brown color.

He had *my* eyes.

"I ain't expect to have to bust my shit while following you today... but I'll protect my sister... it's nothing."

If I didn't think he resembled family before, hearing him call me his sister damn sure confirmed that this man was some kin to me and my family. How though? Did my daddy step out on my mother and have a child behind her back?

"What? I only have two brothers, and they were born at the same time." I removed my hand from Meer, folding them across my chest confused. "Who are you?"

My phone buzzed and I quickly pulled it out my pocket and stared at the screen.

Cappy: *Capella got arrested.*

"Corleone... Desmond and Jean are my parents." My head shot up from replying to Cappy when I heard the words leave his mouth.

Chapter 11
Corleon 'Cor' Bruster

Two years ago...

Moms coughed, catching the blood that spewed from her lips with the napkin she kept clutched in her hands. I watched as she winced while trying to make herself more comfortable. In the hospital bed, she looked so small and child-like. The massive hospital bed swallowed her up, and the shit fucked with me because I wasn't used to her being like this.

"I don't like when you're quiet, Core," she whispered while looking at me sitting in the corner.

I shrugged. "Ma, what you want me to do? Start talking a bunch... I don't feel like talking."

Even as a grown man, seeing my mother in this hospital bed did something to me. It made me feel like I was a child again, and I didn't like it. Especially knowing that I was losing her as each day passed by. No matter how much money I made, nothing could pay or save her life.

"I'm always going to be looking over you. The thought of leaving you down here alone makes this worse for me."

Jahquel J.

"It's just like you to be worried about me when I'm supposed to be worried about you."

She smiled sheepishly while shrugging her frail shoulders. "I'm your mama and I'm always gonna worry about you. It's always been just me and you, Crumb snatcher."

She grabbed the oxygen and placed it over her face and inhaled while laying her head back. Abandoning my seat, I walked over toward her side and took a seat. "Relax. All that talking isn't good for you."

"I...I... have to talk to you about something, Core."

From the way she stared up into my eyes, I knew she had to get this out. "Go slow and use your oxygen when you need it."

She nodded and took one more breath in before removing it from her face. "Core, remember when I told you that you were given to me special?"

"Yeah. I remember. I'm old enough to know how I really got here." I smirked, and she pinched me. Her pinches used to straighten me right up.

Now I could barely feel it because she didn't have the energy to give me one of her infamous pinches. "I've lied to you, Core."

My heart rate increased as the tears slid down her face. "What you mean?"

"I love you, Corleon. Being your mother has saved me in more ways and made me realize that you were meant to be my son."

"Ma, you saying a lot of nothing." I held her hand while she got more oxygen.

With how impatient I was to know what she was gonna say, I was about to give her some of mine. "I adopted you when you were a few weeks old. It was a private and closed adoption between me and a good friend."

"The fuck?"

She held onto my hand as tight as she could, to avoid me

Capri

getting up. "I want you to know that you aren't in this world alone after I'm gone, Corleon."

"I am in this world alone... I don't know those fucking people."

She held my hand close to her chest and smiled. "They're good people, Core... I want you to reach out to them if you need them."

"How could you keep that from me?"

She sighed. "I didn't think I would be in heart failure at sixty years old. Core, I planned to take this to the grave. I can't help but to feel like I'm letting you down by dying... I'm supposed to be your mama forever. Since I can't be... I need you to know your biological family, promise me you will."

I couldn't make any promises because I was still processing all of this shit. Not once did I ever think I was adopted or none of that shit. My mother had always been my mama, and my pops wasn't a factor. Moms always told me that I was so special that I only needed one mama to love me.

Linda Bruster was a force to be fucked with. She worked in IT and busted her ass to provide for me. I attended the best private school, and we lived in a nice condo in Park Slope. Every morning, she made the drive to my private school in Staten Island because it was the best in the state. From there, she drove to Jersey to her job, and we repeated the process every damn day.

I never lacked for anything because my mother was a go getter that made it happen. Every night when she brought her work home, which she usually did, she would teach me things about what she did. Moms was smart as shit, and that was all she wanted for me. She taught me to use my street smarts with my book smarts.

"What's their names?"

"Jean and Desmond Delgato," she went into a coughing fit while struggling to breathe, the nurse came in to sit her bed up and turn up the oxygen.

Jahquel J.

"Linda, you have to rest now," the nurse said as she pulled the blankets up on my mother.

I kissed my mother on the forehead. "Rest, Ma. I'll be back up here tomorrow."

She smiled and hugged me as tight as she could around my neck. "Love you more than you know my sweet Core."

Little did I know that was the last time I would hear those words from my mother. She died through the night, and I got the call in the morning that she was gone. She wasn't just a piece of me, she was my entire heart, and it was broken with that phone call.

As I stared into my sister's eyes as she held her phone in her hand. She was in shock, and the shock wasn't just with her ass. I was in shock because it was like staring at a younger version of my mother. She resembled the picture I had found in my mother's belongings when I had to pack up her condo.

It was a box of a bunch of letters and things that she had been saving. The picture was of a young couple on a beach, and it was noted *Barbados '89*. I couldn't help but see what I saw in that picture in the woman standing in front of me.

My sister looked just like her, as she stared back into my eyes unsure of what to say or do. Shit, I didn't know what to do and had thought about this day since I found out two years ago.

"I...I can't deal with this right now. Um, can we exchange numbers? I really have to go," she stammered, torn between standing here with me and dealing with the situation she had been called about.

"Yeah." She handed me her phone and I programmed my cell phone number into it and handed it back to her.

Soon as I handed her back the phone, it started to ring, and she answered. "I promise I'm going to reach out... I just need to handle this."

"No pressure or rush, just hit me whenever you have the time."

The nigga that just went ape shit had calmed down and looked over at me. "Good looks on holding her down... even though yo' weird ass was following her, too."

I laughed. "Don't even mention it."

He stood by his bike for a minute and waited for her to whip out, and then he followed behind her. I stood there for a second, then decided to get the fuck up out of here since I knew he just bodied that nigga he dragged in there.

Chapter 12
Quameer

"What do you mean you can't locate where they bought them?" Capri screamed into the phone as she paced back and forth in front of me and Yasin.

He was sitting on his bike waiting for the word. As we were leaving, Quasim called me and told me that they scooped Goon too. The shit that worried me was that Goon was on parole, so any situation could land his ass back going up top, and nobody wanted that shit.

"What exactly happened, Sin?" Quasim asked, as he came out of the bar, and leaned on his own bike.

Cappadonna was on his way since he and Alaia were all the way at the lake house when he got the call. I just knew that man was tearing up the highway to get all the way over here.

"He went to press Aimee's cousin or some shit, and the cops came over doing they usual shit... minding everybody else fucking business. That cop had a hard on for him when he saw he wasn't scared of him. Nigga started beating on him and Goon stepped up, and I recorded the shit." He fished in his pocket and showed me the footage.

Chubs was getting hit and wasn't even fighting back. He was eating them hits and it seemed like it was pissing the officer off even more. Each time Chubs didn't react, he would come down with that club harder than the last time.

That was when Goon walked up on him, and the other officer intervened. I handed Sin back his phone and shook my head because that shit pissed me off. I had respect for cops that deserved the respect. These niggas were fucking chumps that got picked on in school and decided a uniform was going to make people respect them.

"Listen to me and listen to me very fucking clear. One of my good friends writes for the *New York Times*. Unless you want the NYPD to be written up for losing two Black men, I suggest you track 'em down and tell me where my clients are now!" Capri screamed into the phone, spit flying from her mouth.

We all just stared at her and said nothing because I ain't never seen her that way. Shit lowkey turned me on, but it wasn't the time for all of that. Plus, she wanted to keep things on the low. I guess she was worried about her brothers finding out. Capri ended the call with whoever she was talking to, and then called someone else, walking further away to have the conversation.

I heard the sound of Cappadonna's engine before I saw him. He pulled up, hopped out and went over to open the door for Alaia. She rushed over toward Capri, while he came over to us.

"The fuck happened, Sin."

Sin didn't bother to explain what happened; he handed Capp the phone with the recording on it. I watched Capp's face take on every emotion there was before he handed Yasin his phone back with his hands shaking.

"Capri trying to figure out where they took them now... they giving her the run around." I filled him in before he could ask the next question.

"Goon on fucking parole... they could violate him for some

shit like this," Capp replied, put his hand on his head and paced in front of us.

I noticed Alaia and Capri walking back over toward us. "My friend is going to represent Goon. We attended college and then law school together, and she's actually a criminal defense lawy—" her words were cut short when her phone rang. "Yeah... oh what do you know... well, I will be there to see my client...uh huh...why? Whatever... I'll be there soon." She ended the call.

"What happened, Baby Doll?"

She sighed. "They took them to two different precincts... I'm going to go to Capella, and I'll send my friend Zoya to Goon. Obviously, they're not getting out until they see a judge. I know I can get Capella home the same day as seeing a judge, but I'm not sure about Goon, which is why I called Zoya."

Capp kissed her on the forehead. "Appreciate you, Baby Doll."

She smiled and looked up at him. "Let me go and see if he's good... because this is a lawsuit. They beat him and he wasn't resisting or anything."

Capp held his hand up. "No lawsuit... too much exposure. Let us handle this how we know how. Get those badge numbers for me, Baby Doll."

Capri smirked. "Got you."

"Yo Capri, text me where he at... I'll meet the lawyer to make sure she's handled."

She nodded before double backing and looking at her brother. "We need to talk, Cappy." It was like she just remembered that we met that nigga that claimed to be her brother.

"The fuck happened, Baby Doll," Capp became even more concerned.

She rushed over toward her car with Aimee behind her. "After I handle all of this, me, you, and Capone need to talk... it's serious."

Capri

"You can't tell me some shit like that and think I'm not gonna be fucking concerned, Capri." Capp didn't ever use Capri's real name. She was always Baby Doll to him, so I knew he was worried.

"You want your son out of jail, right? Let me handle this and then we can discuss that. I'll call you soon as I get to him."

Cappadonna realized that the ball was in his sister's court. He was used to him and Capone running the show, and now they had to sit back and allow their baby sister to handle business. They had no place in Capri's world. If they knew better, they would stay the fuck away from Capri's world.

"I'm gonna follow behind her... Sim, you straight?"

He saluted as he and Yasin took off and headed to where Goon was. Capri started her car and quickly pulled off, while I followed behind her.

"Good looks, Quameer," he nodded his head. I nodded and continued to follow behind her, as she increased speed to where they were holding Chubs.

I sat outside the precinct feeling uncomfortable as shit. Every time a cop walked past, they had to do a double take, as if they wanted to ask me something. Still, I leaned on my bike waiting for my baby to come out.

This whole shit was bullshit anyway.

She had been in there for at least an hour and the sun was starting to set. My phone pulled me from my thoughts. Quasim's name popped up on the screen, and I slid my finger across the screen and answered.

"Yo."

"Yeah. Goon got court tomorrow with Chubs... he gotta sit tonight, but they talking a bunch of bullshit about him trying to fight an officer and shit." Sim sucked his teeth, pissed that this was actually our reality.

"Bullshit... we saw the video."

He sighed. "Yeah... Pri's friend is a shark though. Came in

and had those niggas shook...she said she can probably get him released tomorrow... gotta wait until tomorrow."

"Bet."

"What's going on over that way?"

"Waiting on Suga now... she probably in there going off on them."

Quasim laughed. "If she anything like Zoya, he def gonna be sitting comfortable tonight... I'll see you tomorrow at court."

"Bet... later."

"Later."

Just as I was ending the call, Aimee came out the precinct first. I could tell from her face that she was frustrated and wanted Chubs home tonight.

"This is all bullshit, you know that, right? If I could fucking hack their system, I would fucking... I don't even know, but if I could."

"Why don't you?"

"Um, 'cause this is the NYPD."

"So, you were able to hack into a prison, but not a simple ass precinct?" I stared down at her confused.

She sighed, as if she was about to break it down to some simple person. "That was a low budget state prison. This is the NYPD...do you know how rock solid their systems are? I wouldn't even attempt it because then I'll end up in the next cell from my man."

I chuckled, which caused her to smile. "He good in there?"

"You know Capella, he's going to be good anywhere. I'm just hoping that he's able to be released tomorrow."

We both turned to see Capri coming down the steps on her phone. "Girl, they got me fucked up. Zoy, I don't know... you do this all day... alright, alright, okay. Call me in the morning. Thank you again... did Quasim pay you? Girl, take the money... alright... have a good night." She ended the call and looked at me.

Capri

"Everything straight?"

She took a deep sigh. "He has fucking bruises all over his torso, and they got him in his face, too."

"Oh, somebody dying," I mumbled.

If I knew one thing, I knew that the minute Cappadonna saw his son's face, he was gonna go crazy. I prayed Alaia ain't have no shit to do tomorrow because she was the only one that could control his ass when he got to that point.

"Yeah, my thoughts exactly. Then the whole brother shit... my mind is all over... just tired and wanna go home."

I pulled her closer to me, and Aimee looked at us both. "Um, am I missing something between you two?"

"This my little *yeah don't get a nigga killed*."

Aimee laughed. "Quameer, you know the saying is my little *yeah yeah*, right?"

Capri leaned her head on my shoulder. "No, he means exactly what he said... Aim, keep this between us, please."

"My mouth is shut... I don't speak on nobody's business." She leaned against Capri's car and looked at the precinct. "You know, I haven't slept without him in a long time... don't even know if I can sleep tonight knowing he isn't beside me."

"You can spend the night at my house so we're closer to court." Capri looked over at her, as she continued to lean on me.

"I get the same invitation?" I whispered into her ear before kissing it.

The way her body physically reacted told me all I needed to know. It never got old seeing the way she would shutter, and the goosebumps would form when I was near her. Had that shit always happened, and I just never paid attention?

I knew Capri had me wrapped around her fingers, because that was the shit that kept me awake at night. It mattered to me if Capri Delgato thought I was fucking cool. Anybody else in the world didn't matter, but her, it mattered to me what she thought about me.

"You gonna follow us back?"

"Already know... you tired, Sug."

She smiled. "I got you cheesecake."

I cocked my head to the side. "What you mean?"

"Well, that was how we ended up being followed. I was at Juniors getting you cheesecake... Peach said it was your favorite."

"It's not my birthday though." I smiled while rubbing her cheek and watching her blush while staring into my eyes.

"Nobody should have to wait until their birthday to eat their favorite cake, Meer." She smiled as she walked backward to her car.

Suga didn't understand the hold she had over my heart. Her ass had me smirking and shit in front of this precinct like a teenage boy that just got a date with the popular girl at school. I watched as she and Aimee got into the car, and I got on my bike and rolled out behind them.

To be closer to court, Capp and Alaia were going to stay at their house instead of going back to the lake house. Aimee told Capri to drop her there, and she would ride with Capp in the morning. I followed Suga back to her house and waited for her to pull into her garage before backing my bike in behind her.

Just by looking at her I could tell that she was stressed and inside of her head. While she sat her purse down and washed her hands, I leaned in the doorway watching her. Although she was quiet, her mind was loud. I could hear the shit way over here because her silence was so damn loud.

"Sug," I called.

She finally lifted her head from the water rushing over her hands. "Hmm?"

"Come here." I held my arms open, and she came over and

Capri

hugged me tightly. Her wet hands, wetting the back of my shirt. "Tell me what's on your mind?"

She sighed into my chest. "Zoya has gone in front of a judge. She has done this a bunch of times... not me. I have never gone in front of a judge, and this is my first time doing it. What if I mess up... end up getting him twenty years in prison."

I laughed because she was wild. "Get out your head. Just because you've never done it before doesn't mean you won't be great at it. Every lawyer that will be in that courtroom tomorrow had a first time... feel me?"

She stared up into my eyes. "Yeah."

"I know the passionate Capri who won't let someone fuck over her family. You got that shit in you, and I saw it in action plenty of times... channel that... the legal way." I winked as I kissed her lips.

"Meer?"

"Hmm?"

"I honestly don't know what I would do without you... thank you for always being there for me."

I kissed the top of her head. "You don't ever have to thank me, Sug. I'm here and I'm always gonna be here."

"Until I ruin it," she mumbled, and I removed her from my chest and looked into her eyes. "Can we not get into some deep conversation about what I said."

"I'll give you that." I paused. "You can't ruin something that is meant for you. I'm meant for you... I don't care how much you feel you're not worth being loved, you are, Suga."

She nodded her head. "Okay."

"Go take a shower and I'm gonna order us something to eat since I know you don't have food in the crib."

My chest hurt every time Capri looked at me with those eyes, and felt she didn't deserve to be loved the right way. It wasn't as much as that she didn't believe she was worthy; she was scared. Capri was scared to put her heart in someone else's hands because of how shit ended with both Naheim and Kincaid.

It wasn't as much as Kincaid because their shit was mutual. Suga knew she couldn't see forever with him, and Kincaid knew the same. I didn't respect him for sliding into that situation knowing what she was dealing with. He knew Naheim was out there fucking every damn body and should have separated himself from Capri when he noticed she was becoming closer to him.

She just wanted to feel love, and it didn't matter where that shit came from. Capri was willing to take it from anybody that was willing to give it or pretend to give it. Her past decisions constantly tainted her future because she felt like she shouldn't have that happily ever after and that shit was so far from the truth.

When she came downstairs, I was laid out on the couch watching the news. I ain't have to worry about homie at the motel because the cleanup crew probably already came through and handled that situation for me.

"There is a million and one things that you could be watching, and you choose the news," Capri smiled.

Her hair was curly and wet, and she wore my oversized bike fest T-shirt from an event we had thrown last year. Her nipples were hardened, making my mouth moist. I wanted to put each one in my mouth and remove everything that was going through her head.

Whenever Capri was getting dick, I could tell her mind was blank. She wasn't worried about nothing else. She was focused on feeling good – focused on *me* making her feel good. It was the minute we both came that I saw the thoughts piling back into her head again.

"Gotta stay up on current events." I removed my feet from the couch and tapped the spot next to me. She plopped down while looking at the reporter covering a

Capri

strike that was about to happen with union workers in the city.

"How could I have another brother that I didn't know about?" she blurted, still looking straight ahead at the TV.

I doubted her ass was even retaining information, just staring at the screen while thinking about the man who introduced himself as her brother. "Shit is wild, Suga. I usually call bullshit on a lot of things, but that nigga look like a mix of your father, Capo, and Capp."

It wasn't like I could deny the shit when it was right in front of my face. "I'm so confused because he mentioned both my mother and father's name. I could make sense of things if he mentioned only my father's name... maybe he was out there messing around and had a child. But to mention my mother's name is something different, Meer."

I pulled her over into my arms and she cuddled closer to me. "Only two people can give you the answer to that question. You gotta talk to your parents, Sug."

"A question that I don't even feel right asking them. Not without at least telling my brothers what the hell is going on."

"How you think they gonna take the news?"

She sighed while shrugging her shoulders. "Honestly, I don't even know... a sibling we never knew about. The fact that my parents hid it from us is another thing."

I recognized that she was becoming overwhelmed, so I pulled her onto my lap and started to kiss her neck while she released soft moans. "I think you need to be fucked, Sug."

"I do." She kissed the side of my face and held me around the neck.

That was all I needed to hear as I pulled the shirt up over her head. Her breast sat there perfectly on her chest, staring at me, begging me to suck them while biting them in the process.

"Sug, you know I respect you... right?"

"Yes... I know," she continued to kiss on my neck.

I smirked. "I'm about to fuck you like I don't... ight?"

Capri smirked as she nodded her head slowly, ready for me to put her through it. As much as I wanted to make slow love to her, she didn't need that. All that would do is have her inside her head more.

She needed to be fucked – hard.

Even while still on my lap, I got up from the couch. Suga wrapped her legs around me, as she continued to kiss on my neck, making my dick even harder.

"INY, Meer," she said in-between kisses on my jaw.

I gripped a handful of her ass while crossing the living room into the kitchen. "Don't worry, Sug... I'm about to take care of you right now."

There was no way I was gonna make it upstairs with the way my dick was fighting through my pants. She needed this, and from the soft whimpers, I needed to give it to her to quiet her mind even for a second.

"Meer, this is the kitchen," she moaned out, as I put her down onto the floor.

Biting down on my lip, I spun her ass around and bent her down over the kitchen table. "Arch that fucking back, Sug," I demanded as I held the back of her neck while I loosened my pants and allowed them to drop to the floor.

Capri was nearly on the end of the kitchen table anticipating the dick I was about to give her. I held her waist, slapping her ass hard while pulling her ass apart and slamming my dick into her.

"Me...Meer!" she squealed as she held her head back, and I wrapped her curly tresses around my fist and yanked her head back.

"This is what you wanted, right? Use your words, Sug... tell Pa when you want *your* dick." I said through clenched teeth as I slammed her back onto my dick.

Capri was running so much that I had to hold her in place,

Capri

while moving the entire table where I was. "Baby...ohhh... Meeerrr," she cooed.

"Tell me you wanted this dick, Big mama... tell Big Pa what you wanted." I pulled her head back and sucked on her neck while beating this pussy from behind.

By the time I was done that shit was gonna be swollen from the way I slammed it back onto my dick.

Capri had tears coming down her eyes while staring me in the eyes. "I want your dick, Big Pa... I want it all the time!" she screamed out.

"Suba na mesa, querido, Suga!" I demanded, pulling her head back so she could look into my eyes.

"Baby... what... I... don't know." She continued to try and grip the marble on the kitchen table.

Pinching her hips, I pulled her back harder each time. "Say sim, grande pai," I coached her, as the curls in her hair quickly replaced the water with sweat.

Every time I crashed into her; her ass jiggled which made me continue to do it while licking my lips.

"I...I..."

"Get the fuck on the table and toot that ass up, Sug!" I growled, while helping her up onto the table, pulling the table even closer to us, as my dick found its way back inside of her warmth and tightness.

"Like this, Pai?" she said Pa in Portuguese, and the shit turned me into something else.

Reaching around her, I pulled on her breast as I fucked her from behind. All that could be heard was her screaming and my grunting.

"Just like that, Baby... toss that ass back... you know you pressure right?" I pinched her nipples while she whined out in pleasure. "Fucking answer, me, Capri!" I demanded.

"Yes... ye...Meer," she stammered.

"Say it to me, mama... I need to hear you say it."

Capri moaned while palming the kitchen table, unable to take it anymore. "I'm...pr.... pressure, baby."

I quickly flipped her around and slid back into her, while she stared me in the eyes, wrapping her legs around me. "That's what I wanna hear... damn, Suga... why you so fucking wet? You wet for me?" I smirked, knowing that was the exact reason she was so wet.

She nodded her head while biting down on her lips. "F...for you, Meer... only you."

I stroked her neck before applying slight pressure. "That's what I wanna hear... this pussy is only mine. When you out there, you a reflection of me... mine." I sucked on her lower lip. "You taking this shit so good, mama... look at how that shit stretching for me." I looked down to witness the beautiful site.

I don't know why the fuck I did that because that shit made my dick jump, and I could feel everything rushing to the head. "Can I cum, Pa, please?" Capri kissed my jaw while I continued to stroke her slowly, slowing my pace down.

"Cum for me, mama," I shoved my tongue down her throat, as I mounted her ass down on the kitchen table.

Capri locked her legs around me and started throwing that pussy on me while I continued to suck on her tongue. When I was about to cum, I broke our kiss, holding her leg up, and slamming into her until I exploded.

"Meer..." she said breathlessly, while I was celebrating the victory of quieting her mind for a few minutes.

"Yes, mama?" I rested on top of her while kissing on her neck.

She held me around the neck tighter. "Thank you... I needed that."

Chuckling, I kissed her neck before leaning up. "I know when my baby need to get fucked and when you need to be stroked slowly... I know you, Suga. You never had a nigga that knew you so this shit feel foreign to you."

Capri

Capri looked up at me with that beautiful ass smile on her face. "You don't even know me like that... relax."

"I know you don't need to figure everything out tonight. Being real, you don't have to figure shit out. This isn't your mess or problem to fix, Sug. You gotta stop trying to fix everything... have the conversation with your brothers because they need to know, then go from there."

She gave me a weak smile as she held the side of my face and kissed my lips. "You have good advice when you ain't acting crazy."

"I'm perfectly sane, Sug... just don't do some shit where I have to show you just how insane I can get." I gave her a quick peck on the lips before moving from her to grab the food from the front.

"My trunk, Meer."

"That was light work, Suga... you gotta realize what kind of nigga you fucking with. I know one thing, your friend gonna be tossing that ball from a wheelchair if I see you with him again."

She sat on the table staring at me, and probably wondering what she had got herself into. Then as the smirk came across her face, she knew exactly what she had gotten herself into.

Capri wasn't a fool.

"SEE YOU IN A LITTLE BIT, SUGA." I KISSED CAPRI'S LIPS A few times while she was in the shower and then headed out.

I was meeting her at the courthouse, so I needed to go home to shower and shit. From how quiet she was, I could tell her mind was on a million different things and there wasn't shit that I could do about it. That was how I felt when it came to Capri though. I always wanted to take everything away from her. Those nights we would sit up on facetime drinking, and she would start crying, my chest always felt like it was about to cave in because I was thousands of miles away and couldn't do shit about it.

I couldn't fix her problems because she had to go through them so she could grow through it all. As hard as it was for her to leave, she needed to do it so she could come into her own. The Capri that I knew now wasn't the same woman that was sitting in the backyard of *Fern* with me.

As I pulled my bike out her garage, Brandi called, and I hesitated on answering. The only reason I answered was because she had my daughter. Had Peach been with me, I wouldn't have answered shit for her.

"Yeah," I answered, as I sat on my bike in front of Capri's crib, while waiting for Brandi to get to the damn point. She was always taking forever to get to the damn point whenever she called.

"Why in the fuck did you think it was a good idea to take my daughter to Capri Delgato's lake house for the weekend? Do you honestly think that's okay, Quameer? You didn't call or talk to me about it."

"I'm a grown ass man, and last I checked I'm her father... I can bring her to the fucking moon if I want. As long as she's safe, there's nothing to worry about."

I guess I should have known that Peach would tell her mother about the lake house. When we left, she was so excited, and it was all she could talk about. It wasn't her fault, and I damn sure wasn't hiding it from Brandi. It wasn't her business what I did with Peach when she was with me. It wasn't like she ran everything down to me before she did the shit.

"I'm her fucking mother, Quameer. You should have told me you were bringing her around your girlfriend."

"Who said she was my girlfriend though? I know Peach didn't tell you that because she already knows what it is between me and Capri."

Neither me or Capri came right out and said we were

Capri

together. All I knew is that nobody better had been sliding into her besides me. If she wanted to keep this shit on the low, I was going to allow the shit to happen.

Even though I had our family's blessing, I wasn't trying to rush her into something just because I was ready. Capri wanted to keep things between us, and I was going to respect her wishes.

"You don't go spend the weekend at some random chick's house with my daughter and she's not your girlfriend... I know you, Quameer."

"Shit, it's clear that you don't know me. Did Ryder come back hurt or something?"

"No."

"Swimmer's ear or something like that?"

"N...No," she stammered, confused on why I was asking the following questions about our daughter.

"Anybody put their hands on her? She didn't get hurt or anything, right?"

She sighed. "No, Quameer. She had a lot of fun and loves Capri... go figure."

I put the phone to my mouth. "Then mind yo' big headed fucking business, Brandi. Whoever I'm with or not with isn't your fucking concern. You don't run shit by me when Ryder is with you, and I allow you and that fat bitch of a husband to breathe, right?"

"Wh...what is that supposed to mean?"

"It means, don't fucking question me. When I got something to announce, then you'll be the last bitch to know about it. I'll have my daughter relay the message to you." I ended the call, shoving my phone into my pocket and starting my bike. Her little ten-minute call set me back.

Brandi wanted to know everything I had going on when it came to me. When it came to her, she didn't feel the need to fill me in on shit that was going on. Like when she went to Cabo with her girls and allowed her husband to take our daughter to the Jersey Shore for spring break last year.

When Ryder called me crying because she felt out of place with his family, I got on the next flight and went to get my daughter. Took her ass right off the beach while the family was having a ball, while Ryder was sitting there bored.

It wasn't nothing wrong with Brandi's husband, and Ryder did love her stepfather, she just couldn't vibe with his family, and being as the nigga happened to be back at their shore house working, it didn't make sense for her to be there anyway.

He understood where I was coming from, and I took Ryder home that same day without having to shove my gun in that nigga's mouth. I think he knew more than his wife that there was no limits to where I would go.

It took me nearly an hour to make it to Brooklyn to the courthouse. I parked in a nearby parking lot, and quickly made it inside the courthouse. As I was grabbing my keys from the plastic bins, I spotted Cappadonna standing with Alaia and Aimee outside the courtroom.

"Morning," I said as I walked up on them.

Capp dapped me up. "What up?"

"When is the judge supposed to see them?" I asked, as I leaned on the wall next to where we were all standing.

"Baby Doll and her lawyer friend went back there a little while ago. I came out here because courthouses make me itchy and anxious. Can't sit comfortably up in this bitch. Last time I came in a courthouse, I was saying goodbye to my family before being sentenced and shipped up top."

"I feel you... Chubs got you running through his ass, so you know he's good. This shit a drop in the bucket."

As he was about to say something, we turned when we heard heels stomping against the marble floors. I turned and that's when my tongue damn near rolled out my mouth onto the floor. Capri was talking to some White man in a suit as they

Capri

walked, she walked right by us as they continued talking and I didn't even mind.

The way I was eye fucking her in this hallway should have been illegal. She wore a black dress with black tights, and the highest pair of Louboutin's I had seen, and she was walking in them with ease. In her left arm she held documents, and the right held her Croc Birken bag.

The houndstooth jacket she wore over the black dress had her looking like a sexy Jackie Kennedy. Her Chanel earrings jingled, along with her ass with each step that she took. She was in her element, confident and knew what the fuck was expected of her.

"Oh shit... I'm almost stepped on your tongue," Alaia's smart ass said, pulling me from watching my Suga handle business.

Nothing turned me on more than a woman that handled her fucking business. I wanted to pull that skirt up, rip those tights down and give her something right here and now. "You been hanging with your husband too much." I chuckled.

Capri finished the conversation and then made her way over toward us. Her signature scent tickled my nose as she stood in front of her brother. Even with her highest heels on, we were both still taller than her, especially Capp's big ass.

"He's going to go before the judge, and he will be released straight from here. I'm not having him plead guilty, so we'll have to come back to court in a few months... I told them we had video footage, so I see them dropping the charges before the next court date."

Capp held her face and kissed her on the forehead. "You a fucking beast, Baby Doll."

"I wouldn't say all of that," she downplayed herself.

"Aye, I told you about doing that... you did this shit. Pat yourself on the back because we're proud of you."

"Thanks, Meer." She turned and smiled when she saw

someone. "Zoya!" Capri waved the brown skin plus sized woman over.

She strutted over in heels just as high as Capri, and a navy two-piece skirt set. I couldn't front like she didn't scream she was about that business. Her hair was pulled up in a claw clip, and her purse rested in the crook of her arm.

"Hey. I was about to call and see where you went. Last I saw, you were talking with Henderson."

Capri rolled her eyes. "He was too busy eye fucking me to pay attention to anything I was saying."

"He was what?" I blurted.

"Meer, focus." She discreetly pulled on my pants, and I chilled out while taking note of that man she was walking with.

"Ugh, he's such a creep, but that works out for us."

"Oh yeah...how?" Capp said.

Zoya looked from Capri to Capp. "Big brother?" she smiled.

Alaia took her place beside her husband, and Zoya realized that big brother had a crazy fucking wife. "Zoya, this is my brother, Cappadonna, and my sister, his wife, Alaia," Capri quickly introduced her to Cappadonna and Alaia.

"Nice to meet you... I don't want any problems," she winked at Alaia.

Alaia smiled. "There wouldn't have been any... right, baby?" She stared up into her husband's eyes.

"Never."

"I hear that," Zoya laughed. "So, Goon is going to be released today with Capella... soon as they go before the judge, they will get another court date and then they're free to go."

"Thank you again for doing this for me. I know you're super busy and have a bunch of shit to do." Capri hugged her.

"Girl, anytime... how many times have you saved my ass back in law school?" Zoya smiled, hugging Capri once more.

Capri

"Let's get back in there and hope we're able to get out of here before my wax appointment."

"Seriously, Zoy. I appreciate you doing this for me. I know Jesse has you doing a ton of things."

"Girl, you know she does," she groaned, as I held the door opened and she walked in and took a seat at the front.

While everyone filed in, I pulled Capri back. "You look good as shit, Suga."

She smiled and nuzzled her face against my beard. "Thank you, Meer... now make sure you behave yourself."

"Mr. Henderson gonna have to see me."

"Quameer," she whispered as she walked toward the front where Zoya was already seated awaiting for Chubs and Goon to be brought out.

I sat down in the back row watching people being brought in front of the judge. Most of the cases was some kind of substance abuse cases or a driving under the influence. Each time, the judge seemed to get more annoyed by the second.

Shit, I couldn't even front because I was becoming bored my damn self. Quasim whisked past me, and I did our signature low whistle, and he followed the sound until he noticed me. I scooted over and allowed him to sit at the end.

"My bad. I fucking overslept this morning and then traffic getting into Brooklyn was crazy," he whispered.

"Goon is being released from here. She said it's up to his parole officer to violate him," I clued his late ass in.

Sim nodded his head. "Shouldn't be a problem... he's fucking his probation officer."

"The fuck?"

"Yeah. Told his ass he shouldn't have went down that rabbit hole, but you know Goon... nigga don't never listen."

"Fuck you meannnnn," I snorted.

Quasim shook his head while smirking. "Stupid ass."

Jahquel J.

They called both Chubs and Goon's name. The bailiffs brought them out and I could tell they both were pissed.

> Water head: we're not done with the conversation from earlier.

> Me: stop playing on my phone before I beat your husband up.

> Water head: Quameer, seriously?

When I looked up the bailiffs were taking the cuffs from both Goon and Chubs and allowing them to go with their lawyers. I peeped how Goon kept looking at Zoya while she spoke to the judge.

"This nigga is fucking her with his eyes in front of the judge. He gonna lick his lips off his face with the amount of times he done licked them," Sim whispered.

The judge agreed to release them on ROR, and we were free to get the fuck up out of here. Capp was the first person to greet his son. He hugged him, and then looked at his face, making a knowing nod to Quasim, as we all filed out the courtroom.

Aimee was tied to her man's side, not wanting to let him go. "Aim, I was gone for the night... you missed me that bad," he laughed, as he pulled her close and kissed her on the lips.

"It felt like ten weeks," Aimee's dramatic ass said, as she hugged him around the neck, not wanting to let him go.

"Aimee, you dramatic as shit," Capp replied. "Let's get the fuck up out of here... I'm about to break out in hives and shit."

"Capri, you riding with us?" Alaia asked.

"I got her," I replied, and she smiled.

"We're heading back to the lake house. Try and make it there without getting arrested again." Capp smirked, nudging his son before taking his wife's hand and leaving out the courthouse.

Capri

Chubs came over and hugged his aunt. "Thanks, Pri... always coming through for me." He kissed her forehead.

"You never have to thank me, Sugar Plum," she smiled up at him, and then pinched Aimee's cheek.

"How the fuck we getting home?" Chubs looked over at Aimee.

"I drove your truck, and Capri rode in with me," Aimee explained, as she took her man's hand and they headed out.

Goon and Zoya were over in the corner having a conversation. It was professional on Zoya's end, but Goon looked like he was ready to fuck the two-piece skirt suit off her body. "Yo Gerald, we out," I said, using his real name.

"Aye Meer?"

"What up?"

"Fuck ya." He stuck his middle finger back up, then continued his conversation with Zoya, and I shook my head.

As we walked to the lot where I parked, I held Capri's hand. "Goon look like he want your friend, Suga."

"Zoya has a strict rule about not dating any of her clients so that's not gonna happen." She held onto the handle of my truck and rotated her ankle. "Walking around that damn courthouse all morning has my feet killing me."

I hit the locks and opened the door. Before she could attempt to climb up, I picked her up and sat her in the passenger seat. Taking her foot in my hand, I removed the heels from her feet and kissed the top of each foot.

She giggled as I kissed each foot. "Sexy ass feet."

"Meer, let me find out you got a foot fetish."

"I do."

She looked at me and waited for me to laugh. "You don't have a foot fetish."

"Suga, for your feet... I fucking do. I need you to paint them red and then we'll be good." I continued to caress her feet in this parking lot.

The attendant was staring at us, waiting for us to move so he could go ahead and rent the spot out to the next sucka who didn't have no other choice but to pay his overpriced lot fees.

"Hmm, you gotta pay for them to be putting in color request. I always keep white on my toes," she wiggled them in my face, and I bit her big toe. "Meer!"

"Stop wiggling them if you don't want me to suck 'em, Suga." I finally left her feet alone, and closed the door, walking around to hop in my truck.

She leaned back in the chair, crossing her legs.

"I am so tired... I tossed and turned all night."

"I know... kept tossing that ass on me like you wanted me to handle it again," I smirked, as she rolled her eyes and avoided looking at me.

I whipped out the lot and onto the street. "Close your eyes and take a quick nap."

She was scrolling on her phone. "I need to go over this packing list so I can finish packing for this trip. I am not looking forward to this trip at all," she groaned.

"Doesn't seem like Zoya is either... why the fuck are you going then?"

She turned in her seat. "Even if I explained it to you, you wouldn't understand it. It's a girl thing."

"Oh yeah? Do Jesse return that same girl code bullshit?"

"It's not bullshit," she muttered.

"Answer the question, Sug?"

She let the seat back and pretended to get some rest. "Meer, she's my friend and I have to celebrate her."

"It's less about celebrating her and her returning that favor. Do she celebrate you, Suga?" I asked again, even though I already knew the answer to the question.

Capri faked a yawn and got comfortable in the chair. "I'm tired, Meer. Can we talk about this later?"

"That people pleasing shit gonna end, Capri."

Capri

She folded her arms. "Now I'm Capri. Well, Quameer, I think I might take a nap instead of listening to you run your mouth."

"Go ahead and take a nap."

"I will."

"Aye."

"Hmm?"

"Wake up with a better fucking attitude, too."

She laughed and mushed me. "Whatever, Quameer!"

I watched her get comfortable in the seat and continued to navigate through all this fucking traffic. This was the reason I always preferred my bike over driving.

Chapter 13
Capri

BEFORE I COULD OPEN MY EYES, I RUBBED MY ARMS because the air was blasting on me. I sat up in the chair and noticed Meer wasn't in the driver's seat and we parked in front of a colonial style home. I closed the vent and turned the air down before fixing my seat while trying to figure out where the hell he had us in the first place.

As if God had read my mind, he came out the house holding a bag and with Ryder skipping behind him. I internally screamed when I saw Brandi standing there with her hands on her thin hips. She was saying something to him, and he was waving her off while talking to Ryder who was all too excited to be with her father.

Meer had this cool and calm energy when it came to being a father. Then, he had that side that let you know he didn't play and was raising his daughter to be someone respectful and honorable.

He opened the door and lifted Ryder into the back, and that's when she noticed I was in the front. "Suga!" she hollered, roping her arms around my neck and hugging me tightly.

Goodness, it felt like a warm cup of tea on a cold day. It truly filled me up feeling this little girl embrace me in the way

Capri

that she did. "Daddy, you didn't tell me that you had Capri with you!" she hollered, making me partially deaf.

The second Brandi heard my name, she abandoned that damn step and came walking over toward the car. "Ry, you need to get in the seat and strap in."

"Brandi, ain't no reason you over here telling her something she already knows," Meer replied, keeping his tone neutral in front of Ryder.

Instead of hiding behind his tints, I rolled the window down to make my presence known, and hopefully avoid it being even more awkward. "Hey Brandi." I damn near bit off my tongue even acknowledging her.

"Wow, Capri? How are you doing?" Brandi had always been fake, so I wasn't surprised by her fake ass greeting.

"Hey Brandi. I'm doing well, how have you been? Your home is beautiful," I complimented, because as much as I couldn't stand Brandi, I wasn't a hater.

"Thank you. My husband bought me this house as an wedding gift... four thousand square feet," she gloated. "I'm doing good though, busy with my daughter, who you have met already."

"Yes, I love Peach... she's so sweet."

Brandi nearly had a damn stroke when I said Peach instead of Ryder. "Uh huh... the sweetest. Um, do you have any children of your own?"

Even though we weren't close, and I couldn't stand her, all the girls that attended school with us all kept together in a loop. So, even if you didn't fool with one, you knew her damn business. Brandi knew damn well that I didn't have any children, and this was a little dig.

"Not yet," I heard Meer mutter as he was fixing Ryder's seat. Brandi was too busy in my face to hear what he had said.

"No, I don't have any children. My nieces and nephews are more than enough though... they keep me busy."

"Aren't you married? I know Jesse told me something about you being married." She continued to take small digs that didn't seem like digs, but you knew they were.

If you didn't know her, you would have thought she was making casual conversation. Except, she was probably one of the first people that knew I had gotten divorced.

"Happily, divorced."

"Well, you know me and Jesse actually reconnected. I'll see you at the bachelorette trip, right?"

"Yep. I'll be there."

"Goodie... Ry, I love you and behave yourself."

"Always do, mommy." Meer climbed back into his truck, while Brandi gave Peach Eskimo kisses before shutting the door.

"Later, Meer." Brandi waved, and he nodded before pulling away from the curb, and eventually off her street.

Peach had her headphones on with her iPad, and I looked over at Meer, and his jaw was clenched. "Later, *Meer*," I teased him.

Meer looked over at me while biting his lip. "Why you being messy?" He discreetly ripped a hole in my stockings which caused me to gasps.

"Meer, these are hundred-dollar stockings." I punched him in the arm, and he was unfazed while he kept staring over at me.

"Why didn't you tell me that Brandi was going to be at this little bachelorette trip?"

"What you scared? Been hiding something from me, *Meer*."

He glanced in the rearview mirror to check on Ryder, and she was too busy in her iPad. Meer had a rule that she didn't touch her iPad during the school week. Since her last day of school was last week, she was free to be on her electronics.

"I never got nothing to hide from you, Sug... you know

Capri

that." It was how he said it while staring me directly in the eyes that made me believe him.

Quameer had been open with me during our entire friendship. As we eased into a relationship, I knew he would be the same way.

"Are you coming back to the lake house with me?"

"Nah. I'm dropping you off, then coming back this way."

I pouted as I looked at him. "Don't be a party pooper. Stop at your house and grab some clothes, and then we can grill tonight and take shots."

He chuckled. "I feel like you just want me to cook because you don't want to cook."

"I'm with you when you're right, Meer." I smirked, as he reached over and made the hole in my stocking even bigger.

As I was about to get into his ass, Jesse's name flashed across the screen. I took a deep sigh and then answered.

"Hey Jess."

She was having a side conversation, which annoyed the hell out of me. I hated when someone called me and then proceeded to talk to people in their background. What the hell did you call me for in the first place.

"Hey Capri... quick question."

I just knew what she was going to ask was going to be some bullshit. It never failed with Jesse and her *quick questions.* "Yeah."

"So, they downgraded the villa, and Brandi just called me and asked if she could have her own room."

"Oh, she *just* called you?"

"Yeah... was quite pushy about it too, but whatever. I want to make sure everyone is comfortable, so do you mind giving her your room and sharing with Blair?"

It was crazy how she was making all these accommodations for a bitch that fucked her boyfriend in college. "I don't mind, Jesse."

"Are you sure?"

"I just think you're accommodating someone who you just reconnected with." I said my piece and was going to leave it alone.

"Don't be like that, Capri. I promise we're all going to have the best time... also, I got the invitation to your birthday party."

Erin and Alaia must have started sending them out to the list of people I had given them. "Oh good... did you see the theme?"

"Um, yeah, I don't think I'm going to be able to make it. It's right after we get back, and you know I have so much prep for the wedding."

"Jesse, can I call you back?"

"Of course," she cheerfully replied, so happy to get off the phone and away from the dumb ass excuse of her not attending my birthday party.

Quameer and Blair weren't wrong about Jesse, and it was hard to admit. When you were friends with someone for so long, you naturally accepted them for who they were. You made excuses for them and excused their poor behavior. Jesse had always been the one who needed to be the main attention. We were all pretty and pulled niggas in college, but it was Jesse that always required just a bit more attention than all of us.

I remember one night when we were drinking in our dorms, she had confided in me on how her mother barely paid her any attention, and her father had always been in and out of her life. So, I felt bad for her. I knew how it felt not to be the main priority in your parent's life.

Mostly my mother.

My mother had always been so hard on me about everything. With school, I had to be better and bring home good grades. When it came to being married, she wanted me to be the best wife there was. Now that I wasn't married anymore and chose myself over staying in a toxic marriage, I felt like she blamed me.

It was like I brought shame on her by not being married and playing the field. For a while, there was this small piece of me that tried to keep one foot in with Naheim because of my mother. All you ever want to do is make your mother proud, and it felt like I could never make Jean Delgato proud of me.

So, when Jesse told me about her mother, I could relate to what she was saying. As the years went on, Jesse has shown me that I was the only one pouring into our friendship, while she was staying hydrated.

"She done said some fuck shit, huh?"

I laughed. "Why do you assume that?"

"It's Jesse. I spent enough time with that bitch to know she don't mean nobody good." I hated to even admit that Meer was right about Jesse.

Even though I asked Meer to come up to the lake house with me, I didn't want to intrude on him and Peach's time together. I knew it was important for him to spend one on one time with her, and I never wanted to get in the way of that.

When Peach asked to ride bikes on the trails within the neighborhood, I suggested that the both of them go to spend daddy and Peach time together. While they were gone, I cleaned up the house and started a load of laundry while managing to finish packing.

Meer took out a pack of chicken out the freezer and told me he was going to show me how to fry chicken. As if I didn't know how to fry chicken and didn't learn from the best: my mom. While they were gone, I decided to go over to my parent's house to check in with them.

It had been a while since I had truly checked in with them

since I had been back. Life started happening right away, and I didn't get a chance to sit with my father or listen to my mother bicker over my life.

"What child is getting on my nerves now?" I heard my father yell from his den and laughed as I rounded the corner.

He was sitting back in his recliner with Cee-Cee fast asleep on his chest. It was very clear that my father had a favorite grandchild, and it didn't matter how much he tried to deny it.

"Suga Cane, I damn sure didn't expect to see you round that corner," he leaned forward in the chair, and I kissed his cheek.

"Hey Daddy." I rubbed Cee-Cee's curls and kissed the top of her head before plopping onto the couch across from his recliner. "Now, why is Cee-Cee over here?"

"I went over to grab some beers from her father, and she wouldn't stop crying so I took her with me. Poor baby just needed a nap on her pop-pop."

"She's your favorite," I teased.

He was watching Law and Order while he rocked in his favorite chair and enjoyed a beer. As I stared at him, I couldn't help but to see pieces of him in Corleon. Why didn't he or Mommy tell us that we had a brother out there? What the hell was the story on it, and why was it kept a secret?

I didn't think our family was the type that had deep and dark secrets, but apparently, we were. "Any reason you staring the side of my face off, Capri?"

His words snapped me out of my thoughts, and I smiled. "No reason. I really missed you and mommy when I was away. Guess I missed home... being in your space."

He smiled. "Have you gotten all your traveling out the way?"

I shrugged. "I don't think I will leave for a year again, but I do know I will travel more... the world is beautiful and I'm at peace when I'm in it."

Capri

"Maybe settle down for a bit and figure out what you want to do with your home on the compound."

First, Cappy brought up my house on the compound, and now I had to hear my father bring it up. I wasn't in a rush to build the house because it would be another residence that I would be moving into alone. It was already hard being single and living alone in my current home. I don't think I was ready to build an actual home, and then move into it alone at the end of the process.

The shit was depressing.

"Daddy, I don't know if I want to build my house right away... it makes me sad even thinking about it," I admitted to him.

My father was the calm in our family. You could come to talk to him about anything, and he would never blow up or force his beliefs on you. He was always quick to come up with a solution to fix your problem and give solid advice without flying off the handle like my mother.

The reason their marriage worked all these years was because they balanced each other. They had the perfect rhythm for their marriage, and it always worked out. I aspired to have a marriage like my parents. One where the respect was mutual, and our personalities balanced each other, rather than battled one another.

He grew concerned as he turned his attention away from the episode he had been engrossed in before I came over. "Tell me what's bothering you."

"I never expected to be doing any of this alone. Building a home, having this life with just me. I get sad thinking about the life that I thought I would have, and then the life that I'm living. Guess I always assumed me and Naheim would be doing this together... you know?"

"I do." He shifted Cee-Cee a bit, then continued to look my way. "I also know that building a house on a faulty foundation is a disaster waiting to happen." He gave me that knowing look.

"Yeah."

"I can't sit and pretend to know how hard it was for you to divorce him and move on in life without him. It takes a strong woman to stay, and an even stronger woman to leave. You knew what you deserved, and you choose better. If you need to wait before building your home, then take your time. Do what feels right, Capri. You have a habit of doing what is expected of you... I want you to do what feels right for once. Don't worry about what your brothers or mother think... do what Capri wants."

"Thanks, Daddy."

"If it means anything, I like Quameer for you."

I stared at him confused. "We're friends."

"And me and your mother don't skinny dip in our pool."

I put my hand over my ears and looked at him. "Ugh... I don't wanna hear that."

He chuckled. "I've heard of his nickname for you."

"Suga," I twirled the loose strand of hair around my finger as I thought about whenever he said it.

It was the way he said it in my ear when he was balls deep inside of me. Tossing those thoughts away, I focused on the conversation with my father. "I had a chance to speak to Quameer."

"How did that go?"

"He asked to speak with me and your brothers, and he asked for our blessing to pursue you. I respect the fact that he didn't just sit your brothers down, but he also had his brother and father too. Suga Cane, open your heart up for something real, just one more time. I have a feeling that this time might end up going well for you."

I smiled as I heard my mother yapping on the phone while coming in through the garage. Kissing my father quickly, I went

Capri

into the kitchen where my mother was putting the grocery bags on the counter while on the phone.

She spun around mid-conversation and stopped short when she noticed me standing there. "Jo, you will never believe who I have standing in my kitchen." She put her phone on speaker and sat it on the counter.

"Who?"

"Capri... she has blessed me with her presence after leaving for an entire year." I could hear the shade laced within her words and chose to ignore it.

Even though she never supported me going away, I thought she would have come around and realize that this was what was best for me. I had to get away, I needed to go away for me and to find me again. It had been so long since I felt like myself again that it felt like I was getting to know a new person.

"Hey Mommy," I kissed her on the cheek and started to help her put some of the groceries away. "Hey Jo."

"Hey pretty girl. How have you been doing?"

"I'm good... easing back into life and trying to figure out what's next for me," I replied, putting the ice cream in the freezer.

"We're happy to have you back. I know your mama missed you... Quameer and his little girl are so cute."

"They are. He's such a good father... Ryder is so respectful too. She loves the lake, so I figured they should come again this weekend so she can swim."

"Last summer you had another man staying with you. Now there's a new man staying, and he has a child. What are you doing, Capri?"

I was shocked by her words, and the silence on the phone told me that Jo was too. "Jean don't even be like that.... Oh no, that isn't nice to say to her."

My mother paused, regret entering her eyes as she took a deep sigh before walking toward me. "Jo is right. That wasn't nice of me to say, and I am sorry. I'm just confused on what you're doing with your life, Baby."

"I'm not confused about what I'm doing anymore."

"Naheim is coming up here for the summer. Maybe you two should reconnect and spend time together. He lost his mother, Capri."

When I told my family that I didn't want them to act differently toward Naheim when we divorced, I meant that. I didn't want them to push him away or treat him differently because he was family to me. We had so many memories and I couldn't picture a world without having him there.

Now that I had time to think, I didn't mind Naheim coming around and still being part of the family. I just wanted everyone to realize that just because he was around didn't mean that we would be getting back together.

I wanted his friendship, not him.

"Oh Jean, Baby, you need to let this dream go. That man is with another woman, and he damn near karate chopped your daughter's heart in half. You can't just put them in a room and think the sparks will fly. I've loved a man that broke me in two, and I took him back every time because there was a child involved. I was so broken and lost while trying to make it work. The minute I let him go, I found myself."

"Thanks, Jo."

"I'm going to call you back." My mother now wanted to suddenly rush her off the phone because she wasn't talking about what she wanted.

"Uh huh. Rush me off the phone because I'm not speaking your language. I'll be across the street in another hour or so," Jo called her out and then ended the call.

Jo was like an aunt to me, and I often went to her for advice. Unlike my mother, she listened and didn't past judgment on me. She sat and took in everything that I said, and always had good advice. I understood why Erin was so close to

Capri

her aunt. She was a woman that had experienced life, and because of that, she was wise beyond her years and had so many gems to instill in people.

"You didn't even get to know him before being judgmental," I said lowly.

She held the coconut milk cans in her hands. "I know Quameer, Baby. I know the Infernos very well, better than you think. I don't have anything against him, I know he's a good man. Quinton doesn't play those games when it comes to his boys."

"Then why do you act like you dislike him?"

She sat the cans down. "I guess I can't see you with anyone else except Naheim. I know how much he loves and protects you. He made a mistake, and no marriage is ever perfect."

"Mom, he didn't protect me though. Naheim came home and did whatever he wanted, and I protected him. I held in all the shit we went through because I never wanted you guys to see him differently."

"He put his hands on you, Capri," my mother quickly rushed over toward me, and put my hands into hers.

"No, never. Naheim would never do something like that. I'm just saying, we went through real shit in our marriage, and he didn't always act like the perfect husband that he portrayed to you. I wasn't the perfect wife either."

"I don't know the exacts on what happened, but I do know that you and Kincaid started dating shortly after you and Naheim broke up... you hurt him, too, Baby."

I groaned. "Mom, I hurt him *after* he had already hurt me multiple times. It wasn't right and I own that I made things worse by getting my lick back. However, I am not getting back with Naheim, so I need you to let that dream go."

"Nana! Nana!" Cee-Cee came running into the kitchen, her hair stuck to one side of her head, while my father came in behind her.

"Oh, my little crazy girl," she picked her up and spun her around, kissing her cheek while Cee-Cee giggled, her little glasses becoming crooked while my mother continued to spin her around.

He kissed my mother on the lips, and then held his keys up, letting her know that he was leaving. "I'm gonna head out with you, Daddy."

"Well, look at them leaving us to put all these groceries away. Will you help me, Cee?"

She shook her head and smiled. "Yes!"

Capone and Erin had Cee-Cee in so many different therapies. The minute they found out she had Down syndrome, they were proactive and learned everything they needed for their daughter. In our eyes, Cee-Cee was perfect and so loved. That was my little namesake, so of course she had a special place in my heart.

Me and my mother would resume the conversation another time. I learned a while ago to know when to end a conversation on a good note, and this was a good note to end it on. My father hugged and kissed me before heading to grab more beers from the liquor store.

I headed back across the street and was about to enter through the garage when both Quameer and Ryder both pulled up on the bikes. Ryder cheered, tossing the bike onto the floor to celebrate that she had beat her father in a race.

"Told you that I'm faster than you! I knew, I knew. Did you see, Capri?"

I smiled as I folded my arms. "Sure did. I bet he was talking a bunch of junk too, huh?"

"So much... so guess who has to make a TikTok with me?"

Meer waved us both off as he put the kickstand on the bike, and then walked over toward his daughter. Holding his hand out, she shook his hand, and he bent down to kiss her on the head. "Ryder is the best in the world. She beat her old father,

Capri

who is very old. Ryder is smarter than him too, so he should listen to her more often," he recited as Ryder stood there waiting for him to finish.

"You forgot one."

"Ryder will go viral on TikTok one day."

She jumped up and down while hugging her father. "Thanks, Daddy."

Meer chuckled. "Bring the bike in and get yourself ready for a bath."

She nodded and brought the bike in before going inside the house. I stood there watching him, and he smiled. "When are you going to tell her that you don't even post her videos."

"I post them... they just private. Stop being a snitch, Sug." He kissed me on the lips, and then stood next to me as we watched Cappadonna push Promise on some stroller-bike.

He was on the phone while pushing her up and down the street. "I need to tell him about what happened at the motel."

"I already put him onto game... it would be irresponsible not to tell him that somebody got static with us. He and everybody else need to watch they back... feel me?"

"You're right. I should have told him straight away."

He held my face. "You had a bunch of shit tossed on you, Suga... don't worry about it. I handled it."

I smiled. "Thank you, Meer."

Once again, Meer cooked dinner and it was good. Me and Ryder both had seconds because it was that good. While he went to tuck her in, I grabbed a bottle of wine and Uno and turned the lights on in the backyard.

Right as I popped the wine, he came out with a smile on his face. "You wanna get that ass spanked in Uno, again?"

"Oh, please. You have all this mouth and then be in your feelings soon as someone make you draw a card."

He fished his pockets for a lighter before removing his spliff that he always kept tucked behind his ear. I watched as he sparked it, and then eased onto the couch and waited for me to shuffle the cards.

"How was your bike ride with Peach today?" I asked while I shuffled the cards, making sure he noticed that I wasn't cheating.

"Shit was peaceful. I always enjoy time with her, and it been a little minute since she updated me on her school dramas. We noticed a house for sale a few blocks over and went in the backyard."

"You went onto those people's property, Meer?"

"Hell yeah. I may want to put in an offer... a house for my family to come and relax. I don't know about us buying the whole block, but one house for us all to be together, or use whenever any one of us wants to get away."

"Awe, I love that. Would your mother love something like that?" I questioned, wanting him to open up more about his mother.

He or Quasim never gave much when it came to their family. They were like a sealed vault that you had to crack, and trying to crack Meer hadn't been all that easy.

"As long as she has a window and knows my pops is coming or near, she's good." There was a sadness in his eyes as he continued to take pulls.

I rubbed his hand. "How is Ryder with her grandmother?"

He smiled. "She knows that her grandmother is different and not like her mom's mother. I don't think she understands how serious it is, but she recognizes that her grandmother is different."

It had to be tough to have his mother, who was so young, go through a terrible disease like that. As much as my mother got on my last nerve, I couldn't picture a life with her battling a disease like the one that Meer's mother was battling.

"You know I'm here and you can always talk to me about it.

Capri

Don't ever feel like you're putting heavy shit on me... I'm strong, Meer."

"I'm supposed to be strong for you, Suga... not the other way around."

I looked down at the cards in my hands, then back up into his eyes. "Can we be strong for each other? Is that something that we can both do?"

He nodded his head. "I don't know."

I screwed my face up as my heart propelled against my chest at him telling me he didn't know. "What do you mean?"

"This, Suga... I wanna be all in with you because you are who I want to be with. Some days you give me vibes that we can do this, and then sometimes I feel like I'm pushing this on you."

"I understand... I feel the same way about you."

Now it was his turn to turn his face up confused. "You just be saying shit, Capri. The fuck you mean you feel the same way about me? I been letting you know how I feel about you since day one."

"You have."

I watched him stab the half-finished spliff in the ashtray, knowing he was pissed because he didn't finish it. "Then what the fuck are you talking about, Suga?"

"I've been with Naheim... Kincaid, who is very close to you. What if one day you decide you don't wanna be with the chick who been with all your homies."

He paused to really take in everything that I had said to him, then this man had the nerve to fucking laugh. "The fuck we in high school?"

"I'm being serious."

"Naheim isn't my homie... I only know him because he run with your brothers. We were never close, never had a conversation, and don't kick it with each other."

"Kincaid?"

"We're close not super close so don't know where you got that from. He's IG, and family... I'm riding for him always. Whatever problems he has, we'll talk about them and in the end, I'm doing what the fuck I wanna do, and that's being with you if that's where our path leads us." He moved closer to me and kissed my lips. "I don't give a fuck about who came before me, I just know that no nigga coming after me unless he wanna get a certificate."

"Certificate?"

"Death certificate, Suga. All gas, no sense when it comes to you." He paused. "I just have trouble figuring out if you on the same type of time that I'm on."

"What makes you feel like that?"

"The fact that you wanna keep this a secret... you in the chicken spot with Mason's fucking ass... all that shit tells me is that you want your cake and want to eat it too, and I'm not feeling that. You want me to open up, but I'm not even sure if you're going to stick around."

"Meer, seriously? I wouldn't be here if I didn't want this... I've been here, and that actually hurts my feelings that you don't think I have been."

He shrugged his shoulders. "How much in were you with Kincaid while still sliding back with Naheim?"

I shoved him, getting up. "What the fuck ever, Quameer... way to toss shit back in my face."

He remained calm, and gently pulled me back down beside him. "I'm being honest with you and because you don't like how I'm doing it, your first thing to do is to run... sit down and have the hard conversations. Stop fucking running."

This wasn't the Meer I was used to. He was intense, and serious. There wasn't a smirk on his face to make me feel better. I knew the conversation was serious, but I didn't like this serious Quameer.

"Why bring them up then?"

Capri

"Answer the question."

"What question?"

"How much in were you with Kincaid when you were sliding back with Naheim?" he asked the question a second time, and I winced feeling the knife dig a bit deeper into me.

"I don't know, Quameer. I knew I had feelings for Kincaid, and had fallen for him, but Naheim was my husband. I still loved him," my voice cracked as I looked away.

I wanted him to hug me, make me feel better, and apologize and I got nothing. He sat there staring ahead at the lake in front of us. "And now?"

"Now, what?"

"Do you still love him now?" his voice was eerily calm as he continued to stare forward, not looking in my direction.

I turned until I was directly in his face. "I am not in love with Naheim anymore. That ship has sailed when he left my house that day."

"When it comes to me and Peach, I gotta protect both of our hearts. I can't do the back and forth when it comes to you. I can't afford to have my heart broken again and having to explain to her why we don't come around you anymore." He turned to look at me, and I could tell he meant every word that he said. "Before saying that you want this or you're in this with me, you need to realize that Peach is part of this. Are you prepared for that?"

Ryder had always been part of the package and part of the reason I was hesitant when it came to Meer. I knew how much I liked him, and how much I needed a man like him. The thought of him coming with more than just him scared me.

Even when he saw me off at the airport, I had to consider that it wasn't just him that I could be returning to. Was I prepared to be a stepmother, and build a life with this man? The thought of not having Meer, or building a life without him scared me.

Taking his hands into mine, I looked into his eyes. "I'm in with you, Meer. Is it bad to admit that I am scared?"

"Why are you scared, Suga?" His raspy voice was my favorite thing about him. I reached over and messed with his loose locs that had fell from the bun I had put them in while he was cooking.

"Because I know you are a good thing, and I tend to fuck up things that are good for me." A tear slipped down my cheek, and he swiped it away before pulling me onto his lap.

"Then let's make sure you don't fuck up a good thing." I smiled through my tears as he softly kissed me. "If... I...find... out... you... sliding... with... another... nigga, you really gonna meet the real Meer," he said between each kiss on my lips as I stared into his eyes.

The Inferno brothers both had soft, kind eyes. However, there was always something ominous brewing in them at the same time.

Chapter 14
Quameer

You ever been so deep in a good sleep that any noise that sounded around you, you considered to be inside the dream you were having. I was knocked out with my arm over my face and both the duvet and pillow over my face when I felt someone rip them from me and I opened my eyes.

Thankfully, the room was still dark from the black-out curtains that Suga had in the guest room. Capri stood there with her hand on her hips and my phone in her hand as she stared at me angrily.

"The hell is your problem?"

"Meer, your phone has been going off for the past twenty minutes. Brandi has called your phone a bunch of times... answer the shit," she snapped, turning to head back down the hall to her room.

Since Peach was still here, we slept in separate rooms until I was ready to have that conversation with her. Right now, I wasn't ready to put any of this onto her until we figured the shit out. I know Capri told me she was in this with me, but I needed her to prove the shit to me more. Words meant nothing to me. I wanted her to prove that she wanted everything that came with being with me. I had to feel the situation out more before bringing it before my daughter.

"Good morning to you, too!" I yelled behind her, as she slammed her door back, and I picked my phone she had tossed at me.

Sure, enough Brandi had called me like twelve times back-to-back. It was only eight in the morning, and she wasn't due to get Ryder back until tomorrow. I hit her name and laid back on the bed while waiting to hear her whiny ass voice.

"Quameer, damn, you don't know how to answer the phone?" she barked into the phone, and I pulled it away from my ear to make sure I dialed the right number.

"Before I violate you, what the fuck do you want? Your daughter is sleep, no I didn't fuck Capri while she was here, and I damn sure plan to after I drop her off ... what up?"

I could hear her gasp, and I laughed to myself because her nosey ass wanted to ask all those questions that I had just answered for her. "Whatever you do with Capri is your business... I don't care what you do in your personal life." I could hear the hurt in her voice, and had this been a few years ago, I would have relished in the fact that I had hurt that demon whale's heart.

When we first split, I remember I used to do whatever I could to make her jealous. I wanted her to hurt like she had had me out here hurting. I've long grown from that heartbroken nigga that couldn't think about her without my chest feeling tight.

Brandi didn't know my personal life because I kept it personal. "What do you want? I was sleeping in case you cared."

"My mother flew in to attend my cousin's graduation today. It slipped my mind, but I want Ryder to attend and see her cousin get her degree."

"I can drive her to your house this afternoon."

Capri

Brandi hesitated. "You're on the way to her college, so I figured I could just stop by and grab her from you."

I already knew her nosey ass had been looking at Ryder's location. As a parent, I wanted to know where my daughter was at all times, so I wasn't mad at her for knowing her location. Her ass had planned this perfectly so she could come by here and be nosey as shit.

Putting the pillow back over my head. "Let me ask Capri and see if she's cool with that and I'll hit you back."

"Ugh, you have to ask her if your daughter can be picked up."

I was thankful I had put the pillow over my face. "No, dick breath... this is her crib and you trying to come over, so the right thing to do is to fucking ask her if she's comfortable with you coming to her house."

"The insults aren't necessary, Quameer."

I didn't even bother to reply before I ended the call and checked in on Peach before going to Suga's bedroom. When I opened the door, she was back under all the covers, and I could hear soft snores coming from under the mountains of blankets that were on her.

"Sug, move over," I whispered, and she scooted over as I climbed into the bed and pulled the covers over me.

Capri slept like she was a fucking polar bear. I turned the air up to seventy and she nearly had a damn stroke and accused me of trying to kill her. Soon as I was under the covers, she came back over and put her head on my chest.

"Brandi wants to pick Peach up from here. She claim it's on her way to her cousin's college. You cool with that? If not, I'll have her meet me at a random gas station."

Capri laughed. "You both are not going to do a handoff at a gas station with my girl. This is Ryder's second time being here, so she should know where her daughter is spending her time."

"I don't give a fuck about what she should know. I need to know if you're comfortable because I will make other plans."

She lifted her head to look at me. "Meer, just allow her to come pick her up from here. I am comfortable with her knowing where the house is. Ryder has been staying here, and she's a mom. Maybe she just wants to lay eyes on where her daughter is."

Brandi never cared where I took Ryder in the past. She knew if my daughter was with me, then she was safe. There was never any reason for her to worry because I never gave her any reason to. The only reason she wanted to come pick Peach up from here was the same reason her ass hightailed it to my truck when I picked Peach up the other day.

Being nosey.

Before I could reply to her, we both turned our head at the soft knock at the door. "Come in, Ryder," Capri called, and Ryder slowly opened the door.

She came skipping into the room and hopped up on the bed, sitting on my damn legs. "Good morning. I went to look in the room for you and you were gone."

"I had to talk to Suga about something... how did you sleep?"

Ryder looked at me and Capri, who were both laying in the bed together. "Are you boyfriend and girlfriend now?"

Capri looked at me while trying to figure out what to say. "Well, we—"

"We friends, Peach. Only best friends chill in the bed together," I paused. "Grown best friends," I added because she loved to use my words against me.

I felt Capri sit all the way up as I sent Brandi a text letting her know she could come pick Ryder up from here. She didn't even need to tell me; she felt a way about what I had said and was playing it cool because Peach was in here with us.

Capri

"How about I make some pancakes before your mommy comes to pick you up."

Peach's head snapped in my direction. "Mom is picking me up?"

It always killed me how she switched between mom or mommy. A few times I caught her calling me dad instead of daddy, and the shit hurt. It was a reminder that she wasn't going to stay my little Peach for much longer.

"Your cousin is graduating from college today and your mom wants you to see it."

Peach groaned. "CJ said he would show me the dirt bikes today, Dad... please."

No matter how I felt about her mother, I never allowed her to see it. I didn't want to cut our time short either, but the reason our agreement worked so well was because we both were flexible. There may come a week that I wanted her longer, and Brandi would never deny me because she knew there was times when she did the same thing.

"Next time, Peach. Me and your dad are best friends, so you can come to the lake house all summer if you want."

I side eyed her petty ass, as she held her arms out and Peach fell into them, and she kissed her head. "You promise?"

"Only if your father is alright with it... let's go have some breakfast and then I'll curl your hair so you can look pretty at the graduation."

Peach jumped up out of Capri's arms and hopped down from the bed. "Okay... cinnamon pancakes, right?"

"Yep. Go brush your teeth and wash your face."

Soon as Peach was gone, I went to grab her, and she slipped right out the bed. I was half-asleep and the room was dark, so I didn't notice what she had on. Even though she had on a pajama short set, her ass in those shorts had me ready for her.

As she walked around the bed, I watched her thighs shake

while I avoided biting my tongue. "You don't need to clear anything up with me, Meer."

"What the fuck is that supposed to mean?"

"We spent the other night talking about everything and the first thing you blurt is that we're friends."

I climbed out the bed and stood in the doorway. "What the fuck did you want me to say?"

She turned to look at me while holding her toothbrush. "You said exactly what you wanted to say."

"Suga, what the fuck are you really mad about? Peach don't know what the fuck is going on, and before I introduce her to what could be, I'm taking my time. You not about to make me feel bad about the shit."

"You talk about me being all in and you can't even admit that you don't trust me. Why are you saying things like *what could be?*"

I was talking so damn quick that I didn't notice I had even said those words. "You know what I meant."

"Do I know? You hiding in my damn trunk, whispering in my ear about ending a nigga behind me, but can't tell your daughter that I'm your girl." She held her hand up. "One sec, because I'm not your girl because you never asked me." Capri stared at me, then slammed the bathroom door in my face.

"You ain't have to slam the fucking door in my face, petty ass."

"My bad, *Friend.*"

"Suga?"

"Hmm?"

"Fuck ya."

"Bet you want to," she countered, and I kicked the door before going back down the hall to the shared bathroom with Peach.

As much as our conversation the other night was needed, and I had gotten shit out that I needed her to know, I was

Capri

moving slow when it came to letting Peach know that she was more than a friend to me. I never introduced a woman to her, and Suga only got introduced because she was my best friend.

Had we not been friends first, Peach wouldn't have known anything about her, and that was just me being real and honest about the situation. I needed her to understand that I moved on how my daughter felt and being that I hadn't sat down and picked her brain about Suga, I was taking my time.

Just as we finished eating breakfast, Brandi texted and said she had arrived. Capri called the front gate and gave her permission to come through. Peach went to grab her things while I put the plates in the sink.

"Can I have a hug?"

Capri stopped wiping the counter down. "Of course, Meer."

It was her tone that told me she was about to play games with me. She tried to give me a church hug and I grabbed her ass around the neck, shoving my tongue down her throat. From the way she accepted my tongue into her mouth, I knew she wanted it. Once she realized she was enjoying it too much, she shoved me away.

"Friends don't do that, Meer."

"As you was damn near sucking on my tongue," I whispered as I bypassed her to head to the front because the doorbell sounded.

Brandi's ass knew she could have texted me she was in the driveway. "Peach, your mama here."

I heard her saying something, but I was already making my way to the door. Opening the door, Brandi stood there with a smile on her face. "Hey Meer."

"Why the fuck you at the door and not sitting in that damn car?" Brandi's ass always seemed like she was alone these days.

"Can I use the bathroom? It's another two hours until we make it to the college."

"There's a gas station a few miles down once you leave outta here." I remained at the door, determined not to let her ass up in here.

"Hey Capri," Brandi greeted when she saw Capri coming out of the office. Her head was damn near wrapped around me to look inside with her nosey ass.

"Hi Brandi."

"Um, do you mind if I use the bathroom?"

"Sure. The restroom is down this hall right here... you cannot miss it." Brandi signaled to her mother before I moved out of her way.

Brandi's mother waved at me, then went back to doing whatever on her phone. Her parents were newly divorced, and she had moved out of state. Do you know how much you gotta hate a nigga to move out the state to get away from him?

The feeling was very much mutual when it came to Brandi's father. I still had a hot one waiting in the chamber for that nigga. Peach finally came running down the steps with her bags.

"Capri, your home is beautiful... I bet its more affordable living this far from the city, huh?" she tossed shade, as if I didn't tell her that this was her lake house.

"I only live here in the summers. This is my lake house, and I own a townhouse right near the city." Capri smiled, trying to keep cool because she could sense that my baby moms was being catty.

"Mamãe está com ciúmes," Peach said to me while her mother and Capri were talking. I knew she was jealous of Capri, but I would never allow that to slip to my daughter, so I corrected her.

"Seja respeitoso," I sternly replied.

"Sim, senhor," she looked up at me and then hugged me tightly as her mother walked toward the door.

"Love you more than you know, Ryder. Behave yourself

and I will see you next week," I reminded her and kissed her on the cheek.

"Mommy is going out of town so I will be with grandma this week." Peach loved Brandi's parents, but she never looked forward to spending time with her grandmother because she made her attend Bible school, and church on Sundays.

"You'll be fine, Peach. If you're not, then what?"

"I call you."

"Exactly. I'm riding through to get my Ryder," I winked and kissed her on top of the head, as she ran behind her mother.

"You know the schedule already, right?" Brandi questioned me like she hadn't sent me the rundown via text message already.

I already knew she was heading out of town; I just didn't know that she was going to be with Suga. To be a fly on the wall on this trip with the two of them.

"Yeah."

"See you in a few days, Capri... get ready to turn up." Brandi did a fake little dance while Capri gave her a fake smile and closed the door behind them.

I tried to get another hug, and she ducked around me with an attitude. "Alright, bend the fuck over we need to talk."

Capri stopped short and started laughing. "Meer, please leave me alone."

I dropped my sweats to the floor. "I'm dead ass, Suga. You need some dick to fix that attitude... I can tell."

She stared at me for a minute and then turned to head up the stairs. "All I need from you is a ride to the airport. Might want to pick your pants up because Blair is on her way over here."

"Keep on with the attitude and we really gonna have that talk!" I yelled up the stairs, and she spun on her heels to look at me.

"We don't need to have a conversation because we're friends. You made that very clear, remember?"

"Suga, keep playing with me."

"No, you keep playing with me." She flipped the middle finger at me, and then headed up the rest of the stairs.

"Your brother needs to find him a wholesome quiet girl that will make him happy. Maybe I'm too much for him. You know, with the cancer and all of that."

I looked in the rearview mirror at Blair. "Yeah, you the quiet and wholesome girl that you back there talking about."

She giggled. "Quameer, it's clear that your brother feels very differently than you. Men are stupid anyway, and for the next few days I don't want to think of any man... especially your brother."

"What happened to your boyfriend?"

"He ghosted me after finding out that I have cancer."

"Quameer!" Capri dropped her phone as the car swerved into the other lane when I turned around to look at Blair. "You are driving... did you forget?"

"He fucking did what?"

"When I finally told him that I have cancer, he kind of grew distant with me. I waited to tell him because I wanted to be sure that he was the one, you know." I could see the sadness in her eyes as she tried to shrug it off like it wasn't nothing.

"Fuck him, Blair. Any nigga that can't be there for their woman is a nigga that you don't need to be worried about... alright?"

"Thanks, Meer. I feel like I'm cursed or something. Every time I think I meet the one, something happens and then I'm back at step one."

Capri turned around. "You're beautiful inside and out, and

Capri

when you find the right one, none of those other assholes will ever matter again. God is taking his time giving you the right man, so be patient and try not to question him." She reached back and held her hand.

"God does favor the name Quasim though."

Capri turned back around and pinched me. "Be quiet and get us to the airport in one piece... you already damn near drove us off the highway."

The rest of the ride we were all quiet and listened to the radio. My phone chimed, and Capri's nosey ass couldn't help but look at the message that came across the screen.

> Good neck: miss you, Meer-Meer.

Fuck.

It was clear that the man upstairs didn't fucking favor me right now. Out of all the times Simone's pigeon toe ass could have texted me, she chose to text me right this minute. Capri's eyes dragged from the screen of my phone over toward me. I hadn't talked to Simone in months, and the last time I saw her, I told her that I wasn't on that shit with her.

Why in the fuck would she text me talking about she missed me? The bitch was only good enough for me to shove my dick down her throat, and since I had been celibate, she hadn't even done that. She was acting like we had developed a friendship where we would even miss each other.

"Celibate my ass," she muttered as I drove to departures, pissed that this was the exact moment that Simone wanted to send a message.

"You believing a text message over me?"

"Good neck, Meer? Who gets a message from a chick saved in your phone as good neck? In case you didn't know, you weren't celibate if you were still getting head."

"I wasn't getting no fucking head, Suga... why the fuck you

making shit up?" I pulled up to the curb, and looked at the nigga with a whistle, giving his ass a warning not to blow that fucking whistle my way.

"Oop." Blair finally tapped back in and realized the conversation we were having at the moment. "I'm going to check in my bag and wait for you."

I got out and helped Blair with her bags before getting back in the driver seat. Capri tried to get out and I had hit the locks on her ass. "Why you being like that? You know I didn't fuck nobody... why would I lie to you?"

"Do I know that? For all I know you could have been getting head from headmaster," she cut her eyes at me.

"She got good head; I wouldn't go crazy calling her headmaster."

With the look she gave me, I realized I needed to shut the fuck up because I was making matters worse. "Why is she texting you?"

"You want me to call her and find out."

"Not my place." She reached for the handle, and I pulled her hand.

"Sug, you know the truth so why you being like this? Give me a kiss and have a good trip... when you get back, we'll figure all this shit out."

She decided to keep her brothers in the dark a bit longer until she got back. In my opinion, she needed to go ahead and cancel and handle family shit. Knowing Capri, when she promised someone something, she was going to make sure she came through for them. Even if it was for Jesse's ass.

"Friends don't kiss."

"Give me a fucking kiss and stop playing with me, Capri." She leaned over the armrest and kissed me on the lips. I held her face and stole a few extra kisses. "Stop letting bitches get under your skin... you already know you pressure, Suga. Only person I want swallowing me is right here."

Capri

"Hmph." She tried to act nonchalant, but I could see the smirk on her face as she climbed out my truck.

I helped her with the bags and then pulled her toward me, not wanting to let her go. The last time I hugged her at an airport, I didn't see her for the next year. At least, I knew she had a return date, and I would see her in a few days.

"Be safe and have fun... act like you gotta nigga at home, too."

She hugged me before she joined Blair on the sidewalk. "Big Pri don't have a man at home." Her ass knew she fucked up because when I tried to grab her, she quickly carried her ass into the airport.

"Later, Meer," she winked, while poking her head out the automatic door. I watched as she blew me a kiss.

"You know what to text me if you need me."

"I already know," she said, and then quickly went back inside to join Blair, while I rounded my truck.

"I'm glad we had an understanding, and I didn't have to fuck you up out here," I told the airport security, who hadn't blown his whistle the entire time I was double parked here.

Turning my music up, I whipped away from the curb and the thought about Simone and hit her contact's name.

"Hey Meer-Meer," she cooed into the phone, all too excited that I had chosen to hit her line after that bullshit ass text message.

"Bitch, you know damn well you call me Quameer, so why the fuck you making up pet names like we be on it like that?"

I fucked Simone a few times, but I preferred head because her pussy was trash. Bitch did all this moaning and shit talking and be screaming before I put my shit inside her. And it wasn't like it was a cute moan either, the shit always sounded like she was on steroids or some shit.

"Damn, Meer, I couldn't miss you and let you know that?"

I took a breath as I gripped my wheel tighter. "You don't

fucking miss me, Simone. We fucked or you sucked me off and you go about your fucking day. When have you sat up and talked for you to miss me?"

"Maybe I missed your dick down my throat…. Did you consider that?"

"Lose my fucking number, Simone. I told you I was good when I saw you a few months ago. Respect that shit… next time you hit me up, I'm gonna pull up on you and it ain't to give you no fucking dick, bitch!" I hollered and ended the call.

I had been out of commission when it came to handling business because I was spending time with Peach and Suga. Now that my two hearts were squared away, and I put Simone's ass in her place, I was ready to handle business.

Chapter 15
Capella 'Chubs' Delgato

Since I had got out, Aimee had been up under me like I had served twenty years and not a couple hours. She didn't like that I had been taken from her, and I could understand her point of view. I was all she had and seeing me being tossed behind bars and her being helpless was triggering for her.

I couldn't even blame her lame ass cousin because that scary nigga was ghost before they could even get on his case. It was that fucking cop that just had to prove a point, and now his ass was gonna learn just how grave of a mistake he made.

Cappadonna Delgato went far to prove points and the people he proved them to never could speak about it after the point had been proven. I usually got in my feelings when my pops tried to handle shit for me, but this time I was smart enough to know that this was a situation that I needed to let him handle.

"I'm surprised Aimee let you out the house with the way she been acting with you." Pops laughed as he grabbed the chips he had been looking through. "Do better with the selection of chips and these are fucking expired." He grabbed a bag of salt and vinegar chips and tossed them toward the counter.

Jahquel J.

"She told me she felt like she lost me, even though she knew I would be home the next day. Pops, you already know how it is with her. She doesn't feel like she has family, and then the situation with her grandmother and aunt."

"Aimee's ass needs to stop acting like we ain't been here and would ride for her when she asks. I get she has this dumb ass need to be welcomed by her biological family, but she needs to realize that shit ain't gonna work out. Her ass needs to check her fucking grandmother and aunt. How the fuck they even feel right asking her for that amount of money." I could see him getting upset even talking about the shit.

I got mad thinking of her cousin trying to put his hands on her. If his ass was smart, he better had taken my warning to heart and moved the fuck around. As for her aunt and her grandmother, I was going to allow Aimee to handle that until I needed to step in. I would rather donate to the fucking dolphins fund than to give them money for a house.

Where the fuck did they even believe that shit even sounded right? None of them had been there for her, and they pretended she didn't exist after her mother and brother died. Like the leeches her mother and brother were, it didn't surprise me that her grandmother was the same way. Where else did her mother learn the behavior to pass down to Ace's ass.

"It doesn't matter how much I dislike her family, she gotta see that they fucking bed bugs. Aimee feels guilty, so I know that shit plays a big part."

"I sleep like a fucking baby at night. She gotta stop feeling guilty for people who lived their lives like her pain wasn't relevant. Her mother sat in my fucking face and called her a damn liar."

"Shit complicated."

"When isn't some shit complicated," he opened the chips and dumped half the bag into his mouth.

Capri

"This store holds special memories, Ock." Capone came into the store and smiled as he leaned on the freezer.

"How much you were trapping out of here?" Capp tried to guess what the fuck his twin was talking about.

"I met my baby here. She was right out there about to fuck Timmy's ass up, and Naheim stepped in... I always knew she had that shit in her." He closed his eyes as he reminisced on how he met Erin.

"Soft ass nigga," Capp trolled him.

"Says the same nigga that bought the laundry mat he met his wife in," Capone countered, and Capp couldn't help but to laugh.

As I made my way back out the store, a Benz pulled up in front of Capone's whip, and Naheim hopped out. When he spotted me, he smirked and walked over toward me.

"Look at the little nigga being the big dawg," he dapped me up.

I laughed as we embraced. "They let you back in New York... I hear an accent, huh?"

"Fuck outta here... fucking with NJ, you might hear a little accent or something." He laughed.

Capp came out the store eating the bag of chips I know his ass didn't pay for. "Look what the fuck the wind done blew in." He walked over and dapped Naheim, giving him a hug and looking him over.

"We're straight, Capp. You and Capone had to do what you had to do... I respect it. How is she?"

I half expected the first question he would ask was about Capri. She never asked about Naheim and had been doing her without being worried about him. I could tell that he was more worried about her than she was worried about him.

"I thought you weren't coming in until next week... the fuck happened with that?" Capone came over and dapped him up.

"I missed home, and the plan wasn't to stay down there

forever... moms is gone, and other than my family, I don't have no real reason to stay down there. I'm ready to get back to handling business."

"Erin sent you and Nellie that invitation for Capri's birthday party?"

She called me the other day and told me that Capri wanted to invite me. If you don't want me there, I respect that shit and will fall back.

Capp was messing with his beard. "If Baby Doll wants you there, then ain't shit that neither of us can say. Other than that, you straight?"

I saw how hard it was when it came to both Capri and Naheim. Pops wanted to show Capri that he had her back and stood ten toes behind her, but he looked at Naheim like he was a little brother too. I could see where he mentally struggled but was always going to ride for his sister before anything else.

I could already tell by the sound of the motorcycles that Quasim and Quameer had pulled onto the block. Soon as Quasim rolled onto the block, niggas was nodding their heads and moved their bikes out the way so he could pull through. He pulled up on the sidewalk, killing the engine of his bike, and sitting there for a second. Quameer was right behind him, pulling in behind him, and hopping off the bike as Pops stood there finishing the chips.

"Didn't yo ass get locked up for loitering before?" Quameer laughed as he dapped me up, then walked over toward Capp, and they did their IG handshake.

"Shut the fuck up. I'm surprised to see you out here and not up under Capri at the lake house." The shit slipped, and I saw the look on Naheim's face when the words left my mouth.

"Don't be a hater because we didn't invite you over for dinner," he teased, and then hopped up on the ice freezer while we all chilled. "What up, Naheim?"

Naheim nodded. "What's good, Meer?" The two of them

Capri

had never had a relationship, and it was always tense whenever they were around each other.

"What's the word on this Shmurda nigga, and how we handling his ass?" Quameer asked, as his brother continued to text on his phone.

Capone looked in the opposite direction as a car pulled onto the block. When an older lady got out with groceries, he turned his attention back to us. "The fact that he came after Pri leaves a bad taste in my mouth."

"He fucking did what?" Naheim blurted.

"Chill. She called me, and I made sure it wasn't a problem anymore." Meer shrugged like it was nothing.

I could tell the shit left a bitter taste in Naheim's mouth, but what the fuck could he say? He had a whole girl, and he and Capri were divorced. I don't even think she kept up with him when she was gone for the past year, so this wasn't his problem anymore.

"Those niggas be on Mother Gaston, over near Howard Houses... they run bitches over that way and be busting they little scams." Quasim finally joined us.

He dapped Naheim and everyone else before he leaned on the ice chest next to his brother. "It's clear that nigga wanted a response, so we gonna ride by there and give him one. I don't give a fuck who on the block tonight, they done."

"What scams they be running?" Naheim questioned.

"Phishing scams.... Heard they be bringing in fucking bank doing that shit, too."

Pops smirked while he leaned on his truck. "If there is one thing I can't stand, I can't stand when an old head moves like these little niggas. He should know the game and know that his sons played with me and ended up playing with the angels or the devils. We ride through there and make the block hot since that's where they make their money."

"Fuck with they money... I fuck with it." Capone came and leaned beside his brother, as he looked at all of us.

"Time to start removing plates from the table, Gunna." Pops held his hand out, and Capone dapped him up. "I happen to have a daughter-in-law that could fuck em over without ever being in the same room as them."

I smirked. "My baby can def fuck em over."

"In due time," Pops chuckled.

Quameer's phone started ringing and he hopped down and patted his jeans until he located where his phone was. He scanned the screen before he answered it and held the phone to his face. "This is my daily check in that I have not been kidnapped." Capri's voice came through, as if she was annoyed that he had to keep checking in with his ass.

"Appreciate it, Suga," he walked away, never paying any attention to any of us. Once he saw it was Capri, he didn't give a fuck that we all were in the middle of a conversation.

"What up, Baby Doll!" Pops yelled at his back, as he leaned on the other side of the store talking to her.

Naheim hadn't taken his eyes off Meer since he heard Capri's voice. "Nigga, you might as well go over there and join the fucking conversation," Capone joked, bringing Naheim back to reality.

"They messing around?" he asked.

"None of your business, Nah.... I ain't speaking on another man's business... he right there, ask 'em," Pops replied, walking around his truck.

"You right," Naheim said.

"See you niggas later." He saluted and pulled off with Capone following behind him in his whip.

Soon as Naheim looked my way, I held my hand up and headed to my truck. "Not my business, bro'."

"You acting like I'm asking the impossible... I wanna know if she messing with him." He followed behind me.

Capri

I paused before getting into my truck. "Nigga, why the fuck does it matter? You not with her anymore, so why you care?"

"Chubs, she is my ex-wife. I'm always gonna care about her."

Laughing, I closed the door back and decided to engage further in this madness he was over here conjuring up. "Caring about her and knowing her business is two different things though. Do you even still talk to her?"

"Yeah... we be talking."

I had been blessed with the gift of knowing when a nigga was bullshitting me, and I could tell that Naheim was bullshitting me. It wasn't like I was heavily into my aunt's business where I knew everything going on in her life.

Shit, Capri had become private with everybody since she been away. Even Pops was kept in the dark about certain shit going on in her life, and I respected it. We all witnessed Capri's crash out and go through the worst pain she probably had experienced.

Even while going through her own darkness, she still showed up for every damn body and didn't hesitate to bust her gun in the process, so the fact that she was intentional with what she shared meant that we needed to respect her shit.

"When the last time you talked to her?"

"She hit me for NJ's birthday."

"And then after that?"

"My birthday."

I broke out into laughter in his face. "Nah, leave me the fuck alone... she hitting you up on birthdays don't fucking count."

He shoved me while laughing. "I'm not even on it like that with her though... you forgot I got a whole girlfriend."

"Yeah, did you forget."

He settled on my car and looked my way. "I miss my friend, Chubs. Her light just fills up a nigga's world. I'm not on no funny shit with her either and respect whatever she got going on."

Just like I could sense he was bullshitting when it came to still talking to Capri, I could tell he was being sincere when he said he missed her as a friend. "You need to check all the other shit and lead with that. Don't be all weird watching her and shit, let her rock while you continue to live your life."

He nodded his head and leaned up, holding his hand out. "Appreciate you, C."

"Don't mention it... bring NJ by the lake house to play with Rory. Promise ass be herbing the fuck out my boy, he need to be around some boys his age," I joked.

Between Cee-Cee and Promise, Rory ain't have no other boy around his age to play with. When the twins were born, they would still be too young to play with him. I pictured them when they were older though, and they were gonna be a fucking problem.

"Bet. I'm gonna hit you up.... I'm out Sim," he called to Quasim, who saluted while going back to whatever he was doing on his phone.

I beeped my horn and waved to both Quameer and Quasim. Meer's ass was making kissy faces at his damn screen and all I could do is shake my head and laugh while hitting Aimee's name in my contacts.

"Hey Hun," she answered, sounding like she was out of breath. "Hun?"

"I'm here, Aim... what you doing, baby? Sound like you running around or something." I whipped through the different blocks, thinking about when we had the whole area on lock a few years back.

She giggled. "I am... I finished my last class for the summer, and I was going to get a ride back home with my friend, but she ended up having to leave early."

Capri

I checked her location. "Stay by that coffee shop, I'm on my way to you."

"I don't know who is worse with the location thing... you or your father," she teased. "I'll grab a coffee and wait; do you want anything?"

"Nah... I'm not in the mood to feel jittery."

"Capella," she said in that tone that told me she was about to get on my case for something, and knowing my girl, she was about to.

"Yeah, Aimee. The fuck did I do now?"

"You haven't been taking your medicine in the morning. You left your case out on your side of the sink, and you haven't taken it in three days."

"I missed three days. Shit ain't a big deal, Aim... chill on me."

She sighed. "Capella, you need to take your health and freedom seriously. You act like none of this is serious, as if you can't be take..." her voice cracked. "Taken away from me and your son. I'm begging you to act like you give a little bit of fuck about what happens to me and your son if you're taken away from us."

Every time I heard her about to cry, or when she cried, that shit did something to me. I hated for my lady to ever be emotional because of some shit that I had did to her. Aimee loved the shit out of me, and at times I questioned if she loved me more than herself.

"I'm sorry, Baby."

"I just want you to care. That's all I'm asking... see you when you get here." She ended the call, letting me know she was now pissed.

It took me twenty minutes to make it to the coffee shop, and when I pulled up, she was holding a conversation with some nigga around our age with waves and tattoos. He had a bookbag on his shoulder as Aimee laughed at whatever he had said.

I can assure you nothing that this nigga said was that fucking funny. Hitting my hazards, I hopped out and walked around the car. That was when she noticed me and said goodbye to him, hugging him in the process.

Who in the fuck was this nigga and why did she feel so fucking comfortable hugging his ass. She came out the coffee shop and I opened the door for her, expecting her to kiss me and she just got in.

I yanked her ass back and kissed her on the lips. "Don't piss me off, Aimee."

"Oh, now you give a fuck?"

I allowed her to get in and closed the door before rounding the truck and getting back in. "You on your period or some shit?"

"Why do I have to be on my period for me to care, Capella?"

"Who the fuck was that nigga?"

"He's in my cyber defense class… we're friends."

"Not answering my question, Aim."

"Landon. We're friends, Capella… he's super smart and helps me in class sometimes. Being honest, he's the reason that I got three bands last month."

"He giving you money now?" I damn near drove us into oncoming traffic when she mentioned that she got money from him.

Aimee waved me away. "You are hearing what you wanna hear. I said he's the reason that I made that money last month. If you don't trust me then we can call it quits before even getting engaged… whenever that is gonna happen." She cut her eyes at me.

"You calling me a liar."

"Maybe."

I looked over at her and caught the little smirk. "Aim, you know I'm crazy about you."

Capri

"And you know I'm crazy about you, so stop tripping out when you see me with people that are friends. Capella, I have a life outside of being your girlfriend and Rory's mama... you wanted me to go back to college, and now I'm doing it. Don't put limitations on what I can do."

"Fair."

"Thank you. Can we go to the lake house because I miss my baby. Being away from him this week has been hard." Even with me having to come back out here, I was going to drive her to our baby because I knew she needed to see him. Facetime wasn't enough for Aimee. She was a hands on mother and had barely left Rory since he had been born.

"I know... I missed him, too," I admitted.

She reached over and roped her fingers with mine and smiled. "Love you, Hun."

"Love you, too, Aim," I replied as I made my way to the tunnel so we could go and get our son. It was a blessing having my grandparents, father, and Alaia, because they made it easier for Aimee to do her thing in school without having to pick and choose.

For that, I would always appreciate and love them.

"The fuck do you want, Brandi?" Quameer snarled, as he sat on his bike. This nigga was answering calls like we weren't about to slide on niggas.

"Eww, there is no need for you to act funny like that, baby daddy," Brandi slurred, as Quameer looked at her over facetime.

It was clear she was drunk, and this wasn't something that naturally occurred between the two of them. Quameer never spoke on his shit, so nobody really knew the story with his baby mama, and why he couldn't stand her ass.

Jahquel J.

He stared at the screen with disgust like she had spit at the camera or some shit. "How is it possible your head even bigger over facetime... the fuck you want, Brandi?"

"Well, how big does your little boo look talking to Mason in our section?" I was standing behind him, and I saw as she sloppily switched the camera around, and sure enough Capri was holding a conversation with Mason. He had his arm roped around her as she spoke directly into his ear.

I could feel the fucking heat coming from Meer's body as he squeezed his phone. "What the fuck do you want me to do with that information?"

"Quameer, please. You're the biggest fucking crash out when it comes to the woman you love... Mason Jackson with your girlfriend and you cool?" she taunted, getting a sick pleasure out of seeing this man about to bug the fuck out.

He didn't even reply, he ended the call with her and called Capri's phone. When she didn't answer, he called a second time. He searched his contacts and hit a name.

"Yo Za... I need a favor... get me a jet chartered.... Anguilla... yeah... two... I'mma send the bread over," he replied before ending the call and sliding the phone in his pocket.

"You done fucking cupcakin' on the phone with Brandi's ass?" Quasim asked, as he slid his mask over his face.

"We out when we done with this," he told his brother, who didn't question him. Sim just nodded and then rode by.

Quameer remained quiet while I went to jump in the whip with my father. He was wrapping up a call with Promise when I got into the car. Every night, no matter where he was, he was going to read a book to her and talk to her before Alaia could put her down for the night.

"She went to sleep before you could finish the book this time," Alaia whispered on the phone while my father leaned back with a smile on his face.

This was the shit that he lived for. Being a husband and a

Capri

father was what got him out the bed every morning. His family is why he was out here about to handle business to keep them safe. Capone pulled up with Naheim in the passenger seat and nodded before pulling ahead of us to the meeting spot.

"She been fighting her sleep since naptime. Kiss her for me, Joy."

"You know I always do. I need you to be careful and make sure you handle business so you can bring your butt back home."

He smirked. "I love you."

"Love you more, Roy."

He ended the call and put his phone in the cupholder, looking over at me. "Everybody ready?"

"Yeah. Quameer got the call about Capri with some nigga while on vacation."

Pops laughed. "He wanted Baby Doll, he gotta deal with what comes with her. Meer wanted the blessing; he got that shit. Now he need to handle his shit."

We were in Queens at one of the IG houses that we ran work through. Kincaid pulled up on his bike and hit the IG shake with Capp through the window before he pulled off down the block hitting a wheelie at the end of the block.

Quasim rolled passed the window, giving Capp the signal that we were rolling out. We waited for Quameer to roll behind his brother before he joined his side, and we pulled out. Per usual, all the other IG's circled around us and Capone as we drove slowly through the blocks until we made it onto the Belt Parkway.

The minute we hit the Belt Parkway; we increased speed. Quasim and Quameer were in and out of traffic with Kincaid behind them. Goon saluted as he sped past us, and we switched lanes until we were right behind them.

Capone's whip pulled up beside us before he dipped over two lanes and followed behind Quameer. I cocked my shit back, grabbing our mask from the glove compartment. I watched my father's jaw tighten the closer we got, and he grabbed his mask.

"Don't even give em any chance to breathe... air that bitch out, C."

"You already know."

It was summertime in Brooklyn, so hearing dirt bikes and motorcycles wasn't out the norm. You could always count on niggas riding by on their dirt bikes or motorcycles doing wheelies in traffic. Just like the bikes were out, the cops were also out chasing them down. This shit was all part of a New York summer. It didn't matter what borough you were in; everybody was outside on any block enjoying the nice weather.

On every other block you could count on somebody on the grill and selling plates. The shit always made me proud of my city. Even as we exited off the belt and made our way through Brooklyn. Bitches were out with they asses out, holding a nutcracker and talking to niggas showing off they new whip.

Quameer sped up, hitting a wheelie as he cleared the yellow light, and then dipped down the opposite street from us. Kincaid and Goon dipped down another block, while Sim remained in front of us, with Capone on the side. As we crawled down Liberty Ave and made a left on Mother Gaston, I pulled my mask down and got ready.

Quasim got low on his bike as he held his gun out and let it go, while Capp had his follow up. I ain't let up on that trigger as we cleared the block. On the side of us, I saw Meer come by letting his shit go while on his phone.

This nigga wasn't even phased that we were in the middle of some shit, his ass had the phone cradled between his shoulder and ear as he continued to let his shit go, making a left off the block, he saluted and was out.

Quasim was right behind his brother, as we hit a right and headed right back toward the belt, but we could still hear shit

Capri

getting crazy. This shit was like a fucking soul train line, and everybody was getting a turn to pull they shit. The sound of motorcycles, gunshots and people screaming as they ran was all that could be heard as we gained distance from them.

Capone's name came up on the car's screen. "Yo."

"You straight?" I could tell his ass was smiling.

Capp smirked. "Nigga, you already know… been a little minute. Let em come to us now the right way."

"Facts… we out."

"Copy."

My father looked over at me. "That block gonna be hot for a minute so they gonna rely on they other source of income… time for Aimee to come fuck 'em up."

"With pleasure."

Chapter 16
Capri

WHEN THE GIRLS TRIP FINALLY MAKES IT OUT THE GROUP chat and ends up being the trip from hell. Had I known that this trip would end up like this, I probably would have stayed my ass home. I wanted off this fucking island now.

"All I'm trying to figure out is why you would think it would be a good idea to invite Mason and his friends on your bachelorette trip as a soon to be married woman?" Blair asked, because I was still too fucking stunned to speak.

I sat back with the darkest pair of shades that I packed on as I stared across the table at Jesse in her stupid ass penis sunglasses.

"His *rich* NFL friends," Zoya mocked what Jesse said earlier.

"If you don't like money, just say that, Blair," Brandi decided to add her two cents, which further pissed me off because I already was done with her when she showed up to my house before the trip.

"I don't like you... I'm saying that," Blair snapped.

Jesse took back another shot, her fourth shot since we had been seated for lunch. Since we landed, she had been drinking around the clock, shoving drinks down everyone's throat, then crying once she was fully drunk and couldn't walk.

I came to enjoy the few days we would be here and have a few drinks. Hell, I couldn't even enjoy the few drinks because I couldn't tolerate the damn taste or smell of alcohol, so I had been drinking fruity drinks where I could barely taste the alcohol, or enjoying the freshly pressed juices all the bars seemed to have.

"Mason slid in my dm's and I invited him out here. Why is that such a problem? I didn't think hanging around successful single NFL players would be a problem for you three." She pointed to me, Zoya, and Blair.

"I'm already around successful men all day long and I damn sure don't need your help, Jesse," Zoya countered.

Jesse held her hands up in a mock surrender. "I'm just trying to put all my girls on, and you all are giving me the stink eye about it. It sure didn't look like you minded when you were all on him last night," she smirked as she tried to give me kudos like what she had said had any truth to it.

"What are you talking about? We were kicking it all night while you were tossing yourself all over him. I had a drink, not twelve, so seems like someone forgot."

Jesse and Brandi got so fucked up last night that it took me, Blair, and Zoya to bring them back to our villa. All Jesse kept hollering was how bored she was and screaming like she was arguing with David.

Since we had arrived, I had been wanting to leave and go back home to deal with my own shit. Jesse had made this entire trip about accommodating Brandi. She shoved me and Blair in a tiny ass room right by the front door, so when the staff came in and out the villa, we heard the damn door slam, or them mowing the lawn or cleaning the pool.

This trip wasn't about me, so I wasn't going to complain and took it on the chin. When we went out last night and she got to screaming Mason's name like a lunatic, I was pissed. Mainly because why was he here, and why the fuck did he come here?

Me and Mason hadn't spoken since the night at the chicken spot. Neither of us texted or reached out to the other, which was fine. We were both busy, and Mason was a playboy. He wanted his cake, and he wanted to eat it too, so I knew there was plenty of women occupying his time. I didn't take any of the game he called himself spitting to me seriously because I knew how it went when it came to these athletes.

If his ass knew how Meer operated, he would have left me alone before he was sitting home watching the season unfold without him being the star on the field. What I did respect and enjoy about Mason was how he sensed that his presence wasn't a welcomed surprise, so he wasn't on that type of time with me last night.

He bought drinks for our section and then we chilled most of the night. At the end of the night, he offered to help us back to the villa, and we declined because we pretty much had Jesse and Brandi's drunk asses.

"Tonight, we're going to turn up so hard. We literally have two more days here, and then back to real life. I need you all to start acting like you wanna turn up and for me to have the best bachelorette party."

> Star: Pull up to Miami... me and Skye are down here for Race weekend.

I nearly jumped out my chair when I saw her message pop up on my screen.

Blair noticed me and looked over at my phone and then smiled. "Damn, is she gonna be alright?"

I peeped her lie, and Zoya looked over at me, too. "Oh no... seriously? Capri, I am here for you," she faked along with Blair while Jesse and Brandi looked on.

Capri

The problem I had with Jesse was how she was putting everything on us like we were the only bitches here. Her cousins and other bridesmaids had only been worried about tanning and drinking, not making this memorable for her.

"Is that Quameer?" Brandi blurted, and I looked at her weird, because why the hell was she asking me who was on my phone, and why did she assume it was Quameer.

"Something has come up back home," I lied, purposely ignoring the shit out of Brandi with her dumb ass question.

"Oh no, what happened?" she chugged back another shot, not really concerned for what was going on with me in my life.

"Personal stuff. I'm go—"

"We're gonna have to leave early," Zoya quickly corrected as Blair rubbed my back, and I faked a sad face.

Jesse looked at her watch, then her phone. "Seriously, Capri? What about this trip... we've planned this."

Blair choked. "She has an emergency, and you're worried about why she can't sit around while you get shit face and have fake drunken arguments with David, who isn't even here."

Jesse hated anytime that Blair had something to say, and I was starting to notice that about her. Blair had mentioned it to me a few times, and I didn't brush it off, but I kind of accused her of looking too deep into things, which is something that Blair occasionally did.

As we sat across from Jesse, I saw the way she looked while Blair spoke to her. She was pissed that she even had the nerve to say anything or take my side. "Are you ready for the booze cruise?"

She leaned on Brandi as she stood up from the table, catching her balance. Once she was good on her feet, she went over toward the beach to gather the rest of the girls. I watched as Brandi lingered a bit before she turned back toward the table. "She's really drunk... I know she cares."

"No excuse for her to be a bird," Zoya scoffed.

This was the first time I saw a genuine side of Brandi. Do you know how shitty you have to have been for Brandi to sympathize with me?

"I truly hope everything with your family works out... don't worry about her, I will speak to her," she assured me like I cared.

"Thanks, Brandi."

She headed to follow behind Jesse. "Always fixing her problems like when we were in college... ugh. Why the fuck are we even here, Capri?" Blair rolled her eyes.

"Trying to be a good friend... one day I will learn."

Zoya laughed. "I was here for the free villa, but the fact that she shoved my ass in a shoe closet shows just how much she cared about any of us being here."

Blair looked over at Zoya. "Free villa when your family probably owns several is crazy, Zoya."

The Caselli family was the third founding family on Staten Island. Zoya came from a powerful family that remained private. I had known her all throughout law school, and I had no clue who her parents were. All I knew is that she came from money — lots of money — and her family wasn't anything to mess with.

I casually mentioned her once to Capone, and he gave me a little insight into who her family was. Everyone had enough respect to never mention them and allow them to move the way they did. All I knew is that Zoya wasn't hurting for money, and she had two brothers and a sister. The rest was a mystery and Zoya's ass was like a vault.

For as long as I've known, this has been my life, so I understood why she was quiet when it came to her family. We both attended school and fit in, meanwhile we probably had way more money than half the spoiled assholes we attended school with.

"Free is free, Blair." She flipped her freshly curled hair to

Capri

the back and sipped the rest of her drink. "Are we rebooking flights to Miami, because I know we'll have more fun there than here."

Blair held the phone up and smiled with her confirmation to her new flight. I quickly went on and managed to snag a seat before texting Star back.

> Me: My flight lands in a couple hours.

> Star: My girl.

IT DIDN'T MAKE SENSE HOW QUICK WE PACKED OUR SHIT, got a ride to the airport and boarded our flight. In three hours' time, we were landing in Miami and ready to turn up and continue the fun. There was this small piece of me that was avoiding having that conversation with my brothers. I didn't want to believe that my parents had lied to us our entire life.

I didn't want to believe that my parents were fucking liars at all, and knowing there was a child out there growing up without them kept me up at night. The old Capri would have ignored this and kept it to myself, because it was better to run away from my problems than to face them. I couldn't be like that anymore, and both Capone and Cappadonna deserved to know this information too. This had everything to do with them too, so they needed to know.

Why was he following me around in the first place? These were questions only he could answer, and I had been too chicken shit to even call and try and find out more information. I made a silent promise that once I was back home that I was going to deal with everything and tell my brothers.

"See this is the kind of view I was expecting when we were

in Anguilla. Jesse had us in the damn maid quarters." Zoya took in the view of the bay, and the buildings surrounding our hotel.

Blair popped open the bottle of champagne and poured us each a flute. "To a real girl's trip without the catty behavior and shade."

"Cause if Jesse tossed shade your way one more time... she was gonna have to see me," Zoya clinked glasses with us and took hers back, while I sipped mine and sat it back on the table.

"The question of the day is why Brandi asked about Quameer? Does she know about the two of you?"

"Yeah, I wanted to ask at the courthouse with the way he was eye fucking you." Zoya plopped down on the couch across from me.

"We're not together, but I'm not stupid enough to talk to another nigga."

"And is he not stupid enough not to talk to another bitch?" Blair blurted as she filled her flute back up, then walked over to do the same with Zoya's.

"Honestly, I don't know. I'm trying to trust that he wouldn't do me like that, but some chick texted him before he dropped us off, so I'm having second thoughts."

"Ms. Good Neck," Blair busted out laughing.

Zoya leaned up. "Wait, he had a chick saved in his phone as that?"

"He has names for everybody. Brandi is in his phone as Water Head." Blair couldn't help but to fall out laughing when I mentioned his nickname for Brandi. "He said he hadn't talked to that girl in months, so I don't know what to believe. Why would she text that she misses him."

"Because bitches are petty. Especially when the nigga they want moves on. A bitch will tell you she's pregnant with his dog to get under your skin. It's up to you if you feel like dealing with that." Zoya shrugged.

That chick texting Meer had been in the back of my head. I

trusted Meer with my life because he had proven himself to me, so it was hard trying to believe him and then allowing my inner thoughts to get the best of me. I didn't want to end up being played again, my heart couldn't take that.

"Meer is one of the good men, Capri. He's so honest that sometimes you want him to lie a bit. He honestly looked shocked and pissed that she even texted him," Blair defended him.

"You just want me with him so bad."

"I do, girl... I love the two of you together. He waited for you, Pri... what man does something like that?"

"Not too many," Zoya mumbled.

"Goon would," I teased.

"Gerald is a client and I'm not going to cross those lines with him.... I do know he needs to stop calling me to ask me dumb ass questions."

I laughed because I could only imagine. "Well, you are his lawyer. He retained you for a lot of money I heard."

"Capri, he called to tell me that he J walked. Claim we needed to get a meeting on the schedule to discuss our plans to fight the case."

"The case?"

"He got a ticket for it, and I'm moved to believe that he forced that damn cop to give it to him because cops don't even give you tickets for those anymore."

"He's not wrong... it is illegal," I giggled.

"Goon is fine, Zoya... why you acting like he's not." Blair plopped down beside her and took a sip of her champagne.

"Fine doesn't pay these bills. Gerald is like every client I have defended. They see me, idolize me because I got them off, and then crickets. I made a mistake once dating a client and I'm not going back down that road again."

"Would your parents not approve?"

"My parents are dead. My brother is the one that would

need to approve, and being that Menace is a dick... Me and Kora might be old and gray before he ever approves of anyone we date," she spoke of her sister.

It was how she casually announced that her parents were dead. "Damn, I'm sorry." Blair burped.

"They've been dead since I was seven. My brother raised me along with my siblings. Menace is tough, but he loves hard."

The mood had turned dark, and I laid back on the couch and closed my eyes. "No sleep... we're going out tonight." Blair jumped up off the couch and clapped her hands.

I could have slept here for the next twelve hours if she let me. Star told me where the party was tonight, so instead of laying around, we unpacked and got ready for tonight. I grabbed my phone and sent Meer a quick message.

> Me: Hey.

I expected him to reply right away like he usually did. With me being away, he was probably catching up things that he had been putting off.

Chapter 17
Quameer

CAPRI'S ASS THOUGHT I WAS PLAYING WITH HER ASS. When Brandi turned that camera around and showed me her with Mason, I damn near lost my mind. I let the shit rock because I was her man, that wasn't her man, that would lay any man out behind her. She thought shit was sweet because she was in Anguilla for Jesse's little hoe ass bachelorette trip. Why the fuck was Mason's ass there to begin with?

She should have known I would crash out behind her sexy ass. You don't give me good pussy while moaning in my ear and think we don't go together. With how good her pussy was, I already picked out her engagement ring, the granite in our new crib and named all three of our kids, cause she was giving me three seeds. If that wasn't enough, I was silently debating on which kind of damn doodle dog we would get.

I was jealous and possessive over her, and I wasn't gonna sit back and be the bigger man. Sometimes being the bigger man meant you had to shoot a nigga and let the nigga look up at you from the ground as he screamed in pain.

"I can feel your ass thinking way over here. Was it necessary for us to travel to fucking Miami like it's an emergency.

First it was Anguilla, and now fucking Miami... you need to tighten up."

"It is a fucking emergency," I spat, looking at my brother, who wished he could be anywhere but here.

The only reason we were on our way to Miami and not Anguilla was because my high ass cousin. His ass had the best weed, but he needed to stop smoking that shit. No sooner than I ended the call with his ass, he had forgot what I called him for.

It took both Goon and Quasim to hold me back from putting my foot in his ass when we got to that private airport and there was no jet fucking fueled and ready to go. The only reason I knew she was in Miami was because of Blair's story.

After almost getting his ass beat, Za came through with the jet and making sure we were taking off at the right time. I wasn't playing with his ass, and if he didn't want me to take a shit and light it on fire in front of his house, his ass better had start taking notes when I called his ass.

"This shit not an emergency," Goon sparked a spliff and took a long pull before letting down the window.

"Shouldn't you be worried about how you're in another state when you're not supposed to be." I turned my attention back to my brother. "If you didn't think it was an emergency, why the fuck you came?"

"To make sure you don't do no dumb shit, Meer."

"I got money on Mason this season, so leave his fucking knee alone, lunatic," Goon added as he continued to smoke.

Truthfully, the only reason Quasim's ass was here was because he wanted to run into Blair's ass. He wanted Blair and then acted like he was scared when she gave him some attention. Sim needed to get his shit together because he was starting to give me vibes like his ass played for the other team.

We had landed and were on our way to the same hotel that the girls were staying in. Blair was posting in real time, and that

Capri

was something I needed her ass to chill on. As I watched the video of them riding the elevator down dressed, I could peep something was wrong with Capri. She was withdrawn from the video. Blair had smushed her face against her, hyping her up before she smiled and did a sexy little pose.

"Zoya fine ass with them?"

Quasim chuckled and shook his head. "You know she a Caselli, right?"

"Nigga, her name is on my papers, so you know I saw the shit... she still fine as shit and I want her."

"Want to be free before trying to fuck your lawyer... ain't you fucking your probation officer?" I replied, while getting the play by play on Blair's stories.

"Sim, you real low for telling my business."

Quasim turned in the seat. "The bitch be beating down your door, the shit ain't no secret."

Goon took a pull and laughed. "Fuck you meannn, she doing her job."

I tuned they asses out as we continued to the hotel. Once we checked in, I went to my room to change clothes so we could head right back out. I checked Blair's page, and she posted a picture of drinks.

The next video was Suga smiling while taking a shot, and dancing in her seat at the bar. I don't know what went down, or why she left the trip early, but I planned to get to the middle of the shit.

The club was jumping because of all the races that were going on this weekend. Everybody from back home was out here turning up because this weekend was like a movie. Quasim hit Karter, and he told us he was at the club and told us to pop out.

I spotted Karter in his section, and we headed up there. "Thought you had some other shit to do?" Karter teased.

"This crash out got us stalking Capri."

Karter raised his eyebrow. "You and Capri... when the fuck that happened?" He handed us drinks, and we sat down on the couch.

I had calmed down since Brandi showed me that video, so I wasn't even on that anymore. Once I knew she left Anguilla, I could have chilled and went home. Instead, I decided to come down here since the last time we were in Miami I had to kick a nigga's head off.

Being real, I just wanted to be around Suga. How we left shit seemed good, but I knew her well enough to know that her ass loved to overthink shit and by the time she would have made it home, her ass would have written me off as marrying this chick and fucking her while she was out the country.

I knew my nutcase well, so I wasn't giving her any room to get in that fucking head of hers. She wasn't gonna compare me to Naheim. That man's problems was his own and I wasn't about to pay for them.

From where we were sitting, I could see my Suga perfectly. She was standing by the bar talking to Zoya, Blair, Star, and Skye. They were taking shots and rapping along with the music. "Tomorrow" by Glorilla was playing, and the way Suga did that little lick motion while rapping Cardi B's verse had me ready to go down there now.

Why the fuck was she so damn sexy?

Her outfit didn't make the shit any better. She had on this short ass denim skirt, white Jill Sanders baby tee, and a pair of heels that made her a bit taller tonight. Every nigga in this bitch was looking at them. They were the main attraction in this club tonight. Any bitch that thought she was going to be the center of attention needed to come another night. It was clear from the way those jealous hoes in the section across from the bar was staring at them.

I peeped how they kept looking at them and whispering

Capri

among themselves. This is why I always told her she needed to stop worrying. Suga was that chick, and she made other women jealous. Any room she stepped in, she never had to do much and that was still enough. It wasn't until you spoke to her that you realized she was educated and a fucking bad ass inside and out. I think that was the reason why I was so attracted to her.

One minute she was out here partying and turning up with her girls, then the next she was cuddled up with a book. Suga could read a book in a day and be on the next one just that quick.

Whenever Capri's ass walked into a room, the song "Girlfriend" by Bow Wow and that nigga that be pop locking always played in my head. Except she wasn't mine yet, but I'll break a nigga's jaw for even looking her way.

Capri and Blair were taking back shots like the shit was going out of style. I watched as she danced having the time of her life with Blair. The bitches in the section was still popping off at the mouth, even though the girls weren't even paying them any attention.

I mean why the fuck would they?

As I watched a nigga walked over and whispered something in her ear, too damn close, I leaned up and Quasim held my shoulder. "Play it, P... you bout to go crazy and she pushed his ass away, and he respected it."

"Oh yeah? Why Blair sitting on his homie's lap?"

I had been so busy watching my baby I didn't notice that other nigga's friend slip in. Blair was being extra flirty and sitting on his lap. I could tell both she and Capri were fucked up because they kept whispering in each other's ears, then laughing. Homie kept his hands around Blair's waist, and didn't mind her sitting on him. Even when she tried to get up when Star pulled her up, he kept her right on his lap.

Star pointed up to our section and looked back at the man

and he shrugged, whispering something in Blair's ear, who giggled and told the girls that she was fine. Suga's ass was dancing and rapping all off key like all was perfect in this moment. I watched as she took another shot.

"I'll beat all you hoe's ass!" I read her lips as she pointed to the bitches in the section across from them. That was when I decided it was time for me to go get her ass because Star was pulling her back.

All that P shit Quasim was preaching went out the window when he watched what had just unfolded. I watched Quasim rise, and his ass damn near floated downstairs. Me and Goon followed behind him, playing it cool since I didn't have to knock a nigga out.

He gently pulled Blair out of homie's lap and pulled her dress down that had risen. Blair was drunk as fuck, and I could tell from all the glasses of water on the bar that Star and Zoya had been trying to get both her and Capri to drink water.

"The fuck wrong with you, Gang... we fucking chil—" Quasim grabbed him by the throat, lifting him off the stool as he stared into his eyes.

"Quasim, leave him alone... you not even my mannnn," Blair slurred, as she tried to remove his hand from the nigga's neck. "Meer, help me out... he don't even like me for real."

"Ain't my business, Blair," I looked over at Capri, who was staring at me like she was trying to figure out if I was an illusion or if I was really standing next to her. "Suga, keep yo' ass right here."

"You leaving this club with me, Blair... right?" He applied more pressure to the man's neck, and Blair realized that this nigga was serious.

"I'm not leaving anywhere with you... you ignore me and then come trying to puf—"

"Tell his ass you le...leaving with him," Homie being choked managed to squeal.

Capri

Blair was so damn confused and didn't know what to say or do. She stood there staring at the man and then up into Quasim's eyes. I couldn't help but laugh because Sim had a straight face as he choked this nigga out.

"You leaving with me, right?" Quasim looked her in the eyes as he applied a bit more pressure. The man was fucking red, and Sim didn't give a fuck that he could kill this nigga.

"Yes...yess... I'm going with you," Blair stammered.

Quasim let him go and held his hand out and Blair stumbled over toward him, taking his hand. "We out... I don't ever wanna see you out here drunk like this." He moved closer to her ear. "Do I make myself clear, Blair?"

She stared up at him and nodded while homie scrambled away from them. "Quasim?" He didn't answer, he raised his brow, motioning for her to go on. "My feet really hurt."

Without a word, he picked her up and carried her through the crowd toward the exit. Quasim had always been the quiet brother, not too many met the crazy. Blair was introduced to that shit tonight.

Sim was the crazy that would be chilling one second, then snapping your neck next. I ain't never had a problem doing the most when it came to my woman. I wore that shit with pride and would happily smile in a mug shot. Quasim's ass was in denial about him being the same way.

"What up, Ms. Lawyer." Goon licked his lips as his eyes took down Zoya, who looked from Quasim and Blair leaving to her client.

"Gerald, how in the hell are you even here? Do you know that they could violate you for being in Miami while on parole... did you get permission?"

"Something like that," he rubbed his hands together, hovering over her. He was staring down at her. "You gotta chill with the Gerald, Ms. Lawyer."

It was my turn to turn my attention to Suga, who was

already standing there looking good as shit. "Aye, you gonna learn to stop pissing me off, ight?"

"Meer, whatcha doing here?" Capri laughed, as she went to grab the shot off the bar, and I grabbed her hand. "What the fuck, Meer?" She pulled away, and I pulled her closer, kissing her neck.

"You fucked up, Sug."

She counted on her fingers before busting out laughing, spit hitting my face in the process. "I only had about seven sho... ohhh this my shit." Before she could finish whatever she was saying, she started dancing.

"You got her under control... I'm going upstairs with my husband. They getting too thirsty down here," Star said, as she quickly hugged me and Goon.

Goon made sure he walked her through the crowd before coming back where we were. "Since I know we're about to leave... let's go use the bathroom."

Zoya grabbed Capri as they made their way to the bathroom. I sat at the bar while waiting for them to come back.

"She so fucking sexy... look how she just bossed her way through that fucking crowd... I'll fucking marry her ass... you think she eat swine?"

I looked at Goon while shaking my head. "Nigga, she your lawyer."

Waving over the bartender, I slid my credit card to him to close out their tab. While he was ringing me out, he slid a shot on the house for me. Taking it back, I continued to scan the club out of habit.

"Every good love story happens behind a prison wall or the courtroom," Goon's delusional ass replied.

"Is you straight? 'Cause what the fuck are you even talking about." I signed my name on the receipt and reached in my pocket to bless the bartender with a big ass tip.

Capri

I wasn't clocking how long it took to use the bathroom, but we had been sitting here for twenty minutes and neither Zoya nor Capri had brought they ass back over this way. I abandoned the bar and made my way to the bathroom with Goon behind me.

"Open the damn door... Capri, open the door." Zoya banged on the door, and that's when I increased my speed. "She told you she don't want you... open the door!"

"Please move out my way... I promise you... re...really gonna wanna let me out. This not cute," Capri slurred through the door.

"Stop fronting on me, you been eyeing me all night."

"Negative, bitch. She been eyeing your hating ass girlfriend grilling the fuck out of us." Zoya kicked the door. "Q—"

I held my finger up to my lips and Goon gently removed her away from the door. The frail oak door didn't stand a chance for the way I was about to kick this bitch down.

"Just let me out the bathroom... I can't give you my number... I'm in a situation." I could hear Capri's voice, and she sounded further away from the door.

"He not her—"

I kicked the door so fucking hard that the shit flew open and busted that nigga in the face. He all but screamed with the way I came in that bathroom and stomped his ass out. He was on the floor, halfway under the stall, and next to the door.

"Don't ever in yo' life corner a fucking woman!" I said through gritted teeth. "Especially my fucking woman." I punched his ass in the mouth while he was trying to get his ass into fetal position.

The door wasn't even locked since there was more than one stall in here. His body weight was no match for Zoya to get the door open on her own. Capri was sitting on the sink looking at me with those low eyes as I beat the shit out this man.

"What the fuck are you doing to my boyfriend?" a woman shrieked while pushing me. Her push didn't do shit, but piss me off.

Her man was on the floor groaning in pain, and her ass was about to join him if she touched me again. "Oh, bitch, I don't play about him," Capri hopped down from the sink and rushed over toward shorty.

"Bitch, it's up. You been in my man's face all damn night. I'm gonna black that fucking eye since you think you so cute," shorty started to pull her earrings out, and Capri pulled her arm back and was about to punch her head back, and Goon jumped between the both of them.

"Nah, we not doing that shit here... get your damn man off the floor and get the fuck outta here, lil' mama."

This bitch had the nerve to be all flirtatious with Goon while her nigga was bleeding out on the floor. "Ray-Ray, you got me out here looking stupid as hell... I told you smiling up in other bitches' faces was gonna get you fucked up."

I looked down at my boots and went to leap over on his ass again. "He got fucking blood on my fresh timbs... I'm 'bout to real—"

"Chill the fuck out... We out before this nigga get his pussy ass friends and we gotta stomp they asses out because we not strapped."

"Well, considering you already done broke laws being here, you should have just brought your gun," Zoya replied, leaned on the sink next to Capri.

"Aye, Ms. Lawyer... chill it out with that smart ass mouth."

She blushed and looked in the opposite direction. I grabbed Suga's hand and led her out the club while she kept laughing. Don't ask me why the fuck she was laughing so hard because I didn't fucking know. On our way out I slid the bouncer some bread, and held on tightly to Suga's wild ass.

"Meer Cat, Meer Cat, where are youuuu," she sang out

Capri

while I held her in front of me while waiting for an Uber, since Quasim's ass wanted to take the damn car back to the hotel.

"Meer Cat?" Goon snorted.

"The fuck you snorting at... that's the name my baby gave me."

Capri leaned over me toward Goon. "He loves it, too."

"I don't know about all that, Sug," I held her closer to me while tracking this damn Uber. Her ass was stuck a block away.

Zoya stood with her arms folded. "How the fuck did the night end up like this? We were supposed to be turned... I mean, you way passed turned up."

"The night don't gotta end. We need to work on our case, Ms. Lawyer."

Zoya laughed. "Gerald, you gonna pay that damn ticket and we're gonna try and get this other one dismissed. I don't date my clients, and I don't care if you come highly recommended."

"Put that on our kids."

She stood up to him, trying to make herself taller than he was. "I put that on our... wait a damn minute," Zoya caught herself and laughed.

"Chill with me for a little bit... as lawyer and client, nothing more." Goon was a damn liar with the way he was licking his lips.

Where the club was, there was a bunch of food spots that stayed open late. Zoya looked at Capri, who was dancing to imaginary music. "Is she good?"

"Stop playing with me, Zoya."

She laughed. "My bad, Mr. Inferno... I always said you had a crush on her, and you always lied."

Zoya used to say little slick shit whenever I happened to be around Capri and the rest of the girls. Usually, it was because I was waiting on Brandi's ass. She would always tease me about liking Capri and how I would go out my way just to speak to

Capri whenever I saw her. I used to deny that shit so heavily because I didn't want to believe it.

"My bad, Meer... wifey don't know how to chill," Goon grabbed Zoya by the waist, and she slapped his hands.

"Gerald, keep your hands to yourself or we're not gonna get any food together."

He smirked rubbing his hands together. "See you at the hotel, Meer." We hit the IG handshake, and he grabbed Zoya around the waist, moving her toward the inside of the sidewalk while he walked on the outside.

Our Uber had finally came and it was a quick ten-minute ride back to the hotel. Capri was on the phone with Erin the entire ride. Erin started off the conversation concerned when she heard her slurring. Once she realized I was with her, she calmed down and appeased Capri and her rant about not building on her piece of land on the compound. I don't know what the fuck that had to do with anything, but she kept going on and on about it.

"You staying in my room tonight, Suga," I told her as we walked toward the elevator, and she was skipping in her heels.

From how red her toes were, I could tell she was gonna be in pain tomorrow. "Meer, I gotta secret," she hung around my neck, while we waited for the elevator to take us up to my floor.

"What's the secret, Sug?" I yawned, tired because I hadn't gotten any sleep since Brandi's petty ass had called me.

Capri giggled as she leaned her head on my chest. "I missed my period." She snorted, then broke out into laughter.

My head was leaned back on the elevator wall, and I leaned up to look at her while she continued to be tickled by the fact that she had missed her period. "That normal for you or some shit?"

I knew what a missed period meant, but I also knew that women missed their periods all the time and that didn't mean

Capri

she was pregnant. "Nooopeee," she sang while hitting the running man.

"Bro', you so fucked up," I laughed.

"I am... so bad, Meer Cat," she gagged, and I shot over to the other side of the elevator. I was solid and could hold my woman down with a lot of shit, but vomit made my ass sick.

If she didn't want this elevator covered in both of our vomit, she better had kept that shit in. "Suga, don't you fucking throw up in this elevator."

"I had to burp.... Relaxxxxx."

The elevator doors opened, and she let go of my hand and took off down the hallway. I don't know how the fuck she was running that damn fast in heels. She ran her ass right past my room.

"Yo Sha 'Carri, the room right here," I called down the hall, knowing that I was probably interrupting the people sleeping since it was like three in the morning.

Capri did some football move before she came charging down the hall at me. I stood there trying to decide whether I was gonna let her tackle my ass, or if I was gonna dip into this room. Anytime we got on facetime and got drunk together, she acted all coy and cute.

Her ass was fucking aggressive and crazy as shit when she was drunk, and I was seeing that now. "Alright, my feet really hurt now, and I don't feel good." She slowed down.

No sooner than I helped her out her shoes, she climbed into the bed and was snoring loud as shit. I covered her with the blanket before going out on the balcony to spark my spliff and think about what she said.

A baby was wild.

I wasn't denying the shit because we never used protection. The thought never crossed any of our heads whenever we had sex.

Especially the first time.

Jahquel J.

Neither of us were thinking about protection in the moment. I knew I wanted her bad, and she felt the same way. When I slid up inside of her and nutted inside her, I damn sure wasn't thinking about the blessings that came with that.

I chuckled to myself. "Cappadonna and Capone gonna fuck me up."

Chapter 18
Corleon

> Capri: Hey. Things have been hectic. I'll be back in town in a few days. Can we meet up and talk?

> Me: Of course. Just hit me up when you back.

> Capri: K.

I STARED AT MY LAST MESSAGE EXCHANGE BETWEEN ME and Capri. She had sent it a few days ago, and I was waiting patiently to hear from her when she was back. Finding some shit out like I had told her was a lot, so I was giving her space to sort out how she felt.

"I don't give a fuck if that bitch gave you head, took her head off, spun around on yo' dick, and then landed my jet. Don't fucking charter my fucking jet without my permission, bozo!" Menace, my best friend, barked into the phone and slammed his phone on the kitchen counter.

I leaned up and looked in the kitchen because of the crazy shit he had said. He continued to stab his fork into his eggs that the chef had finished preparing like he didn't just bark on his brother.

"Landon?"

"His ass about to find out why the fuck they call me Menace. Let his ass touch my jet once more, and I'm gonna show his ass... matter fact, Jeffie!" he hollered, pushing the eggs away.

Jeffie was Menace's right hand, assistant, and I liked to call her his handler. She came running into the kitchen with her iPad in her hand. I don't think I ever saw her without her damn iPad in her hand.

"Why are you screaming?"

He took a sip of some red ass smoothie he always had every morning. "Add into my schedule an ass whooping for those niggas at the private airport. Why the fuck they allowing Landon to charter any fucking thing."

Jeffie heaved a sigh, used to the bullshit that her boss pulled on a daily basis. She was used to his shenanigans, and knew he was serious about scheduling some time to whip ass. Menace liked to fight for fun.

The nigga had two hours out of every day where he did some UFC type fighting that looked painful as shit.

"The request came from my computer, so I'm gonna assume your brother hacked into it again."

"Told you about keeping it unlocked around him... he's literally in school for the shit," I remarked, and she rolled her eyes.

"Don't forget to mention yourself, too."

Menace looked from me and then back to Jeffie. "Fuck already and get the shit over with... 'cause when you done, we need to go wring Landon's neck for fucking with my shit. Ain't he supposed to be in school, not fucking Miami turning up."

"Menace, school is out for the summer. It explains why he came over here the other day. I thought he genuinely wanted to intern under me."

"For what? I don't want that sneaky muthafucka working

Capri

under me. He has his role, and he need to start playing that shit when it comes to me. How the fuck is he hacking my shit... I'm the one paying for his education... I'm splitting his shit when I see him."

"You don't mean that shit. When it comes to your sisters and brother, you soft as dough, nigga," I called his bluff.

Menace wasn't one to fuck with, but when it came to his sisters and brother, they could get away with murder. They were his heart, and I knew how he was coming behind them.

"Yeah, ight... why the fuck you over here anyway? Shouldn't you be kissing cheeks with your new family."

Jeffie knew that she wasn't needed anymore and quickly left, as I watched her ass shake in the leggings she wore. "Oh shit... you jealous, Mens?"

He laughed and came into the living room, plopping down on the opposite couch. "Fuck you... why you over here? Matter fact, I need you to stop accessing my fucking house just 'cause you can.... Hacking ass. You a bad influence on Landon's ass."

"Cyber specialist... I like to think of him as an intern. You'll thank me one day," I smartly corrected him.

I was technically a hacker, and one of the fucking best there was. I could get into any system, and I made money by fucking with rich people's money. When you saw a hospital or an airports entire system go down, I was usually the nigga behind the shit. America didn't just run on corruption, the shit ran on money, and they didn't give a fuck about the crime committed, they just wanted to toss any amount of money to fix the problem I had created.

While they got their systems back, I got a big ass lump sum of money wired into a burner offshore account. It was funny because even with me making my money fucking with other people's money, I still owned a cyber security company.

Those who were smart, hired me to make sure their systems and networks were protected from niggas like me. Who better to own a cyber security company? I knew how niggas thought, so I could protect your shit that much better.

I was always one step ahead.

Menace's whole house was run electronically with different codes that switched every other hour. Nothing ever stayed the same in his house, so nobody was getting in this bitch unless he personally invited you, or you were one of his siblings.

Except me.

I knew when to hit that code on his gate at the right time when it was about to switch over, which was how I was on his couch when he came downstairs this morning. He knew my ass was here, so it wasn't like he could be caught slipping. Mens knew there was no way he could stop me, because his ass didn't understand how I did it to begin with.

My mom sent me to a fancy private school and that was where I met Menace. He stuck out like a sore thumb and had a problem with authority. Even as kids, this nigga was running around telling the teachers how to run shit.

By high school, he dropped out because of the situation with his parents, but continued with his education, even while having to raise his younger siblings. The Caselli family was the third founding family in Staten Island.

Case House supplied the highest class of pussy you could get. They didn't traffick women, and force them against their will. There was a fucking waiting list for women to work with Case House. Their escorts drove G-Wagons and owned homes. In return, they serviced high class clients that paid crazy amounts of money to keep it on the low, and it was always kept on the low.

You never heard about a politician, mayor, or governor buying pussy because Case House operated differently. Back in the day, when Menace's pops was running it, it ran off word of mouth. When Menace stepped in as the head, I built a entire cryptic system that couldn't be traced back to anyone.

The money brought in from the system I built was protected by me, because Menace trusted me with his life. Shit, I trusted his ol' crazy ass just as much. When he had to step up and raise his siblings, me and moms was right there with him.

"Clearly you got some shit on your mind, because why else would you be in my shit early in the morning."

"My sister finally hit me up to meet up."

Menace snapped his finger, and the housekeeper came running over with the rest of his drink. "This is what you wanted... you been watching them since your moms told you about them. I told you that you needed to step to the twins first."

"Shit seemed too complicated going to them quick. I've watched them, and a few times they both almost peeped me following."

"How?"

"They could tell I was following them and switched up how they moved. Still don't know where they live... I mean, I can find the information out but that shit creepy."

"Stalking your little sister not creepy?"

"Her shit public record. It took me a little minute to really find her since she's registered under Browne."

"Browne?"

"She's married or was married... some shit like that."

Menace shook his head. "That last name more powerful than some little nigga she married... think you need to have this sit down and then meet your brothers. I'm familiar with the Delgatos. There's a mutual respect. A few times our paths crossed, and it was nothing but respect. I know of Capone more than his twin."

"Yeah. I'm hoping sitting down with Capri will soften things with her brothers."

"Your brothers," Menace corrected. "If I know anything about the Delgatos, I know they ride hard for their own."

"I don't understand why my moms never told me about it.... Like how did the shit even come to be?"

"Only person that can give you the answers is your birth parents. Being honest, it was probably the size of your head that scared them."

I tossed a pillow at his stupid ass. "Fuck up."

"Just saying." He pulled his phone up, and then stood up. "Got a meeting to onboard more women... I do need you to remove access to the police commissioner... was supposed to talk to him, and he seems to be too fucking busy, so maybe this will get his ass to make fucking time."

"I got you. Make sure Jeffie sends me over all the shit on the new women so I can load them onto the site when I get a minute."

"Maybe you should ask her since you want her so bad.... Just fuck and get the shit over with... fucking solves a lot of problems."

"Nigga, just do your job so I can do mine."

I was in charge of loading all the new women that started working for CH. The way we had this shit running, it looked like we had legit employees, so the shit could never come back onto us. When Menace stepped in, he wanted to revamp his father's old tired system and offer something new. If Menace could give, he could damn sure fucking take, and Reggie was about to find that shit out soon enough.

"Make sure you get a suit for the Governor's Ball in DC, too... don't wait until the last minute like you always do." He paused like he was in a deep thought and then smiled, exposing all the gold in his mouth. "How about you ask Jeffie to go with you as a date."

"Nigga, you don't even have a date... why the fuck you think I need one."

Capri

He smirked. "Do you know how many girls I'm gonna have working that night? Pulling a million in on just that night, so I'll have somebody. Gotta bump shoulders with these desperate ass fucks."

"Yeah... get me the information I need, bitch ass."

Menace snickered as he made his way upstairs, and I looked over at Jeffie who was by the pool on the phone. Nah. I couldn't go there with Jeffie... we been cool for too damn long. People never recovered from shit like that.

Chapter 19
Quameer

"Why the fuck you judging what the fuck I'm buying? You already took ten minutes to fucking unlock the cabinet to get me the damn test and now you turning your nose up every time you scan one of my items," I barked, as I tossed my card onto the counter to the clerk.

Her ass was the only one in this bitch, and she was acting like she had a bunch of customers. Miami was dead in the morning because mostly everyone was recovering from their night out. Shit, half the people were crawling down the street to their hotel as I walked to this pharmacy.

"Rum and a pregnancy test is crazy." Her young ass had the nerve to continue with the judgment.

I turned my face up as she slowly continued to scan my items. "Having your baby hair near your eyebrows is wild. You see me saying some shit about it?"

She must didn't like what I said because she tossed the pregnancy test box into the bag harder. "I hope it comes out positive, fucker."

I smirked. "Aww, thank you. I appreciate that."

The fuck she thought I was gonna cry if it came back positive. We didn't plan for this shit, but that didn't mean that I was

Capri

gonna be fucked up over it. I knew what I did, and as a grown ass man I was gonna step up to the plate and handle my responsibility.

I snatched the bag and left the pharmacy. The trip should have been ten minutes, and this bitch made it like twenty minutes 'cause she was dragging her ass. By the way her damn lashes looked, her ass probably came straight from the club to clock into work.

When I made it back to the hotel, I went to sit in the little seating area. There was a few people on their laptops and enjoying a cup of coffee. I felt all mature being up with the early birds. These were the people who woke up at five in the morning and smiled in the mirror.

I don't know if I could ever be that kind of nigga, but this morning I was. All night I tossed and turned while Capri snored like a grown ass man that fucking worked an eighteen-hour shift. Even if I could sleep, the way her ass was cutting up would never allow me to rest peacefully.

Soon as the sun started to come up, I closed the curtains and got dressed to head to the pharmacy. I was a patient nigga, but this wasn't something I could wait to know the answer to. You can't just slip that you're late on your period and think I wasn't going to want to know the verdict.

Plus, Capri was gonna be fucked up today, so I needed to have all the hangover essentials. I already called room service and put in an order for a big ass greasy burger with a sunny side up egg – extra runny – on top.

I got comfortable in the lounge chairs and hit my Gammy's contact in my phone. It rang for a bit before she came onto the screen with a spliff hanging from her lip. It was early so she was on the porch smoking before getting my mom up for the day.

"Om dia bolinho," she greeted.

"Tenho um minuto para mim?"

Jahquel J.

She smiled. "I always have time for you. What is on your mind, and where are you?"

Before Sim, Gammy was my best friend and the person I could always talk to. She was the person that often helped me put shit into perspective because she had lived life on her terms. She was so wise, and I soaked up any advice she had gave me.

Except when she told me about Brandi. I wanted her to be wrong about her so bad, and she ended up being right. Even when I never took her advice, she never got upset or forced me to see shit her way.

She allowed me to make my own mistakes and never had an *I told you so* when it didn't turn out the way I wanted it to.

Gams was the most patient person I knew. Quasim had inherited her patience because I knew I damn sure didn't. "Capri might be pregnant."

Her low eyes widened, yet she remained calm. "How would you feel if that test is positive?"

I shrugged. "I'm not gonna front... I'm scared, Gams."

She gave me that loving look she always gave before she was about to drop some gems. "About what. Give me two reasons you're scared."

"She runs, Gams."

"Next one."

"What if she does the same shit that Brandi did to me? I can't take that shit happening twice to me. I'm not in the business of making babies in broken homes, feel me?"

When Brandi did that childish shit and took my child away from me because she was caught in her feelings, she didn't realize how much that fucked with me. It was one of the main reasons I would kill myself to always make sure I showed up for Ryder. While she thought she was playing immature ass games, she took the chance to be in my child's life from the beginning.

I never witnessed feeling Ryder kick in her stomach, or

Capri

even had a sonogram of her. My baby took her first breath without me being there, and that was some shit you could never apologize for.

Me and Brandi may have been cordial, but I could never forgive her for that shit. I could forgive her for breaking my heart, but the shit with our daughter wasn't something that would ever sit right with me.

"That girl was full of games, and I saw that when it took you ten minutes to get her in my door. Acting all shy knowing she was full of shit." She kissed her teeth. "You remember you told me about Capri's ex-husband?"

"Yeah." I didn't know where Naheim fit into any of this, but I was gonna rock with her and see where she was going with it.

"Quameer, you said that your fear was that she would make you pay for his mistakes. The reason you wanted to remain friends, but your feelings for her became too strong for just friends. Don't make her pay for Brandi's mistakes. She's not Brandi, and you're not her ex-husband. You both need to approach this on a mutual playing field, leaving the past hurts out of your space. You've already created a space where she feels secure and safe."

"I hear you, Gams."

"Does she want children?"

"Says she does... I'm not sure she wanted them right this second. Being real, I don't even know where we stand as far as a relationship."

"Relationship or not... if she's carrying your baby, you will do what's right. I know you and have raised you and your brother the right way."

I smiled. "Of course. She and the baby will be taken care of always."

"Keep me updated?"

"I got you, Gams."

"And maybe I will be able to meet her. I know you keep people away because of your mother. If she's important to you, then she should know your family. If she's the right one, then you'll know by introducing her to your real life."

"I hear you. Thank you for listening to me."

She smiled. "Always gonna be here to give you a listening ear. I just need your brother to be more open."

"Sim is always gonna be Sim."

Gams nodded her head. "I know. It's gonna take a special type of woman to come in and heal him. Healing a broken heart is simple, it takes a special one to heal a shattered one."

When I thought about the kind of woman that my brother needed, I always thought about Blair. I could see her being the woman to pull him out of his shell and love him when he couldn't find it to love himself.

Suga: INY

By the time I made it back to the room, Capri was sitting up on the bed staring into space. Her makeup was smeared all over her face, and her hair was matted to one side. I peeped her phone sitting beside her, which told me somebody had called to wake her up.

"Good morning, party animal."

She winced and held her head. "Can you whisper, Meer? My head feels like I'm about to crack it."

I kissed her on the head, and handed her the ginger ale, Advil, and a liquid IV I picked up from the pharmacy. "I ordered you room service so that should be here soon."

"You're literally the best. So much so that I'm not even questioning why the fuck you are in Miami and not back in New York."

"I'm only here because you keep playing with Mason. Suga, why the fuck do you wanna destroy that man? What the hell did he do to you?"

"Mason isn't even here?"

Capri

"He was in Anguilla though."

She paused and looked at me weird. "How do you know that?"

"Not important."

"Nobody posted that on social media, Meer... how did you find that out?" She pulled the blanket off her legs, while her eyelash sat on her cheek.

"I told you I'm gonna find shit out.... The question is why the fuck was he there when I made myself clear."

"Did you make yourself clear about the headmaster? No... so, don't try and tell me what the fuck I can and cannot do."

I knew eventually that shit was going to end up in conversation. "I keep telling you that her head ain't even on that level."

She yawned as she cut her eyes at me. "Are you going to lie to me or are you going to admit that Brandi told you. Which makes a lot of sense why she was so concerned about if I spoke to you."

"Was she?"

"Quameer!"

"She facetimed me and showed you in the club with Mason, Sug. The fuck you want me to say? I told you about that nigga and you keep doing what the fuck you want."

She held her hand up. "I never invited that man, and I spent the whole night chilling with him. It was no flirting or anything like that... I told him that I had a situation, and he respected that. Jesse's messy ass invited him and spent the whole night throwing herself at him. Is this how things are gonna be? Brandi gonna be your spy? How did you even know I wasn't in Anguilla anymore?"

"Blair's ass need to stop posting in real time." I removed myself from the balcony door and sat down beside her. "Brandi was being petty, and I played right into that shit. I apologize and the shit won't happen again."

"Thanks," she snatched the bag from the edge of the bed.

When she pulled the pregnancy test out, she looked at me. "Meer, what the hell?"

"You told me you were late... go piss on that damn stick, Sug."

"I did?"

"Hell yeah... sang the shit, then took off running down the hallway."

Capri groaned and fell back onto the bed. "Remind me to never drink again. Being pregnant has been on my mind because I am late. I'm never late, Meer."

"You know what that means."

"What does that mean? Do I keep the baby, or should I—"

"Don't make me bug the fuck out in here."

"My brothers, Meer."

"What about them?"

She ran her hand through her hair. "You know how they are... always in my business, and it's hard to keep any business to myself."

I told both Capone and Capp to give me the respect they would want with their own relationship. "That's not gonna be a problem."

"How you figure? Cause you sat down and asked for their blessing."

"Cause I sat down like a grown ass man and told them to respect my shit. You mine, Suga, and when it comes to our shit, it's nobody's business."

She smiled before getting up. Her skirt was up around her damn waist, and her ass was hanging out with the panties she wore, while she limped to the bathroom. I was right behind her with the box of tests, and she turned to close the door. "I been up in there... piss on these damn test so we know."

As she took her piss, I sat up on the sink and read the instructions. This shit was all new to me, so I didn't know how it worked. Capri apparently knew what to do without even

Capri

looking at the instructions. She capped the test and then washed her hands before leaning on the counter beside me.

"Tell God your plans if you really wanna laugh. What am I even doing, Meer. I could really be pregnant. Do you know how bad my mom is gonna get on my case?"

"Shit, you think you stressed. I have to think of another name that goes with Ryder... what you think of Davidson if it's a boy. Ducati?"

Capri looked at me with tired eyes. "Meer, please."

She walked toward the tub and slid onto the floor, pulling her knees into her chest. That was her signature position when she was stressed. I remained seated next to the test as time felt like it had slowed down, making the fifteen minutes feel like two hours instead.

The timer she set on her phone sounded and I looked over at her. "You want me to look?"

She put her hand over her eyes. "Go ahead."

Suga peeked at me through her fingers as I picked the test up. I smirked when I saw that one word. "You carrying a gut full of my sugar, Suga," I laughed.

Her gasp was loud as shit as she quickly abandoned the floor and snatched the test from my hand. "Oh shit."

I allowed her to hold the test and stare at it for a minute before I gently took it from her hand. "No matter how much you look at this, it ain't going anywhere. Those words are there."

"I'm pregnant, Meer," she whispered. "Are you not even a little bit stressed about this?"

I pulled her closer to me and kissed her lips. "I'm not stressed because being a father is one of the greatest joys in my life."

"My mom is gonna be so upset... I'm divorced which she still hasn't gotten over, and now I'm pregnant and not even in a relationship."

"The fuck you mean? The minute I was in you, we were together, Suga. I let you do this little back and forth, but I been solid in my decision when it comes to you. I ain't going nowhere and I mean that shit. We did everything the right way... *our* way. You my nigga before anything, best friend, and you'll be a good ass mother. The way you are with your nieces and nephews, and then Ryder showed that to me."

"I'm not a baby mama, Meer. I was never supposed to be someone's baby mother... I'm a wife." She stared up into my eyes.

"Shit happens not how we want them, but how God wants them to happen. One step in front of the other, Suga."

She smiled. "Did you just refer to this baby as shit?" I pulled her close as she wrapped her arms around my neck and kissed my cheek. "Meer, I'm scared."

"Can I be real with you?"

"Always."

"Me too."

She removed herself from me and searched my eyes. "Why? You've done this before, and you're so good at it. I've never been somebody's mama before."

"Suga, don't take my baby away from me... can you give me your word?"

Capri looked almost offended that I asked her to make that promise. "No matter what happens between the both of us, I would never take your child away from you, or Ryder's sibling away from her... you got my word."

"I hear you."

She held my hand. "I'm not Brandi, Meer. So much shit is happening right now, so I may seem a little off, but I want you. I want to give us a chance... okay?"

I kissed her lips before picking up the pregnancy test. "Shit is wild."

Capri

"Quameer, stop sayin... I was drunk as shit and here I am pregnant... what the hell?"

I laughed because she was chugging back shots and now, we were in the bathroom with a positive pregnancy test. "No more shots for yo' ass."

I kissed her on the lips as she laughed, I kissed her teeth. "Meer, you just kissed my damn teeth."

"I know. You used to other shit from these other niggas. I'm different, Sug... you gonna remember me, and nobody coming after me."

"Word is bond," she threw on an extra thick New York accent.

I laughed. "Word is bond, Big Mama... you really about to be Big Mama, too."

"Starting to think you trapped me, Meer."

"Nah, I ain't have to do that because yo' ass wasn't going nowhere anyway." She hugged me, leaning her head on my shoulder.

"You know I would never take any of these moments away from you, right?" She pulled back, staring into my eyes because she needed me to know.

"I know, Sug."

She rubbed my burn as she looked into my eyes. "I love you, too, Meer."

I grinned. "You heard that, huh?"

She kissed my lips. "I did and I feel the same way."

"Love you, Sug." We shared a kiss before she rested her head on my shoulder, and I rubbed her ass while thinking about how she was gonna have my baby.

This time, I wanted to make sure I did shit right when it came to bringing another Inferno into the world.

Chapter 20
Aimee

SLEEP DIDN'T FEEL LIKE IT LASTED MUCH THESE DAYS. Rory was going through sleep regression, so it was like a newborn schedule in a toddler's body. Capella was keeping late hours, so by the time his head hit the pillow, he was knocked the fuck out and I had to get up and handle Rory. The furniture for the lake house had arrived and this was the first night we were sleeping under our own roof. Me and Capella had never had our own home together, so it felt surreal now having one.

Our house on the compound was almost completed, but we weren't living there yet. We still lived at home with Cappadonna and Alaia, and for the most part I enjoyed being under the same roof. As a woman, I understood that I needed to give Alaia back her home and start the process of running my own.

It was scary to think that I would be in charge of this home. Alaia and Erin ran their homes with such ease. They were able to have their own lives, and still hold down the fort in the same breath. It scared me because what if I couldn't do it as perfectly or seamless as they did. What if I didn't have dinner completed by the time Capella came home, or the laundry didn't get done.

Capri

Alaia did all of those things because she wanted to, not because Capp made her. He was fine with hiring someone else to do it to make her life easier. She enjoyed serving her husband, and it brought joy to her life.

When it came down to it, I was riding with Capella to the wheels fell off, and even when they fell off, we were pushing the car. Some days I didn't think I could be the wife that he wanted, or saw that his uncle and father had.

I loved Alaia and Erin, and respected how they took care of their husbands, babies, home, and then would bust their guns when they needed to. However, I would rather have someone clean my home and have a nanny for those days when Rory overstimulated me.

Did that make me less of a wife and mother because I wanted those things? My eyes became heavy as I laid down my laptop, knowing I had an assignment for a summer class I signed up for. It was virtual, so I didn't have to commute into the city and could take the class from my kitchen.

"Aimee, what the fuck?" Capella roared, and I jumped up from the computer with drool on the side of my face.

"I know, I'm sorry... Capri told me to keep it quiet and I have been... it's hard lying to you," I blurted while looking around the kitchen, my vision in one eye still blurred since I was leaning on one side of my face.

Capella looked at me weird as he sat down the takeout bag from our favorite sushi spot in town. "What the fuck are you talking about?"

I ran my hand through my hair and leaned on the back of the counter stool I had jumped from. "Nothing... was dreaming."

Quickly, I packed up my computer and notebooks and rushed into what would be my office. All I had in there was a desk until I decided on the vision I wanted for in here. Capella wasn't going to let anything go and followed behind me as I sat my things down on my desk.

"Aim, what the fuck were you spewing from your sleep? What you been lying to me about?" He came closer. "You fucking that nigga at the coffee shop?"

I screwed my face up because he had been wanting to ask that question and used this moment to toss it in there. "Yes, I am."

"Because I know you're a sarcastic asshole, I'm gonna let you slide. On the real, I'll fuck you over in the worst way if you do some wack shit like that, Aim."

His voice was low and steady as he smiled at me from across the room. "I am not sleeping with Landon, so please let that leave your head."

"Just making sure we clear on some shit."

I left the office and headed upstairs, since Rory was across the street with his grandfather and his Quack-Quack. A sigh of relief washed over me now that I had successfully made him forget what I had blurted moments ago.

Capri was on a damn world tour, leaving me to hold this secret. I saw that man, and I saw how much he resembled Capone and Cappadonna. I was there and holding this secret had been hard to do.

Hard because I felt like Cappadonna could sniff a secret out of you. All he had to do was look at you, and then the next thing you knew you were spilling your life's secrets to him. It was the reason I had been avoiding him.

"What you been lying to me about?" Capella appeared in the doorway of our closet as I pulled things out the boxes and started to hang them up.

"It was a dream, Capella. Why don't we focus on you taking your medicine consistently." I tried to turn it back on him and he wasn't falling for it.

Capri

"You asked and I been taking my medicine every morning and night... don't bullshit me, Aim."

"Why did I have to ask you to take care of yourself?"

"Aimee, what the fuck are you lying about?" he stood over me, and I looked away from him. "Baby, you don't want me to draw my own conclusions... I promise you don't want me to." He gently pulled my face up toward him.

"Promise you won't say anything," I whispered.

"Depends on what you tell me, Aimee."

I tried to walk away, and he pulled me back toward him. "Promise me that you won't tell anyone. This is going to prove if I can marry you or not."

He laughed. "Keeping secrets from me proves that I might not be able to marry yo' ass." I was so offended that I pinched him. "I'm saying, Aim. You acting like you holding the recipe for the fucking Krabby Patty."

"Jean and Des have another son that they never told Capri, Capone, and Cappadonna about," I blurted, taking a deep breath because it felt good getting it out.

I expected Capella to be moved by the revelation, or even shocked by the piping tea that I just spilled, and he stood there staring at me like I was crazy. "Baby, I know I left that baggie in my laundry... you ain't fucking with that shit, right? Aim, I can support a lot of shit, but fucking with my product gonna make a nigga lose his shit."

"What?" I nearly screamed.

"I'm trying to find the fuck out where that baggie went?"

I snatched a dress out the box and turned to look at him. "To your father. I found it and handed it to him because what the fuck am I gonna do with it?"

"Then what is this crazy shit that you keep talking about?"

I ran downstairs and grabbed my phone from the counter while Capella stood at the top of the steps, still not convinced that my ass wasn't a coke head. I scrolled through my phone and found the picture from that day.

While Capri was talking and trying to piece everything together, I snapped a picture just in case. I figured it would come in handy, and it did because I was about to prove to my baby father that I wasn't a damn druggie.

Capella took the phone I shoved in his hand and looked at it before looking back at me. "Oh shit."

"Exactly. I am not on any kind of drugs." I was still offended that his ass had assumed I was doing his supply.

He left out the room and sat on one of the chairs in the seating area of our bedroom. There was some pieces of furniture that hadn't arrived yet. "What the fuck did my aunt say?"

"She hasn't said much... she was shocked, but you had just got arrested so her mind was on that."

He continued to look at the phone shocked. I was shocked when he pulled that helmet off his head too. "Who the fuck is this nigga? Why the fuck did Nana and Gramps hide that shit?"

I sat on the floor Indian style while looking up at him. "A question that we need the answer to. Can you please keep this between us? Alaia and Erin already tease me and say I can't hold water."

"You really can't though."

"Capella, please. Capri won't forgive me if I let this slip," I pleaded with him because I really wanted Capri to continue to trust me.

I had been doing so good and Capella scared me when he woke me up. "I got you. If she doesn't say shit, then I'm telling my pops and letting him handle it."

I sucked my teeth. "Allow Capri to handle it... sheesh, you be acting like she isn't equipped to handle things too. Is it because she's a woman and gets a period?"

Capella paused examining the picture and looked at me.

Capri

"Take yo' ass back to sleep because you tripping out. I'm not understanding why the fuck you need that damn extra class this summer anyway. You should be spending more time with Rory."

"I do spend time with him... he sleeps all day because he refuses to sleep at night," I countered, slightly offended that he was making it seem like I wasn't present in our son's life.

"Then why didn't you come to his swim lessons this week? I stopped what I was doing to drive back up here to take him all week."

Crossing my arms, I looked away from him. "I called to ask if we could push the time and she told me no."

"Because he only likes to get in the water when Promise is there. Aim, I'm here, and I'm gonna step in whenever I need to when it comes to our son. I support you going back to school, and doing everything you said you were gonna do. At some point, Rory has to come first, too. This summer was supposed to be chill, and you went and took an extra summer course that wasn't needed."

I hung my head because I felt guilty. "Can I tell you something?"

He moved from the chair and joined me on the floor. "You can tell me anything... you know that."

"I enjoy being just Aimee when I'm at school. I love Rory with my whole heart, but when I'm in school I'm not his mother, or your orphan girlfriend with no family."

"Who the fuck said that?" He got upset.

I smiled and rubbed his face. "No one said that.... No one would ever say that. It's just how I feel at times. Like you just stay with me because I chose you over my family so now you have to marry me."

Capella got closer to me and held my face. "Why the fuck you thinking like that? I wanna marry you because you're the love of my life. You gave me my son, a purpose in this life, Aim.

Yeah, you've made sacrifices that you didn't have to make and I'm forever gonna love you for that. My mother never chose me, but you did. You chose me over your own family, and I don't take that lightly. It also doesn't mean that's the only reason that I want you to be my wife."

He softly kissed my lips while hugging me closer to him. "You sure? Capella, I'm not Alaia... I can't keep our home running the way she does for your father. The thought of cooking dinner every night stresses me out."

"Aim, I'm not trying to be my father. What he has going on in his home is his own. How many times do I have to tell you that we will do what works for us. Alaia and Erin do those things because that's how they do shit in their marriages. My uncle and pops have different marriages, and run they cribs differently. I don't need to do what they're doing... this crib is pork free though." He raised his brow, and I laughed.

Even though we hadn't converted yet, we did do small changes to make the process easier. As much as it hurt to tell the lady at the Dunkin Donuts not to add bacon on my egg bagel, I had learned to go on without it. Beef bacon had become a staple in this house, and that was because Capp refused for his grandson to ever have pork.

"So, can we have a housekeeper when we move into the new house?"

"For sure... yo' ass is messy and I can't deal with that shit."

I shoved his ass and then stood up. "Whatever... I have organized chaos."

"Call it whatever you want, that shit messy." He got up from the floor and then pulled me next to him, kissing me on the shoulder. "I love you, Aim. Don't ever question how I'm coming when it comes to you. I just need you to be open and honest with me when you're struggling. I can see why school is an escape. Just know that we love you and we're your family. Don't ever gotta question how much our family loves you."

Capri

"Thank you, Honey." I gave him a quick kiss before going into the closet to finish unpacking our clothes.

"Love you, Orphan Aimee." He smirked.

I flipped my middle finger at him. "Capella!"

"Come on so we can eat, and then I can eat after we finish eating," he winked, as he left the bedroom.

Tossing the hanger on the floor, I ran out the room behind him. All he had to say was a word, and I was right behind his ass. That Delgato walk wasn't a lie, each man possessed that same walk, all having their own signature style about it.

Chapter 21
Capri

THE ROOM WAS BRIGHT, AND I FELT WEAK. AS IF WHEN I stepped down from this bed, I was going to collapse onto the floor. At least, that was how I felt mentally. My body and mental had gone through the ringer, and here they were offering me apple juice and cookies as a prize for basically yeeting my baby out of my body. As if the cookies made walking past the heckling anti-abortionist assholes outside better. I was all for a woman's right to choose, but this wasn't supposed to be me.

I shouldn't have been getting an abortion, and I damn sure shouldn't have been divorced. As I weighed the option on if I should keep this baby and what this would mean, I didn't take it lightly. I wanted to be a mother, but not like this.

Becoming a mother like this wasn't the right way, and I knew nothing blessed could come from this situation. Naheim already have a son, and he was in a relationship. That wouldn't be fair to myself or Nellie. She didn't deserve to find out that her man got his ex-wife pregnant.

That shit was wicked of me to even continue to sleep with him, and then unprotected... gross. The nurse came in with another apple juice, expecting that I had finished the first one,

Capri

when in reality I hadn't moved. I could tell this was normal for her because she had no emotions as she slid the juice onto the tray beside me.

If I had this baby, it would only give more hope to my mother that we could fix this. This wasn't something that could be fixed. Naheim claimed that he wanted us, and to fix things between us. I only heard that talk whenever he and Nellie were on the outs. Soon as they fixed whatever was going on, then I wouldn't hear anything from him. Not until she was pissed with him, and then he was back in my bed while I was making him feel good again.

I craved for someone to make me feel good for once, and messing with Naheim always made me feel worse when it was all said and done. He would roll over and check all the dozen of messages Nellie had sent him, then climb out my bed to get dressed.

He didn't need to cross the room to the dresser or the closet because his clothes were usually sprawled in the corner chair, or on the floor. While he was fixing his belt, he would kiss me on the forehead, and then he left to be with her. I always felt empty when he left, like I was useless, and only good enough to make him feel good. How did I go from being his wife to now the side chick?

When I took that pregnancy test, I knew I couldn't keep this baby. I wanted the experience when I had a child. Being pregnant with someone that wanted me, and someone that would cherish me and this baby. I wanted to have the full experience, and knowing how me and Naheim ended, and how this baby became, I wouldn't want to have that experience with him.

I would look like a damn fool popping out pregnant by a man that humiliated me. Even with me sleeping with Kincaid, I never came back with no damn baby. He slept with Tasha, had feelings for her, and then brought a baby back.

A cute baby that deserved the world – a baby, nonetheless.

As the nurse was explaining aftercare and letting me know about the medication that I needed to pick up from the pharmacy, I started to dissociate while going over my text messages.

Cappy: Meet me and Capone at this address.

He sent his location after the message and I clicked it, looking at the large piece of land he wanted me to meet them at. I quickly got dressed and left the clinic alone, even though the nurse recommended that I have someone pick me up. I lied and told her that a friend would be meeting me down the block. She knew I was lying, but she never pushed me on it. At the end of the day, she had done her job, and it was on me to make sure I was good after I left the clinic. Plus, the clinic was in a shitty part of town, and they damn sure didn't do all their homework before removing this baby. I was still nursing a bullet wound, and they still went through with the abortion.

Before getting into my car, I popped into the liquor store and grabbed a small bottle of Hennessy. I wasn't even a dark liquor drinker, but I needed something to take the edge off me. A few shots back, and I got behind my wheel and headed to the address that my brother sent me.

Baby Doll always showed up for everyone... except herself.

I blamed Jesse Powell for the reason that I had tears falling down my face while I parallel park by this bistro. Every time I heard the song "You," I always thought of what my life could have been. The beautiful wedding, the peaceful pregnancy, and the life that I thought I would have had. Yet, the only thing that came to mind when I heard my favorite song was the bullshit I had been through in my marriage, and all the bullshit I had put him through. I couldn't help but think about the day I had to choose me over the baby I wanted. Nobody knew about the abortion, not even Alaia or Erin and I told them everything.

I was ashamed to admit that I had gotten pregnant by Naheim, and that I even considered keeping the baby. They would never judge me for my decisions, so I don't know why I never told them. Instead, I kept everything inside, and kept myself numb with alcohol and everyone else's problems. It was easier than dealing with my own and having to face reality. God, I was so broken back then and didn't know how I would ever heal.

I sat in my car and mentally prepared to meet my brother – again. It was all that had been on my mind since I been back from Miami. Well, him, and the fact that Quameer had got me pregnant.

I even stole the pregnancy test out the trash to make sure that it didn't switch. Maybe *not* would pop up and we wouldn't have known. How did we allow this to happen? It wasn't like we were preventing it from happening either, however, we damn sure wasn't thinking I would end up pregnant in the process. After having an abortion, I didn't think children were in the cards for me. I thought God would punish me for making such a mistake.

I know for a fact that my mother would have judged and given me the silent treatment for having one. Jean Delgato didn't believe in divorces and abortions, and I had done both. She wasn't even over the fact that me and Naheim were done and divorced. There was still this piece of her that wanted to believe that we would rekindle and fix all the things that had gone wrong between us.

Even though that would have never been a possibility, it died the moment that test turned positive. When I came home, I thought things would be smooth sailing. I would play the field a bit, before deciding that Meer was for me, and then we would ride off into the sunset together.

I damn sure didn't expect for us to be pushing a stroller into the sunset. Not when I felt like he didn't fully trust that I was all in when it came to him. He was still holding out on me, and I was growing tired of having to keep telling him that I wanted to be with him.

Hell, if the damn stomach full of him didn't prove that I didn't know what else would. I quickly fixed my makeup before grabbing my purse and stepping out the car. Capella had court today, and that had been a waste of time. Nothing was dismissed or solved, and they scheduled another court date since the cop that arrested Capella wasn't there.

If it was up to me, I would get on the news with Al Sharpton right next to me screaming for justice. Capella was beat because of who he was, not because he did anything wrong, and the courts didn't seem to care about it.

They wanted to offer him a year of probation and I refused. He did nothing wrong, so why the hell would he even get probation. Capp wanted to keep it quiet and do things his way, so I was stuck attending court dates until this was sorted out. Whether it be in the courtroom or in the streets.

The Bistro was in Jersey City, which wasn't far from the courthouse. I was already running late because it took twenty minutes for them to find out that the officer hadn't shown up for court today. Apparently, he got his days mixed up and was working today, which was insane. He should have been suspended or at least on desk duty.

Walking into the Bistro, I was greeted by a beautiful Spanish woman, who was all smiles. She grabbed some menus and was prepared to seat me until I told her that I was meeting someone. When I explained, she knew exactly what I meant and took me upstairs to the roof top of the Bistro, which was beautiful with views of Manhattan. Corleon was nursing a drink while on his phone when I made it upstairs.

He happened to look up and notice me walking over and smiled. I stopped short when he smiled because it was like witnessing Capone or Cappadonna smile. The hostess stopped with me with a concern expression on her face.

"I promise I'm alright... sorry," I quickly apologized and

Capri

continued over toward the table. Corleon stood up, and he held out my chair for me.

I wasn't sure if I should hug him or what. Instead, I sat my purse down and sat in the chair he had just pulled out for me. This felt surreal, especially since I was doing it alone. Cappy wasn't here to take lead on this.

The ball wasn't in my big brothers' court, it was in mine and for me to figure out. I looked at Corleon and couldn't even make out the words I wanted to say. It was different sitting across from him and seeing all of him in the flesh.

"Am I being weird by staring at you?" I finally broke my silence, the silence he allowed me to have, never pressuring me to speak.

"Call it even... considering I stalked you." He chuckled and leaned back in his chair while staring at me.

"I don't even know the first thing that I want to ask... why would my parents lie to us all these years? Do you want money or are you okay? I don't even know where to start," I started rambling.

"That's a question you have to ask your parents. I don't need any money, perfectly fine when it comes to that area of my life, and you can start anywhere," he replied.

"How did you find out about this?"

"My moms told me before she passed away."

The waiter came over and I looked at him before turning my attention back to Corleon. "I'm sorry to hear that. Were you close with her?"

"She was my best friend... miss her every day."

I finally turned my attention back to the waiter and ordered water. "I just have so many questions swirling and don't even know where to start. How did you find us?"

"My moms wanted to tell me more, but she passed before she could. When I was packing up her condo, I came across a box filled with letters from my birth mother. Every birthday she wrote to my mother, and my mother wrote back. Every accomplishment, she sent it to her. They kept in communication up until I was around seventeen and then it stopped."

"Fuck. I've literally spent every moment since we met trying to think of a moment I missed something. Like, did I miss a sign or something that we had another sibling." I stressed while running my hand through my hair, thankful that I didn't bother to straighten it because of the heat today. "Do you hate them?"

He chuckled to himself while finishing his drink. "Nah. I'm not on that kind of time. Their reasons are their own. I just would like to know their reasons, so it could help me piece some shit together. Honestly, I just want to get to know them... know my siblings, shit like that."

"Why not come up to me and talk to me? Why did you stalk me like a weirdo?"

He broke out into laughter. It was a dry hearty laugh, like he was amused, but it wasn't that funny. "How would I look coming up to any of you and saying some shit like that? I was working out how to do it on my own, and then you seemed to run into some trouble, and I felt the need to jump in."

"I could have handled it on my own... thanks very much." I smiled playfully, while accepting the water from the waiter.

If I didn't know any better, he looked annoyed that all I ordered was water. He stood by the table, as if he wanted to rush us along to order some food. "Why the fuck you standing here guarding the table?" Corleon finally removed his eyes from me and over toward the waiter, who quickly got away from our table. "Nigga been on my ass since I sat the fuck down."

There was no denying that he had the same attitude as the twins. "Did you always know you were adopted."

"Hell nah. My moms put that shit on me before she passed away. Leave it to her to go out with a fucking bang."

Capri

"I guess that helps though... not feeling like you never belonged like other kids do when they're adopted."

He smiled. "It had always been just me and my moms. We didn't have family like that, and they damn sure ain't been around since she passed on."

I reached my hand across the table and touched his. "I'm sorry, Corleon."

"Call me Core," he said as he allowed me to hold his hand. "Capri, I'm not here to fuck with your life or cause drama within your family. If this shit too much, we can pretend it never happened and go back living our lives. I'm not trying to add shit to your family."

"You're a part of our parents. I could never go back and pretend it never happened." I sighed. "I do know I have to talk to my brothers about it, which will be a whole other thing."

He laughed. "I figured that would be the hardest in all of this."

"My parents aren't bad people. I don't know why they made the decision they did, but I'm hoping they clear things up for all of us," I blurted.

As much as me and my mother were always on the outs, she was a good mother. My parents were good people, and I was certain they had a reason for this. It scared me how they were able to keep a secret like this without telling us.

"Don't think they're bad people at all," he reached down beside the table, and he handed me a few aged letters and a picture. "I read through these letters and feel like I know your mother... shit is weird."

"Not weird. You connected with her," I looked at the picture, rubbing my finger across my parents' faces as they sat on the beach with wide smiles on their faces.

He allowed me to sit in silence as I read the letters from my mother. She asked about how he was doing and gave updates on her life. It was before I was born, so she was busy with both Capone and Cappadonna.

"Your parents seem like amazing people."

I smiled. "They're the best... don't get me wrong, they have their shit with them, but if I had to choose again, I would choose them."

He waved for another drink. "A lawyer... they must be proud."

"How did..." I allowed my voice to trail off.

"I find out shit about everybody... we also have a mutual connection."

I put the letters down and paid attention to him. "Who?"

"Zoya Caselli."

"How do you know Zoya?"

His phone buzzed and he ignored the call and turned his attention back to me. "Her brother is my best friend. I'm real close with her family...they're family. I used to help her ass with her school work."

"So, she has kno—"

"Zoya doesn't know anything. Besides her brother, I've kept this tight lipped. Plus, Zoya barely comes home to visit, so she wouldn't know shit anyway. She does her, and lives her own life."

I settled back in my seat and stared at him. "What do you do?"

"Own a cyber security company called Cor Links."

"Nice... must pay well," I noted the Cartier watch on his wrist, and the gold chain around his neck.

"Pays decent."

"Don't be humble."

Corleon laughed. "Pays well."

> 40: coming to the lake house tonight... need to talk.

Capri

When I got that text from Forty, I knew some shit was going down, and it was the text that I had been waiting for.

> Me: K.

"Everything all good?"

"Yeah... just something that I need to handle later."

"Mr. Bruster, can we take your dry cleaning... we can hang it in the back until you're ready." An older waiter came over to speak with Corleon instead.

It was then that I noticed the suit that was draped over the empty chair beside him. "Appreciate it."

"Fancy fancy," I teased.

"I got this ball to attend in DC... hate going to shit like that, but business is business."

"The Governor's Ball... your business has you mixing with the important."

He looked up from his phone. "Matter fact, come with me... we can kick it, and I know you'll know how to act around those stuffy ass people. I'm always fucking up my words around them."

"Seriously?"

"Yeah. If you're comfortable."

I smiled. "Let me get back to you on that. On another note, I'm going to talk to my brothers tonight about you. I've been keeping you a secret."

"Wouldn't be the first time," he teased.

After sitting and talking, Core walked me to my car and saw me off. It felt surreal talking to my brother, who I hadn't known about. I just prayed that Capone and Cappadonna took the news well.

After the day I had, I could drink an entire bottle of wine. Except, I couldn't even do that right now. With the way I got fucked up in Miami, I needed to leave alcohol alone until this baby was born.

Joygottagun: Um, so you gonna come over tonight or ignore us some more?

Alaia sent in our group chat, and I laughed because I had been avoiding them. Only because those bitches were like blood hounds, and they could sniff out anything wrong with me.

Erinwiththecooper: She won't respond... sis too good for us. We boring housewives, Alaia. If you want to join us, you know the little ppl. We're having drinks out back at my house.

I rolled my eyes at them laying it on thick, then went to shower and change clothes before walking across the street to Capone's house. Instead of going in through the front, I entered from the backyard where they were all cuddled up with my brothers with the fire on.

"Baby Doll, feel like you came home, and I don't ever fucking see you." Capp was the first to spot me and stood up to kiss me.

I fell into his arms and hugged him as tight as I could, which wasn't all that tight. He kissed the top of my head while peering down at me. "Hey Cappy."

"You alright?"

"Not really."

His body tensed up. "What happened, Baby Doll... tell me and I'll fix it."

"Well, you're not going to be alright in a minute either," I revealed, knowing that I had to tell them about our brother.

Alaia and Erin both took turns getting up to hug me and check in with me. I could tell from the way they were looking at me that they knew something was wrong. Capone got up and

Capri

kissed my head, and gave me a squeeze, doing his usual check in.

Since I mentioned that Capp wasn't going to be alright, he sat straight up while watching my every movement. "Enough of the fucking hugs. Why am I not going to be alright in a minute, Capri... I gotta have a conversation with Quameer?" He raised his eyebrow while staring at me.

"Don't tell me we gotta fuck his crazy ass up," Capone chimed in, polishing off the rest of his drink while waiting for me to talk.

I found a spot on the couch and looked around to make sure our parents weren't here. "I found something out recently and I don't know how to make sense of it."

"You're scaring us, Capri," Alaia said, as she cuddled closer to her husband, who put his arms around her.

"We have a brother." There was no other way to do it than to just say it, and from the way Capone and Cappadonna stared at me, I was almost sure they thought I had tried coke again.

Capone was the first to lean up and stare me in the eyes, as if he was trying to figure out if I was high or something. "Pri, what the fuck you be over in that house doing?"

"Capone, I am not high... I'm being serious. Mommy and Daddy had a baby after you two and gave him up for adoption. Quameer, Aimee, and Blair all witnessed it."

"Why the fuck Quameer ain't say nothing to me?" Cappadonna asked, skeptical.

"Because he respects not only you, but me too. He realized that this was something that I had to do, not him. It wasn't his place."

Cappadonna stood up and started pacing in front of the fire pit. "Bullshit... I don't believe that shit."

"I met up with him today for lunch."

"You did fucking what?" Capone roared while Capp continued to pace quietly with his arms behind his back.

"He showed me a picture of Mommy and Daddy... letters that Mommy sent to his adoptive mother, in her handwriting. Capone, I promise you this is our brother. He looks li—"

"Just like you and Cappadonna," Aimee's voice sounded from behind us, and we all turned to look at her.

"You wanna get shot, don't you?" Capp asked her, his tone and face serious as she quickly went to take a seat next to Erin.

Capone looked at his wife. "You knew about this, Gorgeous?"

"She didn't know about it, and I didn't tell either of them because I didn't want to put them in a position to have to lie to you for me. Aimee knew because she was there."

"Capella knows," Aimee blurted.

"Well, when the fuck did he find out, *Aimee*," I stared at her, pissed that she couldn't hold down a secret like this one.

"You know I am no good with secrets and it just came out. He promised that he wouldn't tell anyone, and he held his promise."

Capp stopped pacing and stared at all of us. "You had poor Aimee keep this secret knowing she can't even hold piss, then she tells my boy, and he keeps it from me." He held his finger up, stopping me from interrupting. "If none of that was enough, you go and meet this nigga and don't even tell us. You don't know that fucking man, and what if he came at you sideways."

"He didn't come at me sideways when a nigga was trying to shoot me off the road. In fact, he shot at him and helped us get away."

"Moms and Pops wouldn't hide some shit like that from us... the fuck he want? Money or something?"

"Sorry to break it to you, your parents aren't so perfect, and they hid some shit from us. Do whatever you want with that information. I'm just the messenger and as confused as the both

Capri

of you. I do know that he's our brother, and the letters and picture proves it."

Capone was quiet as he leaned forward while Erin rubbed his back. "What's his name?"

"Corleon."

He looked away while processing the name I had just told him. "And he just happened to come to you?" Capp asked, again skeptical of what I was telling him.

"Well, considering I'm the nicest Delgato, he made the right choice. Both of you don't even believe me telling you that he's our brother, so what the hell would you both have done if he came to you."

"Swab his fucking mouth." Capp was the first to break the silence.

As I was about to respond, Jo poked her head out. "Hey. Forty is here."

Capp looked confused as Forty came into the backyard. "Fuck is up, Old Head? Why you here?"

"Damn, I thought I was family... can't come swing by and see the fam." He and Capp embraced.

Forty embraced everyone before sitting down on the single chair and looking at all of us. "Morgan is planning on running for mayor in New York... he hasn't made the announcement yet, but it's coming soon."

"How is he running for mayor when he is a district attorney in Baltimore? Seems like my guy is just tossing noodles at the wall."

"Long as he lives in New York state, he can run for mayor. Bitch was smart and continued to live here, while working in Baltimore."

"Shit. I know his milage on his car is crazy," Aimee muttered, and we all turned to look at her, and she shrugged. "Sorry, that's all I could think about."

"What does this mean?"

"Remember that summer you went crazy and decided to do that judge in??" Forty jogged all of our memories.

"Yeah," Capone replied.

"His whole thing is to stop the violence in New York, and he plans to open old cases. The Baltimore case is a dead end ever since you ceased operation. The higher ups said they're not wasting resources on a dead end," Forty explained. "Which means he's going to start digging up shit. The problem isn't even Morgan."

"Forty, if he finds some shit on Capone... he not taking that fall... that shit on me," Capp said, and Alaia gasped.

"Then I guess we better fucking make sure he doesn't find any shit, Roy." Alaia nudged her husband. Erin was quiet as she held her husband's hand, knowing the life that she signed up for.

"He's a problem for sure... there's a bigger problem."

"What problem is bigger than that dick sucker, Morgan?" Capone snarled.

He had a personal beef with Morgan. This was the man that took his twin away from him for years, so the get back for that man was strong.

I was leaning so far forward that I was sure I would fall off this damn couch. "Rich Parker is the ADA in Baltimore. Guess who has transfer papers to New York and will become the new district attorney here. If you think Morgan was a fuck when he was a detective... imagine being mayor with the district attorney in his back pocket. Still wanna know who he fucked upstairs to get that promotion."

Capp cracked his neck. "Being real, I got too comfortable sleeping next to my wife. Can't see myself getting back behind those walls, but I fucking will if I have to... the fuck we need to do to prevent that, Fort."

He turned his attention to me, and then Aimee. "Tag, Baby

Capri

Doll." Forty winked, and I smirked. "Heard you met someone special, Capri."

Cappadonna damn near touched the sky with how he jumped up. "So, everybody know shit but me... bet."

"Wasn't my business to tell. I respect your parents, and I sat back and allowed Corleon to come to you. You never had to worry; I was watching him... he's good people. Best friends with Menace Caselli."

"He run with the Caselli family."

Forty nodded. "He does. Owns Cor Links... a cyber security company and guess what?" Forty was having too much fun with this.

"This ain't a laughing matter, Fort," Capone said.

"It is when you know what you have on your team... your brother rubs shoulders with the highest in the government. His best friend provides escorts for them, and he has all their information in the palm of his hands."

"Cor Link... I've hit a few licks with them. Landon, my classmate put me onto them," Aimee blurted.

"You've met him before?" I questioned.

"No. Everything always went through Landon... didn't know he was connected. Then again, I didn't know about him until we met him that day."

"He invited me to the Governor's Ball with him."

"You're going... and you're going." He pointed to Aimee. "You're young... men get stupid when they drink. We built this shit brick by brick... the fuck they thought? The Delgatos lay down easy? Aimee has the knowledge; your brother has the connections and is a genius when it comes to this hacking shit... heard he had JFK on a standstill two years ago. Then we have our fucking star... Capri Baby Doll Delgato... or Inferno, who knows. For now, you're Capri Browne." Forty smirked.

"Ugh. I can't escape that man for nothing." I groaned, hating that I would have to keep his damn name.

Jahquel J.

"What we have working for us is that you've moved smart when it comes to social media. Can't find a picture with your parents or your brothers on it. You're not connected unless they know the family personally. Plus, I scrubbed the internet free of anything connecting you three. All your new documents should be ready within a few weeks... you'll be the new ADA, Ms. Capri Browne."

I choked on my gum. "Um, what? How the fuck..."

"When we had that conversation a year ago, I asked you if you were ready. You told me you would do whatever you had to, to keep your brother out of prison. Right now, the city is scrambling because of that scandal with the governor... a lot is flying under the radar, and you my darling, have flew right in, literally popped right up in their system... literally." He winked. "I went fifteen years without seeing you... not going another damn day without seeing you. As a family, we band together and handle this shit. In the streets, we can just pop a nigga, this is different and it's like playing chess. Only the strongest survives, and the Delgatos are fucking strong... only question is... Baby Doll, you ready?"

Everyone turned their attention to me. "I'm ready."

"Fam... nice seeing you." He headed toward the door and then paused. "Oh, yeah... Rich Parker is connected to the Chrome Vipers... reason why those niggas run wild and free out that way. So, as much as we're doing this the legal way... there's some illegal shit that only the Delgato twins and Inferno Gods can handle." He winked, and then headed back inside.

> Me: I'll go to the ball.
>
> Corleon: Knew you wanted to make fun of the boring fucks with me.
>
> Me: Lol.

Cappadonna and Capone looked over at me. "Pri, let us

know if you don't wanna do this... we got you either way. We'll figure out a different way."

All eyes were on me. "I'm not letting this family down... I couldn't do anything back then, but I can now. I refuse to watch my nieces and nephews watch their fathers from behind a wall...it's time for you to meet our brother."

"We'll do our part to make sure you straight, Baby Doll." Cappy stared me in the eyes, hating that I was in control.

He wanted to protect me, as he had always done. "Cappy, I'mma do them in and they not even gonna see it coming." I stood up and looked over at Aimee. "Right, Aim?"

"Facts," she smiled while cracking her knuckles.

"Night, fam... today has been a day."

As much as I wanted to tell my sisters that I was pregnant and soak up their advice and reactions, telling my brothers about our brother had drained me. Then with Forty coming over and dropping that bomb on me, I wanted to go home and be alone for a second.

There was a time when I used to be scared of being alone. I would do literally anything in my power to avoid having to be home alone in my thoughts. Even the first months of traveling had me fucked up. The more time that passed, I was able to become comfortable with myself being alone.

I put the code in and secured the door behind me, kicking my shoes off. As I was about to cross the foyer, I heard a noise and quickly grabbed my gun from the foyer table. Cocking my gun back, I was about to take a step forward when the lights flipped on, and music filled the room.

"Pretty Wings" by Maxwell played softly as Meer came around the pillar that separated the foyer from the rest of the living area. "Should have known better trying to surprise you, Suga."

Seeing his face made my heart jump around in my chest as he came closer to me, and I sat my gun on the table, jumping into his arms. With ease, he caught me and held me while kissing me on the lips.

"I missed you today."

"So why didn't you send me those three letters?"

I shrugged as he continued to hold me. "I didn't want to bother you."

I found myself becoming needy whenever Quameer was near. He made me turn my thoughts off because he handled everything. I didn't feel the need to be so guarded, and strong around him. I was able to feel at ease, move with ease, and never question his motives when it came to me. It had been so long since I had been able to feel safe with a man that it scared me at times.

"Your pretty wings," he sang in my ear as he rocked back and forth, while we listened to the song.

"Meer?"

"What up, Sug?" he said in between kisses on my neck as he swayed slowly to the music while I held onto him.

"You know this song is a breakup song, right?"

"Say word?"

"Word... have you listened to the lyrics?"

He carried me into the kitchen, and I smiled at the bouquet of roses. There were three different bouquets, each a different hue of pink sitting on my countertop. Next to them sat a big box. I blushed as he put me on the counter and took his place between my legs.

"What is all of this, Meer?" I blushed, taking in the effort that he had gone through to make me smile.

He gently took my face into his hand, while staring into my eyes. "I listened to this song damn near everyday while you were gone. Shit made me miss you more, and maybe I took the lyrics differently because I had to let you go. Sug, letting you get on that plane was the hardest thing that I had to do. I had to let you go in hopes that you would come back to me."

Capri

"And I did," I whispered as I swiped away the tears that fell down my cheeks.

Meer rested his forehead against mine and smiled. "You fucking did, Sug,"

"When you came to the airport, I thought you were gonna talk me out of going," I admitted while he continued to rest his forehead against mine. "I would have stayed if you asked me to... you never did."

I just knew when I saw Meer at the airport, he was coming to bring me back home. I was surprised when he let me go, and didn't tell me to stay. There was a part of me that wanted him to ask me to stay, because I would have left the airport with him.

"Would have been selfish of me. How can I be the man that you need moving that way? I had to let you go so you could stand on your own, come into your own as a woman. Learn who you are and be comfortable being alone."

"It was so hard," I whispered.

"Seeing you cry and struggle with it had me ready to come get you every time. Suga, I want you to be here because you wanna be, not because you're afraid of being alone. Remember when I told you that your deck hadn't been shuffled with mine yet?"

A smile came across my face. "I remember."

"Think our cards are finally starting to come together," he whispered in my ear, as I hugged him around the neck.

"I think you're right."

He pointed to his cheek with his burn, and I placed a kiss right on it. "Go pack some clothes... we're going on an adventure."

"Where?" I grew excited.

He knew I was impatient when it came to surprises, so he walked over toward the box. Carrying it over toward me, sitting the big ass box down next to me. I hesitated before opening, and he leaned on the opposite counter and nodded for me to open it.

Pulling the lid from the box, I tossed it to the side while peering down in the box. My hand found its way to my mouth as I looked back at Meer. "A motorcycle helmet."

"You don't have your own when you ride with me."

I pulled the rest of the helmet out and smiled so damn wide I'm sure I looked crazy. "You got me the matching one to your favorite helmet?"

Quameer had a flaming skull helmet that was his favorite to wear. It was all black to match his bike with the skull and flames being white and gray. He got me the exact same helmet, except it was a pink skull and flames.

"You like it?"

"Meer, I love it... you got this for me?"

He moved back over toward me, and I wrapped my arms around him. "I wanna make you smile like this every fucking day. Know why?"

"Why?" I kissed the side of his face.

"Because you deserve that shit, Capri. You deserve for a nigga to keep a smile on your face." He kissed my teeth while I blushed.

"Is this going to be a thing?"

"You know how I'm coming behind you." He nuzzled his nose in my neck while I squeezed him. "Especially now that you carrying my seed... don't do no shit that gonna have me on your neck, Capri."

"How you go from lover boy to lowkey threatening me." I smiled, secretly loving the fact that he didn't play behind me.

"Don't matter... just remember what I said."

I kissed him once more as I looked at the helmet. "Are we really going to do this?"

"You told me that you want me to let you in, so I'm doing

that… go pack a little bag. You coming to stay with me for a few days."

He helped me down from the counter. "Can we get something to eat before going back to your house? I'm starving and haven't had anything all… in an hour," I switched what I was gonna say when I saw his face.

"When's the last time you ate?"

"Like an hour ago."

"You fucking lying, Suga… you starving my fucking baby already." I mushed him in the head and had went to toss some clothes in my overnight bag.

Chapter 22
Quameer

CAPRI WAS SLEEP WHEN WE FINALLY PULLED INTO MY garage last night. The entire ride to the crib she went back and forth debating on what she wanted to order to eat. We were talking about something and then I looked over and her ass was knocked out with drool dripping down the corner of her mouth.

After I carried her into the house and put her in my bed while pulling her shoes off and putting the covers over her as she got more comfortable in my bed. The food I ordered had arrived, so I grabbed it and put it on the counter for whenever she woke up hungry. Za had sent me some stocks to buy, so I went into my office to work for a bit before I would eventually go shower and lay up with Suga for the rest of the night.

My phone chimed and I jumped up and looked at the time. I had fallen asleep at my desk, and I had to pick up Ryder from Brandi this morning. It was technically Brandi's time with her, but I asked her to take her for the day.

I rinsed my mouth out and shoved my feet into my Birkenstocks, and then headed out the door, making sure to secure the doors before leaving. Capri was knocked out when I checked in on her, so I didn't expect her to be up anytime soon.

Since it was morning traffic getting over the bridge, it took

Capri

me a little bit to make it to Brandi's house. Soon as I pulled in, I hopped out and rang the doorbell. We hadn't spoken since she called me and snitched on Capri. I needed to check her about that shit too, because I should have never allowed her to get inside my head like that.

All it did was add to her sick level of satisfaction knowing that she had told on Capri, like she was a child. I could recognize that I crashed out like she was one and flew all the way to Miami. Shit, I was going to Anguilla, but I think God had other plans and used Za's stupid ass.

When she opened the door, she looked like she had been crying and was wearing some short ass shorts. "Peach ready?"

"Morning... toes all out, huh?" she gave a weak chuckle. "Baby Love, your daddy is here to come get you." Her voice was uneven, and she avoided looking at me.

"Stop fronting like my feet not pretty." I flexed my toes, to lighten the dark ass mood I had walked into.

Brandi smiled. "Do you think you can keep her until next week?"

"You never have to ask me, Bran... I got my daughter always," I replied, as Ryder came running downstairs with a bag.

Brandi hugged Ryder and looked into her eyes. "Don't worry about Mommy and Martin... we're okay... promise."

Ryder smiled and hugged her mother around her thin frame. "Okay, Mommy... I love you."

"Love you so much more, Baby Love." She kissed her forehead and gave her a tight squeeze. "Behave with your father, alright?"

"Okay."

Ryder rushed into my arms, and I kissed her a bunch of times all over her face. "Missed you, Peach."

"Hmm, let's see if you feel the same way after I beat you in Uno tonight."

I pinched her. "Go get in the truck."

She giggled and ran to hop in my truck. I turned my attention to Brandi who was smiling watching our interaction with each other. "You're such a good father... I really lucked up with you."

"That's my heart right there... you straight?"

I didn't give a fuck about her marriage, but this was also my daughter's mom, and it was clear Ryder had experienced some shit for her to give her the reassurance that she did.

"I remember when I used to be your heart." She folded her arms and leaned in the doorway, avoiding my fucking question.

"Yeah, that shit was a long time ago."

"Now Capri Delgato is your heart." She snorted, as if she didn't like the idea. As if her ass wasn't the reason we had broken up.

Any time I thought about if me and Brandi did get married, would we have lasted. I think because of the person I was now, and how I had to grow, we probably would have been divorced. As much as it hurt back then, Brandi did me a favor.

"That reminds me... don't call me to tell me about shit about my girl. You being messy and starting shit."

She rolled her eyes as she picked in her nails. "Telling you that your girlfriend is in the club talking to another man is messy? I'm just looking out for you. Especially since you decided to bring her around our daughter."

"What the fuck I decide to do with my daughter, and who I bring around her is my fucking decision. The fact that I've never brought a woman around Ryder until Capri, even then, we were friends."

"Friends don't look at each other like that, Meer. You wanted Capri ever since college and gaslit the fuck out of me when I called you out on it that one time."

"And you were fucking niggas on the football team for your

Capri

school, so why the fuck does it matter? You're married to who you wanna be married to... leave the fucking past alone."

"The past is very much relevant when you're bringing her around our life *now*."

I shook my head, realizing that I wasn't going to get anywhere when it came to Brandi. She was worried about my shit when clearly her life was in shambles. "Boundaries, Brandi."

"Don't forget about Chicago... we both promised Ryder a birthday trip together as a family."

"Yeah. I'm gonna book everything when I get a chance." Brandi smiled. "Your bringing Marty boy?"

Her smile dropped. "Um, no... I thought it was gonna just be us as a family."

"Come on, Brand... Marty boy is family, right? Cool... let me know when you book your flight accommodations... matter fact, I might just charter a jet for our little girl's special day."

Brandi tried to say some other shit and I was already tossing Ryder's bag into the passenger seat and hopping up in my truck. Before she could chase the car down the driveway, I quickly whipped out and headed back to my crib.

"You good back there, Peach?"

"I think mommy and Martin might be breaking up, Daddy."

I looked at her through the rearview mirror and sighed. "Nah. Couples argue and go through things. Especially married couples. It doesn't mean they don't love each other. You know how you get frustrated with your best friend, Piper?"

"Uh huh." She nodded.

"It's the same thing, but your mom and Martin are married. They love each other, but sometimes need space."

"Oh."

"Let them handle their problems and remain my little girl, ight?"

"Daddy?"

"Hmm?"

"Why don't you and Capri argue with each other? Aren't you a couple?"

I laughed because my daughter was nosey, and she damn sure didn't buy that friend card I used at the lake house a few weeks ago. "Why you assume we're a couple? I told you we're friends."

"Daddy, every time Suga calls you start smiling. Even when you see her you get excited."

"Word is bond?"

"Word is bond." Peach laughed.

"Can I tell you a little secret?"

She gasped, leaning forward as much as her chair would allow her. "Yes. I promise I won't tell anyone."

"I'm in love with Suga."

She clapped her hands. "I knew it!"

"You ain't know sh...nothing," I teased her.

"Can I tell you a secret?"

"What's that?"

"Suga is in love with you, too, Daddy." We locked eyes in the rearview mirror as she smiled at me, excited.

"Think so?"

"I know so."

"Think she might say yes if I asked her to marry me today?" My daughter was queen of the dramatics.

I waited while she faked like she passed out in her booster chair, and then woke up like she had actually passed out. "Seriously, Daddy?"

I had already knew I wanted to marry Capri. When we had those deep talks about marriage and how she viewed it differently, I wanted to change that for her. I needed her to see that marriage was beautiful with the right person. I've never been

Capri

scared of commitment, and now I knew why my past never worked out.

I was supposed to wait for Capri. If she said yes, this would be my first time getting married, and her second and last. The way I wanted to make this woman so happy and full kept me up at night. She deserved that shit more than anyone I had ever met.

"I'm serious, Peach. Only if you're okay with it."

She smiled at me. "I love Suga, so yes... ask her... Can I be apart of it?"

"Hell yeah."

"Hells yeah!" she fist pumped the air, and I gave her ass that look. "Too far?"

"Too damn far."

"Sorry."

I decided to drop Peach off at my Gam's house and then go back to get Capri. She wanted me to stop hiding and show her the real me, so I was bringing her over to Gam's house. Today was the day my pops usually came over, so she would get to see him again.

When I returned back to the house, Capri was still knocked out, so I went into my office to finish up what I was doing before my ass fell asleep last night. I was so deep into my computer that I didn't notice Capri standing in the doorway until I briefly looked up and saw her standing there. She smiled with sleepy eyes when I finally noticed her standing there. Rolling back in the chair, I patted my lap, and she came around the desk and sat on my lap.

"Good morning... did you even sleep any last night?"

I yawned. "Nah... ended up getting busy working, then I had to run and pick Peach up to bring her to my Gam's house."

"Oh okay. Are you always this focus when you have your glasses on, Clark Kent. I was standing there for a good ten minutes before you noticed me." She kissed me on the lips.

"Oh yeah. Why you didn't say anything?"

She messed with my locs. "I was admiring you." I felt all warm and fuzzy on the inside whenever she kissed the burn on the side of my face.

"Give me one more." Instead of one, she gave me two more kisses. "Overachiever ass," I snorted.

"What are you doing?" she turned to look at the computer.

I had different portfolios opened because I was sure Za's high ass was telling me to invest in something that I already owned. "Going over some shit... boring stuff."

"You mind?" she asked, and I gave her the green light to go on my computer. Nobody fucked with my computer. Shit, nobody came in my office.

She clicked around all the tabs and files I had opened and was quiet for a minute. My baby was smart, so I knew she understood what she was looking at. "Baby..." her voice trailed off.

"Hmm." I laid on her back while rubbing her stomach while she was bent over the desk clicking around on the computer.

Her stomach was flat as shit, but just knowing she had my baby in there made me fucking excited. "You're a millionaire, Meer... legally."

"Uh huh."

She turned to face me. "Like you're really fucking rich."

"Suga, what the fuck, did you think I was broke?"

I watched as she laughed. "No, like I knew you got money with Inferno Gods, and your brother... all of these investments, stocks and small start-ups you own have nothing to do with Quasim or Inferno Gods."

"Getting money in the streets and not investing is hustling backward... your brothers are on game, too... Quasim, too."

"The more you know. I've always known our family had

Capri

money and where it came from... just thought it was from the streets and obviously the trucking company."

I couldn't help but to laugh because Capone was smart with the way he moved. The Delgatos owned a trucking company, but they were about to get into the import and export business too, which was big fucking money. Capone and Capp were serious about making that step to leave the streets alone.

"They made moves to make sure your family is forever taken care of."

"And you've done the same for you and Ryder."

"Which lets you know that I can and will take care of *our* family. Your brothers have taken care of you, and now as a man, *your* man, I'm stepping up and letting them know that I got it from here."

The money I had sitting in accounts was to make sure my current and future family was always taken care of. The most expensive shit I bought was this house, and that was because I wanted Ryder to have a home, not just some condos that I moved in and out of. She needed stability.

"Our family sounds so..."

"Don't overthink it, Sug."

She kissed my lips. "Not overthinking it... it sounds so warm... sounds like something I've wanted of my own for a while."

I looked up in her eyes, and she hugged me around the neck. "You in this, right?"

"All the way... I mean, you've made sure of that." She leaned back and pointed to her stomach while giggling.

Capri went back on the computer, her back perfectly arched while sitting right on my rising dick. "When you put these shorts on." I pulled the waist band to the boxer shorts that she wore.

"I woke up sweating in your bed... feels like somebody likes it," she did a light bounce on my dick. I pulled her back against me, running my hands up her body until it reached her breasts, and I cupped them, twisting her already hardened nipples. "Hmm, Meer."

"I need some, Suga," I started kissing on her neck while I continued to caress her breast while she tossed her head back. "Come sit on Big Pa," I said between kisses.

She stood up, and I pulled the boxer shorts she wore down, exposing that perfect pussy. Everything about Capri was fucking perfect, and at times she struggled to see that. Suga allowed her mistakes of the past to taint who she was today.

I rubbed her pussy while she struggled to stand still in front of me. Her shit was leaking as she bit down on her bottom lip, giving me that look that made my dick hard. Leaning up, I pulled my shorts and briefs down, showing what she did to me whenever she was near me.

Pressing the buttons on the side of my office chair, I brought them down and motioned for her to sit her pussy right on me. Capri straddled my lap, slowly coming down on my dick while I struggled not to slam her ass down.

Each time she was almost down, she lifted up to tease me while giving me that crooked smirk. "Stop playing with me, Suga," I groaned while holding her hips.

"Sounds like Pa about to cum... hmm?" She lifted up once again, and I gripped her hips, sitting her ass down while she moaned out.

"Stop trying to run shit... I run shit when I'm in there, ight?" I bit the side of her neck while she whimpered and bounced up and down slowly.

Suga held onto the back of the chair while she was whining while biting down on her lips. The sound of her pussy sloshing around while she pounced on me was the soundtrack to my heart. I took her shirt off and tossed it on the other side of the room.

She was fucking me in my office butt ass naked, something

Capri

that I had dreamed of every night when we spoke on the phone. Hearing her soft whimpers in my ear while she kissed and held my neck.

"Meer... this is yours," she cooed, and that shit made me crazy.

It was one thing already knowing that shit, and another thing when a woman told you it. "You dripping, Sug... shit so wet its dripping down on my lap, Baby."

I grabbed hold of her hips and slammed her down on my dick while she squealed, holding onto me. "Please, don't stop... faster, Pa." She clamped down on my neck, using her teeth.

I stood up from the chair, careful not to trip on my pants. Soon as my feet were free from my shorts, I leaned her against my built-in bookshelf, next to my degrees, and delivered that first stroke that had her moan stuck in her throat.

I held onto the shelf while I continued to pump in and out of her while she was throwing that pussy back on me. Sweat accumulated on both of our brows, as she screamed out for me to keep going.

"Don't get fucking quiet now, Sug... scream that shit... I know you could get louder for me."

That moan that was stuck in her throat moments before came out like she was singing opera. Her nails dug into my shoulder as I continued to pound her shit on the bookshelf. "Meeeerrr, it feel.... Uhh. Ummmm," she couldn't finish her words.

"You love me, Sug?" I asked as I thrusted into her, shaking the books on the shelf.

"Uh huhh... yes, Meer."

"How much?"

"So much, Baby... a lottttt."

I kissed her neck, sucking on her neck in the process while balls deep inside of her. "You gonna cum for me?"

"Tell me when, Meer... tell me," she whispered while I kissed her in the mouth, even with it wide open.

"Cum for me right now... look me in the eyes, Sug."

She struggled keeping eye contact as I continued to pound her shit. "Meer, I'm about...please... Can I?"

"Finish for me, Suga... finish me, baby," I sucked on her bottom lip while holding her around the neck.

Applying a little pressure, she damn near shattered in my arms with how hard she had come for me. Her body trembled while she held onto me and wrapped her legs around me tighter. "Can I go back to sleep?" she muttered into my shoulder before kissing it.

"Nah. We need to go shower so you can meet Gams and my mother."

Capri's head popped up. "Seriously? Meer, you can't do this to me and then expect me to go meet your Gams like this."

"With that fresh fucked face." I kissed her lips as I still held her against the bookshelf.

She held onto me tighter, her legs damn near becoming a part of me. "I love you, Meer Cat."

"Love you more, Suga... if you weren't pregnant before, I damn sure put another one up in you."

"When do we tell Peach?"

"Not yet. Let's go to the first appointment before we tell her about it. Peach gets excited, and I wanna make sure everything is straight before telling news like this. Her ass been wanting a sibling for years."

Sug smiled. "Okay... we can wait to tell her."

Chapter 23
Capri

As we slowly turned onto the block, I was certain was his grandmother's, I grabbed his hand and held it, nervous to meet his family. It was easy to meet his father when we were just friends. Even when I met his father, we were barely even friends. This was different knowing that we were together.

Even though I had been on Quameer to open up more, I was still very nervous to meet his family. As he slowed in front of the house, the screen in his truck lit up with Quasim's name. Meer hit the green phone icon and Quasim's low voice came through the line.

"You made it there yet?"

"Pulling into the driveway now... you sure you not coming?"

Quasim became quiet. "Got something that I need to handle or else I would be... kiss Gams and Mommy for me."

"Always do."

"Capri, stop sweating so much. Gams is gonna love you."

I smiled, because how did he even know I was in the car. "Thanks, Sim."

"Hit me up and let me know how everything goes." He ended the call, and I looked over at Meer.

Jahquel J.

"I worry about him."

"Show me someone that doesn't." He got out the car and walked around to help me down from his high ass truck. "You ready for this?"

I nodded my head. "I'm not going to lie, I am nervous... I'm ready though. Meer, I want to get to know this side of you."

He looked down at me before taking my hand and walking up the walkway to the house. I smiled at the wraparound porch, and the beautiful roses that were planted in the front yard.

"My mom loves roses... loved," he corrected himself, as he hit the code to the door, and allowed me to walk in first.

The foyer had a large spiral staircase that had a motorized chair that glided up the steps. There was a huge gallery wall with different pictures of the family, mostly of Peach. There was a little girl with curly hair and light greenish colored eyes that resembled Quasim's eyes.

"That's Harley," Quameer whispered into my ear. "Sim's daughter."

"Oh."

When I first heard Quasim's story, my heart broke in two. No man should have to bury his girlfriend, and then his daughter right behind it. That was enough to break any person, and Quasim was still walking around. It hit different actually seeing the little girl that he had to bury and live without.

"Suga!" Ryder ran down the steps and straight into my arms.

"Peach!" I smiled and hugged her tighter.

When I lifted my head, I saw an older woman peek her head out the kitchen. Quameer went over and kissed her on the head. "What up, Gams?"

It was funny because she had the same curly hair that Quasim, Quameer, and Ryder all shared. While Quasim had black hair, Quameer and Ryder shared his Gam's sandy brown hair. She was stunning with her high cheek bones, low brown eyes, and curly hair pinned on top of her head. Gams was a petite woman, nearly the same height as Ryder.

"Você a trouxe," his Gams spoke to him in Portuguese. It helped me connect the dots that was where he learned the language.

"Ele fez.. ela é bonita, certo?" Ryder replied.

"Gams, this is Capri... the infamous Capri." He smiled, as he pulled me closer to him, as he introduced me to his grandmother.

"Hi Gams!" I greeted her.

She had the biggest smile on her face as she walked over toward me and embraced me. "Hi Capri... I'm so happy that he didn't have to drag you in here."

"Huh?"

"Nothing," Meer said, as he looked over at Peach. "Aye, Peach... come call your mama," he told her, and they went toward the back of the house.

Gams held my hand as we walked into the kitchen. "Take a seat over there and I will give you something to eat. Are you hungry?"

"Starving actually," I admitted.

Gams became excited. "Goodie... I just finished making roasted chicken and rice."

"I'm not picky at all... thank you so much."

I went from being nervous to feeling so at peace in this woman's presence. I had never met her a day in my life, but she made me feel so welcomed. "How did you enjoy traveling around for a year."

"Meer really talked about me to you," I blushed.

She turned around and gave me a warm smile. "He tells me mostly everything, and you happened to be the center of a lot of our conversations." When she winked, it made me wonder if she knew I was pregnant.

"Did he tell you that I'm..." I allowed my voice to trail off, and she picked up the pieces right away without missing a beat.

"He did. Called me before he even knew for sure." She lowered her voice. "Congratulations, mamãe. How has your family taken the news?"

"I haven't told them yet."

"Scared?"

"A little. I want to keep this secret for a bit longer, you know. I've shared so much with my family in the past few years, and I just want something for me. Something for me and Meer for a bit."

My life had been the center of this family over the past few years, and I had lived with everyone having an opinion on how I live my life and feeling like they were entitled to have an opinion on my life and the decisions I had made.

For once, I wanted to have something for myself. I wanted me and Meer to adjust to knowing we were having a baby together before telling my family. As much as I knew Alaia and Erin would be excited for me, I needed to leave them in suspense a little bit more, so I could handle my own thoughts and emotions.

I haven't even fully sat and thought everything through, so telling them while I was still working out my own thoughts would have been jumping the gun.

"You do it on your own time. It has to be when you're ready and comfortable. Don't let anyone pressure you into sharing your business."

"Thank you."

Meer came back into the kitchen and sat in the chair near the pantry. Gams sat a plate of food in front of me and I rubbed my hands together, digging my fork into the chicken that just fell apart.

Soon as the chicken touched my taste buds, the flavors

Capri

exploded in my mouth while I closed my eyes and sat back in the chair. "It ain't all that good."

Gams swatted her grandson and laughed. "I made you more cookies... don't go through these."

"Cookies too?" my eyes widened at the large chocolate chip cookies.

"You can't have none of these, Sug... edibles." He winked.

"This is where you get those cookies from?" I thought he was lying when he told me his Gams made them. I assumed his ass was getting them from a dispensary or something.

"Capri! My hair is tangled!" Ryder came running into the kitchen as I was about to bite back into this chicken.

I wiped my hands as she stood in between my legs. "Relax, we can untangle the knot."

As Ryder bounced from foot to foot, I worked on getting her hair out this knot. It felt like she had something hard in her hair. I got her hair loose from around a ring and held it in my hand. When I turned around to face Gams and Meer, he was on one knee.

In my hand I held a pear-shaped diamond ring that was blinding me. It still had Ryder's hair wrapped around it. "When our paths crossed again, I knew this was God telling me that he wasn't going to give me another chance. He also told me not to rush into it, and to be patient. You know me, Sug... you know I'm not a patient man. I trusted the man upstairs because I needed him to make this happen for me... for us. I know what I want, and I have known since you boarded that flight. Marriage scares you because you've been there and done that. Sug, you haven't done it with me yet." He looked down, then back up into my eyes and I saw the tears fall down his face. "I swore to the man upstairs that if I became a parent again, I would do it the right way."

Ryder walked over toward her father and swiped his tears

away. "Suga, will you marry us? We can have the same last name, too," she added, to sweeten the deal.

I felt a hand rubbing the small of my back, and Gams was standing beside me. "Meer," my voice cracked as I held the ring in my hand. "I love you for the patience that you have had with me. The grace you have shown me when I couldn't show myself it. INY. I can't do it without you... I don't wanna do this without you."

His grin on his face as he stared up at me told me everything I needed to know. "Daddy, my hair really is tangled."

"You'll live, Peach," he laughed. "Suga, you gonna leave me hanging?"

"Yes. I'll marry you." He got off the floor and came to kiss me, swinging me around the kitchen while Peach and Gams clapped.

Meer took the ring from me and slid it onto my finger, and I admired it, looking at the ring finger that I thought would remain bare after I slid off my wedding set after divorcing Naheim. I had made peace that this finger would remain bare, and there goes Meer, showing me that what I thought and what he would do were two different things.

"Shit is fucking beautiful." We turned to the doorway where Meer's father was standing there. "I've always wanted a daughter... the new Lady Inferno," He walked further into the kitchen and hugged his son.

"Thanks, Pops."

"Blaze, it means a lot that you wanted your future wife to wear your mother's ring. Mommy is so proud of you."

Meer looked away and his father hugged him tighter. "Love you, Pops."

"Love you more." He paused, and then pulled me into the hug. "Love the both of you... marriage isn't for the weak, and its hard work. Never give up on each other... life will happen, and

Capri

trust that shit happens a lot, but you signed on to be each other's person. Never lose sight of that."

"I promise I won't."

"Take her upstairs to meet your mother." He held the back of Meer's neck and kissed his head.

I grabbed his hand. "I want to meet her."

He looked down at me. "Then you'll meet her."

We headed upstairs and down the hall to the room. Meer knocked on the door and then opened it. A woman, younger than Gams, but could be her entire twin, sat rocking in a chair. When she turned, I smiled because it was like looking at an older Ryder. The Inferno Genes were so strong.

"Hey lady," Meer walked closer and kissed her on the forehead, while removing her hair from her face.

His mother was more interested in me. She waved him out of her hair, and continued to look at me. I sat down in the empty seat next to her. The view from the seat was perfect. You could see who was coming and going.

Meer leaned on the dresser as I got lost in the view of the neighborhood. I felt soft and cold hands touch mine, and his mother had grabbed my hand. He leaned up when he noticed it, and I laced my fingers within hers.

She gave me a faint smile as she held onto my hand and rocked in her chair. Papa showed up in the doorway, and he smiled while watching us. I offered Meer a smile, and his body language relaxed some as I rubbed the back of his mother's hand while she rocked peacefully. This was going to be my mother-in-law, and everyone in this family protected her, and her privacy. Nothing got out that they didn't want out, and I planned to live by the same rules.

I had given up the Delgato name once before to become a Browne. Now, I was about to give my last name up again to become Capri Inferno.

Chapter 24
Quameer

I hadn't seen my baby for a good two days because of the prep for her birthday party. She was so excited to live out her Roll Bounce dreams, and nothing was gonna ruin it for her. Not if I had anything to do with the shit.

We were keeping our engagement to ourselves right now. That small intimate moment meant more to me than anything. I could have done a big engagement, but I felt my Gam's kitchen was the perfect place. Under the same roof as my mother, and with my father there, even though his ass was late.

If this didn't feel right before, it damn sure felt right after seeing my mother hold Capri's hand. Suga sat in that room for two hours rocking with my mother and holding her hand. She never complained, and it was me who had to drag her out the room because she seemed so at peace. I don't know if my mother could sense she was carrying her second grandbaby, or what. All I did know is that I wanted to marry Capri, and she was gonna become an Inferno. She and our baby would have the same last name.

I made that promise to God that if I was blessed to have another, I would do it the right way, and I was coming through on that promise.

Capri

If it was one thing Erin and Alaia were gonna do, it was throw a party and have a theme with the shit. They rented out the roller rink at Pier 2 in Brooklyn. While you were skating, you had the perfect view of the Brooklyn Bridge and Manhattan right in front of you. They also had the Pickle Ball Courts and basketball courts decorated.

The minute you came in, you were transported to a fucking Passa Passa party. The entire area was decorated with Barbados and Jamaican flags. Shit had me thinking about my teens when I used to be in Brooklyn wilding out on the parkway with my niggas. There was three different food trucks catered to everybody.

They had a Jamaican jerk truck, another one that served Bajan food, and then one with regular shit like burgers, wings, and fries. Everywhere you looked, the shit was done top notch and had me excited for her to see the shit.

The party had already started when we walked in, and everybody was either lining up to grab skates or get on the line for food. Me, Quasim, Goon, and Yasin walked in, and peeped Cappadonna, Capone, and Capella over in the basketball court.

"About time you niggas showed the fuck up." Capone dapped us all.

"Traffic getting over here is crazy. Capri brought the whole damn city out," Goon said, as he and Capp hit the IG handshake, and he signaled to the bartender for water.

Capp laughed. "Wifey made sure we got a cranberry and Sprite bar... it's over there."

"Good looks," Goon tapped his shoulder and made his way across the basketball court to grab a cranberry and Sprite.

I couldn't even front, the combo was good because Capri had put me onto it. "Me and you got a problem." Capp pointed at me.

I already knew it was because of his long-lost brother.

"Wasn't my business, Capp. You respect me because I don't speak on shit that's not mine. I was respecting what my lady wanted to do... can't be mad at me for that."

He looked at me, and I braced myself 'cause this nigga was looking like he was considering dunking my ass in the hoop we were standing under. "This whole give me respect to handle my relationship ain't working with me."

I laughed as I grabbed a shot from the bar and took it back. "She's not a baby no more... she'll always be your baby doll, but she's my Suga... you know she in good hands... I wasn't gonna take her moment from her. Capp, come on, gotta let her come into her own." I reached up and squeezed his shoulder.

"Pissy ass, Meer... can't even believe we even allowing this shit." Capone came over and pulled my loc.

"Stop fucking calling me pissy," I shoved Capone's ass, and he stumbled back while we laughed.

Naheim came over holding his chick's hand and dapped all of us up. It was cool when we saw each other because I didn't have static with the nigga unless he wanted it. Even if he did have a problem with me, he wasn't going to let it show.

At the end of the day, when we were out in the streets, I had to have his follow up. Don't matter if his ex-wife was about to be my new wife, we were all coming home together. Until he proved me otherwise, I was chilling and didn't see the need for the unnecessary beef. In my opinion, the nigga already lost his wife, so his problem wasn't with me. It was still fuck him though.

"Nah Nasty finally out the house," Capone's ass said, and we all turned to look at him because this nigga was tipsy as fuck.

"Nigga, you ain't never in my life call me that name." Naheim started laughing with the rest of us.

"You really nasty though," Capone added while play punching him in the arm.

Capri

Cappadonna looked at his twin. "Aye, you done with the shots."

"Nigga, I'm a grown ass man." He grabbed the Don Julio bottle from the bar and poured both of us another shot.

"How you doing, Nellie... you happy to be back home?"

Nellie accepted the drink that Capone had handed her. "I forgot how much I missed home. I don't miss the prices though."

"Where you looking to buy?" Capp asked like his ass was a real estate agent, and was gonna help them find a damn house.

Jasmine ran over toward Capella and hugged him. The way she was running, it was like she hadn't seen the nigga in years. "Hey Jas." He kissed her head as he hugged her back.

"Hey everybody," she hugged us all before going back over toward her cousin and talking to him.

Kincaid swaggered over after them and dapped us all up. "The fuck is up? We getting fucked up tonight, right?"

"Babe, we are not getting drunk tonight. We have that Tots class for Kaleb in the morning." If I didn't know better, the nigga groaned.

"The birthday girl just pulled the fuck up!" the DJ announced, so we all walked over toward the skating rink while waiting for her to come in.

We spotted Karter and Star, so we went to chill by them while waiting for Suga to come inside. I missed the shit out my girl, and just needed to see her face real quick. Tonight was all about her, so I wasn't on that tonight.

I was cool with playing the back, and just watching her enjoy the party she needed. This wasn't just her birthday party; it was a welcome home to the new and improved Capri. The Capri that was about to be tossed in a tank with sharks and was gonna come back with they fucking heads.

The DJ started playing that old school reggae music as Capri came in laughing with Alaia and Erin. She stopped and looked around at everyone yelling happy birthday and smiled big as shit. I would kiss her fucking teeth if she was closer to me.

She was going crazy looking at all the effort that both Alaia and Erin had put in to plan her birthday party. I watched as she hugged them and covered her mouth with her hands.

That Caribbean was flowing through her ass while she busted a wine while getting hype to the music that was playing. Capone and Cappadonna walked over toward her, kissing her on the head. The photographer came and took their picture, before getting some with Capri alone while she jumped up and down excited.

That was really my fiancée and baby moms.

Capone's ass was feeling too nice because he started dancing with Capri who couldn't stop laughing. He then grabbed his wife, and Erin didn't hesitate to play into his shit and started dancing on him while they danced they asses off to the side.

"Look at wifey... beautiful ass." Goon licked his lips while looking at Zoya, who was talking to Capri, and had dipped off toward the bar. "Let me make sure my baby not drinking tonight." He headed toward the bar where I knew Zoya was gonna call his ass Gerald and wonder why he was out past curfew.

Capp admired his baby sister once more before saying something to her, and then kissing her on the forehead.

"Why you not over there with your baby or are you both still keeping it on the low," Karter asked me.

"Not on the low, tonight is her night... don't need our shit overshadowing that."

Karter held his hand out. "Respect it."

Quasim came over with Naheim and Kincaid and settled by the bar. He ordered a drink while keeping eyes on Blair, who

Capri

waved and smiled at him. He winked and nodded his head at her, and she blushed like he had shared some words with her.

We all hung back and watched her greet everyone, stopping to dance every time the DJ played one of her songs. "Fuck." Naheim whistled while taking in every inch of *my* Suga.

Kincaid hadn't taken his eyes off her since he had come over here. I could tell from the way his mouth was damn near hanging open as he watched her. Suga didn't make it no better with the two-piece sweat short set she wore. Damn shorts were fucking short, and the jacket was cropped.

Fuck.

She had me with my mouth wide opened and tongue hanging out. I loved when she wore her hair curly, and tonight she had it curly with the front pinned back. She had told me her vision was New-New from the movie ATL, and she was giving that and then some. She had a nigga ready to get some *cuddy* in the middle of this fucking skating rink.

"Keep eye fucking what's mine and Ding Dong ain't gonna be the only bad man in this bitch," I snarled, as I stared both Naheim and Kincaid in the eyes, as "Bad Man Forward" played and Capri went crazy dancing with Blair.

Quasim squeezed my shoulder, as I watched my baby continue scanning the room like she was looking for something or someone. Even while dancing, I saw her still looking around the room, as I moved past them, and pulled my pants up while swaggering over toward her.

The minute her eyes landed on me; she had the biggest smile on her face while I made my way toward her. Capri didn't care about who was watching as she crashed into my arms, and I kissed her neck.

"Happy birthday, Suga." I kissed her again, as she wrapped her arms around my neck, and allowed me to swing her around.

"I missed you, Meer Cat."

I smiled and squeezed her tighter. "I missed both my babies. You ate today, and I'm not talking about fucking coffee."

She laughed, which meant her ass hadn't had nothing to eat. "I was busy all day... I spent my morning up at the prison visiting Aimee's father. I wanted to run something by him, and then when I came back Alaia and Erin held me captive."

We hadn't told anyone beside Gams that she was pregnant. We were waiting to tell Ryder when the time was right. I held her hand as I pulled her over toward the food trucks and skipped the line.

"The fuck?" I heard someone holler, and I turned to look at his ass, and he stepped back while I ordered my baby something to eat.

"You gonna skate with me?"

"Hell nah... you not about to have me on the floor. I'll walk beside you because you don't need to be trying to bust it down on skates anyway."

After Capri quickly ate some food, Blair brought over the custom skates they had made for her. She quickly kicked her sneakers off and slid them on while lacing them up. Jaiden rolled his show-off ass over with his skates.

"When the fuck did you learn how to skate?" I asked him.

"There ain't much the kid can't do. Plus, Elliot made a bet with me that I couldn't skate, so had to prove lil' mama wrong." Jaiden laughed while Capri stood up. "I came to get the birthday girl for a skate."

Capri pinched his cheeks like he was a baby, even though he towered over her. "You wanna skate with me."

"Yeah, I have to leave early because me and Erin gotta fly back to Florida for a few meetings."

Jaiden's name was like gold right now, so we all knew he was going to be drafted. "Damn, alright come on... be back, Meer."

I nodded and held her half-finished food. Suga was gonna

Capri

drive me crazy this pregnancy with the way she barely liked to eat, or when she did, she ate like a damn rabbit. "Be careful, Sug."

"I will."

Soon as she hit the floor, her and Jaiden were out as she danced. I trashed the rest of her food and stood off to the side to watch her. "You love her."

I looked over and Capp was leaned on the same railing watching his wife and Erin try to hold each other up.

"With my whole heart, Capp."

"I can tell. You look at her the same way I look at that one over there. There ain't shit I wouldn't do for her."

I chuckled. "I mean, I think you proved that shit plenty of times."

He chuckled. "You would do the same thing for her. Baby Doll deserves a love like that... a protection like the one I provide for Alaia."

"And she has that. You don't never gotta question it when it comes to her... I'm moving in her best interest always."

"I believe that."

After Suga had made her rounds on the skating rink, I took her skates off while rubbing her feet. "The birthday girl has a surprise outside."

"A surprise?"

I helped her up and held her hand as I pulled her behind me as we made it through the crowd. When we made it to the front, Quasim was backing up with my truck. Capri's scream damn near made me deaf when she saw her surprise.

"Quameer, you got me a new motorcycle!" she squealed and jumped into my arms while kissing me all over my face.

"Aye, you missed a spot." She kissed me on my burn and then licked my face. "Chill out, Sug... you can lick me later."

She kissed my lips once more as she jumped down and ran over to the back of my truck where Quasim was unlatching it.

I had got her a Yamaha r7 in a pearl pink. On the side of the bike, I had *Meer's Suga* engraved. "Happy birthday, Sis'." Quasim hugged her as he and Goon got the bike down.

"Can we go for a ride? Please... please." She came back over jumping up and down, too excited about her bike.

I rode my bike to the party while Yasin drove my truck with Suga's bike. "You trying to race...nah."

"Meer, come on... it's my birthday," she batted those eyelashes, and I couldn't say no to her. Not on her birthday.

"Get your helmet out the front."

She rushed over to grab her helmet, squealing because I remembered to bring it. I had bought the bike and got it custom along with the helmet. I just wanted her to get the helmet first. She was so damn excited that she hopped on the bike and revved the engine, excited. Quasim was showing her around the bike, and she listened while too excited that I got her a new bike.

"Know this nigga in love... look at the matching helmets," Goon snickered, while I got on my bike.

"Fuck up," I laughed and looked over at Suga, who was in her moment. She was so damn happy on her bike. "Ready, Sug?"

"Hell yeah."

"Be careful, Pri," Erin called behind her.

Soon as I nodded my head, giving her the signal, she took off down the walk path near Pier 2. It took you right onto the Brooklyn-Queens expressway, and she gunned it once she had clearance. I was right behind her as she zoomed in and out of traffic, and I kept up with her. She did a fist pump in the air, and I laughed because I did this.

I made my baby happy.

In a few months she wouldn't be able to ride this bike, so I was gonna let her live tonight. Capri was in and out of lanes, as

Capri

she was testing out her new bike. A bike zipped right by us, and I turned, peeping three others.

My heart rate increased as I increased speed and did a signal for Capri. I had taught her most of them, so she knew what I meant the moment I held my fist out and rotated my wrist. With one hand, I grabbed my phone.

"What up?" Sim answered.

"Niggas on us... she not strapped. Sim, get the fuck here now," I calmly stated, and ended the call.

I didn't need to tell him where I was because he had my location. Reaching in my back for my gun, Capri kept looking at me for the next move, and I signaled for her to follow me. I wanted her on the side of me so I could see her at all times.

Four more bikes zoomed ahead, bypassing us. When I saw that viper on the side of one of them, I already knew what it was. "Fuck," I said to myself.

I got over a lane where I was closer to Suga, and she flipped her visor up to look at me. "I want you to take the exit that takes you across the Brooklyn Brid—"

RAT TAT TAT!

We both ducked our heads. "Go, Sug... I'm coming behind you.... dust those niggas, Baby."

This time it wasn't bikes; it was two fucking cars trying to trip us up by hitting the back of our wheels. Capri flipped her visor down on her helmet, saluted me and then gunned it down toward the Brooklyn Bridge.

I lowered myself, holding my bike with one hand, and aimed my shit inside the window, letting that shit go. I hit my brake, something that could nearly trip me up, and rotated around toward the other side of the car and hit them again from the other side.

I saw Quasim's bike and pointed toward the bridge, and I gunned it down toward the bridge to get my baby. As I zoomed in and out of traffic, I heard the engines behind me and IG's had my follow up.

I peeped an Inferno Goddess, and she signaled that she was going after Suga, and saluted before taking off with two more behind her.

Quasim and Capp were side by side with the other IG's following behind them. I peeped my baby, and she was still in and out with the car on her ass. Quasim stuck his two fingers up and motioned forward and the rest of the IG's went ahead of us. Kincaid came speeding by on a dirt bike, as the IG's locked down the bridge after Suga had got off.

"I got her... no disrespect."

I nodded, and he took off to get Suga and bring her back to the party. We had one entire side of the Brooklyn Bridge locked down. We didn't have much time before the cops came, so I looked at Capp through the car.

We both smirked, sending bullets from both sides. At the same time, we slid our fingers under our nose and spit in the car at the men riddled in bullets.

Just as quick as we locked it down, we all breezed off the bridge and headed our separate ways. I told Kincaid to bring my baby to the lake house... we couldn't go back to that party.

They came at me with my fiancée, and she pregnant with my baby. Niggas gotta die, and they gotta fucking answer to Blaze.

Chapter 25
Corleon

GOVERNOR'S BALL

Capri seemed like her mind was somewhere else tonight. She was different from the woman that sat across from me the other day at lunch. Every bitch in this ball was someone that worked for Case House. These men had wives, and instead of bringing their wives, they paid thousands to have an escort bring them to the ball. Mostly because they knew how the night would end.

We had been here for an hour and had finally finished making our rounds. Capri sat down at the table, and then scanned the room. She kept scanning the room like she was looking for something. I reached across and refilled both our wine glasses, well mine since she hadn't touched hers.

My phone alerted me that the commissioner was trying to access the app. I smirked, as I hit the decline on the amount of money he tried to wire. Menace wanted that nigga to learn a lesson, and he was teaching it to him. All night his ass was on his phone fighting the urge not to crash out.

"He didn't arrive, so she can't get his phone," I whispered and nudged my sister.

She played it cool, as if I didn't expose her plan. "What are you talking about?"

"Aimee Simmons. You don't think I vet the college students that I allow to work for me? Capri, I know things and can find things out... computer guy here." I winked.

"Is that why you invited me to the ball?"

"Yes and no. I wanted to spend time with my little sister, get to know you. Also want to know why you want the future mayor of New York City's phone... doesn't matter why... I'm fucking in."

Capri smiled while staring at me. "You don't even know what I'm doing and you're in?" She was skeptical, and she had every right to be.

"I mean, I'm supposed to be meeting our brothers... Cappadonna reached out to me. How he got the number to my encrypted phone intrigues me."

"Cappy makes things happen and knows more shit than all of us... older sibling type shit," she shrugged. "You nervous to meet them?"

"Nah... more excited now that he hit my phone." Aimee nodded her head to let Capri know she was going to the bathroom. "She's going to the bathroom," I whispered.

She removed herself from the table and headed to the bathroom, being stopped by some random guy before continuing to the bathrooms. Menace came over and sat down beside me.

"Nigga been trying to corner me to talk all night."

No sooner than he mentioned his ass, Reggie came running over toward the table "How you doing, Commissioner?" Menace snickered.

"My app... it's not working, and I've been sending money through the app, and it's been declined."

I held my phone up. "That's me, Gramps."

Capri

"What is the meaning of all of this?" Reggie was on the verge of being hysterical while me and Menace laughed in his face.

Menace motioned for him to come closer. "I giveth pussy, and I can taketh pussy... now get the fuck out my face before your whip end up blowing the fuck up soon as you start the bitch."

Reggie scattered away all fucked up, and needing pussy more than he needed to breathe. Someone came to grab Menace, and I went to check in on Capri. As I was rounding the corner, we nearly bumped into each other.

Aimee was behind her and stopped short. "I was just coming out there to you."

As I was about to turn around, I felt someone slam into the back of me. "Um, excuse you. Why are you near the woman's bathroom anyway?" I heard a rude fucking voice. Bitch was mad, and she ran into me.

"Jesse?" Capri looked around me and recognized the woman.

"Capri, what are you doing here?"

"I'm here with a friend of mine." She looked up at me, then turned her attention back to Jesse. "You're here with David?"

"No, David is away on business again... I'm here with my father and his fiancée." She sighed.

"Oh, alright... well, call me." You could tell she didn't know what to say and was just trying to end the conversation.

"Come sit with me at my table, please," Jesse held her hand, pleading for Capri to sit with her. "I've listened to the both of them for the entire ride over... plus, we still need to talk."

"I'll meet you over there," she promised her, then looked up at me when she was gone. "Save me, please."

"Just go over there, be nice, and then we can go back to our table." I checked my watch. "Actually, we might could just dip... wanna shot?"

"I'm pregnant... can't drink," she revealed.

"Oh shit... congratulations."

I could tell she was happy by the way she smiled when she said it. "Thank you... now save me."

Aimee dipped into the background while Capri held onto my arm as we made our way over toward the table. Capri dug her heels into the carpet as she looked at the table her friend was waving us over toward.

"Her father is Vincent Morgan?" she whispered, choking back the words.

Aimee was looking at us, and I nodded to let her know he was in the building. She quickly walked over toward the table, and accidentally bumped into him. "I'm so sorry... so sorry." She continued to grab napkins and dab his suit jacket.

"What the hell is your problem? Don't you know how to watch where the hell you're going?" his fiancée hollered and turned to snatch napkins from the nearby table.

"Tasha!" Capri whispered, as she ducked behind me when she looked over this way. The woman, who I assumed was Tasha looked at me weirdly before she went back to helping her fiancé.

To Be Continued